Published by Northwood Publishing

Copyright © 2009 Cynthia Harrod-Eagles

Author's website
www.cynthiaharrodeagles.com

Cynthia Harrod-Eagles has asserted her right
under the Copyright, Designs and Patents Act 1988
to be identified as the author of this work.

ISBN-10 1495449637
ISBN-13 978-1-49544-963-5

A CIP catalogue record for this
work is available from the British Library.

Also available as a Kindle ebook

Pre-press production
www.ebookversions.com

FELL
PURPOSE

*Cynthia
Harrod-Eagles*

NORTHWOOD PUBLISHING

Contents

ONE

Tinkling Symbol

Atherton was singing as he drove.

'If I give my heart to you, I'll have none and you'll have two—'

'What are you so happy about?' Slider asked.

Atherton did his martyred wife impression. 'Just my way of getting through the day.'

'You can't kid me. You're smiling so much you look as if you slept with a hanger in your mouth. It's that good with Emily, is it?' It was good to see his colleague bitten at last, after a lifetime heading the Hounds' Hall of Fame.

'Ah, it's true what they say about women,' Atherton said blithely, laying the car like paint round the corner into Wood Lane.

'What?'

'It's an irregular plural. Anyway, if anyone should be happy, it's you. New wife, new baby—'

'Interrupted Bank Holiday,' Slider concluded.

'Yes. Bummer,' Atherton agreed, finally relinquishing his smile. They had both had the Bank Holiday off. He and Emily had planned to go for a long walk along the Thames Footpath from Richmond to Kew, and have lunch at the wine bar on Kew Green. It had been no part of his plan to pick up his boss at the station and drive out to view a corpse.

Slider had arranged to take his children by his first wife, Kate and Matthew, plus Joanna and the baby, to see his father, who lived out in the sticks in Essex. It was the sort of arrangement that was difficult to make in the first place, with so many schedules to co-ordinate, and was correspondingly harder to have to give up – Atherton at least now had Emily on tap. And his father was getting frail, and he didn't see enough of him at the best of times. Joanna

1

was carrying on with the plan without him, driving all the children down herself, but Slider resented missing out.

'We have *got* to find somewhere to live,' he concluded. Joanna's one-bedroom flat had been tight enough for the two of them, but now with the baby it was bucking for impossible. 'It makes everything so damn difficult when I can't have the children to stay.'

'Well, it's a good time to pick up a bargain,' Atherton said, picking up speed past Television Centre. 'House prices plummeting and all that.'

'We can't even afford a bargain on my pay,' Slider said. 'We'd have to think twice if they were giving them away.'

Atherton glanced sideways at his boss. 'Emily and I will come over and babysit for you some time, if you and Joanna want to go out.'

'Thanks,' said Slider, appreciating the sentiment behind the offer. You needed all the kindness you could get when facing a murder investigation – and all the cheerfulness you could muster on the way to the scene. Underneath the normality of their chat was the tension of not knowing exactly what they would find at the other end, except that it would be horrible.

Wormwood Scrubs was a vast green space, roughly rectangular, almost a mile long by half a mile wide. It was bounded on one long side by the embankment of the main-line railway out of Paddington to all points west. Along the other long side sat the backs of a school, a hospital and the eponymous HM Prison, which all fronted on Du Cane Road. At the western end, where they were now heading, the green was called Old Oak Common, a relic of local history. The prison had been built in a tract of open farmland and common land that stretched all the way from Notting Hill to the tiny village of East Acton. Then the brick tide of London had lapped up and around and past it. Now the Scrubs was the last bit of open ground left, and some of the country's most dangerous criminals were banged up within a stone's throw of little ex-council houses with net curtains and gnomes in their gardens. It was an odd arrangement.

Atherton pulled up behind the other cars in Braybrook Street, which had houses along one side and was open to the common on the other. Slider got out to take in the scene. Already the blue-and-white tape was up, sealing off a large section of the green. The Bank Holiday was fine and warm, for a wonder, though the sunshine was hazy, so it was ideal weather for the locals to be out, early though it

2

was. The uniformed presence was keeping them well back on the other side of the road, where they chattered excitedly about this bit of fame that had come to their neighbourhood. One or two of the older ones still remembered 1966 when, in this same place, robbers had shot and killed three detectives in cold blood and broad daylight. They were predicting that this current murder wouldn't be a patch on that one – but then nothing these days could match up to the old times. The younger ones, Xboxed to a state of advanced numbness where death and mayhem were concerned, were only hanging around for lack of anything better to do.

The press were there, talking aloofly to each other and smoking like kippers, and so far there was just a lone TV camera team – Slider guessed they were from the local news programme. He wondered how long it would take them to catch up with the street's history. He could see the headlines now – Murder Spot Claims Another Victim.

But the action this time was evidently right over at the embankment, where the white-clad forensic support team was already in the process of erecting canvas screens to shield the site from view. Avoiding all eyes, Slider started off, with Atherton at his side, across the grass. He found himself walking over a patch of churned ground, pitted with stud-marks – baked in after a week without rain. This end of the Scrubs was marked out for football pitches, where amateur teams played at the weekends – the football season started in August these days, and he was crossing a goalmouth. He registered automatically the large brick building over to his right, which housed changing rooms, showers and lavatories for the teams, and paused to note its relative position. Was it securely locked, or could someone have lurked in there? Then he turned to take in the rest of the surroundings.

The high, blank wall of the prison was the most obvious feature, with the white-topped turrets of its towers just peeping above. The hospital also had a wall, not so high but just as blank. Beyond that was the stout link fencing of the school playing fields. At the eastern end of the Scrubs, almost a mile away, on the other short side of the rectangle, was another school, and beside it a patch of ground which the council let out from time to time to travelling shows and temporary exhibitions. On Bank Holidays there was always either a circus or a fair, and this time it was the latter: the familiar shapes of helter-skelter and big wheel stuck up from the surrounding circular tent-tops of the other rides and attractions. Public access to the fairground was from the far side, from Scrubs Lane. On this side of it was a dense but orderly collection of parked lorries and the living caravans of the staff. The hazy sunshine glinted off a windscreen or two, as if the fair were winking at him. *Wouldn't you like to know!*

'Too far away for anyone to have seen anything,' Atherton said, noting the direction of his gaze.

'We'll still have to ask questions,' Slider said.

'That'll make us popular,' Atherton said. Fairground people resented, to put it mildly, any suggestion that they were more criminally bent than the rest of the population.

The fair was an added complication that Slider could have done without. 'The press are bound to leap on it,' he said. His frowning gaze returned to the prison's blank façade, where there were no windows to wink. 'Too much scope for speculation altogether.'

Atherton caught his drift, as he so often did. 'But if anyone had got over the wall it would be known about. Meanwhile, there are hundreds and thousands of houses all around us that no one's been watching.'

'Ah, but you don't think in clichés.'

The railway embankment ran the whole length of the Scrubs. It was tall and steep, and had once sported a dense shrubbery mixed with tree cover, but in recent years the track company had cut it back for safety purposes, and acid rain or some other modern blight had thinned the remainder naturally, so now only the lower part of the slope still had bushes growing patchily over it.

Reaching the site, Slider and Atherton passed two of the forensic team, who had just discovered that the screen they were erecting had somehow got torn since the last time it was used.

'Why does this keep happening to us?' one of them complained.

'Awning has broken,' Atherton explained. 'Like the first awning.'

'It's not an awning,' the man replied squashingly. 'Don't forget to sign the access log. And keep to the boards!'

'Tell your grandmother.'

One of Slider's own team, WDC Hart, met them, smart in a charcoal trouser suit and cherry-red shirt, her hair scraped up into a knob on top. She looked upset. They all tried to hide their feelings, but when you worked with someone for a while you got to know the symptoms. Slider gave her a steadying look.

'It's a girl,' she said.

4

'Yes, we were told,' said Slider.

'She's just a kid, guv. Seventeen-eighteen tops.' The emotion escaped her in a burst of anger. 'Who *does* that? Bastards!'

'Let's not get ahead of ourselves,' Slider said. 'Any identification?'

'No, guv. No pockets on what *she's* wearing, and we ain't found 'er 'andbag yet.'

He went to have a look. The victim was lying on her back between the bushes on the lower slope of the embankment, her arms out to the sides, one leg slightly bent. It was a relaxed-looking pose, as if she had just flung herself down to rest in the heat of the day. She had thick corn-blonde hair, shoulder-length, and he noted the night's dew was on it.

She was slim and very young, as Hart had said, but with an enviable figure, with no puppy chubbiness around jaw or waist, and fine skin: not a spot in sight. She was wearing a mauve cropped top with spaghetti straps, and a black skirt, so short it was a mere nod to decency, which fitted round her hips, leaving her navel exposed. The navel sat curled and cute like a winkle-shell – but the winkle-shell of a particularly fashion-conscious winkle – embedded in the smooth honey-coloured mound of her belly. It was appallingly sexual. Why did girls want to dress like that, he wondered, with a background ache of alarm. His own daughter, Kate, bright and pretty as she was, was just getting to the age when she wanted to go out with her friends, all of them looking like hookers – and cheap hookers at that. They might as well have had placards on their backs saying: 'Available for casual sex. No respect required.'

The victim's legs were bare, and one strappy high-heeled shoe was on, while the other lay nearby, its straps broken. The heel had snapped off and was a little further away towards the road.

Hart indicated it with a gesture and said, 'You can see it, guv, can't you? She's running away from 'im and 'er heel catches, down she goes, and he's on 'er.'

'You assume she was running away,' Atherton said. 'Haven't you ever been to the movies? What about playful chasing and light-hearted gambolling?'

'Gambling? What are you talkin' about?'

'There's no reason to think she was running at all,' Slider said impatiently. 'She could just as easily have been walking, or even standing still—'

'Yeah, standing still and struggling,' Hart said.

5

'The ground's too hard for footmarks,' Slider said, but without regret. Footmarks were time-consuming, and hardly ever helpful.

He looked last of all at the face. As Hart had said, she had been pretty, as far as one could tell – perhaps extremely pretty. Now the face was congested; the open eyes spotted with petechiae; the tip of the tongue protruding between the lips, a smear of blood on the chin. Around her neck was a pair of flesh-coloured tights. They were not knotted, just crossed over, but were kept in place by the ridge of swollen flesh on either side. There was also, he noticed, bending closer, a thin red line around the bottom of her neck: a fine cut, as if a wire had been tightened there.

'Strangled with 'er own tights,' Hart said bitterly.

Slider leaned forward. 'You see what she's wearing,' he said, lifting the hem of the skirt back a little.

'A thong,' said Hart. 'I 'ate those things. They're dead un'ygienic. Give you thrush, and it's a bugger to get rid of.'

'The thong has ended but the malady lingers on?' Atherton suggested.

'Sometimes you're really funny, Jim,' Hart told him. 'And then there's now.'

'The point I'm trying to make,' Slider said patiently, 'is that I wonder if she *was* raped. Would a rapist put the thing back on afterwards?'

'Would he take it off in the first place?' Atherton said.

'But what about the tights, guv?' Hart said. 'I fink maybe I was wrong before.'

Slider got the point. 'She obviously wasn't wearing them. She had her shoes on bare feet.' He was trying not to notice that the feet were cared-for and pretty and the toenails were neatly painted with clear varnish. The fingernails, cut short and following the contour of the fingertips, were unpainted.

'So someone brought his own murder weapon with him?' Atherton said. 'That's not so nice. That looks like someone with form.'

Slider sighed inwardly at the thought of a serial killer, but he said, 'It gives us a line of enquiry, anyway. We'll look at the offenders' list and see who's out and about. I can't think of anyone obvious.'

'At least it might misdirect the press,' Atherton said. 'What with the Scrubs being right next door, they're bound to make the obvious misconnection. Finding out who's in there that fits the bill might keep them happily absorbed while we get on with the job.'

'We've got to identify her first,' Slider said, straightening up.

'Look at Mispers?' Hart suggested.

'If we can't find the handbag,' Slider said. 'And there's all these local people to canvass. If only we could take a mugshot, one of them might know who she is, but we can't show them what she looks like now.'

'Murderers are so inconsiderate,' Atherton agreed.

Porson, their superintendent, arrived, wearing his summer tegument, an ancient beige mac: a wondrous thing of flaps and capes and buckles, concealed poacher's pockets, and buttoned straps of unknown purpose. It was so vast and long it looked as if it was taking him for a walk rather than vice versa. His massive and strangely bumpy bald head shone in the muted sunlight, a beacon of hope and a symbol of courage in adversity. He had abandoned his wig when his adored wife died, but was still known by his old sobriquet of 'The Syrup'.

He disappeared behind the screens, had a look, and came back to speak to Slider.

'I don't like it,' he said, shaking his head at the general iniquity of things. 'She's only a kid. What, sixteen? Seventeen? It's nasty.'

Slider had no argument with that.

'The tabloids are going to be all over this one,' Porson went on gloomily, pursing his lips and pursuing something round his teeth with his tongue. 'Young girl, rape and murder. Whose tights are they? Not hers.' The old man was quick, Slider thought. 'Looks like some cyclepath on the loose. They'll love that.' He snorted. 'No one ever lost money misunderestimating the press.'

In his headlong and tempestuous battle with crime, and with life in general, Porson's way was to fling whatever words came first to hand in the general direction of meaning, and hope some of them stuck. It drove the language-sensitive Atherton mad; Slider, who was fond of the old man, found it almost endearing.

Porson snapped his head round and fixed Slider with a gimlet eye. 'Got anything yet?'

'We don't even know who she is,' Slider admitted.

'Someone'll miss her, nice girl like that. She's not a prozzie.'

Slider agreed. Despite the clothes, she looked like someone's daughter. Her skin and hair were well cared-for and well nourished, and her navel wasn't pierced.

'I'm going to go all out to get you resources for this one,' Porson said, 'even if it does jeropodise the budget. It's going to be hell's own job, though, getting the uniforms back, what with the Carnival.' The Notting Hill Carnival, held every August Bank Holiday, sucked police out of the system like a black hole. 'What a weekend to choose!'

'I wonder if it was an informed choice,' Slider said, thinking of those tights.

Porson shuddered. 'If the villains are going to start getting smart, we're out of a job.' He glanced round and said, 'I'm going to go now, before someone tries to interview me. Keep me up to scratch on this. I'll get on with pulling in some extra men. Ask me for anything you want.'

'Yes, sir.' Slider watched him scuttle away, nimbly avoiding the TV cameras. Wise move, he thought. A closed mouth gathers no feet.

He was giving directions to the slowly increasing manpower – some to start the fingertip search, some to the canvassing of locals – when one of the uniformed extras, Gostyn, came up to him.

'Just found this, sir.' He held out something which Slider accepted into his plastic-gloved palm. It was an ornament about the size of a fifty-pence piece, an open circle with a Z inside it, all in diamonds on a silver-coloured metal. 'It was just this side of the bushes, sir, lying in the grass. Think it could be hers?'

Slider remembered the thin red cut on the victim's neck. 'Could be. If it was on a chain round her neck—'

Gostyn got the point. 'And he grabbed it while he was struggling with her and broke it,' he finished for him eagerly.

Slider shook his head. 'He must have grabbed it from behind. The chain cut her neck at the front.'

'So he was chasing her, you reckon?'

'Not necessarily. They might have been talking, then she suddenly got scared and turned to try to escape, and he grabbed her then. If she turned suddenly, that could have been when she broke the heel of her shoe and burst the straps.'

Atherton joined them. 'What's that? Oh, a letter Z. That'll narrow the field.'

'Could be an N, sir,' Gostyn said, trying to be helpful.

'No, look,' said Slider, 'here's the ring the chain goes through. It hangs this way. It's a Z all right.'

'Zöe,' Gostyn said. 'Or . . .' He racked his brains unsuccessfully.

'Zuleika,' Atherton supplied. 'Zenobia. Zephany.'

'Zebra,' said Gostyn eagerly, and then blushed his confusion as Atherton's eyebrow went up. 'I was thinking of Debra,' he muttered. Anyway, since when was Zephany a name?'

'Can I see?' Atherton took it and tilted it back and forth. The stones caught the light and flung it back. 'They look like real diamonds. Small, but not fake. Which means the setting's probably white gold or platinum. Someone didn't mind spending money on her. Pretty good going at her age.'

'If it's hers,' Slider said. 'Find the chain before you jump to conclusions.'

'Yes, oh cautious one.'

'Did you have something to tell me?' Slider asked him.

'Something important,' Atherton confirmed. 'The tea waggon's arrived. Bacon sarnie?'

After a morning and most of the afternoon setting in train the involved and laborious routine of investigation, Slider was back at his desk ploughing through the paperwork when Freddie Cameron, the forensic pathologist, rang. His cut-glass tones, as neat and dapper as his habitual attire, were as stimulating as a yellow waistcoat. He and Slider went back a long way, and Slider had never known him to be other than cheerful, even in the face of the most insalubrious corpses.

'Hello, Bill! How's life?'

'I'm waiting for the movie. How are you?'

'Always merry and bright.'

'Even coming in on a Bank Holiday?'

'The traffic's a pleasure. Absence thereof. And the phone doesn't ring so much.'

Slider smiled. 'I firmly believe if you were being transported to Hades you'd be making cheery small-talk with the Ferryman.'

'Of course.' Freddie put on his unconvincing cockney accent. 'I 'ad that Orpheus in the back of my boat once . . .'

'Orpheus? Didn't we have him up for luting?'

'My God, that's terrible! Let's change the subject. I've got your corpus. Sorry business – poor little beast. Thought I'd give you a preliminary report.'

'Thanks. Was it what it looked like?'

'From external examination it certainly looks as though death was due to strangulation, and the tights fit the pattern on the skin, so they probably are the weapon.'

'Well, that's a start.' Anything straightforward was a relief.

'I'm a bit choked up with work at the moment with half my staff on holiday, so unless there's a particular reason to hurry, I'll have to put off the post for a day or two. I can't see anything out of the way, though. No sign of drugs, but I'll do the usual tests when the time comes. No sign of forcible penetration, or indeed of recent sexual activity – no semen or lubricant traces. But our young lady was not a virgin. In fact I'd say she was probably quite experienced.'

'God, they start early these days,' Slider said. 'She can't be more than seventeen or eighteen.'

'How old were you?' Freddie asked drily.

'I was a country boy,' Slider said. 'We didn't have anything else to do. Any defence injuries?'

'Nothing visible. There might be some subcutaneous bruising. No blood or tissue under the fingernails, unfortunately.'

'Her nails were cut short,' Slider mentioned.

'Yes, and she had strong hands, too – I wonder if she played the piano? Probably the assailant took her by surprise, and instead of hitting or scratching him she tried to pull the ligature away. Pity. But we may find hairs or fibres somewhere. Nil desperandum.'

'I love it when you talk Latin to me. Time of death?'

'I haven't done a liver stick yet, but I doubt if the temperature is going to tell us much we don't know already. I'd estimate she'd been dead about twelve hours when I saw her this morning, which as you know is give or take the usual eight-hour margin.'

'Helpful.'

'But I understand she was found at about seven?'

'Six forty-five. Woman walking her dog.'

'So that cuts it down this end. And I noticed—'

'The dew on her hair?'

'Give that man a coconut. Now, I've done a quick bit of research and dew point would have been at about two o' clock this morning, so given that the ground underneath her was dry—'

'She must have been put there before then. Was she killed where we found her?'

'The hypostasis was consistent with it, though as you know that's only an indicator, not proof positive. But given the trampled grass and her broken shoe and the way the body was lying, I'd say it most likely happened there.'

'That's what I thought,' Slider said. 'It's hard to make a body look natural once you've moved it.'

'Oh, it was a trick question, was it? I'm supposed to tell you things you didn't know.'

'How about her name? That would be a help.'

'I'll send over the fingerprints and dental record as soon as I've done them, but I dare say someone will claim her before you have to use them. Oh, by the way, I understand you found some sort of pendant or charm? Well, we found the chain, broken. It was underneath her when we turned her over. Possibly slipped down inside her clothing when it snapped, and slipped out at the bottom later on, when she was struggling. You saw the cut on her neck?'

'Yes.'

'I thought you would have. It's consistent with the chain. Must have exerted considerable force – I'm guessing it was a sharp jerk to restrain her rather than an attempt at strangulation.'

'Considerable force? So it might have cut his hand too?'

'Possibly. I'll test it for tissue or blood, but don't count on it.'

'I never do.'

'Buck up,' Freddie said sympathetically. 'At least it wasn't a rape.'

'No, just murder,' said Slider. '*So* much more civilized.'

Slider let himself in, very late, to the narrow hall of the flat, and at once Joanna appeared, in her dressing-gown, finger to her lips.

'Don't wake the baby,' she said, coming to kiss him.

'How was he?'

'Perfect. You have a perfect baby.'

'How was the day?'

'It went very well. A good time was had by all, I think.'

He followed her into the kitchen. 'How was Dad?'

'He seemed all right. He's a bit slower about everything, but he's pretty spry, considering, and there's nothing wrong with his mind. He and Matthew were ages out in the garden, talking about the countryside and nature and so on.'

'That's what he used to do with me,' Slider said, smiling faintly, remembering pre-dawn trips to watch for badgers.

'And Kate was wonderful with the baby. She's mad about him.'

'If only we could have the children to stay, she could babysit him,' Slider said.

'I'll go out house-hunting again tomorrow. I'll widen the search area as well.' She eyed him sympathetically. 'You look exhausted. Was it awful?'

'I've known worse. But she was so young.' He told her the bare facts. 'And we don't even know who she is yet. Unknown person, killed by person unknown. I've had people trawling missing persons and runaways, and another lot looking through the rogues' gallery. All without success so far.' He yawned hugely, surprising himself. 'Any phone calls?'

'Just one message for me. They've changed the programme on Thursday to the bloody old Enigma. I hate that piece.'

'But you love Elgar.'

'That's why I hate the Enigma. What a waste of talent! Variations aren't music, they're an exercise: how many different ways can I write this dopey tune? It's like asking Shakespeare how many words he can make out of "Constantinople". Like giving Sir Christopher Wren that puzzle with the three houses and the three utilities, and you have to link them all without crossing the lines!'

'I love it when you get all vehement,' Slider smiled, gathering her in to his chest.

'You do realize what this means, don't you?' she said.

'You're going to have to practise?'

'Some detective you are,' she said. 'Work it out: you, murder investigation. Me, concert Thursday. You were supposed to be home on Thursday night minding the baby.'

'Oh Lord, yes. I can't depend on getting back in time.'

'I know. I've been phoning round all evening. Everyone's away or busy.'

He pondered sleepily. Now he was winding down, Morpheus was catching up, stepping on his heels. With an effort he connected up various threads. 'Atherton said this morning that he and Emily would sit for us some time if we wanted to go out.'

'Nice of him. I'd like to go out with you some day, before I'm old and sere.'

'But he's going to be busy this week too. So maybe Emily would come over – or you could take George to her.'

'Genius. The man's a genius. Why didn't I think of her? I'll ring her tomorrow.' She kissed him affectionately. 'Look at you, you're exhausted. Do you want anything to eat?'

He shook his head. 'Too tired to swallow.'

'Go on to bed, and I'll rub your back for you.' It soothed him when he was tense after a bad day. She let him have the bathroom first, and then popped in and brought the bergamot oil back with her. But he was already asleep, curled on his side with one fist under his chin.

He had surprisingly long eyelashes for a man, she thought, looking down at him. There was a bit of hair on the crown of his head that grew a different way from the rest, and it was hard to get it to lie down. The baby had just the same unruly tuft. She felt the enormous and surprising pang in the loins, that only a woman who has borne a son to the man she loves can feel.

TWO

Tout Passe, Tout Casse, Tout Lasse

Fathom, one of Slider's DCs, appeared at the door: a big, thick-built, meaty-faced lad who looked as if he ought to be slinging hay-bales rather than negotiating the intricacies of a murder investigation. 'Guv, I've had a breakthrough,' he announced excitedly.

Slider looked up. 'Don't tell me you've mastered the photocopier at last?'

'No, guv,' he said, wounded. 'I've got the victim's name. Well, I think I have. You see, I looked up diamond initial pendants on Google, and there were pages of 'em, but none in circles like that one. So I rang up this contact of mine – she does the consumer page in the local rag. She's brilliant – knows where to find anything in the shopping line. Anyway, she put me on to this jeweller's shop in King Street, the only local place they do 'em. And bingo! The bloke remembered the Z because you don't sell many of 'em and he had to order it in special. So he looked up the receipt and it was a Mr Wilding, bought it in May for his daughter when she passed Grade Eight piano.'

'Piano! Freddie, you're a genius,' Slider said.

'Guv?' Slider waved it away. 'Anyway,' Fathom continued, 'it seems the bloke couldn't stop talking about his daughter – proud as a parrot, which is how come the jeweller got to hear so much about her, and remembered the name. Zellah.'

'I didn't see that coming,' Slider remarked.

'I made him spell it. I've never heard of it,' Fathom admitted.

'It's from the Bible,' said Slider, who'd had that kind of education. 'I hope you got an address as well?'

'Yes, guv. Two Violet Street, East Acton. You know?'

'Ah,' said Slider. He knew.

There was a small development of former council houses, built in the thirties and sold off in the eighties, set out in roads with unbearably sweet floral names: Daffodil Street, Clematis, Orchid, Foxglove, Pansy Gardens, Tamarisk Square . . . It was only about a mile as the crow flew from that spot by the railway embankment; although, divided from it as it was by the width of the Scrubs, Du Cane Road, the Central Line rail tracks, and the near-motorway of the A40, it probably felt like a lot further away than that to the residents.

'Then I looked 'em up on the electoral register and the last census,' Fathom went on. 'He's Derek and the wife's Pamela June. No one else living there, just them and the girl.'

'Well done, lad,' Slider said, and if there was a note of surprise in his voice – because Fathom had not exactly shone like true specie so far at Shepherd's Bush – Fathom didn't seem to notice it.

'Zellah Wilding,' Atherton said. 'It sounds positively Brontë-esque. It's an untamed beauty with flowing raven locks, rampaging about the moors in a thunderstorm.'

'I wonder why they haven't missed her,' Slider said, 'if she's been gone two nights.' Knowing the name only made him feel sadder. The unknown victim was now much more of a person: a person whose fate had become his intimate business, but whom he would never meet.

'Maybe they have,' Atherton said. 'You know Mispers don't pass stuff along that quickly when it's older girls. Or maybe she was staying away somewhere. It's still school holidays.'

'True,' Slider admitted. 'Well, someone's got to go and tell them. Want to volunteer?'

'Wouldn't you like to go?' Atherton wheedled.

'I've got too much bumph to clear. You're it. Go thou – and think like me.'

The houses on the floral estate were small, neat, almost cottagey, red brick with white trim and good-sized gardens front and back. Now that they were in private hands, they had lost some of their uniformity, as owners tried to obliterate their council past by changing the doors and windows in usually inappropriate ways, tacking on porches and bays, and in some cases even applying stone-cladding (for which Atherton knew Slider felt the death penalty ought to be re-introduced).

He conceived an embryo of respect for the owner of number 2 Violet Street when he saw that the new double-glazed windows had been made in size and style to match what they replaced, and the new front door was seemly and wooden and painted a modest dark green, in contrast to the all-glass, ali-framed horrors of its neighbours.

The front garden had a neatly trimmed privet hedge, a small square of lawn, and a circular bed of well-tended roses. Behind there would be an unusually large garden, because the street was laid out at an angle, and this house benefited from the corner. Also because of the corner there was a separate side entrance to the back garden, shut off by a high wooden gate. As he got out of the car, the roaring of the traffic down the Westway – as this section of the A40 was called – became apparent. Along this side of the dual carriageway, a row of houses had been demolished back in the eighties for a road development that had never happened, and there was now a strip of wild land, the lost plots reverting to nature. The rear garden of number two backed on to this strip. Atherton wondered how a careful gardener would feel about having to live right next to a riot of seeded grass, bramble and willow-herb, all anxious to escape to civilisation. Well, they would have something worse to think of now.

From the other side of the car stepped Connolly, a uniform who had joined Slider's team as a temporary replacement for Swilley and was keen to transfer permanently to the CID. She was from Clontarf originally, and though ten years in Putney had muted her Dublin accent, the cadences of her home town would never be eliminated from her speech. She was a green-eyed blonde, almost too slender to be a copper; attractive – though Atherton told himself she was not in the same class as Kathleen 'Norma' Swilley, who was away having a baby in the inconsiderate manner of womankind and, incidentally, breaking Atherton's heart. Not that he wasn't happy with Emily: it was just that he hated to see a work of art despoiled. Norma pregnant was like the Mona Lisa with a moustache scribbled on it.

He had brought Connolly along on Slider's orders, because sometimes the bereaved wanted a woman around at a time like this; but on this occasion her uniformed presence, standing beside him, administered such a shock to the pleasant-looking woman who opened the door that he half regretted not coming alone.

'Mrs Wilding?' he asked as calmingly as he could. It was hard to inject warning, regret, compassion, trustworthiness, determination, honour and accessibility into two words, but he did his best.

She was a short woman, probably in her early- to mid-forties – it was hard to tell, because she was overweight, with a round belly straining at the smart grey trousers, and large breasts pushing out the pink cashmere vee-neck jumper. Nevertheless, there was no missing that she had been a beauty once. The face still had it; the eyes, large, blue and heavy-lidded, had known their power. She had full make-up, well applied, and her hands were manicured, with painted nails; she wore a heavy gold necklace, gold earrings and several diamond rings. But her feet, in velvet slippers, showed she was not dressed to go out. This was a woman who liked to look her best at all times. Her hair, cut in a jaw-length bob, was greying at the temples, and the colour was probably helped, but had obviously once been corn-blonde, and was the same texture as the victim's: strong and heavy, and holding together as it moved, like an elastic bell. It was an indication that they were at the right address.

Mrs Wilding had automatically sized Atherton up and begun to react to him as a man, before her eyes leapt past him to Connolly's uniform, and her inviting smile spontaneously aborted for a look of alarm.

'Oh my God, it's Zellah,' she said. 'What's happened? Is it an accident? Is she all right? It's a car accident, isn't it? They went out in the car after all! Oh my God, what will her father say? He didn't want her to go anyway, not to sleep over, but you can't keep them locked up at their age, can you? Sophy's only just got her licence, and Daddy *stipulated* they mustn't go out in the car without a grown-up. He said Sophy was too young, but her father gave her a car as soon as she passed the test, and you can't argue with how other people bring up their children. But Zellah *promised* she wouldn't let Sophy drive her.' She was wringing her hands now. Strange how people really did that, Atherton thought. 'How bad is it? Where is she? Oh, how will I ever tell her father? He dotes on her!'

Atherton managed at last to interrupt the flow. 'Mrs Wilding, we're from Shepherd's Bush police station. I'm DS Atherton and this is PC Connolly. May we come in?'

A new apprehension came to her. 'Detectives?' She stared from one face to the other. 'Not drugs,' she almost whispered. 'Not our Zellah. Say it's not drugs. This'll kill him.'

But she let them in. There was a tiny hallway with stairs going straight up in front of them, a sitting room to the right, and the kitchen straight ahead, with a glimpse of the sunlit garden through its window. There was a smell of washing powder in the air, and the chugging of a washing-machine out of sight in the kitchen. Mrs Wilding walked before them in a rigid, apprehensive way into the sitting room. It was neatly but cheaply furnished, everything clean and polished, with a small upright piano occupying one chimney alcove, knick-knacks and ornaments along the mantelpiece and on shelves in the other alcove, and framed photographs on the walls instead of pictures. Central on the left-hand wall was the largest of them, head and shoulders of a remarkably pretty girl with shoulder-length, corn-blonde hair, smiling straight at the camera. The shirt collar and striped tie visible in the vee of the navy sweater said that this was an enlargement of a school photo. Atherton was impressed. Who looks good in their school photo? Only a real beauty.

'Mrs Wilding, is that Zellah?' he asked gently.

She was standing in the middle of the room, staring at them blankly. New and different fears were coming and going in her face. Her lips moved but she seemed for the moment to be out of speech. She nodded.

'Is your husband at home?' Atherton asked.

'He's out the back, in his shed,' she said. Her words were oddly jerky, as if she didn't have much control over them. 'What is it?'

'Perhaps we ought to get him in,' Atherton said.

'No. Tell me,' she said. 'Tell me first. He won't be able to . . . You don't understand. Tell me first. *What's happened?*'

Atherton took out the diamond pendant in its plastic bag. He had brought it in case extra identification were needed, but now it seemed a gentler way than words to tell her. He extended his hand and opened his palm.

She looked at it, then looked up, appalled. 'No,' she said. 'No, it's not possible.'

'I'm so sorry,' he said gently. She was probably still thinking it was a car accident, but maybe it was better to do this in stages. Dead was the first, but probably not the hardest step, with murder still to come.

He saw her remnant of beauty drain from her face as she read the end of everything in his. She shook her head again, and sat down abruptly, without even looking behind her to see where the chair was. But she must know this small house so well that all the distances were programmed into her body.

'She's seventeen next week,' she said, as if that would get her let off. A plea of mitigation. 'Daddy's going to give her driving lessons.

He said better he taught her himself than someone else and not do it right.'

'Mrs Wilding, I really think we ought to get your husband in.'

'I'll go,' she said blankly, and then looked bewildered as she found she couldn't get up.

So Atherton went.

The question of how a devoted gardener coped with a contiguous wilderness of weeds was answered as he stepped out. The chain-link fencing between this garden and the wild strip had been taken down, and the wilderness tamed. Right at the far end, the blue-painted eight-foot builder's hoarding that cut off the pavement and road beyond was disguised by the original hedge and trees of the demolished house, now grown high and thick. They overtopped the hoarding, and from the road must have given the impression that nothing had changed in here. But to either side, new-looking six-foot-six larch-lap shut off the neighbours, and inside these barriers the extra bit had been incorporated into number two's original garden. It was, of course, slightly illegal, but Atherton thought Slider at least wouldn't have blamed them. Who was hurt by it? The land had been left to rot through twenty years of political dither and budget shenanigans, and as a country boy Slider hated the waste of land. Better, he would think, that the Wildings – or Mr Wilding, probably, because Mrs Wilding with her manicured hands did not look like a gardener – made use of it in neat vegetable beds and grew cabbages and runners and carrots and – what was that? It looked like coriander. *Coriander*?

In the middle of the far end, up against the riotous hedge – it had been privet, but buddleia and elder had seeded themselves into it and waved gaily out of the top – there was a large, stout garden shed, with the door slightly ajar. Not wishing to frighten the occupant by suddenly appearing in the doorway, Atherton called out, 'Mr Wilding,' as he approached, and they reached the door simultaneously from opposite directions.

'Who are you?' the man demanded, with justifiable surprise and faint irritation.

He was a little taller than Atherton, and a lot bigger, bulky about the shoulders, thick in the middle in the manner of an athlete – a rugby player perhaps – gone to seed. He was evidently quite a bit older than his wife, though it was hard to tell by how much. He was well preserved and might have been anything from mid-fifties to mid-sixties. His face was large-featured and had been handsome – they must have been a golden couple, these Wildings – and his straight grey hair was bushily thick and strong, giving the impression of irrepressible growth that would have to be pruned back hard every few weeks. He was wearing grey slacks and a dark-blue check short-sleeved shirt, and he was holding a large screwdriver in one hand. The hands were grey with working dirt, thick-fingered and scarred with cuts and nicks of various ages, the hands of a hands-on workman. Atherton guessed carpenter: his bifocal glasses bore a surface sheen of fine dust; there was a delicate curl, like a feather, of a wood shaving clinging to his trousers, and the unmistakable tang of sawdust was in the air.

'I'm sorry if I startled you,' Atherton said, and introduced himself.

Over the man's shoulder, he caught a glimpse of the shed's interior, well fitted-out as a workshop. There was a good, high bench with cramps and a vice, a heavy plane lying on its surface, and a drill, plugged in to a long strip of sockets behind; shelves loaded with jars and boxes of screws, nails, Rawlplugs, hooks, hinges and so on; a peg-board on the wall with tools neatly hanging. The work in progress was on the bench – a wooden railway engine, about the size of a child's pedal car, partly constructed and lacking wheels yet.

Wilding intercepted the glance. 'I make toys for the Lions Club,' he said shortly, as if to get that out of the way. 'What do you want?'

'I'm afraid I have some bad news. Would you come inside? It would be better to tell you and your wife together.'

He looked angry. 'Is it Zellah? If there's trouble, it will be Sophy and those other girls. Zellah would *never* do anything wrong. She's a top student, all A grades; she plays the piano and flute, she's going to university. She's a *good* girl. If they've done something it's those others who thought it up. I *said* she was too young to be staying over, but her mother insisted. Nobody brings their children up properly any more. They let them run wild. What have they got her into?'

He folded his arms and stood immovably in the doorway of his shed, and obviously was not going to stir until Atherton told him. Perhaps, after all, it was better to tell him first, away from his wife – let him take it to her.

'I'm afraid I have to ask you to brace yourself for a shock,' he said. 'Something very bad indeed has happened.'

Wilding's eyes widened and Atherton saw his nostrils flare. It was an animal's reaction to threat; but no parent could ever be prepared for this.

He hated this bit. But there was no way to say it but to say it. 'I'm so sorry to have to tell you this. Zellah is dead.'

The big, handsome face seemed to shrink together. The eyes were appalled. 'No,' he said faintly. 'No she's not. She's not. She's not.'

But he knew it. The truth was in those staring, naked eyes.

Connolly had made tea, and Mrs Wilding sipped it, more out of automatic social response, Atherton guessed, than because she wanted it. Mr Wilding didn't seem to know his was there. He stared silently into an abyss before him. Mrs Wilding did the talking.

'Sophy Cooper-Hutchinson.' She supplied the name of the girl Zellah had been visiting, and even at such a moment there was a hint of pride in it. 'They have a big house in Netheravon Lane – do you know it?'

Atherton nodded. It was not that far, in fact, from where Slider lived in Turnham Green. It was a small area of very large, mainly Georgian houses close to the river on the border of Hammersmith and Chiswick. It was where rich Londoners in the eighteenth century had gone to get out of town in the summer, the forerunner of the seaside holiday. If the Cooper-Hutchinsons had a big house there – as opposed to a flat in part of a big house – they must be well off.

'Sophy and Zellah are friends at school. Sophy's a few months older than her, and she's got an older sister, Abigail, who's eighteen – she's going to Oxford next month, but she's still at home now – so although the parents are away for the week, we thought it would be all right for them to be in the house on their own. Sophy's quite a sensible girl really, and they weren't going to have a party or anything – Daddy and I made it quite clear there wasn't to be anything like that. They just wanted to be together the way girls do, and you can't wrap them up in cotton wool, can you? I mean, Zellah's nearly seventeen, you have to start treating them like grown-ups some time, and it would have made it very awkward for her with her friends if we'd said she couldn't go when she'd been invited specially. I want her to have friends, the right sort of friends. It's bad enough us living here—'

Wilding lifted his head at that moment and Mrs Wilding met his look and stopped abruptly, obedient, but with a touch of defiance in her expression. She went on, 'The Cooper-Hutchinsons are the kind of people I want Zellah to mix with, not people from round here. I want her to get on, and I wasn't going to embarrass her in front of them and have them laugh at her behind her back because her parents were so out of touch they wouldn't let her come and stay for a simple . . . innocent . . . sleepover . . .'

Shaky breaths that were trying to be sobs broke up the end of the sentence. Connolly gave her another tissue, and she blew her nose, and went on unevenly while dabbing at her eyes.

'They were just going to spend the evening together and cook their own dinner – well, it's good for girls to do that, learn how to be self-reliant, isn't it?' She was going over again, Atherton could tell, the justifications she had used to her husband before the fact. 'We said she could have a glass of wine with it but no spirits. And I expect they'd watch one of their girly films – *Bridget Jones* or something like that – and talk and giggle half the night the way girls do. And then on the Bank Holiday Monday they'd planned to meet up with a couple of other girls and go to the Southbank Summer Festival – you know, by the river, next to the Festival Hall. It's music and dancing and jugglers and mimes and things, and food stalls and crafts. People take their children there, so it's quite safe. Not like the Notting Hill Carnival. We wouldn't have them going anywhere near that: that was made very clear indeed. But the Southbank thing is just good, clean fun. They wanted to go on the London Eye but it turned out they couldn't get tickets. You had to book in advance and it was all booked up. I suppose it would be, on a Bank Holiday.'

She looked at Atherton with a bewildered air, as if something wasn't adding up. Relating the arrangements and the arguments in favour of them had kept her for a moment from realising that Zellah – *her* Zellah, her daughter – had been dead by Monday morning and in no condition to go to the Southbank or Notting Hill. 'I suppose they didn't go in the end,' she said, still not really getting to grips with it. 'The other thing they wanted to do was go out in the country for a picnic, but Daddy said he didn't want Sophy driving a bunch of giggling girls without a grown-up in the car. Zellah knew she wasn't to do that. If Sophy and the others insisted, she was to come home. They were going to go on the tube to the Southbank.' Her confusion visibly grew. 'But it wasn't a car accident, was it? I was forgetting. They couldn't have gone up to London, then. But what was Zellah doing on Wormwood Scrubs? And why didn't Sophy ring us? Zellah was staying two nights, Sunday and Monday, and coming home this afternoon. I half thought she might ring up and ask to stay another night. I wouldn't have minded, though Daddy wasn't keen. But if she wasn't with Sophy, where was she?'

'These are things we have to find out,' Atherton said.

'But why didn't Sophy ring us?' Mrs Wilding persisted.

Wilding spoke up for the first time, his voice harsh with the anger that controlled grief. 'There've been some underhand dealings, that's why. They were never going to the Southbank. I'll bet they went to Notting Hill, and got in with some bad hats, and Zellah's paid the price. We've been lied to, made fools of by the Cooper-Hutchinson girl and her cronies. I knew no good would come of this!' His voice began to rise, and he looked at his wife with near hatred. 'But you – you took her side, like you always do. You insisted, you with your "Zellah has to make the right sort of friends!" Yes, the sort of friends who lie to their parents, conspire behind your back. I *said* she was too young! She wasn't like them – sly and worldly and selfish, like that Sophy creature, and those others that hang around with her. All they wanted to do was to corrupt her – and you connived at it! I blame you for this! If I'd had my way she wouldn't have gone out at all. She'd still be alive!'

Mrs Wilding had whitened to her lips, but she fought back. 'You wanted to treat her like a child!'

'She *was* a child!'

'She's seventeen.'

'She was too young.'

Mrs Wilding blazed, '*I* was seventeen when you—'

Wilding was out of his seat. 'Don't you *dare* bring that up! At a time like this!'

'You didn't think *I* was too young!' Mrs Wilding said viciously, in the manner of one wanting to inflict the maximum hurt. 'Zellah's the same age!'

And in the same manner, he hissed, 'Was! Was! *Was!*'

It was too much for everyone in the room. A hideous silence fell, the Wildings staring at each other with terrified pain and realization, Wilding on his feet, trembling, his wife gripping the arms of her chair so hard her knuckles were white.

Time for a little time out, Atherton thought. There was history here, which might or might not prove helpful to understanding the situation. Think like me, Slider had said; and Slider would have got to the bottom of it. He caught Connolly's eye and conveyed his wishes by eyebrow and an infinitesimal flick of the head, and said, 'Mrs Wilding, I wonder if PC Connolly could see Zellah's room. And we shall need a clear recent photograph, if you have one.'

Mrs Wilding tore her eyes from her husband's like someone peeling off a plaster, and not without pain, either. She stood up, the meat of her face quivering with suppressed rage. 'You want to talk to him on his own,' she said. 'Well, you're welcome to him! Much good may it do you.' A last little spurt of viciousness. 'Much good he ever did me.'

A response almost escaped Wilding's lips, but he held it back, and she walked from the room with unexpected dignity, Connolly following.

In the silence that followed, Wilding remained standing where he was, as if he had forgotten how to sit down. Atherton, trying hard to imagine what he must be suffering, thought he would probably have welcomed death at that moment, so that he would never have to move on from that moment and face what was coming in the future, for the rest of his life.

'Please sit down,' Atherton said eventually, half expecting an explosion. A cornered animal will often attack. But Wilding did sit, blindly, staring at nothing again. Slowly he unfurled his clenched fists and rested them on the chair arms with a curiously deliberate gesture, as though determined to remember where he had left *them*, at least. Atherton sat too, giving him a moment to compose himself.

But Wilding spoke first. The effort of control was audible in the strain in his voice, but it was a very fair attempt at normality. 'I apologise for that. My wife is an emotional woman, and . . .' He didn't seem to know how to end the sentence.

'No apology necessary,' Atherton said. 'This is a terrible time for both of you.'

'We ought to have handled it better,' Wilding said. 'But it's not something you ever anticipate having to face. Please don't pay any attention to what she said. She didn't mean anything. She was just lashing out.'

'I understand,' Atherton said. 'Don't worry about it.'

'I suppose you must be used to it,' Wilding said, looking at him properly for the first time. 'I hope you *don't* understand. Have you got children?'

'No,' Atherton said.

'Then you can't,' Wilding said. 'Though I suppose you've done this before.'

'It's never easy,' Atherton said.

'I suppose not. A strange job, yours. Not one I envy you. You must have seen all the worst aspects of human behaviour.'

'And some of the best,' Atherton said, to encourage him. 'Great courage and dignity.'

'We should have handled it better,' Wilding said again. '*I* should have, as an educated man. But Zellah is our only child. She . . . she was everything to me. You can't conceive how much she . . .' He made an unfinished gesture towards the large photograph on the wall, as if that said what he could not.

'She's beautiful,' Atherton said, deliberately not using the past tense.

But Wilding noticed. 'Not any more,' he said with black bitterness. 'Someone's taken all that away. All that beauty, that talent, that intelligence. All that promise. She was my perfect star.' He was winding himself up again. 'But there's always somebody who can't bear perfection, who has to tamper with it and destroy it. And I know who.'

THREE

Ride, Reading Hood

Mrs Wilding was breathing hard by the time they reached the bedroom, and it wasn't all the effect of the stairs. She was congested with anger as she stalked ahead, leading the way to Zellah's room.

Through the open doors, Connolly could see the upstairs rooms: a double bedroom, with old-fashioned wooden furniture and a silk quilted eiderdown on the bed; a cramped bathroom with a pale-blue suite, Crystal tiles, cheap blue carpet, and matching drip-mat and toilet seat cover in shag-pile cotton; a small spare bedroom set up as a sewing-room, with material and part-made garments spread over a bulky armchair that probably turned into a single bed. It reminded her painfully of her parents' interwar semi in Clontarf: same layout, same taste, just a bit smaller.

The third bedroom, in size falling between the double and the sewing-room – which at home Connolly had shared with her sister Catriona – was Zellah's, and there was nothing remarkable about it at first glance, except that it was unusually tidy for a teenager, and rather young for a sixteen-going-on-seventeen-year-old. There was no computer or television, no sound system except for a portable radio on the bedside cabinet, and a CD walkman on the windowsill. There was a single bed up against the wall under the window, with a menagerie of stuffed toys lined up along it with their backs to the bricks. Cheap, worn carpet partly covered by a home-made rug. Shelves of books and an MFI desk with what looked like homework and school books spread across it. Cheap wardrobe with a door that wouldn't close properly. Cheap dressing table with ornaments and an elderly Barbie mingling with the hair- brushes and a modest array of make-up. Ancient floral wallpaper partly obscured by framed family photographs and two cheap reproduction paintings, one of a cantering horse and one, very faded, of the Margaret Tarrant picture of Jesus with the sheep and the collie dog and the curly-headed children. In the circumstances it was horribly touching.

Mrs Wilding was not looking. She hardly waited to get in there before turning on Connolly to vent her spleen.

'Can you believe he'd talk to me like that, at a time like this? But he's always been the same. He thinks he's the only person that feels things. Him and his education, and his "superior understanding"! What good has it done us, you tell me that! Here we are stuck in a place like this, hardly big enough to swing a cat, and neighbours you wouldn't pass the time of day with. And everyone knows these were council houses. I can't hold my head up. But that's men for you. Promise you the earth, but you end up stuck in a council house, scratching about to make ends meet!'

'Mr Wilding'd be a bit older than you?' Connolly suggested, to keep her going. Not that she needed much encouragement – she was plainly ready to spill everything to another woman.

'A bit? Try a *lot*! That's half the trouble. He treats me like a child, or an idiot. I'm just as bright as him, let me tell you that! Where do you think Zellah gets her brains? He thinks it's all him, but I used to write *poetry* when I was a girl. Always got top marks at school for my essays and things. *I* could have gone to university if I'd wanted to. But I couldn't be bothered with it. Waste all that time getting a piece of paper that's no use to man nor beast as far as I can see? Did you go to university? No, of course not – you've got more sense. I wanted to get *on* with life, get out and have a bit of fun. So I left school at sixteen, did a secretarial course, and got a job. Nothing wrong with that, is there?'

'Nothing at all.'

'I've never regretted it for a minute. But he looks down on me for it now. Didn't mind it at the time, though, did he? Oh no. Couldn't wait to employ me, soon as he set eyes on me.'

'You worked for him, then?'

'That was my first job. Shorthand and general office work at Wildings, Telford Way. A friend of mine's dad worked there, that's how I heard of it, but the employment agency sent me there for a vacancy. It was his own firm, making metal address plates. Not very big, but successful, mind,' she added sharply. 'It was – what do you call that, when you make something no one else does?'

'A niche, you mean?' Connolly suggested, after a moment's thought.

'That's it. Well, like I say, it was very successful, but because it was a small firm he liked to interview everyone himself, to make sure they'd fit in. Oh, he was very grand, you know. The big boss!' She curled her lip. 'But he couldn't keep his eyes off me, right from the beginning. I know the signs, believe you me. Well, long story short, he wasn't getting on with his wife at the time, and before you could say knife he was asking me to work late. Then he started driving me home after. Then it was stopping for a drink on the way, then it was taking me out to dinner. One thing led to another, and – well, you know.'

'Yes,' Connolly assented.

'Of course *you* do, dear,' Mrs Wilding said, in generous acknowledgement of Connolly's not-bad looks. Then she put herself into a different league. 'I was gorgeous then, believe me.'

'I can see that.'

'Thank you, dear.' She simpered a little. 'I could have had anyone, you know. I was seventeen, with my whole life ahead of me. And the next thing I know, I'm pregnant.'

Connolly did a quick bit of maths and tried not to sound surprised when she said, 'And would that be . . .?'

Mrs Wilding waved an impatient hand. 'No, no. Zellah came later. Well, anyway, he'd been talking for ages about leaving Valerie – that was her name, the cow – and finally he had to put his money where his mouth was. He divorced her and we got married, but it was never the bed of roses he promised me. She's been bleeding him white ever since.'

'Valerie?'

'The bitch,' she spat. 'Nothing was too good for her, was it? Lap of luxury, every comfort for her and the boys. *She* got the family house, this gorgeous detached house in Acton. While him and I had to start our married life living in his mother's house. With his mother! I couldn't believe it when he told me that's where we'd have to go. It's no wonder I lost the baby.'

'Oh, I'm sorry.'

'Well, I wasn't. Not really. I was too young to be saddled with a baby then. I wanted to have a bit of fun – and I did after that, believe you me. Dancing, shows, night clubs – I still had too much life in me to settle down to nappies and bottles and all the rest of it. I don't think Derek minded all that much about the baby, either, though he pretended to, because it would have been extra expense, and he was having to work like a dog anyway, with Lady Muck to support, not to mention school fees for the boys – though why they had to go to private school *I* don't know. Like leeches they were, the three of them, sucking the life out of us. No, I was twenty-five when I fell for Zellah, and *that* wasn't planned, but at least I'd had a bit of pleasure by then. Though it's goodbye to all that when you've had a baby. Your figure goes, and you're tied hand and foot. But I never resented it. She was a gorgeous baby from day one, and she just got more gorgeous as she grew up.' Her eyes filled with tears as reality struck another blow. 'I can't believe it. I just can't believe it. Who would do such a thing? This'll kill him, I'm not kidding you. He thought the sun shone out of her eyes. He'll never get over this.'

She stared at Connolly, her large eyes swimming, tears slipping over in an almost theatrical way; but it was not theatrical. There was a world of genuine pain, the real, gritty, unbearable sort that only happens in real life, not on the screen. 'She wasn't raped?' she asked pathetically. 'You promise me she wasn't raped?'

'The doctor said not.'

'And he didn't cut her? This maniac? He didn't – disfigure her?'

Connolly shook her head. 'No, nothing like that.'

'But – the other thing,' she went on. 'The thing he did. You know.' She didn't want to say the words. 'Strangling. Does it hurt? Did she suffer?'

Connolly made a helpless gesture. How do you answer a question like that? 'Mrs Wilding . . .'

'I want to see her,' she said. 'I'll know if I see her. I have to know.'

'You can see her, of course. And somebody will have to identify her – you know, formally. Either you or your husband could—'

'It had better be me,' she said, suddenly sounding strangely calm and capable. 'He'd go to pieces. Him and his superior education! He's never been able to cope. The divorce, Valerie – he never stood up to her, just gave her anything she asked for. It was me that was short-changed – having to settle for second best, while she got the big house and everything. And then when she died, it turns out she owned half his company, more than half. She left it all to the boys. *They* didn't want it, of course – just wanted the money. So he had to sell. She'd poisoned their minds against him, of course. They took the money and ran. Alan's in Canada and Ray's in New Zealand. Good riddance, as far as I'm concerned. But he practically killed himself building up that firm and putting them through school and everything, and when he had to sell it – well . . .' She shook her head. 'It knocked the stuffing out of him. He's never really been the same since. After that, the only thing he cared about was Zellah.'

'And you,' Connolly suggested.

Her eyes became bleak, and she said, in a different voice from any she'd yet used, a plain, sad, matter-of-fact voice, 'No, I don't think he ever really cared about me. He thought I'd trapped him into marriage, you see. Well, we both lost out. I don't know which of us lost more. Until now.' Her lips trembled. 'My Zellah. You've got to find who did this. And then let me have ten minutes alone with him.'

Wilding had to take a few turns about the room to deal with his emotions before he could speak with a semblance of calmness.

'I had two other children,' he said at last. 'Two boys. I don't see them – haven't seen them for years. The divorce was acrimonious, you see. Pam is my second wife.' He stopped pacing and looked at Atherton, who nodded receptively. 'You probably noticed she's a lot younger than me.' He gave a snort of non-laughter. 'Well, I suppose I wasn't the first fool to go that way and I won't be the last. I threw away everything. I had my own engineering company, with a combined office and factory on the Brunel Estate.'

This was a small industrial park at the back side of East Acton, about half a mile from the Scrubs, in an otherwise unlovely area defined on all sides by railway lines and bisected by the Grand Union Canal. The Wildings' lives had certainly been local, Atherton thought.

'Pam came to work there,' he went on. 'She was young, beautiful – you've only got to look at Zellah to see how beautiful – and I . . . well, I don't need to spell it out for you. It's a common-enough story. There was a divorce, I lost my boys, my house; ultimately I lost my business, everything. You see me here with all I have left. How are the mighty fallen. I don't blame anyone but myself. But it was a disappointment to Pam. She feels I let her down. She's always cared more for the . . . the outward signs of success. If she spoke harshly just now – well, I wanted you to understand.'

'Of course,' Atherton said.

'I think that's why she wants Zellah to have those things – why she's always trying to get her into a more exalted social set. Don't mistake me; I want Zellah to have everything, too. She deserves it. But Zellah's not just a beauty. She got Pam's looks, but she inherited my brains. She could do anything, be anything. I don't want her to think that marriage to some rich idiot is her only goal.'

'What school does she go to?' Atherton slipped it in.

'St Margaret's. You know it?'

It was the all-girls school at the far end of the Scrubs – next to where the fairground was presently set up. 'I know it,' Atherton said. 'It has a good academic reputation.'

'One of the best in the country,' Wilding said. 'It used to be a grammar school, but when the government abolished them it went private. But it's also a church school – Anglo-Catholic. Fortunately we're in the church's catchment area. It's one of the reasons I bought this house.'

'You're Anglo-Catholic?'

'I am, and Pam was willing to be, in a good cause. We've brought Zellah up as one. I always had my eye on St Margaret's for her because of the academic excellence, but you had to be regular communicants. We couldn't have afforded the fees, but Zellah won a bursary, and it's been wonderful for her. The standard of scholarship is as high as in any public school. The downside,' his expression soured, 'is the kind of girls she's had to mix with. Empty-headed rich kids like Sophy Cooper-Hutchinson and Chloë Paulson, who poison her mind with trash and trivia – boys and make-up and pop music and all that rubbish.'

'What school did Zellah go to?' Connolly was asking upstairs.

'St Margaret's,' Mrs Wilding said, and pulled a face. 'All *he* cares about is exam results. He doesn't give a damn about her getting on and meeting the right people. With her looks she could be anything – a model, an actress, anything. The sky's the limit, but these days it all depends on having the right contacts. *He* just wants her to be a bookworm and ruin her eyes with reading and have no social life and end up a sour spinster with four cats. Fortunately, a lot of very nice girls go to St Margaret's, so it's sucks to him. Girls from well-off families, whose fathers can afford the fees,' she added acidly. 'Zellah's clever, but she's also got a bit of common sense. She wants to have fun, same as anyone else. She wants to be a normal girl, not a freak of nature.'

'Does she have a boyfriend?'

'*He* won't allow it,' she said, making another face. 'Says she's too young. Well, it's hard for her when she can't go out whenever she wants to, like the others. Never on a school night, and at weekends it's questions, questions, questions, and where are you going and what time will you be back? I mean, the poor girl's watched like a criminal. And she couldn't bring a boy back here. There was one boy, Mike Carmichael, brought her home on his motorbike once, very good-looking lad, and the ructions! Derek caught them kissing in the porch. Made them come in and – well, talk about the Spanish inquisition! Poor Zellah was mortified. And nothing the boy could say would satisfy Derek. They ended up having a row, and Zellah was forbidden to see him any more. She was in floods. Well, so was I. I mean, how's she ever going to get married if he chases off every boy that looks at her?'

'I suppose he'd be being protective,' Connolly said.

'Protective? He's a . . .' Her voice cut off as she remembered again.

Connolly felt a pang of sympathy. It must be one of the worst things, the way you kept forgetting, and then remembering again. Every remembering must be like having it happen all over again for the first time.

'It didn't do her any good, did it?' Mrs Wilding resumed bitterly. 'Maybe if he'd let her go out more, she'd have been a bit more streetwise, known a bit more how to protect herself. What was she *doing* out there at that time of night? That's what I want to know. She'd have known better than to go there with a strange man if only he'd treated her like a normal teenager.'

'Did Zellah have a boyfriend?' Atherton was asking.

'No,' Wilding said. 'I didn't allow it. She was too young, and I didn't want her distracted. She had her whole life for that sort of nonsense, but you only get one chance at schooling.'

'It must have been hard, though. I mean, girls of sixteen and seventeen naturally want to go out with boys.'

'She understood. Despite her mother trying to fill her head with rubbish, she knew what her own best interests were.' His face hardened. 'There was a boy who came sniffing round her. I sent him away with a flea in his ear. I told you I know who you should be talking to: a yob by the name of Michael Carmichael. A greasy Lothario with a motorbike. A boy from a sink estate in Reading, whose father's a jailbird! And he thought he was good enough to lay his dirty paws on my daughter! He brought her home once on his damn motorbike, and I caught him fumbling with her outside the front door. I brought him in and read him the riot act. Of course, Pam took his side against me, and there was a row. Poor Zellah ended up in tears. He stormed off, uttering threats against me. The only reason I didn't report him to the police at the time was because I didn't want to embarrass her any further.'

'What sort of threats?'

'Oh, nothing specific. Just that he'd get his own back on me and that I'd be sorry, that sort of thing. And two days later someone broke our front window in the middle of the night. I've no doubt at all that it was him.'

'Did you see him?' Atherton asked.

'No. I told you, it was the middle of the night. I was asleep until the noise woke me up. By the time I looked out, there was no one there. And a couple of weeks later both the wing mirrors were ripped off my car. Pam said it could have been anyone, but I knew who did it. Bad blood will out.'

'How did you know his father was in jail?'

'He told me so himself, that night he brought her home. Practically boasted about it.'

'It's an odd way to introduce yourself to a girl's father.'

'He *said* he didn't want me to find out and think he'd kept it from him. I asked why he should think I was interested, because he was never getting within a mile of Zellah ever again. Then he started calling me names; Pam started shouting and Zellah burst into tears.' He stared morosely at the carpet.

'So when did all this happen?'

'A couple of months ago.' He looked up, remembering the point they had reached, and his face hardened again. 'You go and interview Mr Michael Carmichael of the Woodley South Estate.'

'We'll certainly do that,' Atherton said, his interest quickening. Everyone had heard of Woodley South, the bane of the Thames Valley Police: one of those bare and ugly estates, cheaply run up in the sixties to get families out of central London, which had degenerated into far worse slums than the evacuees had come from, a place of blowing rubbish, burned-out cars, un-employment, boarded-up windows, late night joy-riders, and hooded drug dealers.

Lately the Reading police had undertaken a 'clampdown' to try to make a dent in the crime figures in advance of an application for central funds for a regeneration project. Their methods and results had been widely written up for, and discussed in, the Job, which was why the name resonated with him.

It always amazed Atherton that anyone managed to live even a near-normal life in such circumstances, and yet from his own experience there were always some decent families among the lowlifers in these places, desperately clinging on to standards, doing their best and getting precious little help from the authorities. It was possible young Mr Carmichael was one of the good guys, and his outburst in the Wildings' front parlour was from frustration at being judged on his appearance and postcode. On the other hand, there was a better than even chance he was one of the bad hats, and there was nothing more attractive at this stage of an investigation than a bad hat. It gave you something to follow up, a mote in the otherwise clear eye of all the unknowns.

'Reading's a long way,' Connolly said. 'What was Mike Carmichael doing over this way?'

'Well, he had this motorbike,' Mrs Wilding said, drying her eyes again. 'He could get about on that all right.'

'What I meant was, how did Zellah come to meet him?'

'Oh, I see. Well, he had some friends who shared a house in Notting Hill, and one of them was Chloë Paulson's brother. That time he brought Zellah home, they'd all been out together, a whole crowd of boys and girls. You know how they do. It wasn't that way when I was young,' she added in a complaining voice. 'You went out in couples, or maybe a foursome, none of this all hanging around together in a gang. It just makes it harder to know what's going on, to my mind. I mean, it isn't natural for boys and girls to be friends like that, is it? They're supposed to date and fall in love. You don't marry someone you're friendly with. But I suppose it was better for Zellah, in a way, because her father would only let her go out in a crowd, so she wouldn't have met any boys at all otherwise.'

'Did she see this boy more than once?'

'No, Daddy forbade it. But she seemed to go off him anyway. She didn't mention him ever again.'

If it was me, Connolly thought, *I wouldn't have mentioned him, even if I was seeing him.* A girl had to learn to manipulate in order to get her way. Anyway, from what the doc said it was obvious that Miss Zellah had been getting the ride off some fella or other, whatever her parents thought. 'Do you think you could find me that photograph now?' she said. She would have a quick look round the bedroom while the oul' one was getting it; see if there was a diary or any letters.

'What a life,' Atherton said, when they had given Slider their various accounts. 'I wouldn't blame her for cutting a rip with biker boy.'

'It's the devil when parents try to relive their lives through their children,' Slider mused. 'There's father wanting her to be an academic success and probably end up with her own business, while mother just wants to relive her youth and beauty vicariously, and probably hopes her daughter will be a model and marry a film star. Impossible expectations.'

'And what about being forbidden to go out with boys?' Connolly said indignantly. 'Janey Mac, she was *seventeen*.'

'Right,' Atherton said. 'You can't keep 'em down on the farm after they've seen Paree. What would you have done?' he asked Connolly.

'Pretend to go along with it and run mad behind their backs,' Connolly answered. 'If they want to carry on like Ignatius Loyola, what can they expect?'

'Tyrants make liars,' Atherton said.

'Well, that's one way to look at it,' Slider said, from the point of view of a father. 'But was that what Zellah was doing?'

'She *was* out on the Scrubs late at night when she should have been somewhere else,' Connolly pointed out.

'We know she was rebelling,' Atherton said, 'because of what Freddie Cameron said about her having had a lot of sex. And I must say she must have had considerable moxie to defy her dad like that. I wouldn't like to try it.'

'Moxie?' Slider queried vaguely, out of a train of thought.

'Balls. Spunk. Chutzpah.'

'I know what it *means*. I just don't know why you're using it.'

'I'm a Red Sox fan.'

'You are not.' Slider shook his head. 'Try to be duller,' he advised.

'I can't help it. I spent my formative years at the pictures.'

Connolly suppressed a grin. This was why she wanted to get into the CID. They were all pure mad in the Department. 'Sir,' she said to Slider, 'I've been thinking about the clothes she was wearing.'

'Yes, I've been wondering about that too,' Slider said. 'I wouldn't have thought her parents – her father, anyway – would have let her go out showing that much flesh.'

'No, sir. That's what I thought. And I had a good oul' look in her wardrobe while I was in her bedroom, and there's nothing else like that in there. It's all Sunday School stuff, skirts and ganzies your mammy would buy you. I'm wondering if she borrowed those clothes from her friend.'

'Sophy Whatsit? It's a thought. And if she did, then Sophy must have been in on the whole thing,' Slider said. 'Which would mean she'd know who it was Zellah was seeing that night.'

'It's obvious the Sophy thing was a front,' Atherton said. 'Either for some kind of group outing to a *place* the Wildings wouldn't approve of, or for Zellah to go out with a *person* ditto ditto.'

'That Mike Carmichael sounds the lad,' Connolly said. 'The Woodley South's a total kip. Drugs, stolen cars, smuggled fags and booze. Unemployment about ninety-eight per cent. What's a skanger from a place like that doing, hanging around the likes of Zellah Wilding?'

'Yes,' said Slider. 'I do wonder what the connection with the smart girls is. How did he know Sophy Whatsit's brother and his friends?'

'Oh, I think we can all guess that,' Atherton said wryly. 'What do larging-it youngsters do with their money these days?'

'We can all guess,' Slider said, 'but I'd prefer to know.'

'I take it an early interview with biker boy is a priority,' Atherton said. 'The hood from the 'hood.'

'First of all,' Slider went on, 'we need to speak to this Sophy girl. She may be the one person who knows where Zellah was going and with whom.'

'Do you want me to do it?' Atherton said.

'No, I'll go myself,' Slider said, stretching his shoulders. 'I need to move. I'll take Hart with me. They'll think she's cool.'

'*I'm* cool,' Atherton protested. Connolly made a snorting noise, and he turned on her sharply to find her face rigidly controlled. 'What?'

'Nothing, sir,' she said.

'I think PC Connolly thinks you're more hip than cool,' Slider explained kindly. 'Anyway, you two have got your notes to write up. Get the photograph copied and circulated. Oh, and you'd better arrange for the Wildings to identify the body. Get them to come in, and take their statements down, such as they are.'

'We can send someone there for that,' Atherton said.

'It'll do them good to get out of the house,' Slider said, and Connolly gave him a pleased look for having thought of it. 'What did you think of the father?'

'Obsessive,' Atherton said. 'Transferred all his love to his little princess when he realized he'd married a pudding.'

'Right,' said Slider. 'On the principle that it's always the person nearest what dunnit, get him to write down where he was and what he was doing.'

'That poor man?' Connolly protested. 'He was heartbroken!'

'For elimination purposes,' Slider said. 'Always bread and butter first, before you can have any cake.'

Mad as bicycles, Connolly thought admiringly.

FOUR

Bedlam Sans Mercy

'So, what's the griff with this one, guv?' Hart asked, deeply gratified to have been chosen to accompany the boss. She glanced sideways at his profile as he drove. He still gave her a flutter, though she accepted he was off limits now. She liked older men, and there was just *something* about him . . . Sexy, she thought with an inward, wistful sigh. Definitely a hottie.

'That's what we're going to find out,' he said.

'No, but I mean did she go putting herself about to get one over her dad, and get picked up by a low-life, raped and murdered?'

'She wasn't raped.'

'Oh, yeah, I was forgetting.' She frowned. 'Well, how does that work, then?'

'It complicates things,' Slider admitted.

'Why strangle the cow when you've drunk the milk?'

'What a dainty turn of phrase you have. Anyway, it's useless to speculate with so few facts.'

'Yeah, but it passes the time.' He didn't look at her, but she saw his lips twitch in response.

The house was big, handsome, well proportioned; probably built in the 1820s, Slider thought, of solid London stock and slate, with the tall sash windows beloved of people who had enough servants to clean them. There were wide steps up to the front door over a semi-basement, and what had been a large front garden was now mostly gravelled parking, but with a shrubbery softening the edges, and a couple of lofty ancient trees for beauty. Parked on the gravel were a black sports-model Golf, a red Mazda X5 and a big Mercedes station wagon.

'Bet the Golf's the birthday present,' Hart said as they pulled in alongside. 'Lucky girl.' She climbed out and looked up at the house.

'Well, obviously they've got money, a house this big in this part of the world.'

Slider got out at the other side and pointed upwards. 'That's the other side of the coin,' he said, as a 747 roared slowly over on its way to Heathrow. 'All these lovely houses are under the flight path.'

Hart shrugged. 'Wouldn't bother me. I grew up with two bruvvers who loved reggae. A jumbo's a breeze compared to that.'

They walked up the steps. There was the sound of slamming music from somewhere inside. Slider rang the bell, waited a moment, and rang it again. A dog's barking came closer, retreated, advanced again until it was just behind the door. Slider rang again, then knocked for good measure, and the dog exploded with urgency.

At last there was movement inside, and the door was opened by a girl with wet eyelashes and a towel wrapped in a turban round her head. Beside her a golden retriever was woofing madly. Behind her an elderly mongrel of largely Labrador descent was scenting the air and wagging its tail, and further back still a grey whippet and a black toy poodle lurked, poised for flight. The music sounded louder now, but was still distant, upstairs somewhere.

'I'm sorry, did you ring more than once?' she said with the instant, confiding friendliness that Slider thought her generation's nicest trait. 'I was washing my hair, I couldn't hear for the water.'

'Are you Sophy Cooper-Hutchinson?'

'Good God, no!' she said, as if it was out of the question. 'She's my little sister.'

'You must be Abigail, then,' Slider said, produced his brief, and introduced himself and Hart.

Abigail looked alarmed. 'Oh God, what's she done now? If she's got into trouble my parents will kill me. But I don't see how I'm supposed to control her,' she complained, her pretty face turning sulky. 'She never listens to me. I've got a life of my own, anyway. Why should I have to hang around taking care of her like a nanny? It's not *fair*. What's she done, anyway?'

'Nothing, as far as I know,' Slider said. 'She isn't in trouble. We just want to ask her a few questions.'

'God, that sounds ominous! That's what they say on the TV, and the next thing there's a chase and a gun battle.'

'Well, this is real life, and believe me, it's nuffing like TV,' Hart said. 'Is that her upstairs? Can we go up, then?'

'I suppose so,' Abigail said with a shrug, stepping back and abandoning all responsibility.

The retriever had long exchanged barking for sniffing Slider's trousers with every intention of becoming his lifelong companion, and it frisked beside him as he stepped in. He had that effect on dogs, Hart noted.

'Second floor, on the left,' Abigail said. 'Follow the noise. She's supposed to be doing her practice but I wouldn't bet on *that*.'

Slider climbed the stairs with the dogs surging about him, perhaps in the hope that he could be persuaded to take them out for a walk. Hart followed. The music grew louder, until the banisters trembled. At a turn of the stairs, when Slider was facing her for a moment, he raised his eyebrow enquiringly and she said, 'It's Foxxy Roxx. Wiv two exes.'

'Where?'

'Everywhere. It's metal.'

'Heavy metal?' he said, to show he knew what she was talking about.

'No, it's more like Glam Metal,' Hart said. 'Still a bit crusty for a kid, though.'

'You think she ought to be listening to Perry Como?'

She looked blank for a beat, and then said helpfully, 'There's a band called Epic Coma, but they're more Gothic.'

'How do you know all this metal stuff?'

'Me bruvvers grew out of reggae.'

On the second floor the door to the left was open. Through it the music pounded, and they could see a slim young girl dancing about. She was wearing a black leotard and pink footless tights and a grey sweatband round her head, but above it her short coal-black hair stood up in waxed spikes, and she wore heavy black make-up about the eyes and near-purple lipstick. There was a heap of clothes on the bed, and her dance, all in time to the music, involved picking up garments, taking them to a full-length cheval mirror to hold them up against herself, and rejecting them on to a pile on a chair. She moved very well, Slider thought, and had obviously trained in dance, but ballet practice this was not. The contrast between the girlish occupation and the savage music was slightly disturbing.

The room was a cornucopia of possessions, electronic goods, sports equipment, hobby paraphernalia – evidence of past fads requiring considerable financial investment, before interest waned and a newer, shinier preoccupation took over. There were outgrown toys, ornaments, souvenirs, and clothes not only on the bed and chair but bulging out of the wardrobe and hanging on the back of the door.

William Whiteley opened a department store with less stock, Slider thought.

He banged on the door, but she didn't hear him through the music, which was beginning to give him a neck ache. But the dogs had surged past him and attracted her attention, and then she caught sight of him in the mirror and whipped round so hard it was practically a *fouetté en tournant*. In a gesture of unexpected modesty she clutched the garment she was holding to her front, high up at the neck. Her lips moved to say *who are you*, but their sound could not compete with Foxxy Roxx.

Slider held up his badge while Hart beside him lifted her hands in a placating, we-won't-harm-you gesture, and then pointed to the CD player that was pumping out the decibels. The girl went to it crabwise, keeping her eyes on the intruders, and a moment later a blissful silence fell, surprising the dogs so much that one of them barked involuntarily, and then looked embarrassed.

'Sophy Cooper-Hutchinson?' Slider said with comfortable formality. 'I'm sorry if we startled you. Your sister let us in and told us to come up. I'm Detective Inspector Slider from Shepherd's Bush police station, and this is Detective Constable Hart.'

'But I haven't done anything!' she cried, dropping the dress she had been holding. She had a tattoo like a pattern of thorns growing up around her neck from under her leotard, unpleasantly violent-looking against her young skin. She saw Slider notice it and said impatiently, defensively, 'It's just a transfer. It washes off. I'll take it off before my parents get back. It's just a bit of fun.'

'Was that what you were doing with Zellah Sunday night – giving each other transfers?' Hart said.

'Oh, she's so lame, she wouldn't even do that, in case it wouldn't all come off,' she said contemptuously, and then with an instant change of tone and sentiment, 'But it's cool, she's my mate, she can do what she likes. It's a free country.' Slider was still blinking at this volte-face when her face changed again. She scowled and demanded, 'What *is* this? What do you want, anyway?'

'So you haven't heard about Zellah, then?' Hart asked.

'Heard what? What are you talking about?'

She was no more than averagely pretty, Slider thought, so perhaps her extreme make-up was her way of giving herself distinction; but under it he saw no fear or consciousness in her expression. She genuinely didn't know – and was probably not interested to know, either, which was that generation's *least* attractive feature.

'When did you see her last?' he asked.

'See her last? Oh fuck, she's not run away, has she?'

'Just answer the question, please.'

'Yeah, and can the language, babe,' Hart added for him.

She looked wary now. 'Well, she came over for a couple of days. Her mum and dad knew about it. She stayed Sunday night and last night and went home this morning.'

Slider shook his head. 'Don't you know it's a very serious matter to lie to the police?'

'I'm not lying,' she said, her eyes flitting from Slider to Hart and back.

'We know you are, love,' Hart said, 'so don't make it worse for yourself. We know Zellah wasn't here this morning. She was found dead yesterday.'

'Dead?' Sophy received the word with absolute blankness. 'You're joking.'

Hart winced on Slider's behalf. 'It's nuffing to joke about, is it, girl? She was murdered. Somebody strangled her. Got it? Now are you going to sit down and answer our questions and try and help your mate, or d'you wanna get nicked for obstruction? It's up to you.'

'She can't be dead,' Sophy said, but she sat down on the bed, her demeanour compliant now. 'She's younger than me.'

A glance at Slider told Hart he wanted her to ask the questions, so she sat on the chair, pushing the clothes to one side, while he remained standing by the door. The poodle and whippet took the excuse to jump up on the bed, but the two bigger dogs remained on faithful-hound duty at Slider's feet.

'Never mind that,' Hart said. 'Just tell us about Zellah's visit. We know what her mum and dad thought was happening, but what did you really plan on doing?'

'It's not as if it was anything bad,' Sophy said in wounded tones. 'We just wanted to go to the Notting Hill Carnival yesterday, but Zellah's dad won't let her do *anything*. Every time she wants to do something it's "no, you're too young". I mean, she's nearly seventeen! But he says not the Carnival, it's too *dangerous*.' She exaggerated ludicrously. '"You might meet nasty, *rough* people, you can't go." So we made this thing up about the Southbank Fair.'

'You weren't actually going to the Southbank, then?'

She rolled her eyes. 'Duh! Of course we weren't. Lame or what? Mimes and jugglers and roundabouts? What am I, nine? No, that was just the cover, to get him to let her come over. About the only time she gets off the leash is when she comes to see me, or stays late at school, like for a club or an extra class or something, or Saturdays when we have a ballet class and we can go somewhere afterwards. Or sometimes she says there's a class when there isn't, and I cover for her. I mean, it's pathetic that she has to pretend like that, but what can you do, with dinosaurs like them?'

'So you were actually going to the Notting Hill Carnival?'

'Oh yeah, we were going all day, then in the evening, if we didn't get invited to a party or anything, we were going clubbing. That's why she was staying last night as well, so we could stay out late. Her dad would've wanted her home by ten.'

'Who was going – just you and Zellah?'

'And Chloë. Chloë Paulson. She's at school with us. She came over Sunday night and we were just going to hang out here.' She blushed at a memory.

'What?' Hart said.

Sophy looked defiant. 'Chloë had this book of cocktails she found in a drawer at home, and we were going to work our way through them. My dad's got all the ingredients in the drinks cupboard.'

'What did your sister have to say about that?'

'Abi wasn't here. She was staying with her boyfriend. Anyway, she's cool, as long I don't bug her.'

'And your parents are away?'

'They're skiing in the Andes. Abi's got a contact address for them, but we're not supposed to bother them unless it's an emergency.'

'Any other brothers and sisters?'

'Hector and Theo are at camp in Colorado. They're younger than me. And Oscar's hiking in Chamonix with his girlfriend. He's at Durham, so he's hardly ever here anyway.'

She sounded sulky, and Hart said sympathetically, 'So everyone gets away except you?'

'Yeah, I get left to look after the dogs!' She rolled her eyes in a martyred way, but quickly lost the attitude and said, 'I don't care, though. I like being on my own. I could have gone to Chile but I hate skiing. It's more fun here. And I thought it'd be nice for Zellah to have a bit of fun too. Only she had other ideas,' she added morosely. 'As it happens.'

'What d'you mean?'

'Well, it turns out she was never planning on going to the Carnival anyway. She came over Sunday about six, the way we arranged. Chloë was already here. We'd been out in the afternoon – Zellah's dad wouldn't let her come earlier, said Sunday was a family day or some such shit.' Another eye roll. 'Anyway, she turns up, and Chloë says, "OK, girl, let's get wrecked," and then Zellah calmly tells us she's got a date.'

'A date? With a boy?'

'Of course with a boy! But she wouldn't tell us who. We kept asking but she just shrugged and said nobody we knew.'

'Was it Mike Carmichael, do you think?'

The question didn't surprise her, but she shook her head. 'Why wouldn't she have told us if it was him? But she wasn't still seeing him. She did for a bit, after her dad told her not to – well, you've got to, haven't you? – but I razzed her about him because he was such a dork and she dropped him'

'*Was* he a dork? I heard he was cool.'

'Per-leese! He comes from a council estate. He's got a motorbike. He's, like, some old greaseball rocker. I wouldn't go out with anyone that doesn't have his own car,' she added proudly.

'So she didn't give you *any* hint about who it was?'

'No, like I said, she was being all mysterious and wouldn't-you-like-to-know, as if it was someone really good.'

'Was she excited?'

She frowned. 'I wouldn't say excited, exactly. More sort of tense. Well, if it was the first date she would be nervous. Anyway, I said, "you can't go dressed like that." All her clothes were terrible, like a kid's clothes, and she had hardly any make-up. Her dad wouldn't allow it. She said it didn't matter, but I said she couldn't go on a date looking like that, not from my house. So we had a bit of fun, dressing her and making her up with our stuff, and Chloë made a few cocktails while we were doing it, so it was all right, we still had a good time. Then she went off.'

'This date didn't call for her?'

'We'd have seen him if he did, wouldn't we?' she said, with a sigh at Hart's stupidity. 'She said he was meeting her outside the Black Lion, in the car park.'

'And you were expecting her back that night, were you?'

45

'Yeah. She was still coming to the Carnival with us. She said she might be late back, so I gave her a spare key, in case we were asleep.'

'And you were in the whole evening?'

'Yeah. We did think about going to the pub, but in the end we just stayed in, talking, having a laugh, a few drinks. Just hanging out.'

'What time did you go to bed?'

'I dunno. About one o'clock, I suppose. Zellah wasn't back, and when we got up she still wasn't. Chloë said, "She's doing all right for herself." We just thought she was staying over with him.'

'Did she phone you at any point?'

'No.'

'And the next day you went to the Carnival without her?'

'Well, yes.' She looked as if she was being accused of something. 'We hung around a bit, but she didn't turn up, so we just reckoned she was spending the day with the bloke, whoever he was. And why wouldn't she? She doesn't get many chances like that. We reckoned it was up to us to cover for her, with her parents. I was scared they'd ring to check up on her, so I was glad we were out all day, but there was nothing on the answer-machine when we got back. So we did a quick change and went out clubbing. Chloë went home from the club and I got back here about four this morning, and there was still nothing on the machine, so I went to bed. Unless I heard from her I was going to say she left here this morning, the way we planned, and after that it was up to her. I mean, you can only do so much.' She shrugged. 'But she never rang or anything, so I reckoned she must have gone home.'

'So the last time you saw her was when she left for her date at . . . what time?' Slider asked.

She looked at him as if she'd forgotten he was there. His presence reminded her that this was serious, and her voice shed its attitude as she answered. 'It was about half-seven, quarter to eight, I suppose.'

'Was your sister here yesterday?'

'Abi? No, she came home this morning, about half-eleven. She woke me up coming in.'

'So, once more, to be quite clear,' Slider said, 'you have no idea where she went on Sunday night, or who she was with? Think very carefully. It's very important you tell us everything you know.'

'Yeah, love,' Hart said, 'if you've got an idea, it's not dropping anyone in it to tell us. We don't know it was the bloke she went out with that did it. She might have gone somewhere else afterwards, and he might know where.'

Sophy's eyes grew round for once, and she looked younger than her years. 'I don't know, honest. If I knew, I'd tell you. I swear. I want to help. She was my mate.' Suddenly enormous, childlike tears welled up in her eyes and rolled over, through the black stuff. 'I can't believe it. Who would do that? Who would do that to her?'

'That's what we're trying to find out,' Hart said.

Outside, she saw that Slider was preoccupied and took a chance on it, went round to the driver's side, and when he automatically went to the passenger side, held out her hand across the roof and said, 'Keys, guv?'

He tossed them to her without seeming to notice he had done it, and she unlocked the car and got in with a small, satisfied smile. In the absence of any orders, she headed back towards the factory. 'Well, wasn't *she* a little sweetheart?' she said after a while. 'Little rich princess pretending to be street – as long as it's in the safety of daddy's big house. Ballet class and Goth tattoos! Pur-leese!'

'That's a very unattractive expression, Detective Constable.'

'It was ironic, that time,' she explained. 'But I'm crushed we gotta start again. I was really fancying Biker Boy for it.'

'We've only got Sophy's word for it that Zellah wasn't seeing him. She may not have told Sophy everything. Would you?'

'No, you're right. And Sophy did say she razzed her about him. Maybe that's why she was being secretive. After all, why would she want to keep a new man secret? She'd want to boast about it, if she had a new boyfriend, wouldn't she?'

'Unless he was also someone Sophy would disapprove of. A nerd or a lamo.'

'Guv, where'd you get language like that?' Hart said, shocked.

'I don't think we need to eliminate Mike Carmichael yet. While bearing in mind she may have had another boyfriend altogether. Maybe her other friends would know.' And he sighed at the thought of having to interview another bunch of Sophys. What a depressingly trashy girl she was. Despite all her advantages of money and education, blokes, clothes and getting wasted seemed to be the summit of her ambition. And where did they learn this contempt of grown-ups? Every generation had always thought its parents 'didn't understand', but they hadn't despised them for it. It was unsettling.

'I just wish I knew what she was *doing* there – on the Scrubs,' Hart was saying. 'I mean, it's such a weird place to go.'

'Hmm,' said Slider, thinking. They did now have Zellah's own clothes, in a bag in the back – not that they would tell them anything, but the Wildings would want them back – and a description of Zellah's handbag (pink fabric with Lurex threads and a thin pink shoulder strap) which had not been found yet.

Damn – he'd remembered something. 'Give me your phone, would you?' he said. Hart passed it over and he phoned Atherton. 'Have you done the Wildings yet?'

'They're here now. I was just going down.'

'Ask one of them for the number of Zellah's mobile, will you? Assuming she had one. I meant to ask the Sophy girl and forgot.'

'OK. Anything else?'

'Not that I can think of. We're on our way back.'

Wilding was reading over his short statement. Zellah had left at about five. He went to his shed and did accounts and paperwork for the parish council and Neighbourhood Watch, while Pam watched the television. He had fetched his own supper at about nine o'clock and took it back to his shed, where he had worked on the wooden loco. He liked to work at night – it was quiet and he didn't get disturbed. He didn't sleep very well at nights anyway. He worked until about two, and then went to bed. Pam had been already asleep when he went up.

'By the way,' Atherton said, as he reached the end, 'did Zellah have a mobile phone?'

Wilding looked up. 'Yes, I did buy one for her. I wasn't wholly in favour at first, having seen how much time they waste with that silly texting. But I hope and believe Zellah was a bit more sensible than that. And her mother felt that these days a girl ought to have one, in case she gets stranded somewhere. You can't depend on finding a phone box any more. Not that she's out very often, and never late at night, but Pam said she'd feel happier if she knew Zellah could get in touch any time. So I agreed.'

'Have you got a recent bill we could see?'

'It was a pay-as-you-go one. You don't get a bill.'

'Then can you give me the number, please?'

Wilding looked surprised. 'Why do you want that?'

'Well, it may help us locate her handbag, which we still haven't found.'

'How can it do that?'

'Every mobile phone gives out a radio signal that can be tracked,' Atherton said, recollecting patiently that Wilding probably didn't read much popular fiction or watch cop shows on the telly. He probably thought *The Vicar of Dibley* was cutting-edge.

'I didn't know that,' Wilding said.

'So if the phone is in her bag we'll be able to pinpoint it. And there may be something in her bag that will help us as to where she went on Sunday night – a cinema stub, say, or a receipt from a café,' he added to forestall the next question. 'So if you can tell me the number . . .?'

'Hmm? Oh, yes.' He seemed utterly distracted, and Atherton, who had accompanied them to the morgue earlier, was not at all surprised. What a rotten business it was. As Slider had said during another case, parents weren't supposed to outlive their children. It was something from which you could never wholly recover.

'Right,' said Porson, 'you've identified the body and the family's been informed. So we can release the name, get the photos out, do the appeal. What's happening now?'

'Everyone's still out doing the fingertip search and canvassing the neighbours,' Slider said. It was eerily quiet in the CID room.

'Anything from that?'

'Not yet, sir, but it's early days.'

'It's the early day that catches the worm. What else?'

'We think the boyfriend, even if he is an ex-boyfriend, is worth pursuing.'

'Oh, always,' Porson agreed. 'Has he got form?'

'Nothing much, but he is known. Joy-riding when he was a juvenile. A couple of tugs for possession. The local police have suspected him of dealing, but they never got anything on him, and apparently he's not been much in evidence lately – they think he's operating somewhere else.'

'But nothing for violence – affray, carrying a knife, anything on that side of the septum?'

'Nothing like that, and no sexual assaults, either. But Doc Cameron says she wasn't raped, so it's not strictly speaking a sexual assault anyway.'

Porson stopped his pacing to look at Slider sharply. 'Strangling's always a sexual assault,' he said. 'And sexual assault's never about sex; it's about domination and destruction.'

'Yes, sir,' Slider said. The old man came out 'orrible sensible sometimes.

'There's more than one way to butter a parsnip. Whoever was having sex with her, strangled her; that's my view. Pity there isn't any semen to get the DNA from. Let's hope Cameron finds a hair or something. Anyway, follow up the boyfriend. What else?'

'We have to check at the Black Lion if anyone saw the girl, or saw who picked her up. Bearing in mind, of course, that she may have met somewhere else entirely, and just used the Black Lion to throw Sophy off the scent. She seems to have been quite mysterious about it all.'

'Right.'

'And we ought to make questioning the fairground people a priority.'

'You think someone there might be involved?'

'It's not that; it's the question of why she was on the Scrubs at all. It's only a mile across the grass from the fair to where she was found. Maybe she was at the fair that evening, and maybe someone saw her, that's all.'

'All right, go for it. Anything else?'

Slider sighed. 'I think we have to interview her school friends and find out if she said anything to any of them about a new boyfriend, or about her plans for that weekend.'

Porson eyed him sympathetically. Interviewing young girls was nobody's favourite job. Boys were much easier. They gave you lip but, as with horses, after the wild bucking generally came submission. But with girls you never got to the end of the attitude, and if you tried to press them they took refuge in tears, hysteria or, worst case, accusations of mental or physical assault.

'Well, don't get hung up about it. It's a rotten job but somebody's got to do it. Just make sure you don't get left alone with any of 'em. I can do without any of my officers being suspended on the say-so of some little madam with more mummy than sense.'

FIVE

All Creatures Grunt and Smell

It was late when Slider got home, but Joanna was there to greet him with a kiss, and there was a welcome fragrance of cooking in the air. He understood completely why married men were said to live longer than single ones.

'I bet you haven't eaten all day,' she said. 'I made a big soup. It's all hot and ready, on the table as soon as you like.'

He only had to shed his jacket and tie and wash his hands. Joanna's soups were a meal in themselves, so packed with good things you practically needed a knife and fork to eat them. After a large bowlful, accompanied by the heel end of a chunky loaf (she always saved the heels for him, though he suspected she liked them herself – she took wifehood very seriously, he realized humbly), he was feeling revived enough to pay proper attention to a morsel of cheese, with which she thoughtfully put out a glass of Bruichladdich. He sighed and looked at her. 'I'd marry you if you weren't a married woman.'

She batted her eyelashes. 'I love you, too. So, how's it going?'

'Too early to say. Thousands of canvasses to go through, lots of sightings of young people and young couples in and around the area but nothing stands out yet. One obvious suspect but only because he's a bad hat and he knew her. We've nothing on him.'

'Oh, well that all sounds wonderfully positive,' she said. 'You look bushed. Another Brutal Laddie?'

'Just a tiny one. Have one with me?'

'Just a tiny one.'

'I interviewed the victim's best friend today,' he said while she poured. 'Or I should say "mate". God, it was depressing. Girl from a well-to-do middle-class family, attending a fee-paying school, and she talks and behaves like a trollop. It made me think of Kate. I don't want her becoming like that, but I suspect there's nothing anyone can do to prevent it. I don't suppose the Cooper-Hutchinsons planned their Sophy to be like that, but the culture is stronger than the people.'

'Don't be silly – the culture *is* the people,' she said briskly. 'Mostly people are too indolent. It's a huge effort to take a stand over things, and they can't be bothered. They'd sooner be friends with their children than try to discipline them.'

'Tough talk.' Slider smiled wearily at her. 'I can't even influence Kate now, let alone discipline her. We really have to find somewhere with another bedroom, so I can have them to stay. I can't be a part of her life when I can only see her for a couple of hours at an amusement park like a Divorce Dad. Did you have any luck today?'

'Oh, I saw the details of a lot of properties, but nothing *we* can afford. One estate agent recommended looking at the auction sites. There are a lot of repossessed properties coming on at the moment, at rock-bottom prices. I've got the details of a couple of sites. I'll have a go at it tomorrow when the baby's napping.'

'Talking of the baby, have you found a sitter for Thursday night?'

'I asked Emily, and she jumped at it. You'd think I was doing her the favour.'

'Oh good! Funny Atherton didn't say anything to me.'

'She probably hasn't spoken to him, any more than I spoke to you,' she pointed out kindly. 'She's thrilled about it, bless her. Says she's never looked after a baby before, and can't wait.'

Slider stirred. 'Never looked after a baby? Is that a good idea, then?'

'Good practice for her, for when she and Jim get at it.'

'I think they're at it already.'

'Parenthood, rather than mere vigorous bonking.'

'But I meant, is it a good idea for the baby?'

'Oh, what could go wrong?' she said. 'Worst case he howls all evening, which won't hurt him, and will prepare her for the realities of life.'

He smiled. 'I love your cavalier attitude to our only offspring.'

'You're a worrier. Probably comes from being an only child. When you come from a big family like me, you're expected to get on with it and survive. *My* older sisters used to use me for netball practice,' she boasted largely. 'Never did me any harm.'

'I used to sit in for the smoking beagles for pocket money,' he capped her.

She smiled, glad to see he had relaxed: that tense, grey look had gone out of his face. 'I'm ready for bed,' she said. 'How do you feel about sleeping with a married woman?'

He pretended to consider. 'Sounds good to me. Have you got her number?'

'I've got *your* number, you Lothario. Leave the dishes,' she said, standing up. 'I'll clear it in the morning. I want my cot.'

He caught her up, slid an arm round her waist, and nibbled her neck. 'How do you feel about making love with a married man?'

'As long as you don't wake up my baby.'

They headed for the bedroom, where the bedside lamp was already on to guide them home. 'I can't help feeling,' he said, 'that learning how to do it really quietly has got to come in handy some time.'

Detective Inspector Douglas 'call me Duggie' Sweyback of Woodley Green nick (which had responsibility for the Woodley South Estate) had trotted out the tea and biscuits – custard cream, coconut ring and Abbey Crunch – as soon as Slider arrived, and was plainly spoiling for a chat, so it was some time before Slider was able to get down to the matter in hand.

Sweyback's name owed more to Nabisco than Quasimodo, as he had revealed during an etymological discussion at a junket they had both attended: in fact, he was as tall and straight as a reasonable man needed to be, taller and more heavily built than Slider, only somewhat under-endowed in the follicular department – something that was often on his mind. Slider had more than once heard his treatise on Why Bald Men Don't Get On (subheading No Bald Man Will Ever Be Prime Minister Again). Sweyback regarded Slider as a bit of a soul mate, largely because it was unusual for an older copper to remain at station level rather than levitating to the SOs, or copping out to the cushy desk jobs. When they turned up at the same do, as happened from time to time, Sweyback would hasten to Slider's side with the glad eagerness of a German tourist spotting a sausage, and would bend his ear about the sheer awfulness of the Job these days.

The last such occasion had been a seminar on Policing By Intelligence, and Sweyback reverted to it now, dunking his Abbey Crunch in the PG Tips, and reeling out a few things he had thought of since and hadn't had a chance to air to anyone yet.

'Policing By Intelligence? What we need is policing *with* intelligence, but fat chance of getting any of that these days! You know what the other thing means: crouching over a computer all day, never going out on the street, fiddling your figures to make it look as if you're doing your job properly. You can't police from a desk. But these youngsters don't know what I'm talking about. Do you know, I haven't got a single person over thirty-five on my firm? I'm saddled with kids still wet behind the ears, and of course that's the way they've been brought up. If it's not in the computer they don't want to know. You talk about knowing your own ground and knowing your own villains and working up your own snouts, and they look at you as if you were talking Chinese. *You* know what I mean, Bill. You're like me. We're from the old school. I'm a copper's copper, and I'm not ashamed to say it, I don't care who's listening. But the Job's going to the dogs. I don't know why I carry on sometimes. They won't *let* you catch criminals, and when you do catch them, the CPS won't prosecute. Did you see that statistic in the paper the other day? Only fifteen per cent of serious crimes end up with a jail sentence.'

Slider listened patiently – he agreed with much of what Sweyback said, but hearing him saying it was a useful lesson to take on board about not sounding like a disgruntled old fart. He waited for him to run down (it was never much longer after the 'I'm a copper's copper' bit) and occupied the unused part of his brain with wondering whether Duggie's teeth were natural or not. They were so white and even, it either suggested tremendous lifelong care, or the old Royal Doulton job.

Eventually Sweyback reached the bit about having had it up to here and thinking about early retirement, and Slider was able to say, 'Go on with you, you'll die in the saddle. What would you do with retirement – play golf and collect beer mats? You'd miss Woodley South too much.'

'Miss it? It'll be the death of me!' But it was enough of a reminder. Sweyback pulled himself together and said, 'You're interested in one of my home-grown villains, aren't you? Young Michael Carmichael.'

'Yes, what can you tell me about him? What's he like?'

'Cocky young devil. Too much of this.' He flapped his hand in the 'mouthy' gesture. 'Too clever for his own good, that'd be my verdict. He's bright enough, could have made something of himself, but like all these kids he's lazy – wants everything *now*. So he goes the easy route.'

'He's been in trouble for possession, I understand.'

'Yes, and I'd bet my last biccie he's dealing, but we've never been able to nail him for it. He can spot a ringer too easily, and he seems to know by instinct when we set up a surveillance, and just melts away. But I know for a fact he supplies his mum. Well, who else'd do it? Lilian – Lilly – Atwood's her name. She's a big user.'

'Not Carmichael, then?'

'I don't know that she ever married Michael's dad. He *calls* himself Carmichael, but anyway what's in a name, as the Bard says. Atwood's her third, the one after Carmichael. He's inside now – Atwood is – doing a ten stretch for armed robbery. He was the one that was around while Michael was growing up. Her first one, O'Dade, he's dead, killed in a pub fight donkeys' years ago. That was about my first case when I came to Woodley Green. Old Lilly was quite a looker in those days, not that you'd know it now. She'd already started drinking too much and putting herself about when O'Dade snuffed it. Then she had this brief thing with Carmichael. Could have gone respectable at that point – he was a rep for a paper company, Bowman's of Bracknell. But he took off when she got in the club. He'd seen the future and it didn't work. Then not long after she had young Michael she fell in with Atwood. That was her downfall. He's a nasty, violent piece of shit. In and out of chokey, drunk more often than not, belted her and the kids – she had three more by him, one whenever he was out. They're in care, now. First she went on the sauce, and now she's doing drugs. She's hanging round the pubs most nights, bumming for drinks.'

'Prostitution?' Slider asked.

'She used to make quite a living that way. When she's not monged she's one of those women they call lively – which means she's noisy, got a foul mouth and she laughs a lot – but there's a lot of men on the Woodley South don't ask for more. But she's not often straight enough these days to make a living at it. It's low-level stuff now. She'll do it down an alley or in a car for the price of a wrap. We've taken her up for soliciting a few times – more to move her on than in hope of a prosecution. But she'll do it anywhere with anyone. They call her Lilly the Pink. I'll leave you to work out why.' He paused a beat, and added in conclusion, 'Not too much of a surprise that young Michael went wrong.'

'He's still living there, is he, with his mother?'

'You tell me,' Sweyback said, scratching delicately at his pate. 'I haven't seen him about as much the last few months, but he's still there sometimes. Bringing her the doings, I suppose. Who knows where these youngsters hang out nowadays. It's not like when we were kids – they all sleep on each other's floors. Anywhere's home. To be frank with you, if he's not on my radar I'm not worrying about him. He's the kind of lad that, when he finally goes over, it'll be big trouble for everyone. You know some kids just potter along being a low-grade nuisance, and in some ways they're the worst because you can't do much about 'em. But there's others marked out for glory, as the Bard says, and they eventually go down hard for something really big. Carmichael's that sort. He's a storm brewing, he is. A disaster waiting to happen.'

'Is he violent?'

'Quick-tempered, I'd say. Quick to take offence. And handy with his fists. Well, with a dad like Atwood it's not surprising. That's all he's known – when in doubt, lash out. He's been in a lot of fights but we've never had him for anything more than that. And being a fighter's kept him out of the gangs, which is one blessing: the only thing we've got over *them* is they're all pig stupid, and someone like Michael could pull 'em together into a real menace, if he was interested. What's your interest in him, by the way?' He gave in at last to the curiosity that had been burning him for the last ten minutes.

'We think he might have known our latest murder victim.'

'Oh, that girl on the Scrubs? I saw that in the papers, wondered if it was yours. You fancy him for it, do you?'

'Haven't got that far. But he was going out with her at one time.'

'*Was* he? Sinning above his station, eh?'

'Did he have a reputation that way?'

'What, for girls? They couldn't get enough of him.'

'And did he smack them around?'

'Never had any complaints against him. Of course, he grew up seeing it at home, and often they repeat what they know. But he never had to force anyone, I can tell you that. Good looking, leery sort of lad. Always had a girl on his arm. But I'll say this – I can see him killing a girl in a temper, if she got across him the wrong way.'

Slider nodded. 'It looks like that sort of murder.' *Except for the tights*, he thought uneasily. The tights were a real thorn in the woodpile, as Porson might say. 'Well, thanks a lot, Duggie. You've given me quite a graphic picture of him. A great help.'

'Murder, eh?' Sweyback said thoughtfully. 'Well, I said when he went, he'd go big. Are you going round his mum's house?'

'Yes, in the hope that he might be there. What does she do, by the way?'

'Drugs? Well, she'll do anything she can get. Dope, coke. Scag – she smokes that. Booze when she can't get anything else. Haven't seen the boy around lately but he comes and goes, and you might get something out of her about where to look. Probably a good time to catch her,' he added, looking at his watch. 'After she wakes up and before she goes looking for the next fix.'

'Right,' said Slider.

Sweyback rose to his feet and extended a hand like a ham for Slider to shake. 'If I spot him around, or if one of my snouts spots him, shall I tug him for you?'

'That would be grand,' Slider said. 'Thanks a lot, Duggie.'

'No trouble. Us old 'uns have got to stick together. There aren't many of us left.'

The Woodley South was as depressing as he had known it would be – a wasteland of mean houses, boarded-up windows, broken fences and dying hedges, trampled front gardens full of junk, the rotting corpses of dead cars that the boy vultures were taking a long time devouring. Slider had brought Fathom and McLaren with him in case of trouble – Fathom because he was big and meaty, and McLaren because he was tough and whippy and quick in a fight. He collected them from the Woodley Green canteen where they had been wiling away the time he was with Sweyback. McLaren, at least, had understood that the purpose of the canteen stop was not to fill up the tea-tank – though he had managed to take on board a cheese roll and a massive chunk of coconut cake, and was now finishing a giant Mars Bar in the car while Slider drove.

But he said, 'I got it from one of the woodentops in the canteen that Lilly Atwood's shacked up with a black bloke at the moment.'

'Don't slobber chocolate down my neck.'

'Sorry, guv. Anyway, this bloke's half her age, name of Leonard McGrory, Lennie, local Reading lad, got a bit of form, TDAs, shoplifting, possession, and done time for malicious wounding – he knifed some dealer that was trying to stiff him. Got six months for that. God knows what he's doing with Lilly the Pink, but maybe it's got something to do with Mike Carmichael, if he *is* dealing.'

'Well done,' Slider said. 'Always useful to know what we're facing. What did you find out, Fathom?'

'I didn't know we were supposed to be finding stuff out,' he said, a touch sulkily.

'He spent the time smoking too much and watching me,' McLaren said.

'I didn't know we were on duty,' Fathom complained.

'You're always on duty,' Slider said. 'And if you don't know that finding stuff out is your job, you shouldn't be in the CID.'

'Sorry, guv.'

'Mind you, watching McLaren eat is always an education. But if he can eat and work, you can watch and work. You should have got chatting to someone.'

'Lazy, that's his problem,' said McLaren, who had raised inertia to an art form.

If anyone was going to criticize Slider's troops, he'd do it himself. To balance the books he said to McLaren, 'If you applied to women the expert attention you apply to food, you'd have to become a Mormon.' McLaren was famous in the firm for not having had a date for years. He slowed the car. 'This is it. What a name for a road like this – Applelea.'

'This used to be called the Orchard Estate when it was first built,' McLaren said. 'Bloke in the canteen told me it was all farmland, orchards and stuff, up to the sixties. So they gave all the roads farmy names. Gawd 'elp us.'

Slider had noticed. Apart from Applelea they had passed High Garth, Hay Wain, Cherry Orchard Lane, Plum Tree Lane, Tithe Road, Orchard View, and Blossom View. A rural paradise, care of central government post-war planning. As McLaren so aptly observed, Gawd 'elp us.

Number fourteen was just as tatty and desolate as its neighbours, but it was obviously inhabited: all its windows still had their glass and all were curtained. The curtains in the downstairs window were drawn shut, rough-looking red cloth hanging slightly askew, though the upstairs ones were open. There was a sheet of hardboard nailed over the glass portion of the front door, and the house number was missing, though a paler outline in the dirty paint showed where it had been. They walked cautiously up the path, and when they neared the house they saw that the front door, though pulled to, was not completely shut. The wood of the frame, however, was not splintered. It had not been jemmied or kicked in: it must either have been left open deliberately, or had been pushed carelessly by the last person in or out, who had not checked that it had latched.

Slider pushed it cautiously, and it swung back. A narrow, dark hall led straight back to a kitchen, whose open door revealed a scene of dirty crockery, fast-food boxes, and general rubbish in greater amount than you would have thought possible in a room that small. The stairs, narrow and steep, were to the left. To the right was the single downstairs room, whose door was slightly ajar, enough to see it was dark inside, the curtains closed and no light on. Pop music was sounding in there at medium volume from a radio station. The carpet underfoot and up the stairs was filthy with footmarks and spillings, and in the air was a smell of dirt, feet, fat, hashish and rancid garbage.

That living-room door had the look of a trap to Slider. Had they seen him coming, and were luring him in? But he thought of Lilly the Pink and her half-age shack-up. People like that rarely showed cunning. They just reacted belatedly when something came at them. A movement from the kitchen caught his eye and he could tell from the sharpness of the chill down his neck how tense he was. A rat was sitting on top of the heap of plates and cardboard boxes on the draining board, working on a Kentucky Fried Chicken bone. Slider forced his shoulders to relax. He wished the rat no ill. Anyway, it was the only one in this house who was doing any clearing up.

There had been no sound or movement anywhere, so indicating for Fathom to stay by the door, in case there was anyone upstairs, and for McLaren to keep close, he pushed the living-room door all the way open. Even in the dim red light filtering through the curtains he could see well enough to pick out a scattering of cheap furniture, a television – turned off – and a sofa bed in the pulled-out position taking up most of the room. The floor and other surfaces were a mess of clothes, fast-food boxes, bottles, glasses, empty beer cans, overflowing ashtrays, and general litter. The radio was sitting in the hearth of the boarded-up fireplace. The smell in this room was intensified by the addition of bodies, sweat and stale cigarette smoke.

And two people were asleep in the bed, tumbled together with a grubby sheet to cover their modesty. One of them was snoring throatily, interspersed with an occasional wet gulping snort, like a pig enjoying apples.

Slider positioned his men, stepped to the window and pulled the curtains. He half expected an explosion of movement from the bed, but all that happened was that the tangled heap stirred and grunted, and after a moment the male half of it sat up blearily, rubbing its head with one hand and scratching under the sheet with the other.

'Wassappenin?' It rubbed its eyes, and then registered Slider and McLaren. 'Wassgoinon? Who the fuck are you?' Belated alarm widened the eyes, and he began fumbling about under the pillow.

Slider suspected a weapon under there, and said sternly, 'Stay still. We're the police. We just want to ask you a few questions.' He went on fumbling. 'Don't do it, son. You're not in any trouble – yet. Let's keep it that way.'

But it was cigarettes that came out. At the same time, the female half mumbled itself awake – or half awake, at any rate. She turned over on to her back, frowning against the light, smacked her lips and groaned. 'Whafuck's going on? Put the light out.'

'Wake up, Lil,' the man said urgently, jabbing her ungently. He was sitting up, covered from the waist down – always thankful for small mercies, Slider thought – and from the undeveloped nature of his bare chest he looked to be no more than twenty. He was of West Indian stock, with longish hair, tattoos on his upper arms – a spider in its web on the right and a ghost on the left – and rings through both eyebrows and the left nostril.

Lilly dragged her eyes open, and then sat up slowly, instinctively pulling the sheet up with her to cover her breasts. She looked at Slider carefully, and then yawned widely. The yawn turned into a prolonged and hacking cough, which nearly dislodged the sheet, after which she wiped her nose on her fingers, her fingers on the bed, and said, 'Can't you fuckers leave me alone?'

'That's enough of that language,' McLaren said, and threw her a T-shirt from the floor at his feet. 'Put that on. We just want to talk to you.'

She inspected him, smiled unpleasantly, picked up the T-shirt and deliberately dropped the sheet so that they had a brief introduction to her womanly frame before it disappeared under the soiled cotton.

The youth, to do him credit, looked angry with her and muttered, 'For fuck's sake, Lil, it's the filth.'

'Well, they can get the fuck out of my house,' Lilly said, feeling around in the bed. 'Gimme a fag, Len, for fuck's sake.'

'I said that's enough of that,' McLaren said.

'Oh, get lost,' she said with weary irritability, taking a cigarette from Lennie and sucking at the light he offered. She looked, Slider thought, anything between fifty and sixty, but he knew how drugs aged people, so she was probably only in her early forties. Her face was sickly pale, with brown circles under her eyes and an uncomely spot coming up on her chin, and her hair was limp and greasy, flat to her skull and straggling over her shoulders. But she might once have been good looking: she had a strongly sculpted mouth (though it was turned down disagreeably now), a determined chin and a straight nose. But just now, sucking on the cigarette in between phlegmy coughs, she looked like an old bag.

Slider showed his badge and told them who he was. 'I'm looking for Mike Carmichael,' he said.

Lennie looked cautiously at Lilly, who said, 'I don't know any Mike. So you can piss off out of my house. What's *he* want?' She directed her verbal energy suddenly towards Fathom, who had appeared in the doorway, unable to bear not seeing. He didn't speak, and she stitched an appalling smile on and said, 'You got any change, love? I'm short me rent. Come on, love, a coupla quid. Give us twenty and I'll give you a blow job.'

Fathom looked taken aback and she went into raucous laughter. 'Your face!'

Lennie looked embarrassed and said, 'Can it, Lilly, for fuck's sake. It's the police.'

'Oh, don't you think coppers do it? I've had plenty of them in the past, I can tell you. You want names?' She leered at Slider.

'Just tell us where Mike is, and we'll leave you in peace.'

'I don't know any Mike. So get out.'

'Your son, Mike. Michael Carmichael.' Slider had seen the candle, spoon and glass straw on the mantelpiece, the tackle for chasing the dragon, which was evidence enough to arrest the pair of them – not that he wanted to. He gestured to McLaren to pick up the piece of silver foil from the floor – obviously the wrap the H had come in. McLaren picked it up and showed it to them.

'There'll be enough traces on this to show what was in it,' he said. 'We've got a field test kit in the car. Possession of scag is a serious offence – and what'll we find if we search a bit more?'

It was enough to alarm Lennie. 'Mike's not here,' he blurted.

'Shut your mouth, you stupid little shit,' Lilly growled at him.

'Look, it's her, not me. I don't do scag.'

'I'll kill you, you fucking rat!'

'You let me go, and I'll tell you.'

'Tell me, then,' Slider said calmly. 'Where can we find Michael Carmichael?'

Lilly flung herself at her lover with an incoherent scream, and Fathom leapt into action, throwing himself at her and grabbing her arms. McLaren had to go to help him, while Slider gestured Lennie back as he jumped out of bed, and warned him not to try to leg it. Fathom and McLaren were at a disadvantage with Lilly, since they had to fight fair, try not to hurt her, and keep from being bitten or scratched – God knew how toxic she was. McLaren could have felled her with a tap to the chin, but they weren't allowed to do that. After a bit she got tired of the business and stopped struggling, otherwise they could have been fighting for hours. She slumped back on the bed, coughing. They kept hold of her arms, panting, but she said, 'Let me go. I gotta find my fag, before the bed goes up.' And when they let her go, she gave herself to rummaging about for the lit cigarette that had fallen among the sheets in the struggle.

Slider said, 'All right, Lennie. Where's Mike?'

In the interval, the naked youth had put on a pair of sweat pants from the floor, and now was standing with his arms wrapped round his chest, watching, his eyes flitting about as if calculating the odds of escape.

'You'll let me go?' he said now.

'I promise.'

'Well, he ain't here. He don't live here no more. He's got these friends up town – rich kids. He hangs about with them now. We're not good enough for him,' he added scathingly.

'Where does he live?'

'I don't know the address. It's in Notting Hill, that's all I know. He wouldn't tell me.'

'Shut your face, you little shit!' Lilly said angrily. 'I'm warning you.'

He looked at her with a wrench of contempt. 'I've had it with you, you rotten slag. You're always calling me names. I don't owe you nothing.' He looked at Slider. 'Mike's got it good up there, selling coke to these rich kids for big money. Well, why wouldn't he? Better than knocking stuff out round here for half the price. He doesn't like me and I don't like him. You should hear what he said about me and Lilly. He thinks he's too good for the likes of us now. Well, stuff him! And stuff you, Lilly! You and your skanky son. I'm not getting in trouble for either of you.'

Lilly screamed at him incoherently, and Fathom and McLaren had to restrain her again, while Slider was having to persuade Lennie not to deprive them of his company just yet, which was how he excused himself afterwards for not having heard anything from outside. But suddenly all the ruckus stopped as if by magic. Someone had appeared in the doorway. Slider turned to see a young man in leather jacket and jeans standing there.

Lilly saw him too, stopped writhing, and cried urgently, 'Mikey, have you got the stuff? Have you got the shit for me, Mikey?'

The man disappeared with amazing speed. Slider flung himself after him, feeling, rather than seeing, McLaren coming behind.

But the fleeing man had jumped astride a powerful motorbike parked at the kerb. Because the engine was hot, it caught at once. Slider only managed to touch a sleeve with fingertips as he swerved out of reach. McLaren passed him running as the bike roared up the road, but he stopped after a few yards, seeing it was hopeless. The bike turned the corner and was out of sight.

Slider ran to the car. There wasn't the faintest chance of catching him with that sort of start, but the gesture had to be made. The others piled in, and he drove off with a squeal of rubber.

'Anyone get the number?' McLaren said.

No one had.

'It was a Harley Davidson,' Fathom said.

'Yeah, we got that,' McLaren said witheringly.

'But he must be making big money, to have a bike like that,' Fathom offered.

'Yeah,' said McLaren, 'and better than that, we know we're on to something, or else why did he run?'

SIX

One Ring Leads to a Mother

Sergeant 'Nutty' Nicholls, the handsome, polyphiloprogenitive Scot from the far north-west, took the trouble to come upstairs to Slider's office from the front desk to report that there was a woman waiting to see him. 'She says she's your victim's headmistress.'

'Oh? Well, I'd better see her. She might have an insight to share. What's she like?'

'Posh. I doubt she's ever seen the inside of a polis station before. She spoke to Harris ve-ry slo-owly to be sure the puir heathen understood what she was saying.'

'We'd better not slap her in an interview room, then,' Slider said. 'Can you get someone to wheel her up here?'

'My thought exactly. She's the sort that'd tell on ye in a minute. Years of working with children warps your mind. It's a bad business, this, Bill,' he went on, suddenly serious. 'With six girls of my own, I hate it like fire. Any leads yet?'

'Not really. But we've got everyone out asking questions, and someone will have seen something. They always do.'

'Aye. Well,' he sighed, 'not to be suggesting anything, but I don't know if you knew that Ronnie Oates is back in circulation.'

'The Acton Strangler?' Slider said, and then distracted himself. 'I can't believe we've got a serial killer called Oates.'

'God has a strange sense of humour,' Nicholls acknowledged. 'But I'd remind ye that he's never killed anyone.'

'I beg his pardon,' Slider said. Oates had indecently assaulted five women, and although the assaults themselves had been fairly minor, he had a proclivity for choking his sexual partners during the act, which had eventually got him into trouble when one of them complained. It had also finally brought him to the notice of the press,

65

who could not resist giving him the sobriquet. 'What did he get last time?'

'Four years. He was a good boy and got out after eighteen months. That was a couple of months ago, and Arthur told me when we swapped over that he's been seen around East Acton again, where his mother lives.'

'Arthur' was Paxman, the sergeant on the night relief.

'How come he always knows everything?' Slider complained.

'People tell him things. He's like the river that king in the legend stuck his head in, to whisper his secret. He flows.' Nicholls demonstrated a beautiful smoothness with one hand. 'Men may come and men may go but he goes on for ever.'

'Well, thanks for telling me, anyway,' Slider said. 'Oates liked to use the women's own tights, didn't he?'

'That's why I thought you ought to know right away,' said Nicholls. 'The trouble with people like him is that they escalate. The sin loses its edge so they have to sin a bit harder to get the same thrill. And he's just stupid enough to want to earn his sobriquet. He may have finally crossed the line, Bill.'

'Yes,' said Slider. It was a dismal prospect.

'I'll wheel up your woman,' Nutty said. He got to the door and turned back to say, 'His ma used to tie him up when he was bad, you know – Oates. When he was a wean. Used to tie him to the banisters by the neck so he wouldn't struggle. Used to use a pair of her old tights.' He shook his head. 'The things we do to our children.'

The woman moved so briskly across the room that Slider only just had time to get to his feet before she thrust her hand out to be shaken.

'Elizabeth Finch-Dutton, head teacher of St Margaret's,' she said crisply. 'Zellah Wilding's head teacher. They tell me you are the officer in charge.'

He'd forgotten they didn't call themselves masters and mistresses any more. 'Detective Inspector Slider,' he said. Despite the warm day, her hand was cold and dry, and the grip was hard and brief, like a politician's, and quickly withdrawn.

'I heard the dreadful news this morning, on the radio. I'm so shocked I can hardly believe it. Is it true the poor child was murdered?'

'I'm afraid so.'

'But – how? I mean, what—?'

'I'm afraid I can't go into any of the details,' Slider said.

She pulled herself together. 'Of course. I understand. It's just so *incomprehensible*. In the absence of information the imagination tends to run wild.'

Let it run, said Slider's sturdy silence.

'I thought I'd better come here and see if there was anything I can do,' she said meekly. 'It's good of you to see me, when you must be so busy. But if I can help in any way, I will gladly rally any forces at my command to find out who did this dreadful thing.'

Slider gestured to her to sit. She was tall and thin, in her late fifties probably, with cropped grey hair, large glasses and a professional smile – a ritual baring of teeth. It seemed to be coming and going rather randomly, as if she kept finding herself doing it automatically and then realizing it wasn't appropriate to the occasion. She was not as much in control of herself as she wanted to appear, and Slider liked her the better for it.

'Any background information you can give me?' he suggested. 'What was your impression of Zellah?'

'She was one of our *stars*. A *very* able girl. She was a *prefect*, you know, and she was under consideration for *Head Girl* next year. Exemplary behaviour *and* academic prowess. *Such* a good example to the lower forms. We *all* thought a great deal of her.' Her accent was crisp and her enunciation perfect, and she spoke with an emphasis carefully placed on one word in each phrase – a learned trick of rhetoric, presumably, but which made her sound authoritative. What she said would be the last word on any subject. 'It's so terrible to think of all that *potential* cut short in this *senseless* manner. She was the sort of girl we *all* long for but *rarely* get through our hands: a girl with a real *academic* intellect. Her A levels were sciences, you know.'

'I expect that's unusual.'

'More so every year. One feels so for the Wildings, because they encouraged her *just* as they should, and that's even more rare. Mr Wilding,' the smile flashed out briefly, like a lighthouse beam passing, 'is *quite* one of our treasures. He's on the Board of Governors; he involves himself in all our projects, always willing to help in the most *practical* way. I believe he does a great deal of charity work outside as well, and sits on various committees – residents' association, parish council, Neighbourhood Watch and so on. He's a pillar of society.' She used the phrase as if it were placed in inverted commas: a cliché, you were to understand, but one that could not be bettered. 'And a most conscientious communicant. We expect all our parents to attend service regularly, but one can't command the spirit in which they do it. But Mr Wilding is a true Christian in the best sense. And he recognised Zellah's abilities and was most anxious that she should study serious subjects and do well at them. Most of our girls,' she said with a sad shake of the head, 'want to go into media studies, fashion, journalism, the soft options, and their parents encourage them. They want them to make easy money and good marriages, nothing more, as if the height of their ambition is to see their daughters emulate Victoria Beckham. Thirty years on from so-called Liberation, and women's minds are still not valued in the least! I sometimes think it's impossible to educate adolescent girls at all. And then someone like Zellah comes along and restores one's faith in the species.'

It seemed a lot to be resting on one girl's shoulders, Slider thought. 'So you would say she was a serious-minded girl. Was she a . . . a good girl, for want of a better phrase?'

'I understand you. And yes, she was a good girl. That was why we made her a prefect. But she wasn't, shall we say, dour and humourless. She had great charm and vivacity. And her intellect was very well rounded. We wish our girls to be balanced, and Zellah's science subjects had their counterpoint in the arts. She took part in many of the after-school activities. She was a member of the choir, the drama society – she took a leading part in our play at the end of the spring term. Her father helped make the scenery, by the way. I believe she did ballet, though of course that was outside the school. And she had quite a talent for art. *Quite* a talent. Our art master, Mr Markov, thought the world of her.'

'So, it sounds as if she was the ideal pupil.'

'The ideal student,' she corrected. They didn't say 'pupil' any more, either. 'She will be a great loss to the school. And of course to her poor parents.'

Slider nodded, thinking. After a pause, he said abruptly, 'Did you like her?'

There was a small hesitation. Then she said, 'I never allow myself to become emotionally attached to any of my girls. You will see the necessity. Affection is not in my remit, and indeed would be too likely to affect my impartiality were I to permit it to develop. And Zellah was in many ways a very private person, hard to get to know. But she was a credit to the school, and the manner of her death has come as a great shock. A great shock.'

Was that a long way round of saying that she *didn't* like her? Was there something a little intimidating in all that perfection? Or perhaps that Finch-Dutton simply had not known her well enough to like or dislike. A head teacher these days was probably fairly remote from the pupils, stuck in an office with reams of paperwork and government returns to fill in. Or, another possibility, Miss Finch-Dutton – he was sure it was Miss – didn't really know what liking a girl felt like.

But there did seem to be quite a discrepancy, he thought when he had seen her out, between the jewel of St Margaret's crown and delight of Mr Wilding's eye, and the girl Sophy Cooper-Hutchinson described as her mate. It was a large crack for the real Zellah to get lost down, and Slider, who would never now meet her, felt an aching need to know what she had been like.

Meanwhile, there was Ronnie Oates, the Acton Strangler. He got up to go and see Porson. Leaning on a pervy little sex-offender was the kind of policing an old-fashioned copper like Porson would feel comfortable with, and Slider liked his bosses to be happy.

Chloë Paulson had evidently modelled herself on Sophy Cooper-Hutchinson to a large extent. Though her hair was mouse-fair, it was cut short and teased into moderate spikes on top of her head, and she wore purple lipstick and nail varnish, though the black around her eyes was much more subtle. Perhaps the fact that her parents were not in South America, and that her mother was actually at home, had moderated her fashion statement somewhat.

The Paulsons lived in a large Edwardian semi in Stamford Brook, the quality of whose paint-job alone declared them to be wealthy and sophisticated. Mrs Paulson was in her well-preserved fifties, slim and very smart, dressed and made up as if she was going to an important meeting, though it was evident she was just hanging about at home. But within seconds of Slider and Connolly arriving she had managed to get them into her kitchen and apprise them of the fact that it had been newly refitted at the cost of £80,000. It looked it. Slider could almost feel Connolly quivering with desire beside him. Strange how women felt about kitchens; and it seemed to him, the less they actually cooked the more desperately they wanted a vast culinary temple full of the most cutting-edge gadgets. He had seen Connolly eating, and while she was nowhere near being a female McLaren, he was convinced nobody who willingly chose to ingest a chutney-chilli-cheeseburger from Mike's stand at the end of

Shepherd's Bush Market could be interested in the art of haute cuisine. Yet here she was, practically drooling over the six-burner Aga-style gas-stove, the double stainless-steel sinks with jet hose attachment and pre-chilled drinking-water tap, and the island unit's integral butcher's block with the range of cook's knives sunk into slots along the back, including everything from an aubergine peeler to a marrow-bone splitter.

A glance at Mrs Paulson's nails suggested she didn't do a lot of hands-on cooking either, but the two women were as one in regarding this vast hymn to the domestic art as the peak of their desire. It stretched right across the back of the house and was extended outwards under a glass roof, so it measured about twenty feet by sixteen. He thought of Joanna cooking for them in her dark little six-by-six cubbyhole, with a sink, stove and about two feet of work surface her only comforts, and felt uneasily that he had let her down in some essential duty of manhood.

Mrs Paulson also managed to mention that her husband was an investment banker and that she had been a high-powered financial analyst until child-bearing took her out of the loop, but that she now did 'important charity work', whatever that might be. The need to impress even such lowly specimens as police officers suggested a level of loneliness and frustration that made him sad. But it did leave her open to the suggestion that she talk to Connolly in the kitchen while she made coffee for them all, while Slider interviewed Chloë alone (although in sight, beyond the triple sliding glass doors out on the patio). Slider wanted a franker talk with Chloë than he was likely to get with her mother listening.

Chloë was a bouncy girl, too energetic to be fat, but with roundnesses where Sophy and Zellah – perhaps because of their ballet classes – had none. She was wearing a stretchy halter top which stopped just under the breasts, and shorts that hugged her around the hips. Everything in between was bare, and as brown as if she had been basted and roasted – which he supposed after all was what sunbathing was. His daughter Kate would have called her 'a chub', a dismissive adjective she applied to everyone in the world apart from herself and a couple of approved skinny chums. Chloë's little round belly looked like the nicely egg-glazed top of an apple dumpling, and the ring in her navel might have been put there on purpose to lift it by. She had a round face, plumply pretty and even less suited to the Goth make-up than Sophy's, especially as her default expression seemed to be one of wide-eyed surprise.

70

She seemed thrilled by the attention of a real police detect-ive, and was eager to talk to Slider, especially when he said he hoped she would be frank.

'Oh, I don't mind telling you *anything*,' she said. 'Try me.'

She confirmed the times and substance of what Sophy had told him about the weekend, adding her own gloss. She agreed Zellah had refused to say who she was going out with, but added that she had said 'he was a man, not a boy'. Chloë had asked her if he went to St Martin's, the neighbouring boys' school whose playing fields they shared, but that Zellah had said she was way beyond St Martin's boys.

'Sophy said she was nervous about the date. Is that how you saw it?' Slider asked.

'I wouldn't say *nervous* exactly,' Chloë said. 'More, like, jumpy. But excited as well. Once when Sophy was out of the room I said to her, "Come on, Zellah, we're mates. Tell me who it is." Because Sophy can be a bit, like, pushy, you know? And I thought she might tell me when she wouldn't tell her. But she just looked at me, kind of, like, *sparkly*, and said she might have something important to tell me next time I saw her. But after that Sophy came back in and she clammed up and wouldn't talk about it at all.'

'Did you conclude from that that it was someone you knew?' Slider asked.

'There's no one we know that any of us would get excited about,' she said simply. 'Sophy thought she was just trying to make herself important, making out she'd got a better boyfriend than us.'

'So you don't think it was Mike Carmichael?' he slipped in.

She merely looked surprised. 'That was ages ago. She wasn't still seeing him. Sophy razzed her about him so she gave him up. I mean, he didn't have a car. Sophy says you can't go out with a bloke without a car.'

Sophy seemed responsible for most of Chloë's ideas, Slider thought. 'What's the importance of a car?' he asked.

'For copping off,' she said, as if he ought to have known that.

'Copping off, as in—?'

She blushed a little. 'Well, you know, snogging and that.'

Slider was beguiled that expressions of his youth like 'snogging' – along with 'cool' – had come back into vogue.

'Where else can you do it?' she went on. 'My mum and dad would never let me have a boy up in my bedroom. Sophy's the lucky one. Her mum and dad are really cool. They go away a lot, and even when they're at home they let her do whatever she wants. They're great.'

'Is that what constitutes great parents? Letting her do what she wants?'

He got the stare. 'Well . . . They give her shedloads of money, too. She's always got all the latest stuff and, like, loads of clothes and everything. It's cool.'

He was realizing his fundamental failures as a father. 'What about Zellah's parents? Were they cool?'

He got the stare *and* the head jerk this time. 'Duh! That's what the whole weekend was about. They're *awful*. They never let her go anywhere. And they've got, like, *no* money. Zellah had, like, hardly any pocket money, and no new clothes.'

'Did you ever meet them – her parents?'

'Not really *meet* them. We didn't get invited round her house. But I'd seen them, at parents' day and sports day and prize giving, things like that. Her dad wasn't so bad – sort of hunky, in a way – only *way* strict. I was scared of him. But her mum was *fat*!' She added the last in tones of breathless horror as the worst thing that could be said of any human being.

'If her dad was so strict, how come he didn't check up on Zellah the whole weekend?' Slider asked.

'He used to,' she said. 'It was, like, *so-o* embarrassing. Zellah, like, trained him out of it. Her mum was all right, she wanted Zellah to have fun – it was her picked the name Zellah. How cool is that? I wish I had a great name, instead of crummy old "Chloë". Everyone's called that. There are three Chloës in our year at school. What was I saying?'

'About her parents checking up on her.'

'Oh, right. Well, her dad used to phone up all the time, until when she turned sixteen she told him if he didn't leave it off she'd leave home. She said you can by law when you're sixteen and your parents can't make you come back, and he was so scared he agreed not to call her when she was out, as long as he knew where she was going. Well, she could tell him anything after that, as long as it was something he'd approve of, like that dorky Southbank Fair.'

'So he believed her when she said she'd leave home?'

'You don't know Zellah. She'd have done it all right. She didn't care. She was really cool. She was the first one of us to go all the way with a bloke.'

'Was that with Mike Carmichael?'

Her eyes slid away from his. She put her hands between her thighs and squeezed them together, rocking forward and back in her chair. 'I shouldn't't've said.'

'Come on, Chloë. I thought we were going to be frank.'

She looked at him. 'This doesn't get back to her mum and dad?'

'Zellah's dead,' he reminded her.

'Oh, yeah. I'd forgotten.' She seemed remarkably unaffected by it. 'Well, I s'pose it doesn't matter then. Yeah, she went all the way with Mike.'

'How did that work, if he didn't have a car?'

'He's got his own place. But she said she'd have done it anywhere with him. She was nuts about him. And the way she talked about it, she was really hot for, you know, sex. It was funny really, her being like that and her mum and dad being all proper and churchy. She told Sophy once the only reason she stayed with them was she wanted to finish school and she didn't have any money so she had to.'

'In that case, why did her father believe she really would leave?'

Chloë looked blank. 'I dunno,' she said at last. 'I suppose she just kind of *made* him believe it.'

'Through force of personality, you mean?'

'Yeah, like that,' Chloë said

'So you and Zellah and Sophy go around together a lot?'

'Yeah, we're, like, mates. We're tight. We've had, like, this gang since the fourth year. There used to be another girl as well, Frieda, Frieda Mossman, but she got all stupid when we started going out with boys, so we dropped her.'

'You mean she didn't approve?'

Eye-roll and jerk. 'Couldn't pull one herself, so she was jealous. Said she was saving it for marriage. Sophy said "nobody's going to marry you, girl, so you might as well spend it while you can", and she got all upset and, like, stormed off.'

'That was pretty cruel, wasn't it?'

'Oh, Sophy doesn't care what she says. She's great. Frieda shouldn't have been so sensitive. But she was a bit fat and she has this frizzy hair.'

Slider couldn't decide if this was justification for the nastiness, or the reason for being over-sensitive. He was fascinated, though appalled, at this glimpse below the gleaming surface of these girls. In the kitchen he saw Connolly deep in conversation with Mrs Paulson, with Mrs Paulson doing the chin-work, but he could also see the coffee was ready and only needed pouring, so he had to get on.

'Tell me about your brother,' he said.

'Which one?'

'The one who lives in Notting Hill.'

'What, Oliver? He's cool.'

'What does he do?'

'He's a foreign analyst for a firm of brokers. City stuff, you know. He earns shedloads of money. I mean, him and his mates are all making out like *bandits*! He shares this great flat in Lansdowne Crescent with these three other guys – you should see it! It's gorgeous. And he wears these beautiful suits. Boss, Armani. Totally great threads. He had this girlfriend Tara who was actually an earl's daughter. They've broken it off now, though. Sophy says Tara's a dorky name, anyway. She says it's, like, a name you give a pony. But Oliver never had trouble pulling girls anyway. He's gorgeous looking, and he has, like, this great sense of humour.'

'So how does he know Mike Carmichael? It seems an unlikely sort of friendship, given Mike's background.'

The round face was innocent of guile. 'Oh, I don't think he knows him that well. He just lives in the neighbourhood. I think they met at a party of a mate of his.'

'And how did Zellah meet him?'

'Round Oliver's. Zellah and Sophy used to go up Oliver's on Saturdays after ballet class and I'd meet them there. I don't do ballet. This one Saturday Oliver was taking us all to lunch. He does that sometimes. He's great. And Mike was there, so he came with us. Mike's all right,' she added, free of charge. 'Sophy doesn't like him, but she's a snob. Mike's a laugh. I could see right off Zellah liked him. Sophy said that's because of Zellah's chav blood. It takes one to know one, she said. But I reckon she fancied him herself, Sophy did, only you could see it was Zellah he was into. It, like, pissed her off, Sophy, so she never had a good word to say for Mike after that. But I don't think she would have gone out with him if he *had* asked her,' she concluded, 'so I don't know what she had to get snarky about.'

'Do you know Mike's address?'

'No, but I know he's got this flat in Ladbroke Grove, over this cool shop that sells, like, tarot cards and joss sticks and mystic books and stuff. I'd love to have a flat over a shop. It's so cool.' She returned from her dream to ask, 'Why d'you want to know about Mike? Zellah's not seen him in months.'

'Oh, we have to talk to everyone who knew her. You never know what you might find out.'

She observed him with interest. 'You don't think *he* killed her, do you?'

'I don't think anything yet. I have to gather the facts first. Why, do you?'

'*Me*? I don't even know the bloke. Well, hardly. It would be, like, cool, though, knowing a murderer.'

Slider ended the interview and excused himself. He could take, like, no more.

Slider was comfortable with Connolly beside him in the car. She exuded the same sort of confidence that Swilley always had, but with the addition of something of her own that was relaxed and easy, which made her good with distraught victims and agitated villains. Sergeant Paxman had the same sort of quality, only developed over a longer career than Connolly's. Nicholls had described him as a tranquil stream, but Slider saw him more as a black hole into which all over-wrought emotions were sucked, leaving peace and quiet behind.

'You're not related to Sergeant Paxman, are you?' he asked her now, idly.

'No, sir. You don't think I look like him?'

'Hardly,' he said, with a sideways glance.

'I like him, though. I always like being on his relief. And . . .'

'Go on.'

'No, I don't want to bang me own drum.'

'Oh, don't be coy.'

'He said he'd be sorry to lose me if I did get into the Department.' She turned a wistful face to him. 'Do you think there's a chance I could? I mean, there's a vacancy, right enough?'

'Because DC Anderson isn't coming back?' Anderson had been on secondment to an SO for over a year, and Slider had recently heard that it was being made permanent. It left him even shorter-handed than usual.

'Yes, sir. And then, if Kathleen doesn't come back . . .'

Slider had never heard anyone call Swilley 'Kathleen', and it took him a moment to realise who they were talking about. Everyone on his firm called her Norma because she was a better man than they were – so much so that she didn't even mind the nickname. Odd to think of her now doing something so essentially womanly as having a baby. 'Don't you think she will?'

'Oh, I haven't heard anything,' Connolly said, 'but it must be hard to leave your baba every day. And then there'd be the late evenings and the weekends and everything. I can't see how she'd crack it.'

'Her mother lives nearby. I understand she'd take care of the baby.'

'I didn't mean physically. I meant how she'd crack it emotionally.'

'So when you marry and have children you'll leave the Job?'

'I'm never going to get married. And I definitely won't have kids,' she said, with a sureness that intrigued him. 'You've only got to look at Mrs Paulson to see where that carry-on leads.'

He wanted to know whether she didn't think that would mean a very lonely future, but he couldn't go probing into his people's private lives. He'd had enough of that with Atherton's serial involvements, particularly when he'd been dating one of Joanna's friends and breaking her heart.

He said, 'How did you get on with Mrs Paulson?'

'I hardly needed to ask her anything – she was desperate to talk. Bored mental being a stay-at-home mammy. Mostly she went on about being worried about Chloë – the shock from Zellah being murdered and the fear that it would happen to her kid as well. She's convinced it's a serial killer targeting schoolgirls. She says that Sophy Cooper-Hutchinson's the driving force of the group, and it was her led Chloë and Zellah astray. She's sorry about Zellah. Thought Zellah was a good girl, couldn't understand why the Wildings let her hang out with Sophy.'

'If Sophy's so bad, why does she let Chloë associate with her?'

'I wondered that, sir – hinted around it as tactfully as I could. But it seems that the Paulsons and Cooper-Hutchinsons have been best pals for years, ever since their oldest sons were at school together. Joint family holidays, outings, dinner parties and all that carry-on. The children know each other from the cradle. So no criticism of the Cooper-Hutchinsons possible, and no way to keep the children apart. But I gathered that Mrs Paulson is a bit feeble, anyway, doesn't feel she has any influence over Chloë, no right to tell her what to do. She was critical of Mr Wilding, but admired him on the side. On the one hand said he was too strict with Zellah and maybe that was what led her into trouble—'

'Trouble as in . . .?'

'Oh, getting murdered – and on the other hand said she wished she could be strict like that with *her* children. But then, she says, the Wildings have but the one kid, so it's easy for them.'

'You did well, getting all that out of her,' Slider said.

'It wasn't hard,' said Connolly. 'She wanted to talk.'

That wasn't what Slider had meant: people can talk all they like but the listener had to be hearing them. He was liking Connolly more all the time. 'What did she think about Mrs Wilding?'

'Didn't like her. Too much of a chav for her taste.'

So that was where Chloë got the idea of 'chavvy blood', Slider thought.

'She hinted,' Connolly went on, 'that Mrs Wilding was her husband's secretary once, and they'd had an affair, and Mr Wilding left his first wife for her. Seemed to think that was a bit beyond the pale. What bothered her was not so much the affair, but the secretary thing.'

'Too much of a cliché?'

'Yes, sir, something like that. It made Mrs Wilding too common to mix with the likes of the Paulsons and Cooper-Hutchinsons. I thought it was interesting,' she added, 'that she didn't seem to think Mr Wilding was tainted with the same brush.'

'I can clear that up for you,' Slider said, wincing at the mixed metaphor but letting it pass. Nobody was perfect, after all. 'Chloë revealed to me Mrs Wilding's cardinal sin, and the source of her chavviness.'

'Yes, sir?'

'Apparently, she's fat.'

Connolly whistled. 'Janey, dice loaded against her, or what?'

SEVEN

Fair Words Never Won Fat Lady

The fair was not open until the afternoon, but as it was school holidays, there were quite a few kids hanging around already. The coffee stall was open, and the hamburger-and-hotdog stand had fired up for the vital dispensing of hot grease. The air was redolent with the particular mixture of diesel, burned fat, rancid onions, trampled grass and sawdust that was a quintessential part of childhood dreams. It was Paradise – if you could stand it.

Some of the fair people were engaged on routine maintenance of the rides, others on cleaning and household chores, though some caravans still had their curtains drawn, indicating a lie-in after the late night. The side panels were off the merry go-round, and a knot of fascinated juvenile idlers was gathered round two pairs of oily overalled legs sticking out from under it. The horses, frozen in mid-leap, flared their crimson nostrils in their eagerness to get galloping again; the cockerels strode out on their strong, ridged legs like Road Runner.

'Yeah, what is it wiv them cockerels?' Hart asked in wounded tones. 'I never got that. What's the connection?'

'It's one of those sweet, insoluble mysteries of childhood,' Atherton told her. 'Don't breathe on the magic.' A man was tinkering with the pipe organ, and it sounded an asthmatic note or two, mournful and joyous as a steam locomotive. 'This must be one of the few go-rounds that still has a proper organ, not just recorded music,' he said, betraying his enthusiasm.

Hart looked at him with fake fondness. 'You big kid. You love all this. For two pins you'd be begging 'em for a ride.'

'My good woman, it costs a lot more than two pins these days. Come on, stop gawping. We've got a job to do.'

The fair people were already doing a good job of ignoring the hangers-about, and somehow managed to ignore Atherton and Hart even more intensely because they were police, narrowing eyes that were already narrowed and turning away faces that were already averted, like cats punishing an errant owner. Sometimes their questions were answered by a grunt, more often by complete silence. When words were forthcoming, it was, 'Don't know nothing about that.' They were armed with photos of Zellah and of Mike Carmichael but could hardly get anyone to glance at them, let alone recognize the faces.

The first proper response they got was at a snack stall, presently closed up, where a stocky man in shirt-sleeves and braces was around the back, spanner in hand, connecting up a new Calor gas canister. He had a cigarette clamped in his mouth, a cap clamped down over his head, and two days of white stubble sprouting from the whole lower half of his face. He stopped and straightened when they addressed him, though it seemed more to stretch his back than for their benefit.

But then he rolled the fag to the other side of his mouth, glared at them through narrowed eyes, and said, 'Why don't you piss off, copper?'

It was the friendliest thing anyone had said to them. Atherton felt pleased and encouraged. 'Just look at this picture and tell me if you saw her here,' he said beguilingly.

The man grew angry. 'Is that the girl that got murdered? Why d'you come asking *us* questions? We don't know nothing about it. You people never leave us alone.'

'Take it easy, mate,' Hart said, letting her accent slip a little further towards the of-the-people end of the spectrum. 'We don't fink you had anyfing to do wiv it. Course we don't. We're just trying to work out where she was Sundy night. We fink she might've been here, thass all. It ain't no grief for you. Did you see her? Have a look at the picture, go on.'

He squinted unwillingly sideways at it, and then, as Hart urged it at him with little pushes, took it, looked once properly, and then thrust it back at her as if unwilling to be caught holding it.

'Might have been here. Lotter people here Sundy night.'

Hart glanced at Atherton. In these-people speak, that was a yes. 'We reckon she might've been here wiv her boyfriend. This is him.' She held out Carmichael's picture. He didn't touch that one. He removed the cigarette from his mouth and spat out a shred of tobacco on to the grass. 'That who you reckon done it?'

'Yeah,' Hart said, and Atherton let her. If it took the heat off . . .

'I seen her. She was wiv a bloke. Coulda been him. Never saw him proper.'

'Thanks. That's great. What was he wearing, d'you remember?'

He shrugged, and turned back to his barrels. He muttered something, and Hart bent forward, 'Say again?'

'Rifle range,' he mumbled. Then he turned back sharply and glared at them. 'Sod off. I got work to do.'

The man at the rifle range was just taking the covers off, in between stretching, yawning, scratching himself, and trying to light a roll-up that would not catch. He was younger than snack-stall man, lighter skinned, with greasy mouse-brown hair and a puggy, cockney face. 'Cor, you ain't 'arf stirred up a few people,' he said as they approached. He was not exactly friendly, but did not seem to be suffering from the same congenital hostility as the others. 'They don't like your sort round here.'

'We noticed,' Atherton said.

The man shrugged. 'Well, I don't care. I ain't one of them. Pikey bastards! They keep themselves to themselves. I'm a gayjo to them, even though my dad was in fairs forty years, and I've had the stall twenty. You can't ever be one of them unless you're born in one of the families. Fuckin' gyppos. Well, they can keep it. I don't care. I'm as good as they are. I make me money and stay out of it. You looking for that girl that was killed?'

'That's right. This is her. Did you see her?'

'She was here all right. Pretty girl. Couldn't miss her. Having a great time, she was. Screamed her head off on the waltzer and the atomic rocket. Having too much of a good time, if you get my drift.'

'Showing off? Drunk?'

'Both, I reckon. She was with this bloke. He was showing off as well. Took her on the dodgems, show her what a great driver he was. Banging into everything. Danny on the dodgems had to warn him. Had a couple of goes on my range. Not a bad shot,' he conceded with professional grudgingness. 'I let him win a teddy bear for her. Do me bit for our side.'

'Our side?' Atherton queried.

'Men,' Hart elucidated.

The rifle man nodded. 'He was trying to pull her, but it wasn't working. I could see that. She was flirting with him, but she wasn't going to put out. I could've told him. She had the cold eye, for all her screaming and hanging on to him. Ended up having a row.'

'*Did* they?'

'I wasn't surprised. I reckon he worked it out in the end, realized he was spending his money for nothing.'

'Did you hear what they were rowing about?'

'Nah. Just arguing back and forth, yap yap yap. At it for quite a while they were. Then she walks away. That's all I seen.'

'Did he follow her?'

'Nah. He went off in *that* direction.' He jerked his head towards the entrance on Scrubs Lane. 'He might've come back, though. But I never seen him.'

'Did you see her again?'

'Not after that. But I wasn't looking out for 'em. I had other things to do.'

'And do you know what time that was? When she walked off?'

He scratched his head again. 'It was just getting busy. I reckon – maybe half-nine, ten o'clock.'

Hart and Atherton looked at each other. That was awfully early. They must have got together again afterwards. She showed him Carmichael's picture. 'Is that the man she was with?'

'Could've been. Looks like him. I wasn't that interested in *him*, tell you the truth. Had a leather jacket on, though. I saw that. Could've been him.' He passed the photo back. 'You won't get anything out of the others. They don't talk to the cops. But Gary on the waltzer'll remember her, and Danny on the dodgems. They won't tell you, though. They're all giving me filthy looks for talking to you, but I don't care. My family's bin in the fairs as long as any of them. We're as good as them any day.'

He was half right. They couldn't get anyone else to talk to them, though one or two of them looked at the photos and grunted before freezing them out. To counterbalance that, and to dispel any suggestion the fair folk were going soft, Danny on the dodgems crawled out from under a maintenance panel with a two-foot-long spanner in his hand, which he slapped suggestively against his other palm, while his brindled pit bull advanced snarling to the end of its chain and burst into a fusillade of barking, effectively drowning out any possibility of conversation.

They worked conscientiously towards the back of the fair, where the living vans and lorries were parked, between the rides and the open space of the Scrubs. No one in the caravans would speak to them either, and many of them would not even open the door. Eventually they got to a large van parked right on the edge of the lot, its open door towards the Scrubs, where a woman was sitting on the step knitting what looked like a string dishcloth, and smoking a roll-up wrapped in liquorice paper. She was so massively fat she looked like a shipping hazard, but she might have been beautiful once: the face above her accumulation of chins suggested it, with striking dark eyes and abundant black hair done up in large rollers all over her head. Her hands were like a couple of pounds of pork sausages, but they flashed away nimbly, and were decorated with a large number of gold and diamond rings. She was wearing an ankle-length skirt and voluminous smock-like top, probably because nothing else would have fitted her, and the lobes of her ears were pierced and carried thick, heavy gold rings which had enlarged their holes over the years into hanging loops of skin. But her plump bare feet, protruding into the sunshine from the hem of the skirt, were surprisingly small and rather pretty, with gold rings on three toes of each.

'Excuse me, sorry to disturb you, but have you—?' Hart began politely, but she looked up at them unsmilingly, while her fingers never ceased to knit.

'Making fools of yerselves,' she said, in the strange accent of the fair people, which was like East End London mixed with Essex, but with a different, more exotic tinge to it, which made them seem slightly foreign, like the tinge of sallowness to their skins.

'Just doing our jobs. A young girl was killed,' Hart reminded her.

'Oh, I seen her. She passed by here.' The fingers reached the end of a row and switched the knitting over all on their own. They weren't so much like sausages now, Atherton thought, as like plump bald feral animals munching at something they had hunted down. 'She went off that way.' She nodded towards the open space.

'Was she on her own?'

'She had a row with him, didn't she? Tall chap. Brown hair. Older than her. Bit like you.' She nodded towards Atherton. 'She was angry. He was trying to pretend he didn't care, but he was angry all the same. Harsh words was exchanged, then she went off. Running, she was. Took her shoes off so's to run. He went back that way.' She jerked her head towards the fair. 'Didn't see me, either of 'em. I was looking out me winder, having a last smoke.'

'*Last* smoke? What time was this?'

'Midnight, near enough. I don't stay up till we close, not these days. Near two o'clock, time my son comes to bed. But we was still open. Be about midnight, give or take.'

That was much better. Atherton said, 'Did you see him go after her later?'

'Nah. I watched till she stopped running, see if she'd come back, but she went trudging on, away over the common. I'd finished me smoke so I went to bed. Never saw neither of 'em again. Now I told you all.' Her face grew a fraction sterner. 'So don't you come saying it was one of our chaps what done it. Don't you try that. She was just a gayjo tart, nothing to do with us.'

'We never thought it was,' Hart said. 'Thanks, ma.'

The woman turned her face away, staring out at the green grass under the smudgy August sky, her fingers chumbling away at their woolly carcase. 'What for? I never told you nothing.'

Slider picked up the phone and said, 'Slider,' but was answered only by breathing. 'Hello?' he said impatiently.

His father's warm, burring tones came back to him. 'Sorry, son. I was debating whether to hang up, you sound so busy.'

'I am busy, but don't let that stop you,' Slider said. His father hardly ever rang, and never at work before. 'Is everything all right, Dad?'

'Oh yes, don't you worry. I'm fine.'

'Joanna said you wanted to talk to me about something. I'm sorry I haven't been able to ring you, but I'm not getting home until late and I know you go to bed about half past nine.'

'Don't worry about it. I'm sorry to bother you but there's something that has to be decided, and I need your opinion first. I'll get right to it. I'm thinking of selling this house.'

There were many things about that statement that required questions to be asked, but the one that got its nose in front was, 'But you don't own it. How can you sell it?' The house he had been born and brought up in had been a tied cottage, for which his father, a farm worker, paid a peppercorn rent.

There was a soft chuckle down the line. 'Bought it years ago. Just didn't tell you. It was going to be a nice surprise for you when I popped off. Make up for losing me and all my helpful advice, see.'

It was one of Dad's jokes. 'Nothing could make up for losing you. But how come you bought it?'

'It was when old Mr Davies died. He said in his will I was to be offered it. Afraid if the estate was sold off I'd be chucked out. He was always very good to me and your mother.'

'Why would the estate be sold off?' Slider couldn't help asking, even though he didn't want to slow his father down in getting to the point.

But Mr Slider said with commendable briefness, 'Going through a bad patch. As it happened, they come out of it, eventually, but at the time young Mr Davies was happy enough to let me have it. Nobody else would've wanted it, anyway. Not modern enough, and too far out of the way. Well, I had a bit put by, and there was an endowment policy come in just about then, and it was enough. He didn't want much for it.'

'So you've owned it all these years?' He reckoned back to when the estate's owner – the 'old lord' – had died. 'That must have been twenty years ago.'

'That's right. Bit more, even.'

'So why do you want to sell it now?' A thought occurred to him. 'You *are* all right? You'd tell me if you were ill or anything?'

'No, I'm fine son. Don't worry. But I'm getting on a bit now, and the garden's getting a bit much for me. I don't need that much land. It's near-on four acres, you know.'

'*Is* it?'

'Well, I bought the fields either side of the lane. Thought at one time I might keep a few chickens, sell the eggs, but I never got round to it. I just let 'em for grazing. But you're busy,' he collected himself. 'You don't want to hear all this. Fact is, it's a long way from anywhere and a bit isolated, so I'm thinking it's time to be selling up. I just wanted to be sure you didn't mind.'

'Why should I mind?'

'Well, it's your childhood home. Lot of memories. You might've wanted it for yourself. Holiday house or some such.'

'I'd love to *live* in it, but it's far too far to commute. And it would be wonderful for a holiday cottage, but I can't afford it. I can't even afford a flat for Jo and me and the baby. But if you sell, where will you live? Oh damn.' He added the last as Mackay, one of his firm, appeared in the doorway with a look of triumph on his face.

'What's that?' his father said.

'Someone wants me.'

'That's all right, son. I won't keep you. Just wanted to be sure you didn't mind if I sold it. We'll talk about it some other time.'

'I'll give you a ring. As soon as I can. It won't be tonight—'

'Don't you worry,' his father said soothingly. 'I know how it is. We'll catch up when you've got this case out of the way. Don't worry till then. Everything's all right, I promise.'

'All right. Thanks, Dad.'

'God bless, son.' And he was gone.

Mackay had been down at the Black Lion that morning, canvassing the staff, with a copy of Zellah's photo to show round. 'I've got something, guv,' he said.

'Somebody saw Zellah?' Slider said.

'Well, guv, I wasn't that hopeful, if she was picked up from the car park and didn't go inside. But as it happened, one of the barmen recognised her photo right away. Course, she *is* good-looking, the sort that turns heads,' he added. 'Anyway, this bloke, name of – hang on, I wrote it down.' He pulled out his notebook and read, 'Vedran Kosavac. He's from Croatia.'

'No fooling,' Slider said drily.

'Speaks perfect English, though,' Mackay added. 'Anyway, apparently he was on duty Sunday night and Zellah comes into the pub and looks around, like she's looking for somebody. He notices her right away because she's such a babe, but also because he thinks she looks a bit young, and the management is very hot on not allowing under-age drinking. He hates having to ask borderline cases for ID because half the time they haven't got any, and there's a row, and it all takes time and they're busy anyway. I'm telling you all this,' he added, looking at Slider, 'to show he really did remember her.'

'Fine, go on.'

'Yes, guv. Well, after a bit she comes up to the bar and says excuse me, and he's just bracing himself to ask her for ID, when she asks him where the Ladies is. So he's all relieved. She goes off in that direction, and a few minutes later he sees her come past again and go out into the front car park. So he reckons she must have been drinking out there – because they have those bench-table things and there were a lot of customers out there that night – and someone else was buying her drinks, which all right as far as he was concerned, as long as he didn't have to worry about it.'

'So did he see who she was with?'

'No, guv, he never went out there and he never saw her again.'

'So we're no further on than we were,' Slider said. 'All we know is that she went to the Black Lion as she said she was going to. We still have to find someone who saw who she went off with.'

'No, guv, it's better than that,' Mackay said. 'They've got a security camera trained on the car park, and when I told the manager what we wanted to know, he took me in the tape room and we went through the videos. Luckily they keep them a week before they tape over them.' He drew a video cassette out of his pocket and laid it on Slider's desk with the air of a successful conjuror.

Slider's shoulders went down and he sighed with satis-faction. 'You weren't kidding when you said you had something.'

'Well, the quality's pants, like they are, but you can see it's Zellah all right, though it's only her back view as she comes out of the pub. She stands around for a bit, looking round, fidgeting, like she's nervous or impatient. And then this motorbike comes in.'

'A motorbike,' Slider breathed. It was almost too good to be true. A car might have been anyone, but a motorbike was almost certain to be their best candidate for suspicion.

'With this bloke on it in a leather jacket,' Mackay went on, 'and it looks like jeans. Zellah runs straight over to him. And she gets on the back and he drives off with her.'

'And can you see that it's Carmichael? I know these tapes are poor quality, but sometimes they can be enhanced enough to—'

'Well, guv, you can't really see his face. He never takes his helmet off.'

Slider made a whimpering noise.

'But you can see part of the number plate,' Mackay said, like a comforting father. 'We might be able to enhance that enough to get a partial reg number.'

'All right, Mackay, thanks. You've done well. And at least we know she went off with a biker who we can *assume* for working purposes was Carmichael, even if we can't prove it. It gives us a handle.'

'I could go back tonight and see if any of the customers saw her getting on the bike,' Mackay offered. 'Someone might have seen him well enough to identify him.'

'What beer is it there?' Slider asked innocently.

'Adnams, Theakston's Black Bull, Bombardier . . .' Mackay stopped abruptly as he realized he had given himself away.

'I wouldn't put you through that again,' Slider said kindly. 'You've done your duty, lad. If a return visit is necessary, I'll make someone else take the strain.'

'Brought you a sandwich, guv,' Hart said cheerily as she appeared in his doorway, with Atherton behind her. 'I bet to meself you hadn't eaten.'

'You're not my mother,' Slider said repressingly.

Hart was unabashed. 'Have you seen the time? We stopped down Mike's and got you a sausage sandwich, wiv termata sauce, the way you like 'em. And a jam doughnut from Fraser's on the way back. And I'll get you a proper tea from the canteen, if you like.'

Slider weakened. 'In a proper cup.'

'Of course, guv,' Hart said. 'How long have I been here?'

'So what's all this excessive thoughtfulness about? Have you done something wrong? Or is it bad news?'

'Neever. It's a celebration. We got two sightings at the fairground. Zellah and Mike the Bike. And bloody hard work it was, too.'

'That's why you get the big money. Fairground people unwilling to talk?'

'You'd get more chatter out of a depressed Trappist monk,' Atherton said. 'But the rifle range proprietor had a grudge against Romanies, not being one of them, and was bursting to co-operate. He ID'd our couple from the photographs, said they had a row and parted the ways.'

'And then this old woman, with a van right at the back of the lot, said she'd seen a couple quarrelling, and the female half of it walked off across the Scrubs alone,' Hart concluded. 'She wouldn't look at the photos, though.'

Slider told them Mackay's news. 'Can't ID the biker, but it's definitely Zellah, so we can assume Carmichael picked her up by prior arrangement and took her to the fairground.'

'Where they had fun until a row blew up,' Atherton said.

'When she blew him off and ran off across the Scrubs,' Hart concluded. 'That all fits pretty nice. Then he goes and gets his bike, reckons to catch her at the other end, they have another row and he kills her.'

'It does explain everything,' Atherton said.

'Except the tights,' Slider said, getting depressed again. 'Whoever killed her took them with him, which makes it premeditated.'

'Well, wait a minute, guv,' Hart said, thinking hard. 'Maybe she carried a spare pair in her handbag.'

'Spare pair? She wasn't wearing any to start with.'

'No, but they could've been in there from another time, and she just forgot to take 'em out.'

'*Do* girls carry spare pairs of tights around with them?' Slider asked.

'Well, I've knew girls that did,' Hart said.

'And she helpfully told him about them, handed them over, and then stood around waiting while he got them out of the packet, to make it easier for him?'

Hart continued to look unabashed. 'Maybe they weren't in a packet. And he saw them when she was looking for something in her bag. I'm only saying it's *possible*, that's all.'

'*Anything*'s possible,' Slider said. The heavenly scent of his sandwich drifted up to him, reminding him it was getting cold. 'We'll go over all this at the meeting. You said something about tea?'

'Righty-oh,' Hart said obligingly.

By the time he started the meeting, Slider was feeling more positive about things, though that may just have been the essential greases reaching his system. He reported on the developments of the morning, including his own interview with Chloë Paulson.

'So we've maybe got a partial reg for Carmichael's bike, then,' said Hollis, his other sergeant, who was office manager. 'That's a start.'

'Michael Carmichael. What a name!' Atherton interjected. 'The things people do to their children.'

'His mother named him,' Slider said, 'and I don't think she was bursting with lucidity. Besides she never married Carmichael. He took the surname because he hated his stepfather.'

'Then he shoulda called himself Bikemichael,' Hart said. 'He never had a car.'

'Moving on,' Slider said, 'we also have a partial address. It ought to be easy enough to find the right place, now we know it's over a tarot shop.'

Atherton gave him an old-fashioned look. 'We *are* talking about Ladbroke Grove. Tarot and crystal shops are as plentiful as black beetles in a basement. It'll have a Moroccan restaurant on one side, and a shop selling velvet scarves and clothes with little mirrors sewn into them on the other.'

'I can't see the point of tarot,' Hart said. 'Even if you know the future, you can't change it.'

'No, and it's a strain to keep looking surprised. So, we are going after this Carmichael type, then?'

'We've got him placed with the victim on the night in question, and a row between them,' Slider said.

'But you still don't think he's the murderer?' Hart said, disappointed.

'There are problems. The tights, for one thing. And the witness discrepancy about the time the quarrel happened.'

'I don't think that's a problem. Both are correct. They just parted for a bit and then got back together for the second round,' Atherton said.

'We also have to take into account that Ronnie Oates has been seen back on the ground,' Slider added.

'What did Mr Porson say about that when you told him?' Hart enquired. It was a rhetorical question, but Atherton answered anyway.

'I'd take a modest bet he said, "That's more like it."'

'Someone is going to have to go round to his mum's house and see if he's there,' Slider said, 'and if he isn't, find out where he is. It needs the right handling if it's going to get a result. His mum may not be firing on all cylinders, but she won't want to drop her son in it. Hollis, I hate to take you away from your work, but I really think this is one for you. She'd trust you.'

'Whatever you say, guv,' Hollis said, looking pleased. He was tall, and so thin he had to run around in the shower to get wet. He had pale green eyes like over-cooked gooseberries, a truly terrible moustache, and a curiously strangled Mancunian accent, but somehow or other, people, particularly old people, trusted him and told him things they wouldn't tell someone who looked more like a paid-up member of the human race. It made him an invaluable interviewer, and Slider often regretted that, by his own choice, he was always office manager, the member of the team who stayed in the CID room pulling everything together. But the fact was he was very good at that, too – and no one else liked doing it.

'So, it's off to Ladbroke Grove to look for Biker Boy, then,' Atherton said, summing up, 'and East Acton for Ronnie Oates. What else?'

'There are all these canvasses to trawl through. Did anyone get anything interesting?'

They discussed the more hopeful sightings, though none was sufficiently definite, particularly in regard to time. Several people had mentioned a blue or black car parked under the railway bridge late at night. A couple of people had complained about a motorbike going round, making a noise, but that was a common occurrence and a common grouch. A girl had been seen walking on the Scrubs on her own, a 'weird-looking' man ditto, and there had been a couple snogging by the changing rooms – though that also was a frequent occurrence. It was, after all, the Sunday night before a Bank Holiday, so there were a lot of people about, and Londoners were trained not to look too hard at each other, for the sake of everyone's privacy. The car, for instance: under the railway bridge away from the street lamps was a place where those who could do no better were accustomed to have sex *in vehiculo*, so in politeness nobody would have approached it too closely or looked directly at the occupants.

'When we've got a possible scenario,' Hollis said, 'it'll be easier to filter out what might support it and go back to them. We're working in a vacuum at the moment. And we still haven't found the handbag. Possibly the murderer took it with him, in which case it could be anywhere.'

'Widen the search,' Slider said. 'If we find the handbag we might find her mobile phone, and that would tell us who she'd been talking to. We can't trace it by the signal because it's apparently switched off.'

'Funny that, though, isn't it, guv?' Connolly said. 'Why would she switch it off?'

'Maybe the murderer did it, if he took the bag,' Hart said.

'Only if he was savvy enough to know it could be traced that way. And why would he want the bag anyway?'

'I dunno. Souvenir?' Hart said. 'Or he was just plain daft.'

'But if he was daft he wouldn't know to switch the phone off.'

Slider interrupted this unfruitful speculation. 'It's odd the way Zellah's headmistress and her parents thought she was an angel, while Sophy and Chloë saw her as a goer.'

'Probably one side or the other was deluded,' Atherton said.

'Maybe she was somewhere between the two,' Connolly said. 'Neither angel nor divil. People like to exaggerate.'

'Or maybe neither side really knew her,' Slider said, 'and she was something quite different from either. The other thing that's said about her was that she was a private person. I'm getting the image of a girl who is whatever is expected of her, different things to different people. And yet,' he checked himself, 'she was willing to deceive her parents over the weekend with Sophy. I'd like to know whose idea that was, initially. Maybe she was a master manipulator.'

'Well, it seems certain that she did have sex with Biker Boy,' Atherton said, 'so she was a goer to that extent.'

'Maybe there were others,' McLaren said. 'What about this Oliver Paulson type?

'Yes, I wouldn't be surprised if he knew a bit more about Miss Zellah than is necessarily apparent,' Atherton said. 'Besides being a probable consumer of Biker Boy's little wraps. I like snapping at the heels of rich kids who think their money entitles them to break the law. Who knows what we may find in his fabulous flat?'

'While agreeing with you that it's fun to taunt those better off than ourselves,' Slider said, 'it doesn't necessarily get us any closer to an answer. I wish I had the slightest bit of evidence against Carmichael, other than that he knew Zellah and has a shady past.'

'And a shady present – we know he's a drug dealer,' McLaren said.

'We've been *told* he's a drug dealer, which is not the same thing.'

'That Harley he rides around,' McLaren said, not without envy. 'How does he afford that, if not from dealing?'

'Even if he is dealing, it doesn't make him a murderer,' Slider said.

'Well, at least he's a bit closer to it than anyone else we know about,' Atherton said cheerfully.

EIGHT

Whale Sandwich

'We released the victim's name this morning, so we've had to put someone on the house to keep the vultures off,' Porson said.

It was always a delicate decision to make, when and how much to release to the press, and Slider was glad it did not fall to him to make it. On the one hand, there was the danger of clues being lost under the inevitable media stampede; on the other hand, it was the quickest way of reaching people at large, and people at large might know things that were useful and come forward with them. They never released the name until the family were told, and in this case it had meant they had had the first day to themselves; but now the feline had been defenestrated, every gawper and gutter hound in the region would be hammering round to Violet Street as fast as his cloven hooves could carry him.

'But we're not telling 'em any more than her name and that we're treating it as murder. Don't want them getting prurient about it. Her parents have got enough to be coping with, without the sex angle.'

'It will leak out that she was strangled. The dog-walker who found her will tell.'

'It'll get out in time, it always does, but that's not our providence. You can't make an omelette without breaking step. So what are you up to? Got any lines?'

Slider told him where they were on Carmichael.

'Looks like the evidence is stacking up on him all right,' Porson said. 'I'll get on to Woodley Green, ask them nicely to keep an eye out for him, especially at his mum's house. You've got people out in Notting Hill?'

'Yes, sir, looking for a flat above a tarot shop.'

'Be a few of those,' Porson said, echoing Atherton. 'Can't chuck a brick round that way without hitting some of that dippy mystic stuff.'

'We'll find it, sir.'

'And what then?'

'If he's there, we'll arrest him for questioning. We've got enough to nab him, given that he ran away.'

'And if he isn't there?' Porson moved restlessly back and forth, unwinding a paper clip and then bending the resultant length of metal back and forth in his big, chalky fingers until it snapped. 'Can't search his gaff without a warrant, and it'll be hell's own job getting one without more evidence than that. If it was on our own ground that'd be one thing, but you know what our brothers in Notting Hill are like. Don't like people raining on their shed without all the eyes crossed and the tees dotted.' He selected another paper clip and resumed the exercise. 'He's got to come home sooner or later,' he concluded. 'If he's not there, put someone on obbo and nab him as soon as they see him.'

'Yes, sir.'

'And meanwhile,' Porson went on, 'what about Ronnie Oates? Now there's a little toerag you can get your teeth into.'

'I'm sending Hollis out to see his mum. He'll get it out of her where Ronnie is. And we've got a sighting of someone who fits his description hanging around the Scrubs that evening.'

'Good. Excellent. I'd like to get him put away properly. They didn't jug him half hard enough last time, and if it *was* him . . .' The paper clip snapped audibly. 'That pretty girl, not even seventeen . . .' His eyes lifted to Slider's. 'Sometimes I hate this job.'

'At least we get to do something about it,' Slider said, offering his own comfort, 'even if it isn't enough.'

The steel re-entered Porson's soul. 'Is that you sympathizing with me?' he barked.

'No, sir. Just passing a comment,' Slider said hastily.

'When I want pity, I'll ask for it. And it'll be a warm day in Hull before that happens, I can tell you.'

'I know that, sir.'

'Well, get on with it, then. No use to anyone standing round like a spare plate at a wedding. Get weaving.'

Slider was hardly back in his office when the phone rang.

'Is that Inspector Slider? It's Derek Wilding here, Zellah's –

Zellah's father. I understand you're the person to talk to.'

'I am the investigating officer. I'm so sorry for your loss, Mr Wilding. Is there something I can help you with?'

'I hope perhaps I can help you. The other officer – I think his name was Atherton?'

'Detective Sergeant Atherton, that's right.'

'Well, he asked about Zellah's mobile phone, asked me for the number and make of it. Said it could be traced from the signal.'

'That's right. Unfortunately, we haven't been able to trace it because it seems to have been turned off.'

'Yes, Mr Atherton said it could only be traced if it was turned on,' said Wilding. 'The thing is, I've just found it.'

'You've found the mobile?'

'Yes, it was here in her room. In the drawer of her bedside cabinet. I was just – I was in her room. Looking at things.' He swallowed audibly, and resumed, his tone pleading. 'Her things are there. It's all I have left. It still . . . smells of her.' His voice broke altogether, and Slider fought with his own pity to remain steady and grounded.

'I understand, Mr Wilding. Please don't feel you need to explain. Now, this mobile – you're sure it's hers?'

'Of course I am. I bought it for her.'

'I'm just surprised she didn't take it with her.'

'She must have forgotten it.' His voice wobbled again as he said, 'It's terrible that she didn't have it with her that night. I can't help thinking—' He cleared his throat and regained control. 'What if she wanted to call me, and she couldn't? What if she was frightened? What if I could have saved her?'

'You mustn't think like that,' Slider said. 'There were lots of houses within a few yards of where she was. She could have knocked on any door for help.'

'At that time of night? Everyone would have been fast asleep.'

'But there was no report of any disturbance or shouting or anything like that. I think it happened very quickly, and she wouldn't have had time to telephone you, even if she'd had her mobile with her.' It was a perilous way to try to console a father: there wasn't much comfort in it whichever way you sliced it. He didn't want Wilding to think too deeply about what he had just said, and went on, 'I'd like you to put the mobile into a bag – an ordinary freezer bag will be fine – and we'll collect it. And don't handle if, if you'll be so kind. Pick it up by the end of the aerial stalk and drop it into the bag.'

'You're thinking of fingerprints? But – what fingerprints can there be on it, if she didn't have it with her?'

'It's a very long shot, of course, but it may have been someone she knew and they may have touched it at some point recently. We have to go through the routines.'

'I see,' he said dully. 'Of course, I touched it when I took it out of the drawer.'

'I understand. I'll send someone round to fetch it, and we'll be able to get a record of her calls, at any rate. We'll know who she was in the habit of calling.'

'Very well,' he said, resignedly. 'I expect it will just be her school friends. And this number here. It won't tell you anything.'

'We're doing all we can,' Slider said kindly, answering the thought behind the words.

Atherton took the news with more interest than Slider had shown. 'Wait, wait, this could be something,' he said. 'What girl *ever* goes out without her mobile? They're surgically wedded to them. The only way to stop a teenager texting her pals is to prise the phone from her cold, dead fingers.'

Slider winced. 'A happy turn of phrase. I agree with you in general, but even a teenage girl can be absent-minded on occasion. She just forgot it, that's all.'

'That's what I'm saying, she wouldn't have. Never in a thousand years. She'd have put it into her handbag as automatically as her door keys.'

'Well on this occasion she didn't. Why are you getting so excited?'

'Suppose the murderer brought it away from the scene with him?'

'You want Wilding to be the murderer?'

'I don't *want* him to be. But it usually *is* the victim's nearest and dearest, and he was hugely controlling of her. Maybe he followed her, discovered what she was up to, sex-and-smut wise, had a violent row and strangled her.'

'With tights he just happened to have brought with him.'

'He may have found out beforehand that she wasn't the little angel he had always believed in, and went out to execute her, to save her soul from worse to come. There would have been plenty of tights in the house, his wife's and his daughter's. Look,' he said to Slider's rejecting expression, 'we know he's a religious nut—'

'He's a churchgoer,' Slider said indignantly. 'Why has everyone with a religious belief got to be a nutcase?'

'Well, they don't have to be. But he's too good to be true – all that charity work and helping out at the school and being on committees and going to church. Yet he wasn't above stealing that piece of land behind his garden – because that's what it comes down to. And he knocked off his secretary, which involved immorality and deceit. Old Wilding's not as squeaky clean as he likes to seem.'

'It's others who praise him,' Slider pointed out. 'He never said he was a saint.'

Atherton waved that away. 'And look at the way he treated Zellah – wouldn't let her go anywhere or do anything for fear of her purity being sullied. Brooding away out in his shed about disgusting youths putting their hands on his lily-white treasure. You've got to admit it's a compelling scenario. I mean, the shed alone condemns him. Men who spend all their leisure hours alone in a shed at the bottom of the garden have got to be up to no good.' He was only partly joking. 'And if he hasn't got a stack of hygiene magazines in there, then what *is* he doing?'

'Woodwork,' said Slider. As he said it, he remembered with a horrible chill another shed in another garden, which *had* belonged to a religious nut. The smell of new pine and old sweat pierced his memory. It was always smells that brought back the past the most vividly. He had been tied up by a man with a knife who was going to kill him; and instead it was Atherton who had been stabbed, near fatally. He met his subordinate's eyes and knew he was thinking of the same thing. He said, 'Even allowing your analysis for the moment, what are you supposing happened?'

'Don't you think it's suspicious that it's only after I tell him the phone can be traced that it turns up? He hadn't thought of it before – it was certainly news to him at the time that you can trace a mobile with pinpoint accuracy from a signal. So he dashes home and switches it off before we can start looking, and then decides the safest thing is to tell you he's found it in an unexceptional place.'

'But why is it there at all?'

'After he killed her, he took her handbag away with him. To conceal her identity, probably,' he said in anticipation of Slider's next question, 'to give himself time to work out his story. He disposed of it somewhere – or maybe hid it in his wardrobe.'

'Or his shed?'

'Yes, better. Wifey might find it in his wardrobe, but I'll bet he locks the old wooden hacienda when he's not using it. Then he was alerted that the phone would lead us straight to him. He's probably destroyed the handbag by now – might be interesting to ask the neighbours if he was burning leaves on Tuesday afternoon.'

'Burning leaves? In August?'

'Well, whatever gardeners burn in August. By the way,' he short-circuited himself as he remembered, 'what would he be growing in his vegetable patch that looked like coriander?'

Slider thought for a moment, and then said, 'Parsnips, you philistine. So if he burned the handbag, why didn't he get rid of the mobile at the same time?'

'You can't burn a mobile. Maybe he was going to take it out and dump it down a drain somewhere, but then he thought it would be better for us to have it.'

'Why?'

Atherton looked triumphant. 'Because if she was regularly telephoning a gentleman of the male persuasion, it would make *him* a suspect.'

'Oh, you're clever,' Slider said bitterly. 'You've got it all worked out.'

Atherton looked wounded. 'Why do you want it *not* to be Wilding?'

'Because he's her *father*,' Slider said. He was silent a moment, and then said, 'You're right, I'm not being objective. And there is one thing.'

'Tell me, tell me.'

'He was imagining her fleeing the murderer in terror and not being able to phone daddy, so I said there were lots of doors she could have knocked on. And he said, "What, at that time of night? Everyone would have been fast asleep." We've never released a time of death. We don't even really know it. It could have been any time after about ten p.m.'

'He could have just assumed it was in the dead of night,' Atherton said.

'Now you're being perverse. It was you who wanted him.'

'Just playing your part.'

'Well, don't. You were right that we have to consider every possibility. We ought to look into Wilding. If he did know, or even suspect, that she was getting away from him, he might feel strongly enough. He was certainly passionate about her. And it is odd, at least, that she left her mobile behind. We'll have a completely objective goosey at him, ask the neighbours what they thought of him, check what he was doing that night. It won't be easy without making him think he's being accused of something, and if he's innocent, that's the last thing I want.'

'Salt in the wounds?'

'More like boiling lead.'

'Nobody said this was an easy job,' Atherton commiserated. 'First thing is to send someone for the mobile, I suppose.'

Slider was pondering. 'I think I'll go myself,' he said. 'I haven't met the man – I'd like to get a look at him, and at the shed. And I'd like to have a look at her room.'

'What do you hope to find there?' Atherton asked.

'Some clue as to who she was.'

'Angel or devil?'

'She won't have been either. Nobody is. But I can't see her clearly, and I want to. I think,' he concluded sadly, 'that I would have liked her if I'd known her.'

'You always say that about everyone,' Atherton said. 'You're just an empathizer.'

Hollis knew Ronnie Oates was living at home because his mother opened the door at once when he rang, and said, 'Left your key behind?' before she saw who it was. Then her face sagged like a disappointed child's. 'Who're you? I don't know you.'

'Yes you do, love,' he said kindly. 'Sergeant Hollis from Shepherd's Bush. You know me from when Ronnie had his last little bit of trouble.'

'Well, he ain't done nothing this time,' she said, but yielded anyway to Hollis's body language and let him in.

It was a ground-floor council-owned maisonette in a tiny terraced house in East Acton, in a turning off the A40, where the traffic thundered past night and day like the migration of the mastodons. Hollis was fortunate in not being cursed, like Slider, with a sensitive nose, or like Atherton with a refinement of taste, but even he quailed a little before the Oates establishment. It was filthy, and it stank.

The front door opened directly into the single living room, whose far end, under the window on to the garden, was the kitchen. In this end there was a sofa, two armchairs and a television set, but all the furniture was hidden under a silt of clothes, fast-food packaging, sweet wrappers, food residue, and saucers containing dabs of left-over cat food. The kitchen end festered under a silt of dishes and rancid food. The window to the garden was open and a succession of cats hopped in and out. The place smelled of urine, cats, and the sweetish, eye-burning odour of dirty bodies, which was also Mrs Oates's *parfum du jour*.

She was a shortish woman, wide rather than fat, with dirty grey hair held back from her face by a child's pink plastic hair-slides. She had a startling number of missing teeth, but when you saw the condition of those remaining, this seemed rather a cause for celebration than otherwise. She was dressed in a wrap-over floral cleaning overall, so amply stained it looked as if she had spent the day butchering piglets, and below the hem her tights hung in festoons on legs that disappeared into battered carpet slippers. She wore the slippers everywhere, inside the house and out in the street, and besides being stained each had a hole in the top where her big toe had poked through, on account of her never cutting her toenails, which were long and sharp enough to geld the piglets with.

'So your Ronnie's staying with you, then,' Hollis said.

'No, he ain't. I dunno where he is,' she said automatically. A look of cunning entered her face. 'He's in jail. My Ronnie's in jail.'

'Don't be daft, ma. You know he came out in May. And I know he's staying here because you've got the sofa bed out. Who's sleeping on that if it's not Ronnie?'

She looked for a costive moment at the sofa – thought did not come easily to her. The sofa was pulled out into a bed, taking up most of the space in the tiny room, and 'made' with a muddle of blankets and dirty sheets. Finally she said with an air of triumph, 'I am. I'm sleeping on it.'

She looked pleased with herself for precisely the few seconds that elapsed before Hollis said, 'Because Ronnie's got your bed, right? He's not in, is he, ma? Mind if I have a look?'

A door to the right led to the rest of the maisonette: a tiny hall, too small to swing a cat without killing it, with two doors, one leading to the tiny windowless bathroom – the smell in there was indescribable, and the bath was full of several years' worth of old newspapers – and the bedroom, dominated by a double bed and an upturned plastic beer crate which served as a bedside table. Hollis only glanced into each to be sure Ronnie wasn't there before returning to the living room.

'So where was your Ronnie on Sunday, then, ma? This Sunday just gone.'

'Out. He was out,' she said quickly. 'He weren't here.'

'Oh, so you can't vouch for him, then?' Hollis said innocently. 'Can't give him an alibi?'

She looked dumbfounded, but recovered to say, 'No, that's right, he was here all day. I 'member now. He never went out at all. He was watching telly all day, and – and – I give him fish and chips for his tea.'

Hollis was impressed with this piece of invention from a woman who was so dense that light bent round her. He needed to disarm her and get her to talk. He wished he could sit down, but he was afraid for his sanity. Instead he moved a little way from her and leaned against the wall, folding his arms, and said benignly, 'Come on, ma, you can tell me. If he's in trouble again, I can help you. You don't want this to get out of hand, do you?'

She stared at him anxiously. 'He's a good boy, really,' she said. 'He never meant to hurt nobody. It was them girls that led him on. They was bad girls. Especially that last one, that Wanda. She was the one got him into trouble that last time. He'd never have thought of a thing like that. It was her what told him to do it. My Ronnie's a good boy. It wasn't true what they said about him in the papers.'

'I'm sure it wasn't,' he said soothingly.

'I kept 'em all,' she said proudly, short-circuiting herself. 'Every one what had his name in. Pages and pages there was about him. Pictures, too.' Her eyes clouded. 'The pictures wasn't good of him, though. Not one good one in the 'ole lot. Wouldn't you think newspapers could take a better picture 'n that?'

'It's a shame,' Hollis said. 'So he went out Sunday lunchtime, did he?' It was just a guess, but it primed her all right.

'Went down the pub for his lunch,' she agreed, 'but he come back after and we watched telly, and then he went off out again.'

'Went to the fair, did he?'

'I dunno. I dunno where he went.'

'I heard he likes fairs.'

'Yeah, he does. Likes the lights and the noise and all that. Waste o' money, I call 'em. But Ronnie likes 'em. I spec he did go to the fair. Never come in till late, any 'ow, that I do know.' In her confusion, she seemed now to think it was a good thing for him to have been out, the longer the better.

'What time did he come home, then?'

'I ain't got a clock,' she said simply. Then, 'I was in bed.'

'Right,' Hollis said. From memory, she stayed up watching the television until all hours, so this wasn't much help, except that it suggested it was well after midnight. Mind you, the old bat was so wonky she wasn't to be trusted on anything, and it could just as well have been Monday night he was out, or a fortnight-last-Whitsun. You could never use her in court. Still, she might be right on this occasion. And if Ronnie was out Sunday night, it led to a promising area of speculation, especially as a strange-looking man had been seen wandering around the area.

He was working out his next question when there was the sound of a key in the lock and the hair stood up on the back of his neck. Ronnie had been too dopey to be dangerous the last time Hollis had seen him, but that was before he had done a stretch as a sex-offender among the high-powered criminals in Wormwood Scrubs. There was no knowing what he might have learned in there.

The door opened and he slouched in, flinging a newspaper down on the nearest surface before he registered that there was a strange man in the room with his mother. His jaw dropped, and he stared, trying to work it out.

'Hello, Ronnie, remember me? I just dropped in to have a little chat,' Hollis said as unalarmingly as possible.

Ronnie Oates, the Acton Strangler, was undersized and thin – though he had put on a bit more flesh with good prison feeding – and his head looked slightly too big for him. He had large, pale-blue eyes etched about with a mass of fine lines, while the rest of his face was quite smooth, which gave him the curiously old-young look which was the hint to the wary that he was of limited mental acuity. In fact, his record gave his age as thirty-four. His hair was straight, limp, and fair, but thinning on the top. His hands, like his head, seemed over-large, and hung rather uselessly at the end of his arms. He was wearing the jacket of a dark- blue suit with trousers of buff cotton, a blue T-shirt and plastic sandals. Just a glance at his clothes would tell you he wasn't dealing from the full deck; but in fact, since he combined the IQ of a glass of water with strong sexual urges and – according to the various female victims he'd exposed himself to over the years – a johnson the size of a Lyon's family Swiss roll, he was not quite as harmless as he looked.

'Sergeant Hollis, Shepherd's Bush,' Hollis helped him out, smiling comfortably. 'Just popped in to see how you're getting on.'

You could almost hear the gears grinding inside Ronnie's skull; faint wisps of blue smoke from the burning oil drifted from his ears. 'I never done nothing,' he said. 'It wasn't me this time.'

'Not you this time?' Hollis said encouragingly.

'It weren't my fault. She wanted me to do it.'

'Who did?'

'That Wanda. She wouldn't leave me alone. Kept asking me and asking me. She *made* me do it, Mum,' he flung at his mother, who was watching the exchanges with her mouth partly open, like someone at a ping-pong tournament.

'You gave her money to let you do it, Ronnie,' Hollis reminded him.

'She asked me for it. She asked me for money.'

Wanda Lempowski had been a prostitute, so Hollis didn't doubt that. 'But you shouldn't have strangled her,' he pointed out.

'She said I could. She liked it. I asked her and she *said* I could squeeze her neck.'

'Not as hard as that, though.'

'I never meant to. She said she wanted it, then she started screaming, so I pressed a bit harder to stop her, and then she hit me. She hit me *hard*. It really hurt,' he complained.

'She was scared, that's all,' Hollis said soothingly.

'Anyway,' Oates said sulkily, 'my mum said I wasn't to do that no more.'

'That's right,' said Mrs Oates, 'and he won't. He promised. You won't, will you, Ronnie? I told him he wasn't to get it out no more, never again.'

'That's right, Ronnie,' Hollis said. 'Not unless you're on your own in the bathroom.'

He stuck his lip out. 'It don't hurt 'em just showing it to 'em.'

'But the probation man said you're not to, Ron, never no more,' Mrs Oates said anxiously.

'All *right*, mum,' he said irritably, and turned to Hollis. 'Anyway, I never hurt *her*.'

'Who's that, Ron?' Hollis asked, catching the change of tone with a quiver of interest.

'The other night.' He lowered his voice to keep it from his mother. 'I was going to show her my porker. She was lying down. Maybe she was asleep, so it wouldn't have mattered. She wouldn't have minded if she was asleep. I wanted to show it her. But then I never.'

'Why not?'

'I thought someone might come. And I'm not supposed to get it out no more.'

'That's right,' Hollis said. 'So was that on the Scrubs? By the railway embankment?'

'Yeah, in the bushes. People go there to *do* it, y'know. All sorts. I like watching. I bet that's why she was there. Like that Wanda. They're all scrubbers, all them girls. Teasing and asking for it and *making* you, and then screaming.'

'But if you squeeze their necks hard enough they can't scream, can they?'

'She never screamed,' Ronnie admitted. 'She never made a sound.'

'I'm going to have to ask you to come with me, Ronnie,' Hollis said gently. 'Just to have a little chat and write down what you've told me.'

He looked alarmed. 'I never done nothing! I never hurt that girl.'

'No, of course not. I just want to have a chat where it's comfortable, and write down what you've told me. Tell you what, I'll ring the station and they can send a proper police car. You'd like a ride in a police car, wouldn't you? With the lights and the siren going? You like the lights, don't you?'

'Can I ride in the front?' he asked suspiciously.

'We'll see. And when we get there, you can have a nice cup of tea and some biscuits.'

'Cake,' he stipulated, playing hard ball.

'All right, cake.'

'A lot.'

'As much as you want.'

'Fruit cake,' Ronnie said firmly.

You said it, Hollis thought.

When Oates had been removed, Hollis was free to search his room, loath as he was to disturb any layers in there. Apart from the signature dirty clothes, crockery, food waste and general rubbish, Ronnie's interior decorating style was eclectic, gathering souvenirs from wherever he went. Anything he came across in the street during his wanderings was grist to his mill. Bits of wood, half a broken nameplate from someone's front gate, several hubcaps, a washing-up bowl with a hole in the bottom, a garden gnome with a chipped nose, a cracked tea plate decorated with violets, a set of pram wheels, an umbrella whose fabric had parted from half its spokes, a wire supermarket basket, a split cricket bat. In a cardboard box in one corner there was a whole collection of bits of broken glass that had once been part of headlights and tail lights of cars that had been in collision – he must have picked them up out of the road, along with the hubcaps, from the scenes of accidents. In another box was an amazing assortment of plastic cutlery of various sizes and styles. Perhaps more sinister was a box full of Barbie dolls, every one of them damaged, some with missing arms or legs, some with missing heads, some bald, all of them battered, dirty and naked. He must have gleaned them from dustbins or perhaps rubbish tips. They lay tumbled together staring up from their box in a way that, Hollis decided in the end, was more pathetic than sinister after all.

Overall it was a weird and far from wonderful collection but there was nothing helpful there, except insofar as it confirmed that the lad had the intellect of someone who bungee jumps off low bridges. Hollis left the bed until last, from an unwillingness to discover what it was like. When finally he turned over the sheets, he found they were not only dirty but suspiciously stiff. Ronnie had evidently used a generous interpretation of the word 'bathroom'. But reward was there for the dedicated archaeologist, for underneath the pillow he discovered a female's handbag, pink fabric with shiny threads woven through it, small and oblong, with a thin shoulder-strap.

'Oh, Ronnie,' he said aloud, shaking his head in dis-appointment. 'You daft pillock. It's just no fun at all if you make it too easy.'

NINE

From Bad to Verse

Slider went downstairs while they were processing Ronnie, and the sergeant on duty, O'Flaherty, stepped away to talk to him. He was a vast and beefy man whom copious pints of the Guinness and his wife's traditional cooking maintained at a glossy peak of solidity, like a prize breeding bull. He, Slider and Nicholls had known each other a lifetime, and had seen each other through various vicissitudes – many involving top brass, pointless changes in working practices, and mad political directives descending from on high like the proverbial brown shower. O'Flaherty, whose nickname of Flatulent Fergus was both true and affectionate, had often said that coppers at the sharp end coped with crime in spite of, not with the help of, their seniors. Like Slider, he approved of Porson, who got them left alone to a remarkable degree.

'Dis is a bad business, Billy,' he said, unusually serious for him. 'I always thought Ronnie was going to escalate one day, but I didn't think it would be this soon. Mind you, I wasn't in favour of him going down for that Wanda Lempowski thing. She was a nasty piece o' the divil-in-a-skirt, and I don't doubt she pushed him in the hope of getting more money out of him. In th'end she hurt him more than he hurt her. She's twice his size, and she packs a punch like an army mule.'

'That's not really the point, is it?' Slider said, a faint smile twitching his lips.

'Ah, sure, I know that. But psychiatric was what he needed, not a spell inside learnin' to be brutal.'

'Well, he'll get it this time,' Slider said. 'If he's found guilty his brief will plead insanity and he'll be locked up at Her Majesty's pleasure. And that'll be that.'

Fergus cocked an eye at him. 'What's up wit' you? Don't tell me you're developing a liking for smelly little flashers who go on to murder?'

'God, no! It's just so depressing. And what'll happen to his mother?'

'Ah, don't you worry about her. She's too t'ick even to realize he's gone. Are you going to interview him yourself?'

'No, I think we should let him settle in first. Get him comfortable, get some good grub inside him.'

'So he'll sing like a contented canary?'

'Right. One thing with Ronnie, you don't have to worry that he's using the time to think up answers. He couldn't make up a story if he used both hands and a tool kit.'

'Well, we'll be a while processing him anyway, so by the time he's had his supper he'll be ready for bed. You can safely leave him till the morning. And I bet he'll sleep better than you.'

'I don't doubt it. Thanks, Fergus.'

'How's your wee boy?' O'Flaherty asked as he was turning away.

'I wish I knew,' Slider said.

Porson called him in as he passed his room. The television was on in the corner.

'Look at this!' he barked. 'Have you seen this?'

Slider looked. It was the twenty-four-hour news channel. The sound was turned down, but the newscaster was mouthing to a background piece of film of the Oates house in East Acton with the squad car parked in front of it, its light revolving, and Ronnie coming out walking between two uniformed officers. The rolling ribbon at the bottom of the screen said: 'Breaking news – police make arrest in Zellah Wilding case. Ronnie Oates, the Acton Strangler, taken into custody.'

'How the hell did this get out?' Porson demanded.

'From the quality of the film, and the angle, I'd say it was a neighbour using a camera-phone leaning out of a window,' Slider said. 'I suppose there must have been neighbours who knew who Mrs Oates was, and knew Ronnie was back.'

'Well, we can't deny it now,' Porson said. 'And the vultures'll have a field day with this. It'll be all over the evening papers. "Acton Strangler strikes again." I've had to ask for more uniform to guard that old bat as well. Why couldn't you take him quietly? What'd you have to send a squad car for?'

'Ronnie likes riding in them. He likes the lights. It was a way to get him in without a fuss.'

'It was a way to alert the world and his wife that we were there!' Porson stared at the screen in disgust for a long moment, and then straightened his shoulders. 'Well, we might as well get all the queue-doughs we can out of getting a quick result. There's no other pleasure catching a nasty little Herbert like him. He's a sausage roll short of a picnic, that one, and the press are going to go to town on why he was wandering the streets in the first place.'

'It wasn't our fault he was let out,' Slider pointed out.

'Maybe not, but the public thinks we ought to be watching all these nonces all the time. It'll be our fault he was let to kill again.'

'He's never killed before.'

'Are you just going to stand there correcting me? Go and put a case together. He was seen in the area, he does it with tights, and you've got the handbag. What more do you need?'

The old man was unusually irritable, Slider thought as he escaped – but he took little pleasure in catching a brainless, hopeless, useless little git like Ronnie either.

He went the short way to his room through the CID room, entering in time to hear McLaren say to Connolly, 'Here, Rita, here's a good one – what do you call that useless piece of flesh at the end of a penis? Ronnie Oates.'

Connolly didn't react. She was on the telephone, and looked up as Slider appeared and said, 'He's just come in. Sir, it's Sergeant Atherton for you.'

'I'll take it in my room. McLaren, get me a cup of tea, will you?'

'Anything with it? They got bread pudden up there today.'

Slider's stomach groaned. It was a long time since the sausage sandwich. 'All right, I'll take a slab. Thanks.' He looked at Connolly. 'What are you doing?'

'Going through the canvasses again, for anything that could be Oates, sir.'

'Good. Find out who the Oateses' neighbours are. They'll have to be interviewed, in case they saw him go out or come in. One of them filmed him being arrested, so we can assume an interest.'

'Right, sir.'

Atherton sounded elated. 'Well, we found it, and it wasn't easy. When Chloë Paulson said Ladbroke Grove, obviously she was talking generically about the area, not the road itself. There was one likely shop on Ladbroke Grove, right opposite the station, but the flat above it was untenanted. We asked the proprietor about other similar shops nearby, and she said there was one in Portobello Road, so we went down there. In fact there were three operating in the general area of retailing mystic crap to mugs, but it wasn't any of them. Finally we found it on the KPR near the junction of Talbot Road. Man in the shop recognised the photo, and the second-floor tenant confirmed the bloke in the flat below was called Mike, and nodded to the photo as well. But there was no answer from his door – of course.'

'Where are you now?'

'Outside. I came out to ring you. We saw on the pub television that you've arrested Ronnie Oates.'

'What were you doing in the pub?'

'Relax. We went into the Castle to ask about more tarot-type shops, and they had the telly on.'

'Is that all you went in for?'

'And for Fathom to use the loo. You *are* suspicious. Anyway, the point is, do you still want to tug Mike Carmichael now you've got Oates? Lawrence said you'd found Zellah's bag in his room, so it looks pretty conclusive.'

Slider had been thinking about this ever since Hollis rang in. 'Yes, I think so. He was with her all the last evening and they had a row. We've got to construct as full a case as possible. And if Ronnie *was* at the fair, he might have seen him hanging around watching her. Also,' he added, 'he ran away, and he's given us a lot of trouble to find him.'

'We haven't found him yet – only his drum.'

'Exactly. I want to inconvenience him at the very least.'

'Attaboy! Take him in, keep him hanging around, harass him and put the wind up him for dealing.'

'You've got to catch him first. Start Fathom and Mackay on obbo. You can come back here and organise the rota.'

'Are you off out again?'

'In a while. I'm going to call on Mr Wilding.'

'You're still going to do that? Even though you've got Oates?'

'I'm being thorough,' Slider said.

'I know you,' Atherton said. 'You just want to poke about in Zellah's room.'

'That's being thorough.'

'No, that's being weird.'

'Thank you. I'll remember that come annual assessment time.'

Slider had forgotten about the media circus he had been warned was gathered around the Wildings' door. It was probably much less than it had been – a lot of them would have beetled off to the Oateses' when that news broke – but there were enough who would hang on like grim death in the hope of a 'personal touch' interview, a good photograph of a grief-stricken face at a window, or the now traditional tearful parents' appeal to anyone who knew anything to come forward. It was part of the loathesome apparatus of a murder investigation, the way the media would demand, on behalf of 'their' public, that certain things would be done, and be done the way they had made sure was expected.

His arrival caused a stir among the waiting hounds. Cameras were raised, pencils flexed, questions shouted. He rarely now had to make statements to the press – it was usually done in the media suite in Hammersmith by a team trained for the job – but of course they all knew who he was. It was their business to.

'Have you made a breakthrough?'

'Any comments on the arrest?'

'Is Ronnie your man?'

'Have you come to tell the Wildings about it?'

He passed through them without comment and without meeting any eyes, and they didn't make too much of a fuss, because he was known for being tight-lipped and they were resigned to getting nothing out of him. They crowded forward instead to see if they could get a good grief-shot when the door was opened. But the constable on the door – it was D'Arblay – rang the bell for him, the door was opened a crack, and he sidled through without seeing who was on the other side.

'Oh, it's you,' said Wilding, without noticeable enthusiasm. 'Can't you do anything about them?' he demanded at once, with a gesture towards the front gate.

'We're doing all we can,' Slider said. 'We're keeping them to the pavement outside.'

'We're prisoners in our own house,' Wilding said angrily. 'We can't go out. We can't even look out of the window. There was a man on next-door's roof yesterday, photographing the garden. I went out to dig some potatoes and I had to come back in again without them. He started shouting questions. Do you want us to starve to death? My wife can't go out to buy food – we're living on what's in the freezer. Why can't you make them go away?'

'I'm afraid we don't have the power to,' Slider said. 'It's a free country and we have a free press. We can keep them off your premises, but the road outside is a public right of way.'

'Free country! What freedom do we have? We're supposed to be the victims here, but it's us who are being punished, hounded by those brutes, locked up here day and night. The only freedom is for murderers, let out of prison so they can go on murdering other people's children!'

So they had heard about Oates. He supposed they were bound to be watching television, confined to the house as they were.

'This man, Oates,' Wilding went on. 'Why was he let out to kill again?'

'He had never killed before,' Slider said. 'It was the press who called him the Acton Strangler. He was in prison for indecent assault, not murder.'

'He still killed my little girl. Why did we abolish hanging? He ought to die for it. What are you going to do to him?'

'It's early days yet,' Slider said. 'We have a lot of ground to cover.'

'But you know it was him?' Wilding said insistently, glaring into Slider's face. 'You've got the right man? We want this over so we can go away. My wife's distraught. I want to take her somewhere away from here, as soon as possible.'

'I promise you we are doing everything we can to bring this to an end,' Slider said. 'I have to ask you just to stay put a bit longer and try and be patient. I know it's hard for you.'

'You know nothing – nothing at all. You can't imagine what we're going through,' he said bitterly. 'What have you come for, anyway?'

'To collect Zellah's mobile,' he reminded him. 'And I'd like to have a look at her room, if I may?'

'What for?' he said sharply and suspiciously.

'It's part of the routine I go through in every case. You never know what will be helpful.'

'My daughter was killed at random by a sex-offender who didn't even know her. What will her room tell you?' Wilding said angrily.

Was he very keen to keep Slider out? Or just a grieving father? Hard to tell. Slider used all his calm, assertive energy. 'If you please, sir,' he said steadily.

Wilding tried to stare him down, but Slider was good at that game. After a moment the weary, red-rimmed eyes faltered and fell, and he turned away with a gesture almost of despair. 'Oh, do as you please. Just don't talk to me any more. I've had all the talk I can stand.' And he went into the sitting room and shut the door hard behind him.

Slider went up the stairs and, with a fair knowledge of the layout of houses like this, found Zellah's room first shot. The door was closed, and as he opened it his sensitive nostrils caught a faint breath of perfume. He remembered Wilding saying the room still smelled of her, and pity rocked his heart. Wilding thought he didn't understand, but he did. He had a daughter of his own and, yes, he *could* imagine – only too well – what it must be like.

It was a plain little room. He compared it in his mind with Kate's, cluttered now with consumer trophies that his ex-wife's rich new husband had poured on both children in the hope of winning their love, or at least their acceptance. He thought of Sophy's over-filled treasure trove, typical of the well-off middle-class child. He appreciated all over again how strict Wilding must have been with Zellah, to keep her in this state of mercantile innocence. No television or DVD player, no computer, no vast hamper of outgrown toys; just a wardrobe of plain, service-able clothes, a little modest make-up on the dressing-table instead of the groaning board of unguents of any other sixteen-year-old. No eyelash curlers, curling tongs, hair straighteners, exercise machines – few possessions of any sort, in fact. *What had this girl been?* He felt frustrated. She had rebelled outside the house, he already knew that, but she had meekly bowed the neck within. How had Wilding dominated her so successfully? Had he abused her? And how far *had* she gone when she was out? Was her headmistress right or was Sophy? The parents or the friends?

He sat down on the bed, resting his arms on his knees, his hands dangling between them, and stared at the carpet in helpless thought. And after a moment he saw something white poking out from under the mattress – a small white triangle. Hastily he stood up. The bed was made in the usual way with an under sheet and duvet. Something had been pushed between the mattress and the divan, presumably to hide it. Carefully he lifted the mattress and drew it out.

It was a sketch pad. He turned the pages. There were a lot of horses to begin with, just figure studies, standing, walking, a rather unsuccessful one grazing – the length of the neck looked wrong – and then, as skill grew, trotting and cantering. At the end of this group a more finished page showed a horse cantering in open country with trees and hills in the background. Slider thought it was pretty good. Then there were some pages of still-life drawings – the usual groups of vases, flowers and fruit; a geranium in a flowerpot; a French loaf, cheese and a bottle of wine on a table with a gingham cloth. Competent but dull. Some ballet sketches reminiscent of Degas – copies perhaps? And finally some drawings of people in the nude. Life studies, wasn't that what they called it? A woman, reclining, from the back; a girl seated on a table, knees together, hands supporting her weight on the table edge, head dropped forward; more of them, pages of them, some in pencil and some in charcoal. Slider was no expert but he thought them beautifully done, not just accurate in terms of proportion and anatomy, but with a line and grace and feeling to them that suggested an artistic talent, not merely a draughtsman's skill.

He remembered the headmistress saying Zellah had real talent, and that the art master thought the world of her. No wonder she hid the book under her mattress, though. All that bare flesh? He would like to bet that Wilding didn't know his daughter was drawing nudes at her art classes. Then his thoughts arrested him. That corner of white showing. Someone had been careless putting it back. Would Zellah, with everything to lose, have been careless? If Atherton's theory was right, perhaps Wilding did know. Perhaps he had found the sketch pad and that was what had started him off on a quest to find out what his daughter really did when she was out of the house.

He was about to restore it to its home when he thought to check the rest of the book. There were a bunch of empty pages, and then, on the last one – on the back of the sheet so that it was face down to the cardboard back cover – was a poem. It was written in pencil in the round, unformed hand of the present-day teenager.

My self breaks its wings on the bars of my heart,
Sings, at the stirring of spring,
Like a frantic thrush, sobbing in darkness
Songs meant for the sun,

Whence it was ravished and has long forgotten.

It was the usual teenage stuff, he supposed. All teenagers who wrote poems wrote about how lonely and misunderstood they were. It was probably no better and no worse than any other adolescent offering. Not that it had been offered. It was hidden away at the back of the book, and the book was hidden under the mattress. Zellah had seen herself as a frantic thrush sobbing in a cage. Was it her father she saw as having imprisoned her? Or was it just her hormones making her restless? He wished he knew. He wished he had known her. The poem made him shiver, however good or bad it was, for she was dead, and it called to him from beyond the grave, from someone who had seen herself as imprisoned and helpless. Well, she was free now.

He replaced the book carefully, smoothed the bed where he had sat on it, and went downstairs. The Wildings were both in the sitting room – he could hear the television behind the closed door, and the rest of the downstairs was silent. He walked through the kitchen to the back door and looked out from the glass panel. Yes, there was the shed – and even from here he could see that it was locked with a large, stout padlock. To see inside he would have to ask Wilding for the key, and suddenly he had had enough. He had nothing on the man except Atherton's idea, and the tradition that it was always the nearest and dearest who did it. To ask him for the key and search his shed would only be giving him more pain, which he probably did not merit.

He walked back towards the front door and was startled when the sitting-room door opened suddenly and Wilding was there, towering over him.

'Seen all you want?' he asked abruptly.

'Yes, thank you,' said Slider.

'You wanted this.' He held out a freezer bag with a mobile phone inside it. Not a camera phone, just the basic ring-in-an-emergency sort. Even in choice of mobile he had been controlling.

'Thanks,' said Slider, feeling mean about his last thought. Probably the poor bloke couldn't afford anything more. He had lost his business, after all.

'Not that it will tell you anything,' Wilding said, glaring at him. 'It will have my fingerprints on it. And probably Zellah's. But if you want to waste your time, obviously I can't stop you. You'd do better to concentrate on that strangler you've caught, if you want *my* opinion. Don't make a mistake and let him go again.'

He dropped the bag so that Slider had to catch it in mid-air, stalked back into the room and slammed the door. Slider's sympathy dwindled a little. So anxious to put it on to Ronnie Oates? So quick to pre-empt the fact that his fingermarks were on the phone?

'And it's fingermarks, not fingerprints,' he addressed the closed door conversationally. *Frantic thrush sobbing in darkness.* So unhappy? Not the nuts-to-you rebel Sophy described? There was something about the words that stuck, he thought, opening the front door to let himself out. She had a talent. And the nude drawings were beautiful.

Atherton, perched on Slider's windowsill, his favourite pose for a bunny, still looked immaculate at the end of a long hot day, where Slider felt grubby and rumpled. He had crossed his ankles and was contemplating with satisfaction the fraction of silk sock that was revealed. 'Interesting,' he said, when Slider had finished. 'I wish we hadn't got Ronnie Oates, now. We can't really run three suspects at once, and Oates is so much more likely.'

'Likely?' McLaren said, leaning against the door. 'Try definite.'

'We're getting people ringing in with sightings,' Connolly said, 'now he's been on the telly. I'm keeping a log and sorting out the most likely ones, but it looks as though he was at the fair, guv. Three people have said they saw him there.'

'I expect people will have seen him everywhere from Glasgow Central to Piccadilly Circus,' Slider said.

'Yes, sir, and if it was only the one I'd have discounted it. But three separate witnesses? *And,*' she added quickly to stop anyone thinking that was a real question, 'the barman in the North Pole said he was in there drinking that evening, and the North Pole is only across the road from the fair.'

'That's a better identification,' Atherton told her kindly. 'Passing someone in the crowd is one thing, but facing someone sitting at a bar for a couple of hours . . .'

'That's what I was trying to say,' Connolly said with a faint look of annoyance.

'Don't sweat it, love,' Hart said. 'He's just trying to bring you up right. Part of his seduction technique – he thinks correcting people is erotic.'

'I thought you understood by now that I'm no longer in the market,' Atherton said loftily.

Hart grinned. 'Yeah, it must be queer having to turn women down, eh, Jim?' She winked at Connolly. 'The nearest he ever got to saying "no" to a woman was, "not now, we're landing".'

'Man was never meant to be monogamous,' McLaren offered.

'Or in your case,' Hart turned on him, 'even ogamous.'

'Do they always go on like this, sir?' Connolly appealed to Slider.

'I let them let off steam now and then,' he said. 'Meanwhile, let's you and I have a sensible conversation. Did you get anywhere with the neighbours?'

She consulted her notebook. 'It was the man at number six that took the film, sir, and sent it to the BBC. He's retired, ill-health, so not much to do but watch his neighbours out of the window. He was a bit excited about Ronnie Oates coming back to his mum's. Pretended to be angry about it,' she said, lifting her eyes to Slider's, 'but you could see it was the best thing in his life for years. So when he saw the squad car he grabbed his camera phone and started filming.'

'But on the night in question?' Slider prompted her.

'He saw Ronnie go out about lunchtime, come back in about three to half past, and go out again about eight. But he didn't see him come back in. Said he went to bed about half-eleven.'

'He wasn't watching out the window all that time?' said Hart.

'No, but he said the walls of those houses are so thin you can hear someone coming in, especially if they slam the door, which Ronnie does, and he didn't hear him come in. So if you allow for him dozing off, that means he probably didn't come in before midnight.'

'Getting the truth out of Ronnie won't be easy,' Atherton said.

'That's why I've left him to get comfortable and relax,' Slider said. 'The less he thinks, the more likely we are to get the truth. All right, we've got the watch set up on Carmichael's flat, we've got Ronnie tucked up for the night. We'll need a statement from the barman at the North Pole—'

'Sir, I live out that way. I could do it on my way home,' Connolly said.

'All right, do so. Anything else?'

'You thought about questioning the Wilding neighbours,' Atherton said. 'In support of my theory.'

'It's hardly a theory,' Slider said. 'More a wild stab in the dark.'

'We've investigated a few of those,' Atherton nodded.

'Yeah, Sat'dy night down the Shepherd's Bush Road,' McLaren said. 'Outside the Jesters Club. I hate bloody knives.'

'And they're always bloody,' Atherton finished. 'But to return to our *moutons*, which is to say Wilding – in the interests of being thorough, as someone we know and revere once said . . .'

Slider remembered, uneasily, the drawings, the poem, the corner of white sticking out from the mattress. You could only see it when you were sitting above it, as he had been. Whoever put it back that way would not have realized it was showing. Even so, would Zellah have been careless, when she was taking care to hide her secret life? She had drawn the cantering horse naked, too, he remembered, running free, without even a head collar. *Had* her father done more than clip her wings?

'All right, you can question the neighbours. But for God's sake be subtle about it. And don't let the press see you. The last thing we want is to start public speculation about it.'

'The press are having a field day with the Acton Strangler,' Atherton said. 'They won't be looking for any other explanation.'

'I dunno why *we* are,' McLaren said. 'Have you seen the *Standard*, guv? They've got an interview with a geezer 'at shared a cell with Ronnie in the Scrubs. Claims he was talking about getting his revenge on the establishment when he got out, and offing a posh girl.' There was a chorus of protest. 'All right,' McLaren said, unabashed, 'even if he didn't use the word "establishment", there's no reason he couldn't've said something like that. It's just as likely as not. And there she is, dead. What more do you want?'

'World peace,' Atherton enumerated. 'The perfect Yorkshire pudding—'

'And lipstick that don't come off on your glass,' Hart concluded.

TEN

Stupid Like a Fox

Slider had a bad night, too tired to sleep, his mind revolving uselessly round the facts and speculations, trying to make sense of them, and interrupted constantly by disjointed images that seemed terribly significant in the dead of night, but whose meaning eluded his grasp. He was almost glad when young George woke up and began crying. It wasn't like him: he was usually a good sleeper. Perhaps it was the start of another tooth coming through. Or perhaps he had picked up his father's restlessness.

Joanna stirred, and he told her to go back to sleep. 'I'll see to him.' She murmured and sank back instantly into her warm slumber. Slider got up, collected the baby from the cot at the foot of their bed, and carried him out to the kitchen, where he at once became wide awake, intrigued by the novelty of being up at this hour and fully intending to do the situation justice. After a lively session involving drinks of water, half a banana Slider found in the fruit bowl, and a scientific investigation of the contents of every tin on the kitchen counter (tea, coffee beans, rice, lentils, pasta shells, and – good Lord, Father, what's this? – didn't know they were here – rusks!) the scion of the house consented to settle down on the sofa in the living room and be read to out of his favourite book, which Slider had dubbed 'The Three Little Pigs In Escrow'. And it was here that Joanna discovered them in the morning, curled up together and fast asleep. To her fell the unhappy duty of waking up her beloved and telling him he was late.

Slider drove to work with that detached, arm's-length-from-reality feeling you get after a broken night. He told himself he did some of his best thinking in that condition, and himself was far enough gone to believe it. He hadn't had time for breakfast at home, so he sent for a bacon butty from the canteen and consumed it while he did his essential morning paperwork. Then, a little fortified (because under relentless pressure from the troops the canteen had at last got the bacon butties perfected) he went down to conduct his interview with Ronnie Oates.

Nicholls was on duty. 'Ronnie had a quiet night,' he reported.

'More than I did.'

'Wean giving you trouble?'

'Let's just say there's nothing I don't know about designing premium anti-wolf housing for porcine triplets.'

Nicholls was quick on the uptake, a multiple father himself. 'Wait till you get on to the gingerbread man. I'm surprised they're still allowed to print that, as a matter of fact.'

'Too gruesome?'

'Too homophobic. All that persecution of a ginger. Talking of which . . .'

'You don't think Ronnie's gay?'

'It's what all the psychologists would tell you. Repressed homosexual urges leading to hostility towards females, who represent his mother, at once forbidden and forbidding. It's classic.' He observed Slider's alarmed expression indulgently, and concluded, 'I'm just winding you up. Ronnie's too dumb to be gay. Anyway, he's a happy bunny this morning. Enjoyed his supper, solid night's sleep, big breakfast, and now he's having a fag and reading the paper. Well, looking at the picters, anyway.'

'I'm so pleased we've satisfied him. Maybe we'll get that third star this year.'

'We managed to get him to shower, as well, and put him into overalls, so he's considerably more fragrant than heretofore. Clothes are bagged up. Probably what he was wearing on Sunday – I think he only changes with the seasons – so there might be something interesting on them.'

'Interesting, but repulsive,' said Slider. 'All right, wheel him in there.'

Slider had Hollis with him, as the least scary of his firm, and the one with whom Oates had already established a relationship. Hollis held the door for him and he carried in two mugs of tea, one of which he put down before Oates, already seated at the table. The pale-blue overalls matched his pale, surprised-looking eyes. His complexion was slightly less grey after the shower and the plentiful food, and he looked extremely chipper.

'There you are, Ronnie,' Slider said. 'Two sugars, that's how you like it, isn't it?'

'Two sugars, yeah. Ta.' He took a noisy slurp.

'I'm Inspector Slider, and you know Sergeant Hollis, don't you? We just want to ask you a few questions, all right?'

'Yeah,' Ronnie said easily. 'You got a fag on you? Only I run out.'

Hollis, who didn't smoke either, knew the routine and had brought a packet in with him. He handed it, and the matches, to Slider, who extracted a cigarette, gave it to Ronnie, and lit it. Then he put the pack down between them, at an ambiguous distance from Ronnie, who eyed it speculatively and with an edge of greed.

'Better?' Slider said, as Ronnie blew smoke out from his mouth and nose together with a sigh of content.

'Yeah.'

'What did you have for supper last night?'

'Steak 'n' kidney pie an' mash. It was top. Could've done with a pint, though,' he added slyly.

'Sorry, can't manage that in here. Never mind, have a nice cup of tea instead, and tell me about Sunday. What did you do on Sunday?'

'I dunno,' Ronnie said vaguely. 'Which was Sunday?'

'You went down the pub for your dinner,' Slider suggested.

'Oh yeah.'

'Which one?'

'Down the Goldsmiths,' he said. The Goldsmith's Arms in East Acton Lane was about two minutes' walk away from the Oates house.

'What did you have?'

'Roast pork,' he said. 'An' syrup pud an' custard. They do a good dinner there of a Sunday.'

'And then you went home for a bit, and you went out later.'

'I dunno. Don't remember.'

'You went to the fair, didn't you?'

'Oh yeah. I like fairs.'

It was all too easy to lead him, Slider reflected; but how else to get anything out of him? His reply was always that he didn't remember, and he probably didn't, without clues. 'Tell me about the fair. Was it a good one?'

'Yeah. It was big.'

'Did you go on the rides?'

'Nah. I just walked about. I had a hot dog and onions,' he remembered suddenly. 'With mustard.'

'And did you notice a girl?'

'What girl?' He sounded wary for the first time.

'Any girl.'

He thought for a minute, smoking, and Slider tried to project a deep pool of calm and confidence. Finally a bulb lit inside Ronnie's dim brain. 'There was one on the waltzer,' he said. 'She was screaming fit to bust. She done it on the rocket an' all, and the chairoplanes. Screaming her head off.'

'You followed her round,' Slider suggested. 'Was it fun, hearing her scream?'

'It was fun looking up her skirt,' he said slyly, grinning to himself. 'She had them knickers on that's just a kind of string. Like dirty girls wear.'

'Do you think she was a dirty girl?'

'Yeah, I reckon she was. Cause she went up the bushes after, where people go to do it.'

He had come most obligingly to the point. 'So you followed her to the embankment, did you?' Slider asked casually, as if it didn't matter in the least.

'Nah. She had a bloke wiv her. He took her on the dodgems. Can't see up their legs on the dodgems. I was firsty, so I went over the North Pole for a pint.'

'That's right. Did you stay there a long time?'

'Where?'

'In the North Pole.'

'I had a couple of pints in there,' he agreed, then frowned. 'I dunno when that was. Was it Sat'dy?'

'It was Sunday, when you went to the fair.'

'The fair was good. It was a big one. Lots of lights. I like the lights. They're best when it gets dark, though.'

'So what did you do after the North Pole?' Ronnie looked blank. 'Did you go back to the fair?' Slider tried. 'To see the lights again?'

'Yeah,' he agreed – too easily? 'I walked about the fair a bit.'

'Did you see the girl again? The one that screamed?'

'No, I never see her. Not there.' He frowned again with effort, and managed, 'I was hungry. The hot dogs smelled nice, but I didn't have no more money, after the pub. So I went home.'

Something occurred to Slider. 'What way do you go home from there, Ronnie?' He looked bewildered, not understanding the question. 'Do you go on the bus?'

'Me mum's got a bus pass,' he said vaguely.

'What about Sunday night? Did you take the bus home?' Ronnie shook his head vaguely. 'Did you walk home, maybe? It was a nice night, warm, not raining. Nice for walking.'

'Yeah, I walked home,' he agreed. 'I never had no money left for the bus, so I walked home.'

'Along the streets?' Slider offered, trying not to hold his breath. 'Or did you go over the grass? Across the Scrubs?'

'Yeah, I went over the Scrubs. It's quicker that way.'

'It's a short-cut,' Slider said, breathing out with relief. They were back on track. And it was absolutely true. From the fair to Ronnie's house across the Scrubs cut off a big corner and saved a walker somewhere near a mile. It was the most natural thing in the world for a lad who had lived in the area all his life – and was too thick to be afraid of walking across dark commons at night – to go that way. And it fitted with the witnesses who said they had seen a strange-looking man wandering across the Scrubs. Ronnie was not the sort to yomp along briskly, heel to toe and head up. His natural gait would be as woolly and indefinite as his thought processes. He would have 'wandered' all right.

'Did you see that girl while you were walking over the Scrubs?' he asked. 'The one that screamed?'

'The one with the rude knickers,' Ronnie said, and chuckled. 'No, she wasn't there. She'd gone before I left.'

'How d'you know that?'

'Everyone'd gone. They was closing down when I left. I don't like it when they turn the lights off.' He frowned, but hadn't the vocabulary or brainpower to describe why he didn't like the lights going out. Slider could imagine. The glorious, bright, multicoloured gorgeousness of the fairground depended on its lights. When they went off, there was just wood and canvas, dullness, drabness, blown rubbish, and the dark of night creeping in.

But more importantly, Slider thought, they were getting something like a timing now, which was always difficult with a man like Ronnie, who had neither watch nor sense of time. 'So you stayed at the fair until it shut down?' he said. 'You stayed all the time until they put the lights out?'

'Yeah,' said Ronnie. 'I didn't like it when they put the lights out. The dodgems man told me to clear off,' he remembered suddenly. 'So I cleared.'

What had the fat lady said in Atherton's report? It was near two o'clock when her son got to bed. So the fair probably shut around one in the morning, maybe half-past. Ronnie was walking across the Scrubs between one and one-thirty-ish, and Zellah died some time before two o'clock. And he had seen her at the fair and thought her a dirty girl, the sort like that Wanda Lempowski who let him do things if he gave them money. *But he didn't have any money.* And Zellah was not, in fact, a dirty girl.

'So when you got across the other side of the Scrubs,' Slider said, 'what did you do?' The blank look again. He couldn't answer non-specific questions. 'You didn't go straight home, did you?'

'Nah.' He looked sly again. 'Sometimes you see people round there. I like to watch 'em. Once this couple broke into the changing rooms, and I watched 'em through the window. And people in cars.'

'Was there a car there that night? Under the railway bridge?'

'Nah. There wasn't nobody. Everyone'd gone home. But I found a thingy there, under the bridge. One of them things you wear on your porker. A fresh one,' he added with a relish to which Slider managed not to react. Ronnie sat back complacently, and then a vague look of unease came over him. 'You won't tell my mum?'

'We won't tell her anything,' Slider said warmly. 'Promise. We're all men together here, aren't we?'

'Yeah. All men. Women don't understand. My mum don't like all that stuff. She gets cross with me if I talk about it.'

'So what happened then, Ronnie?' Slider said, easing him back to the scene. 'After you found the thingy under the bridge. Did you see that girl?'

'Yeah, I see her.'

'Was she walking home, like you?'

'I dunno.'

'What was she doing when you saw her?'

'She wasn't doing nothing.'

'Did you ask her if she was walking home?'

'She w'n't *walking*,' he said, as if Slider should have known that. 'I told you, she was asleep.'

'Asleep?'

'Yeah, she was lying in the bushes, asleep.'

'What were you doing in the bushes?'

'I went to see if there was any more thingies. People do it in the bushes, and they leave 'em around. I see her lying down. I was gonna show her my porker, but my mum said I mustn't do that no more. So I come away.'

'Did you go right up to the girl?'

'Nah, I never.'

'How did you know she was sleeping, then?'

'Well, she was lying down.'

'If you didn't go right up to her, how did you get hold of her handbag?'

'I never,' he said. 'I never touched her.'

'We found her handbag in your room, Ronnie. Under your pillow. A nice pink one. You must have taken it from her.'

He stared at Slider for a long, congested moment, and then another light bulb flickered in his head. 'I found it.'

'Found it where?'

'I dunno. I just found it.'

'Now, Ronnie,' Slider said, stern but fatherly, 'you've got to tell me the truth. Otherwise I might have to tell your mother.'

Ronnie looked alarmed. 'No, don't tell Mum. I won't never do it again. I promise.'

'What did you do to that girl, Ron? You can tell me. Tell me the truth and I won't tell your mum.'

'I never done nothing to her.'

'You squeezed her neck, didn't you? Like you did to Wanda?'

'No, I never done *that*,' he objected. 'I just looked a bit. At her legs.'

'You squeezed her neck until she fell asleep, and then you took her bag.'

'I never. I found it. Finders keepers, my mum says.'

'Where did you find it?'

'I dunno. It smelled nice so I took it. I put it under my pillow for in the night.'

Slider had a depressing vision of Oates masturbating over the smell of Zellah's handbag. But they were no further forward.

'Tell me about squeezing her neck,' he said.

Ronnie looked sulky. 'She told me to. She said I could if I give her money.'

'No, not Wanda, the other one. After the fair, on Sunday. The one in the bushes. Tell me about squeezing her neck.'

'I never. I never touched her.'

'What did she say to you?

'She was asleep.' He paused, searching the airwaves for inspiration. 'I see her knickers, though. On the chairoplanes. She had them dirty-girl knickers on.'

And so the world turned.

In the end, it was Slider who tired first. Ronnie, with no apprehension and no sense of time, could keep it up all day if necessary, but Slider, being carbon-based, wore out. Ronnie was taken back to his cell – pleased to have been given the pack of ciggies – and Slider climbed wearily to his office, with Hollis beside him.

'We're not going to get it out of him yet,' Hollis said. 'He's too cunning.'

'Cunning as a jar of chutney,' Slider said. 'I've had more intelligent exchanges with my shirts.'

'He's out of the shallow end of the gene pool all right,' said Hollis, 'but he's just clever enough to stick when he gets to the dangerous bit. He's not bright enough to make up a story. He just says he don't know or he can't remember.'

'Unless he really doesn't remember. Defensive amnesia.'

'I'm sure there's something there,' Hollis said thoughtfully. 'Something he doesn't want us to know. But whether it was killing the girl or not . . .' He shook his head.

'On the face of it, it could have been the way he said,' Slider agreed. 'She could have been already dead, and he took her bag as a souvenir. But then why does he deny going right up to her? And what was he doing in the bushes that he won't tell us?'

Hollis screwed up his face. 'Well, guv, what's his favourite hobby? Say he saw her already dead and got excited, gave himself a hand shandy on the strength of it. He's told his mum he won't get Horace out except in the bathroom, so he doesn't want to tell us in case we tell her.'

'It's possible,' Slider said. 'All too depressingly possible.'

'And he picked up the bag as a souvenir, but doesn't want to say he took it from her body because that's part of what he's ashamed of.'

'It makes sense. Unfortunately.' They reached their floor. Slider paused. 'On the other hand, it makes just as much sense that what he's hiding is the murder.'

Hollis shrugged sympathetically. 'We'll have another go at him later. Maybe we can walk him up to it gently and get him to cough.'

'Maybe,' said Slider.

'Or we could pretend this is the seventies and beat it out of him,' Hollis said blandly.

'Eh?'

'Just joking, guv.'

Porson was not pleased. 'He's leading you round the Marlborough bushes. Where do we go from here? The clock's ticking, you know, Slider. Sooner or later we'll have to get him a lawyer, and then there'll be no getting anything out of him. His brief'll scream diminished responsibility and that'll be that. Have we got enough to charge him?'

'He'd still have to have a lawyer,' Slider pointed out.

'But at least we wouldn't be on the clock.' He lifted a hand and used the fingers for points. 'We've got his usual *modus bibendum*, he admits following her around at the fair, he admits he was on the spot at the right time, and he's been found with her handbag.'

Slider shook his head. 'We could charge him but it's not enough for a case.'

'On what we've got, a jury would go for him like buttered teacakes.'

'I don't know, sir,' Slider said. 'A good barrister would point out that everything we know could equally be explained by what he says being true. He could just as easily have found Zellah when she was already dead. Unless we can prove he was lying – if someone actually saw him doing something to the body. Or if we got anything off his clothes—'

'Well, get on with that, anyway. Meanwhile, keep at him. A confession would solve all the other problems.'

'I'm just giving him a rest, sir, then I thought I'd let Hollis have a shot. He knows him pretty well.'

'Hmm. Does Hollis think he did it?'

Slider hesitated. In spite of everything, he had the feeling that Hollis had doubts. 'He doesn't think he didn't,' he said at last, and for a wonder Porson accepted that without comment.

When he got to his room, Connolly was there, fresh as a daisy and twice as tasty.

'I had a crack at the barman at the North Pole, sir. Name of Dave Beswick. He knows Ronnie by sight – apparently he goes in there quite a bit. Your man says he's never any trouble, sits over a couple of pints, doesn't talk much. Beswick didn't realise who he was until he saw the arrest on the telly with the mugshot. He never knew Oates had a past. Remembers the Acton Strangler case, but didn't put the two together. Why was he called the Acton Strangler, anyway, when he was from East Acton?' she diverted.

'More euphonious,' Slider said. 'Like the Boston Strangler. The East Acton Strangler just doesn't cut it.'

'Does sound a bit culchie,' she agreed.

'What does this Dave Beswick think of Oates?' Slider asked.

'Only that he's a quiet bloke, no trouble, sir. Thought he was a bit of a denser, that's all.'

'Did he give you any times?'

'He said Oates went in about ten o'clock. They'd got extended hours for the Bank Holiday weekend, so closing time was midnight. Oates made two jars last till then. Didn't speak to anyone while he was there, apart from Beswick, and then only to order the bevvies. Not much of a gas, your man,' she added, with a cocked look at Slider.

'Oates says he didn't see Zellah when he went back to the fair after the pub, and we've got her having a quarrel and walking off about midnight, so it's possible she had already gone at that point. He could be telling the truth.'

'Does it matter, sir?' Connolly asked. 'After all, we know she wasn't killed at the fair. Whether he followed her or went on his own, we know he was on the scene where she *was* killed.'

'True. But with someone like Oates you need all the confirmation you can get of anything he says. It's the only way to filter fact from fantasy.' He frowned, going over the interview again in his mind.

'So – what now, sir?' Connolly asked, after a moment's sympathetic silence. 'What do you want me to do?'

'Re-interview anyone from the canvasses who said they saw anything, and see if they can identify Oates at the scene, and if so, get some times.'

'Righty-o.'

'Anything useful from the people ringing in?'

'Not yet. The ones that seem genuine are people who saw Oates at the fair, but that doesn't get us anywhere. The rest just seem like over-excitement.'

'There's a lot of it about. Keep fielding them, anyway. And you can go and see anyone from the canvasses you think is promising. Do you know where Sergeant Atherton is?'

'He went to Ladbroke Grove to check the surveillance team, then he was going to interview the Wildings' neighbours.'

'Right.'

'Are you going to have another go at Oates, sir?'

'I'm going to let Hollis have a crack at him,' Slider said. 'I'm going to see a man about a horse.'

'Sir?'

'And a still life, and a whole series of nude women.'

'Sounds like fun,' she said uncertainly. You never knew with the CID geezers when they were joking and when they were serious.

'Fun? I don't know,' he said. 'How do you tell when a person is waving and when they're drowning?'

'You have me there, sir.'

'It's all right. You weren't meant to understand,' he said.

ELEVEN

Ars Longa, Vita Sackville-West

Markov, the art master, lived in a smart new block of six flats in Bravington Road, a run-down area now being renovated, which, being on the far side of the railway and the Harrow Road, came under the title of Kensal Town, though it was only a stone's throw from Ladbroke Grove, and resembled it in style and demographic.

A quick bit of research on the St Margaret's website – it still slightly amazed him that schools had websites – had armed Slider with the knowledge that Markov's name was Alexander – Alex; he was thirty-eight, married to Stephanie, an intensive-care nurse manager at St Charles's Hospital, and his hobbies were skiing, and holidays in Italy where he liked to sketch old masters in situ. A photograph showed him as handsome, smiling and debonair, and it was no surprise to Slider to read that his nickname among the girls was 'Magic Markov'.

The three-storey block had replaced two large nineteenth-century houses, and the flats were of the sort termed 'luxury' by estate agents, because they had two bathrooms and the sort of street door you had to be buzzed in through. Where once there had been two front gardens, there was now a neat bit of paving with parking spaces marked off in brick. Only one was occupied – by a black Toyota, as Slider noticed automatically – so presumably everyone else was at work. He wondered briefly how much the parking habits of Londoners helped burglars in their trade.

He was duly buzzed in, and instructed to come up to the top floor, where Markov met him at the top of the stairs. 'Just wanted to warn you we have to be quiet,' he said in a low voice. 'My wife's a nurse and she's on nights this week, which means she's sleeping now, so I don't want to wake her up. I hope you understand.'

'Of course,' Slider said. 'It's good of you to see me.'

'Oh, no problem, no problem at all. I couldn't be more shocked about poor little Zellah. I couldn't believe it when I saw it on the television. But come in. If you don't mind we'll talk out on the balcony. We're less likely to disturb Steph there.'

The flat, despite having developers' proportions, was decorated in a modern and luxurious style, open-plan, wood-block floors, pale walls and lean, painfully modern furniture. There was a showpiece sofa covered in taupe suede – you'd have to be wearing freshly dry-cleaned clothes *ever* to sit on that, because it would show every mark, and getting them off would be the devil. There were modern art pictures on the walls, and some equally obscure bits of modern sculpture (or were they called 'installations' now?) on stands and shelves. The Markovs, Slider decided, must be doing all right. The place said taste, money and modernity. More importantly to Slider, it smelled nice – of cleanness and light furniture polish.

Markov led the way through to the balcony, which was the width of the sitting room and just deep enough to take chairs and a small round table. It looked out at the back over the gardens of this road and the next, which included some glorious big trees. Markov was evidently pleased with the view, because he turned at the railings and looked expectantly at Slider. 'Nice, eh? It was one of the reasons we bought this place.'

'Very nice,' Slider said.

'Can I get you something to drink? Tea, coffee – a glass of wine?'

'That's very kind of you, but no thank you. Nothing for me.'

'Oh. Well, I'm going to have a glass of wine. It'll be back to school for me next week, so I might as well make hay while the sun shines.' He gave a little, unconvincing laugh. 'Sure you won't join me?'

'No, really. Thanks all the same.'

The bottle was evidently open, for he was back in no time with a large glass of chilled white in his hand. He leaned against the railings, facing inwards, to sip it, so Slider was able to get a good look at him. He was tall and well-made, though not ostentatiously muscled – working out at the gym was obviously not one of his hobbies. He had thick, toffee-brown hair, expensively cut (Slider recognised the symptoms from Atherton) in a sort of floppy, public-school style, and shot with blonde streaks which were either the result of all those Italian holidays, or put in artfully for a hundred and sixty quid by a bloke called Adrian. He was wearing stone-coloured chinos and a denim-blue shirt, open at the neck and with the sleeves rolled up, showing tanned forearms. But the lean, classical face was neither as young nor as handsome as the photograph on the website had suggested. He had not shaved that morning, and his eyes looked bloodshot and pouchy, while his smile and debonair manner seemed effortful.

'So, to what do I owe the honour of this visit?' he asked at the end of a large-ish swig.

'I wanted to talk to you about Zellah Wilding,' Slider said.

The smile wavered, but stuck gallantly. 'So I imagined. But I don't know how I can help you. It's school holidays and I haven't seen her for a month. I have no idea where she was or what she was up to.' He swigged again.

'I didn't suppose you had,' Slider said. What was the man so nervous about? 'I saw some drawings that she did, and they impressed me with their skill. I'm not an expert, of course, but they did seem to me to have something. I wanted to ask you your impression of her, as a person.'

'Oh,' he said, but didn't immediately go on.

Slider thought he'd better prime him. 'Your headmistress said you thought the world of her, and believed she had talent.'

'Betty's a mathematician,' he said with a throw-away laugh. 'She has no eye for the visual arts. Her idea of beauty is a quadratic equation.'

'So, you *didn't* think Zellah had talent?'

He seemed to pull himself up. 'Oh – well – I didn't say that. Yes, Zellah had talent. She was a very bright child all round. She could draw nicely, and had a good eye for line and colour. Whether it would have gone on to develop into anything more than that, one can't say. Lots of girls can draw nicely, but they don't all become artists. And her father wanted her to go into engineering. I doubt he'd have been happy with a painter in the family.' His expression changed. 'Anyway, we'll never know, now, will we?' He emptied the glass. 'Sure I can't tempt you?'

'No, thank you.'

He went into the house, and returned quickly with the glass refilled. Slider was beginning to understand the eyes and the unshaven slackness of the face. Perhaps he was more upset by Zellah's death than he wanted to show. If he had based his reputation on buccaneering good looks and insouciance, he might be unwilling to reveal a sentimental side, especially to another man, who might see it as weakness. Or perhaps he had other troubles in his life.

'So, what were these pictures of Zellah's that you saw?' he asked when he had settled again. This time he sat on one of the wrought-iron chairs and crossed one leg over the other, resting the ankle on the knee in the classic Englishman-abroad pose.

'I found a sketch pad of hers in her room at home, which she had gone to some trouble to hide. There were drawings of horses—'

'God, yes, those horses! She was horse-mad, like all these girls!'

'And some still-life things, and then some drawings of nude figures. Life studies, is that what you call them?'

The smile disappeared. 'Yes. I arrange classes out of school hours for the girls who are serious about art. Teenage girls being what they are, it's difficult to hold them in school time without a lot of sniggering idiots making a noise in the corridor and trying to look through the glass door panel. Prurient little beasts.'

'Yes, I understand,' Slider said.

'Do you?' He sounded unexpectedly annoyed. 'It's not even just the kids; it's the parents, too. The human form is a thing of beauty: clothes are not. Just that. But the *hoi polloi* fasten on to the nudity aspect and make a vulgar song and dance about it. It's ignorance, pure and simple.'

Slider forbore to mention that 'hoi polloi' meant 'the people' and to say '*the* hoi polloi' was a tautology and a mark of ignorance. This man had probably had to field a lot of complaints from parents over the years, and specialists often got annoyed with ordinary people who didn't understand their specialism. *You should hear policemen talking about the great General Public*, he thought.

'There's a long and honourable tradition of painting the naked human form,' he said soothingly.

'I paid for the models myself, out of my own pocket,' Markov concluded, with a steep descent into bathos. 'I don't know what they had to complain about.'

'Look,' Slider said encouragingly, 'I'm not here to criticize your teaching techniques. I'm only saying I understand why Zellah hid her sketch pad from her parents.'

He looked relieved at the sympathetic approach. 'God, yes! That philistine of a father of hers! I met him at parents' meetings and school events and so on. Onward, Christian soldiers! He was an absolute ogre. No wonder Zellah was terrified of him.'

'Was she? I'm trying to understand her, you see. Different people give me different accounts of what she was like. You obviously knew her better than her other teachers—'

'Why do you say that?' he interrupted.

'Well, you saw her out of school hours, with your art classes.'

'As a teacher.'

'Quite. But I'm sure she revealed things about herself through her drawings. That's what art is for, isn't it?'

'Oh – well, yes, I suppose so.'

'So, how would you characterize her?'

He took another swig before answering, and stared thoughtfully at the middle distance. 'She was a clever girl, as I've said. But a quiet one. It wasn't easy to get anything out of her. She never talked about herself.'

'Her friends say she was a bold spirit, defiant of convention,' Slider said. 'Sexually active, for one thing.'

'Well, I wouldn't know about that.' He glanced at Slider and away again. 'You know how schoolgirls like to show off and exaggerate.'

'You mean her friends are exaggerating about her? Or that she exaggerated about herself?'

He hesitated. 'You saw her life-study drawings? What did you think of them?'

'I thought they were very good,' Slider said. 'I thought they had a great deal of feeling, not just technical accuracy.'

'Yes,' he said. He paused, as though thinking something out. 'Zellah did talk sometimes about boys, the way girls of that age do, but I always thought it was – well – a way of trying to fit in with the others. Because of her parents she was rather cut off from the other girls. I think she felt like an outsider. But those drawings showed the real Zellah.'

'Meaning . . . what exactly?'

'Meaning I think she was attracted to other women,' he said, returning his gaze almost reluctantly to Slider, and surveying his face as if for reaction.

'You think she was a lesbian?' This was a new turn.

'Oh, I wouldn't go that far. I don't know, but I would guess that she was still a virgin. But young people of that age are often puzzled and confused about their sexuality, especially if they've had few chances to experiment. Perhaps she was just beginning to feel these feelings – finding women attractive – and worried about being different from other girls. So she joined in the girl talk and the boasting with her friends, to hide her real self from them. But in her drawings she could only be honest. That's where the real Zellah came out.'

Slider pondered this for a moment. It made sense in its own psychological terms, all right; but he knew Zellah had not been a virgin, so whatever she may or may not have felt about it, she had certainly put her money where her mouth was. But those lyrical drawings of females nudes – *was* that what they were saying? He had thought the nakedness was in direct line of descent from the naked horses; that the freedom from clothes represented a greater, spiritual freedom – the freedom denied to the caged thrush. Though of course, longing for spiritual freedom and a suppressed attraction to women were not mutually exclusive ideas.

After a moment he asked, 'Did you think her a happy person, at the bottom?'

Markov looked grave.

'No, I thought her very unhappy. In fact...' A hesitation. 'In fact when I first heard she was dead, just for a second it flitted through my mind that she might have committed suicide. But from what the media seem to be saying that wasn't the case.' He finished on what was almost a wistful note, as if he hoped that somehow or other Slider could tell him it *was* suicide after all.

'I'm afraid it wasn't suicide,' Slider said.

Markov sighed. 'But you've caught the man, anyway, haven't you?' he went on, more briskly. 'It was on the news last night. Some ghastly serial killer, who picked on her at random. Dreadful thing – awful. But at least there's no mystery about it, is there?'

'No,' Slider said. 'There's no mystery about Ronnie Oates. What we don't know is what Zellah was doing in that place at that time.'

'Walking home from the fair, probably. No buses that time of night. Taking a short-cut.'

'How do you know she was at the fair?' Slider asked.

He blinked. 'Well, there's nothing else around there. And it said on the news report that's where the murderer – this Oates man – had been. So I just assumed.' He stared at Slider an instant and then laughed loudly. 'That wasn't one of those Columbo questions, was it? "But I never mentioned what the murder weapon was, sir." Oh dear, you can't possibly think *I* did it! What possible reason could I have for wanting to kill poor little Zellah?'

'I wasn't thinking that,' Slider said calmly. 'It was a simple question, nothing more.'

'Well, if the next question is, "where was I that night?"' he went on, still laughing, 'I was here at home, painting. But I'm afraid my wife was working so I can't call on her for an alibi. So you'll just have to take my word for it. I can produce the painting I was doing, if you want to see that.'

'That won't be necessary, sir,' Slider said. He thought the laughter was rather overdone, but the man was down the bottom of the second large glass, and he doubted they had been the first two of the morning. He stood up. 'By the way, the car outside, parked on the hardstanding – is that yours?'

'I don't own a car,' he said. 'It's hardly worth it in London, with the cost of parking and everything. One of the reasons we bought this flat is it's so handy for both our places of work. My wife can cycle to the hospital from here. She works at St Charles's. Why do you ask?'

'No reason in particular. I'm just interested in cars. Well, thank you for giving me your time, and your opinion of Zellah. It was very helpful. One of the hardest things about an investigation like this is that one never gets to meet the victim. And there's something about Zellah that haunts me, I don't know why.'

'She was a sweet kid,' Markov said seriously. 'And I must say it's refreshing to hear you talk like that. One somehow assumes that you policemen all get so hardened to stuff like this that it doesn't affect you any more.'

'It affects us,' Slider said. 'You learn to cope with it, but you never stop feeling it.'

Atherton was being regaled with tea and biscuits by the Wildings' next-door neighbour, who was plainly thrilled to bits with the whole affair and couldn't wait to be asked her opinion. She was a woman in her sixties, thin, with a tight perm. Her face – so wrinkled it looked like a dry river bed – was thick with foundation and powder; she wore crimson lipstick, and the strong lenses of her glasses emphasized that she was wearing not only eye-shadow but mascara. Done up like a Christmas turkey, Atherton thought, in case there was any chance of getting on the telly or in the papers.

But the media pack had mostly dispersed. When he arrived there were only two of them left, a weedy youth with an adenoidal look who was from the *East Acton Times* – a lowly subsidiary of the

Acton Gazette – and a very young, plump girl with a camera whom he didn't recognize, and took for a freelance. They were beguiling their lonely vigil by chatting to each other, and getting on so well they barely glanced up as Atherton drew up in front of a house two doors down. Mind you, neither did the policeman on duty, who seemed too sunk in lethargy to care about movements outside his own immediate line of sight.

So it was balm to the Barretts' souls when Atherton introduced himself and asked if he could ask them questions. Or rather to Mrs B's soul – she practically abducted him into the over-furnished, over-stuffed sitting room, barking out an order to Mr B, cowed in formal suit and tie and highly polished shoes, to fetch the tea. The kettle must have been on the boil and the tray already laid, for it all arrived in double-quick time, after which Mr B subsided in one of the armchairs and sat mute, stroking the black-and-white cat which ambled in from the garden and jumped on to his lap.

Apart from appealing to her husband from time to time for confirmation, which she never waited for, Mrs Barrett ignored him. She had stuff to say and she was going to say it.

'I never liked them,' she said, 'and I never trusted *him*. Thought himself so superior, that Mr Wilding! Thought himself better than everybody else, that's the truth of it.'

Atherton got it: the greatest damnation you could offer in this present age. To think yourself better than other people was the sin of sins.

'I suppose he *was* educated,' Mrs Barrett conceded with the deepest reluctance, 'but so were other people. My husband was an accountant, you know – weren't you, Gordon? Well, a bookkeeper, which is the same thing. Double entry. Forty years with the Co-op – they'd have been lost without him. They gave him a plaque when he retired. Anyway, if Mr Wilding was such a great businessman, how come he lost his business? Everyone knew Wildings. Up Telford Way, it was. My sister worked there at one time, and my niece, and one of my cousins was a machine operator. I never worked, of course. My hubby couldn't do with a wife at work, could you, Gordon? And I was married straight from school. That's another thing – *she* didn't have anything to brag about, that Mrs Wilding. Just a typist, she was, though she called herself a secretary. *And* he was already married when she got her hooks into him. Ramshackle business *that* was, whichever way you look at it. But I was sorry for her, if you want to know. *I* wouldn't have wanted to be married to that man. Something very sinister about him, that's what I always said, didn't I, Gordon?'

'In what way, sinister?' Atherton managed to ask. The armchair was so old and soft he had sunk almost to the floor, and his knees were in danger of banging his chin whenever he moved. There was no way he could get his teacup to his lips, so he went without. Shame, because he was thirsty. It was a hot day outside, and while the room was on the shady side of the house, it was absolutely airless and smelled faintly of dust. It was like being trapped inside a Hoover bag.

Mrs Barrett bridled and touched her hair. 'Too good to be true! That's what I always said. What was he hiding? All that do-gooding and churchiness. And *High* Church at that! Bells and smells and bowing and scraping. I can't be doing with all that mumbo jumbo. Plain vanilla, that's how we like our religion, don't we, Gordon? Next door to Catholics, his lot. All that fancy dress, robes and hats and gold embroidery. Hypocrisy, that's what I call it. Sheer hypocrisy. If I want to worship my God, I can do it naked in a field, that's what I always say.'

Atherton tried not to imagine this. 'So you think he wasn't really a Christian?'

'Well . . . I don't say that,' she said with the air of one determined to be fair at all costs. 'He *may* have been a Christian. But he thought himself better than us, and that's not a very Christian attitude, is it? Refused our invitations – our Christmas drinks party, Gordon's birthday, any number of things. Barely gave you the time of day when you passed on the street. And the way he treated that girl of his! Wouldn't let her join in anything! When my nieces were staying, I always asked her to come over, because it must have been lonely for her, being the only child. But he wouldn't let her. My nieces weren't good enough for his daughter, oh no! Wouldn't let her go anywhere or do anything. Watched and spied on, she was, all the time, which isn't natural for a girl. No wonder she got into trouble.'

'Did she?'

Mrs Barrett was short-circuited for a moment, and then resumed indignantly. 'Well, if you don't call getting murdered by a sex-fiend "getting into trouble", I don't know what is! I wouldn't have liked one of my nieces to be seen in public dressed like that. Ida Sharp on the corner said she spoke to someone who knows someone who was there when she was found. That Zellah Wilding was dressed like a tramp, she said, with a skirt so short it left nothing to the imagination. And what was she doing there at that time of night, that's what I want to know? So the Wildings have got nothing to be snooty about. My nieces would have known better than that, wouldn't they, Gordon?'

'Now, dear,' Mr Barrett began in mild reproof.

But she was off again. 'And what does he do in that shed of his all night, night after night? Charity work my foot! There's something suspicious going on in there, you mark my words. Night after night I see the light on, and his shadow moving about, two in the morning sometimes. Built it right down the bottom of the garden, so no one could see in – and he'd no right to that land. Calls himself a Christian but he's not above breaking the law when it suits him. I had a word with him about it when he took down the fence – or Gordon did, didn't you, Gordon? And he said he had to do it because the weeds were invading his garden. As if his garden's any better than anyone else's! And complaining about our poor Lucky every time he sets foot in it. Chased him with a garden hose, he did once. I'd a good mind to report him to the RSPCA. Mrs Delancey on the other side lost her cat, and I wouldn't be a bit surprised if he hadn't killed it and buried it somewhere. Always digging in his vegetable patch. I said as much to Mrs Delancey, and she agreed with me. She never liked him either. He shouted at her once about her Sooty – a poor old lady like her! You could hear him right across the garden. He had a temper on him all right, despite claiming to be a Christian.'

'Was he violent towards his wife and daughter?'

'Well,' she hesitated. 'I can't say for sure if he was violent, but I wouldn't be surprised. I've heard him shout at them many a time. And the life he made that poor girl lead, with no friends and no fun, that was tantamount to abuse, wasn't it? No, there's something queer about him, that's for sure.'

'Now, dear—'

She turned on him. 'What about his night wanderings, then? What's a decent man got to do with roaming around the streets at night? If he wasn't in his shed, he was out in his car. Picking up prostitutes, as like as not. It's always those churchy sorts that are the worst.'

She had gone too far for her husband. He must have tensed, for the cat shot off his lap as he said with surprising sternness, 'Now, Ruby, that's enough!'

Not as far as Atherton was concerned. 'What's that about roaming the streets?'

She turned to him with relief, glad to have the chance to justify herself. 'He goes out in his car at night. Sneaks out straight from his shed – I'll swear his wife doesn't know he's gone, because she never stirs once she's in front of the telly. He goes down the shed of an evening, and then as like as not he creeps out and down the path to the side gate, and when I look out of the front window the car's gone.'

'Perhaps he has evening engagements,' Atherton said mildly. 'Social engagements.'

'Not him. Refuses everything he's invited to. Besides, when it's one of his committee meetings or whatever, he goes out the front door like a Christian. No, this sneaking out he does is something shady, you mark my words.'

'Now, Ruby—'

'You don't see it,' she turned on him. 'You wouldn't notice anything if it was right in front of your face! But I've been watching him. Sneaked out on Sunday night, didn't he? Down to the shed he went, but he wasn't in there more than ten minutes when he sneaked out again, got in his car and drove off.'

'Did he?' Atherton said with interest. This was good – this was gold! 'You wouldn't know what time that was, would you?'

'I don't know,' she frowned. 'I suppose it might have been about half past five, that sort of time.'

'And did you see what time he came back?'

'No,' she said with reluctance. 'I was watching television in here – wasn't I, Gordon? I looked out at about ten o'clock when I went to make a cup of tea, and his car wasn't there then. And it wasn't there when we went up to bed, which would be about half-past eleven. I said as much to you, didn't I, Gordon? I said he was out again, on the prowl, didn't I?'

'Did you, dear?'

'The car was back the next morning, but he could have been out all night for all I know, and it wouldn't be the first time. Up to no good, you mark my words. Well, now they've gone, and good riddance to them, that's what I say.'

'Gone?' Atherton said, trying to sit up and failing entirely.

'Yes, left this morning, early. With bags. Gone to stay with her sister in Basingtoke, I wouldn't wonder. That's the only family I've ever heard her talk about. But it's good riddance to bad rubbish as far as I'm concerned. I don't care if they never come back.'

Skipped, by God, Atherton thought.

Outside, he realized the Wildings' dark-blue Focus was not in its accustomed place and cursed himself for not having noticed that when he arrived. It was the unfortunately named PC Organ on duty on the door. It was a muggy day, and sweat was rolling round his neck under his chin, and a trickle was easing down his cheek from under his helmet. Atherton stood in front of him, to mask any possible reaction from the press – their interest in each other still seemed to be greater than in the possibility of a story, but you could never depend on the press to remain indifferent when you wanted them to.

'What's this about the Wildings leaving this morning?' he asked, low but urgent.

'Yes, sir,' said Organ. 'Went off about eight o'clock. I've got the key, though, if you want to go in. Mrs Wilding left it with me in case.'

'In case of what?'

'She didn't say, sir. Just in case.'

'And when are they coming back?'

'She didn't say.'

'And where have they gone?'

'She didn't say. But they had overnight bags with them.'

Atherton rolled his eyes. 'It didn't occur to you to stop them, then?'

'No, sir.' He looked wounded. 'I was here to keep the press from bothering *them*. I wasn't told to stop them going out if they wanted.'

'And it didn't occur to you to let anyone know they'd gone?'

He looked even more wounded. 'No, sir. Why should it? They're the victim's parents, not suspects.'

Atherton turned away.

'Sir,' Organ called after him. 'Do I still have to stay on the door, now they're gone? No one's said anything.'

'I think you might be on duty here a while longer, Constable,' Atherton said.

TWELVE

What a Difference a Dray Makes

Slider would have liked to round things off by talking to Oliver Paulson – whose flat was only a hop, skip and jump from Bravington Road – but of course Paulson would be at work in the City, and would have to be an evening call. Instead, he decided to look in on his obbo team.

At present on duty outside Carmichael's flat were Hart and McLaren, and as Slider came along he was pleased to see that they blended in with the background nicely. He only knew them because he knew them. McLaren was leaning against the wall between the two shops opposite, eating a drippy meatball sub, and given that everyone on London's streets under the age of fifty seemed to be eating all the time these days, it made him inconspicuous. Hart had abandoned her smart work suits for a cropped top and a pair of hot pants, and if men walking past were looking at her it was not because they thought she might be a cop. She was wearing an iPod and earphones, an inspired piece of costume because it gave her an excuse to jiggle about a bit and disguised the fact that she was staying in the same place.

Slider didn't want to go up to her and blow her cover, but he saw her spot him, so he went into the tobacconist's next to the tarot shop under Carmichael's flat, and bought a pack of cigarettes and a box of matches. When he came out, he found Hart there, having sloped inconspicuously across.

She saw the cigarettes in his hand, as he had intended, and said, 'Got a fag, mister? Go on, give us one. Be a sport.'

'You're too young to smoke,' he said, and took his time unwrapping the pack to give her time to make her report to him.

It didn't take long, however. 'Nothing,' she said. 'Nothing in and nothing out. I wonder if he's on to us?'

'Surely not. You blend in so well,' Slider said.

'Not *us*,' Hart said with superb self-confidence. 'That pillock Fathom we took over from. Just one look at his shoes'd tell you.'

And then suddenly she wasn't there. There was a little whisk of air, and she was running like a hare down the KPR. Across the road McLaren had also sprung into action, hurling the remains of the sub into a waste bin as he passed – it was *that* serious, then. Slider went after them, only then seeing their quarry, who must have come out of the flat door while Slider was concentrating on the cigarette pack. Evidently he had seen Hart clock him and, with admirable perspicacity, put two and two together and taken off.

Hart was fleet and nimble, but Carmichael was young and fit and a good runner, and she was only keeping up with him, until he started across the road towards Westbourne Grove, presumably hoping to cut through to the Portobello Road and lose them among the stalls. At that moment a flat-bed fruit and veg truck pulled out of the turning, heading him off and losing him most of his lead. He turned right instead, down Stanley Gardens. Slider, who was some way behind, turned down the parallel Ladbroke Gardens and then left into Stanley Crescent, hoping to cut off a corner. He saw Carmichael emerge from Stanley Gardens into the crescent. Carmichael spotted him and hesitated a fatal second, wondering which way to run, and by the time he turned left, away from Slider, Hart was on him.

She brought him down to the pavement with a satisfying smack, using the whole weight of her body. Carmichael was no taller than her, but he had a man's weight and muscles against a woman's, and by the time Slider reached them, his breath dragging at his lungs, Carmichael was in danger of getting away again. Movies always made subduing a struggling man look easy, but in real life Slider had seen one drunken sixty-year-old woman require the services of four burly policemen to hold her down. But with Hart lying full length on top of him, Carmichael was hampered for breath after his run, enough for Slider, and McLaren when he arrived seconds later, to grab an arm each and pin him to the ground.

'Get off me!' he gasped. 'I haven't done nothing!'

'Stop struggling,' Slider panted, hanging on. McLaren had got the handcuffs out and was trying to get one end on the other wrist. 'You'll just hurt yourself. Give it up.'

'Lemme go! I ain't *done* nothing!'

'Then what did you run for? Keep still, you idiot. We've got you now.'

But not until the cuffs were on did he stop thrashing, and even then Slider suspected it was lack of air rather than lack of ambition. 'Get *off* me! I can't breathe!' he was moaning.

Hart eased herself off, taking hold of the handcuff chain for precaution as she rose. Slider and McLaren took an arm each and heaved the lad to his feet. He was about five-foot-seven, lean, good-looking, in his early twenties, though he looked younger because of his slight build. Despite the warm day he was wearing his black leather jacket over jeans and boots. His longish dark hair was all over the place, and he had a red mark down one side of his face where it had been pressed to the pavement, which slightly detracted from his air of sophistication – and no one looks their best in handcuffs. But Slider could guess that in good times he had the air to attract the girls and make the boys envy him.

He glowered at Slider. 'I haven't done nothing! Take these things *off* me!'

'You've run away from me twice, son,' Slider said. 'That's enough for me.'

'You'd run away if people were always after you. You cops never leave me alone.'

Hart gave his chain a yank. 'Stop dealing drugs and we'll leave you alone.'

'I don't deal drugs,' he said. 'Just 'cos I was in trouble once. You never give anyone a chance. Anyone from the estate, you're down on. You're all the same, you—'

'Oh, stop whining,' she said. 'You're nabbed. Take it like a man.'

Slider almost snorted, but the approach seemed to work with Carmichael. He sagged a little and looked sulky. 'So what're you arresting me for?'

'We'll think of something. I'm sure when we have a little look in your flat we'll find something interesting,' Hart said.

'Plant it, more like,' he muttered sullenly.

Hart winked at Slider. 'There y'are, guv. Out'v his own mouth. He wouldn't've said that unless there *was* something up there to find. I knew he didn't run for nothing.'

'Why don't you bastards leave me alone?' Carmichael almost wailed. 'Why don't you go after the big players?'

'Because we want to talk to you about Zellah Wilding,' Slider said.

'Who?' Carmichael said.

'Your girlfriend,' Hart said. 'You must remember her.'

'She's not my girlfriend,' Carmichael said. 'We broke up.'

'It was off, and then it was on again,' Hart said.

'I tell you I haven't seen her in months.'

'Well, in that case,' Slider said, 'we'll arrest you for lying to us. We've got a dozen witnesses that you were with her on Sunday night.'

'Oh shit,' said Michael Carmichael.

'That's what you're in, all right,' said McLaren.

'You didn't half go, guv,' Hart said to Slider as McLaren was putting Carmichael into the squad car they had summoned. 'I was well impressed.'

'Do you really think I'll respond to blatant flattery like that?' he said severely.

'What sort of blatant flattery *will* you respond to, then?' she asked cheekily.

He ignored that. 'You, on the other hand, brought him down with a tackle that could qualify you to play for England.'

'Thanks, guv. I'll take all the flattery I can get; any sort.'

'I don't understand how he got *into* the flat, however, when it was being watched twenty-four hours a day.'

Hart met his eye. They both knew the answer. He had been missed going in. But Hart nobly didn't even say, 'It wasn't us.'

'You and McLaren can give the flat a good going over,' Slider said.

'Righty-o. I bet we find enough in there to put the pressure on him. But I can't see why he wouldn't tell us the trufe anyway – about Zellah, I mean. Once he knows we don't think he killed her. We don't think he killed her, do we?' she added on a faintly puzzled note. 'I mean, it was Ronnie Oates done her?'

'It looks that way.'

'So we only want him for corroboration?'

'So it seems.'

She cocked her head at him enquiringly. 'Guv, I can't help feeling you've got reservations about this case.'

'I can't help feeling there's something I've missed,' Slider confessed

'That's just normal paranoia,' Hart said comfortingly. 'Everyone on the planet gets that. Don't worry, some 'orrible snag will come up and blow the case to bits and you'll have to put it back togevver against the clock with the big brass breathing down your neck, and everything will seem nice and normal again.'

'Thanks, I feel better now,' said Slider. 'I'm going back to the factory.'

His room looked like a public place within the meaning of the act. There were so many people in it he couldn't get through the door, and when enough of them spotted him and melted away to give him access, he found Joanna in there, with young George Slider sitting on the edge of his father's desk holding court. With a rusk in one hand and a pencil in the other, he was waving his arms swoopingly at his fans, like Solti conducting Debussy, except that Solti, though equally bald, had never smiled so seraphically at an orchestra.

Joanna looked guilty. 'Sorry. Is this a completely inappropriate time? I just picked him up from the baby-minder after rehearsal. I was on my way home when I thought that, as you'll be late again this evening, you'd like to see him awake for once, so I popped in. But I can pop out again just as quickly.'

George had spotted his father now and was beaming in delight, showing his new top incisors, which he was growing to match the two at the bottom. 'Mumurummmum,' he said.

'I didn't realize it was that late,' Slider said.

'It isn't. We finished early. I think the conductor had somewhere more exciting to go.'

Slider picked up the baby, who signalled his approval by pushing the damp end of the rusk into his father's ear and saying, 'Blum mum num.'

'I'm glad you came,' Slider said. 'But I can't spare you long. We've just brought someone in and he'll need questioning.'

'I know, don't worry. I should go home, anyway. There's a mountain of ironing I've been putting off. I can get some of it done while he's having his nap.'

'I wish that I could take you out to lunch,' Slider said wistfully, 'but...'

'We'll catch up when all this is over. I just wanted my boy to know he still has a father.' She smiled as she said it to show she was not complaining.

'I slept with him last night. What more does he want?' He grinned at his son, who tried to grab his nose, so the pencil in his hand came dangerously close to Slider's eye. He removed it gently. 'I'm glad you brought him.' It helped to keep a person grounded. He made that noise with his lips that all babies find irresistibly funny, and George responded by demonstrating his award-winning chuckle. 'If we could bottle that, we could sell it for a fortune,' Slider remarked, making him do it again.

'By the way – I meant to ask you – did you speak to your father?'

'Yes. He rang me here yesterday morning.' Good Lord, was it only yesterday? 'He's talking about selling the house.'

'Yes, he said something about it when I was over there on Monday.' She hesitated. 'Reading between the lines, I think he'd like to move nearer to us.'

Slider sighed. 'I wish he could, but London prices being what they are . . .'

'I know.'

'I worry about him.'

'I know. But he can look after himself. He's a big boy. And talking of big boys . . .' Through the windows on to the CID room, she had seen that Atherton had come purposefully in and was heading towards the communicating door. 'Let me have him. I'll get out of your hair.' She took the baby back, shouldered her bag, and pecked her husband on the cheek in passing. 'I'll leave something out for you to heat up, in case you're hungry when you get home.'

'Have a good concert. Drive carefully,' Slider said.

She departed through the door to the corridor, George watching his father over her shoulder with a slightly disconcerted air, and reaching out for him in farewell with the damp rusk. 'Bloo,' he said.

Atherton came in at the other door, unaware that his big entrance had been upstaged by one of the world's great exits, and said, 'Wilding's flitted. That's one for my side!'

'It's not exactly flitting, is it?' Slider said, perched on Atherton's desk for a change. 'They were under siege from the media, angry and distressed. When I saw him on Wednesday he complained they were prisoners in their own home. They'd probably just had enough.'

'It'd drive anyone mental,' said Connolly.

'Ah, but wait till I tell you what the neighbours had to say,' said Atherton, and gave him a summary of the Barretts' evidence. 'Now, leaving aside all prejudice for bad neighbourly relations, Wilding was out in his car on the night Zellah died, and didn't tell us. When I interviewed him he said he was working in his shed all evening until quite late and then went to bed.'

'Yes,' said Slider. 'That is a point. And if it's true that he often slipped out without his wife's knowing . . .'

'It puts things in a different perspective.'

'Yeah. Wandering about at night—' Mackay began.

'Driving,' Connolly corrected him.

'I was gonna *say*,' he went on, giving her a look, 'he's probably down Paddington picking up tarts. He's a kerb-crawler.'

'Why does it have to be something to do with sex?' she objected.

'It always is,' said Mackay with some justification. 'I mean, what else would he bother to hide from his wife? He's got some sex-habit he needs catered for.'

'S and M, most likely,' Fathom agreed. 'He looks the type. He's out nights finding a Miss Whiplash to give him correction.'

'He's a pillar of society,' Connolly said.

'They're the worst,' said Mackay confidently. 'All pious and holy when anyone's looking, then creeping out at night murdering prostitutes. Look at Reg Christie.'

'We're not talking about murdered prostitutes,' Slider reminded him. 'However, in fairness to the "here comes a churchgoer, let's chuck a brick at him" brigade I seem to be fostering in my midst, it does make you wonder whether his repression of his daughter was ever taken any further.'

'I wondered about that,' Atherton said. 'I asked the neighbours if he ever knocked his wife and daughter about, but they only said they'd heard him shouting at them. And if I was married to Mrs Wilding I'd probably shout. But they obviously don't know what went on inside the house.'

'And neither, I suppose, will anyone,' Slider said. 'That's the problem with a family that never lets anyone else in. He *could* have been abusing her, but if he was, I'd imagine it was only the psychological sort of abuse.'

'*Only?*' Atherton queried, with a pained air.

'You know what I mean. Physically abused children tend to be too quiet and don't do well at school. They're not described as live wires by their friends. They don't go to ballet classes and extra-curricular drawing and shine at lessons.'

'But then,' Mackay said, 'what was Wilding doing out in his car on the night Zellah was murdered, and why didn't he tell us about it?'

'Following her,' Atherton said. 'That's my bet. If the old bat next door is right, he left not long after her. He was following her to see what she got up to when she was out of his sight. And I would be surprised if he hadn't done it before.'

Slider nodded unwillingly. 'It *is* suggestive. He obviously liked to keep a high level of control over her. And Mrs Wilding said he was very against her staying over at a friend's house. Perhaps he wanted to make sure that *was* where she was going to sleep.'

'Suspicious brute,' Atherton said.

'The question is, how long did he follow her, how much did he witness, and what, if anything, did he do about it?'

'Say he followed her to the Black Lion an' saw her go off with Mike Carmichael, when he'd forbidden her to see him again,' Connolly said.

'And he went mad with rage,' Fathom went on, 'and decided to punish her.'

'You don't punish someone by strangling them,' Slider said. 'Strangling is always intended to kill.'

'Perhaps,' Atherton said – and the tone of his voice told Slider that he wasn't happy thinking this – 'he decided she was so far gone in sin it was the only way to save her soul.'

Slider wasn't happy thinking it, either, because there was something about Wilding's towering person and character that made it seem plausible. Each man kills the thing he loves – and who had loved Zellah more? 'There's still the problem of the tights,' he said.

'As I said before, there must be lots of pairs around at home,' said Atherton.

'But if he went home to get a pair,' Slider said, 'how did he know where she would be? And in any case, why would a man in a homicidal rage bother, when he's got a pair of large, strong hands at the end of his arms?'

There was a little silence. The hands came before Atherton's mind's eye, strong and grimy with a workman's little nicks and scratches. *Had* he got those from carpentry? But it was true, he wouldn't need to go and fetch a pair of tights. 'Unless,' he said slowly, 'he'd already had enough evidence that she was going to hell in a hand basket, and he took the tights along with him in case execution proved necessary. In which case it wasn't just spur-of-the-moment homicidal rage.'

'In which case,' Mackay agreed, 'he's seriously bonkers.'

'It's a lot of suppositions,' Slider said. 'But there are certainly important questions to ask him. The trouble is, we don't know where he is, do we?'

'The old bat next door said they'd probably gone to his wife's sister's,' Atherton said, 'so we'll start by trying to find her.'

'How?'

'Bit of this, bit of that,' Atherton said airily. 'The wonders of the internet, plus the Wildings' address book. Leave it to me.'

'That's what I was thinking of doing. But make it quick, wonder-fingers. If – and it's only an if, but all the same – if Wilding did kill Zellah, he's dangerously deranged, and his wife could be the next target.'

'If it had been me,' Atherton said, departing, 'she'd have been *way* up the list.'

Meanwhile, Slider went to see Porson.

The new Wilding development caused the Syrup's massive eyebrows to hurtle together above his nose as if for comfort. 'This is not good,' he said. 'I don't like it. A man driving secretly round the streets at night, and not telling us. And then flitting. He's got something to hide, all right.'

'And then there's Michael Carmichael,' Slider said. 'He denied knowing Zellah, then said he hadn't seen her for two months. Why? We know he was with her that evening and that they had a row, after which she walked off. And local residents in the Old Oak Common area said they heard a motorbike roaring round late that night. It could have been Carmichael looking for Zellah to finish the row, having fetched his bike and gone after her round by road. He finds her, they go at it again, and he ends up strangling her, the only way to shut her up.'

The eyebrows huddled even closer together. 'That's plausible. But it would have to be a really serious row to go that far. And what about the tights? Where would he get those?'

'The tights are always a problem,' Slider said.

'Not with Ronnie Oates,' Porson said. 'If we assume he went out looking for his own brand of fun and took them with him.'

'But he's never done that before.'

'He's never had to. Prozzies have tights to hand.'

'Then why would he assume this time he'd need to take his own?'

'*I* don't know,' Porson sighed. He walked over to the window, scratching gently at his scalp as if he hoped to stimulate thought within. 'Damn it, Slider, now we've got *three* suspects! Normally you'd be grateful for one, but now we've got a plethora.'

Slider was so startled the Syrup had used the right word in the right context, *and* pronounced it correctly, that he couldn't immediately assemble an answer.

'Wilding's got the best motive,' Porson went on. 'Righteous rage, possessiveness, thwarted love and all that sort of thing. But Carmichael is young and we've been told he's got a temper, and they *were* argy-bargy-ing. On the other hand, Oates doesn't need a motive. She's his random victim. And he's got previous. All right, he's not murdered before, but it's the same method. You can't teach an old leopard new spots.'

Slider relaxed, back in the comfort zone.

'I don't know,' Porson concluded unhappily. 'You'll have to go after all three of 'em until something breaks. If it was Wilding, he'll have tried to cover his tracks. But the criminal always makes one carnal error. With Carmichael it'll be more a matter of breaking him down and catching him out. As for Oates—'

Porson's door was almost always open, and at that moment Hollis appeared in the doorway and tapped politely to attract their attention. He looked tired, and his tie had been loosened and pulled awry, while his impossible hair was at its liveliest, suggesting a certain degree of frustrated finger-raking had recently taken place.

'They told me you were here, guv,' he said to Slider, but his eyes moved on to Porson. 'Ronnie Oates has confessed.'

Porson looked as if he'd been thrown a lifeline. 'That's more like it. Confession is as confession does. I don't like it when they don't cough. What sort of state's he in?'

'He's fine, sir,' Hollis said. 'Quite cheerful. Thinks himself no end of a buck, if you want my opinion.'

'Good. We don't want the defence claiming we beat it out of him.'

'No, sir. He's all right. Better than me.'

Porson looked at his watch. 'Has he had anything to eat?'

'Not since breakfast, sir, though he's had several cups of tea.'

'All right. This is what we'll do. Read him his rights, get him a solicitor, and make sure he gets a good lunch before the brief arrives. Whatever he likes best. Keep him in a good mood. Then get him to do it again on tape with the solicitor present. That way there's no argument.' He pulled out his handkerchief and mopped his brow and round his neck. Behind him the window was open, but not a breath of air came through, and the sky was blankly grey. 'Meanwhile, follow everything up, get everything corrobolated, leave no grindstone unturned. If we're going to stand Ronnie Oates up against the bleeding hearts brigade, we need a cast-iron case, no loose nuts.' He put his handkerchief away. 'Too damned hot today. Wouldn't be surprised if it rained later. Oates is in the coolest place – can't accuse us of cruelty. Well,' he concluded in a bark, 'what are you standing there for? Get on with it!'

Slider turned away. He wouldn't be surprised if there wasn't a storm later, and not only meteorologically. This case was like a typical British summer, he thought. Three hot days and a thunderstorm – with a period of unease in between.

'I'm going to leave Oates to you,' he said to Hollis as they walked down the corridor. 'Can you manage that and office manager?'

'Yes, guv,' Hollis said, with a question naked in his face.

'I'm going to interview our friend Carmichael,' Slider said. 'As the Old Man says, we don't want any loose ends.'

'Curiosity,' said Hollis gravely, 'got the early cat the cream.'

THIRTEEN

Another Day, Another Dealer

Running was Carmichael's undoing. DI Phil Warzynski at Notting Hill accepted it, when Slider phoned him, as proof of villainy, and with his good word in support the duty muppet coughed up a warrant to search the flat. Hart and McLaren came back with cheering news. They had found things of interest.

'It weren't a bad pad,' Hart commented. 'Clean, done up nice. I dunno if he spends much time there, though. There wasn't many clothes, no telly, just a sound system and some CDs. No food to speak of in the fridge, just the empties of a six-pack and a Chinese takeaway in the bin. He must have gone out last night and took it back in with him.' She rolled her eyes slightly to show what she thought of the other team allowing him past. 'Anyway, I couldn't picture him sitting around there of an evening. It was more like a drop-in.'

'Expensive drop-in,' McLaren said. 'Anywhere decent round there costs a bomb.'

'But we reckon he was making *well* enough to afford it,' Hart went on. 'I knew we'd find something as soon as he started talking about "planting" stuff. They always say that, the dipsticks. And right away we found a whole lot of little squares of white paper in one cupboard, and a couple of packets of white powder in another.' She grinned. 'He'd put 'em in two tins marked rice and flour. I reckon he's got a sense of humour.'

'But they weren't rice and flour?' Slider prompted gently.

'Kensington an' Chelsea,' Hart said.

'Calvin Klein,' McLaren put in, not wanting to be left out of the hip-talk stakes.

K&C, or CK, was ketamine and cocaine, the latest drug of choice for young people wanting to get off their faces. Ket, the veterinary tranquiliser, was cheaper than charlie, and while the high didn't last as long, there was no paranoid come-down as with cocaine. It was more like being hilarious drunk for a couple of hours, leaving you with nothing worse than a mild hangover. At the lower end of the social scale, the users were abandoning coke for financial reasons along with high-price cocktail bars and nightclubs, and taking ket with friends at home, which was a lot less trouble for everyone (including the police). The better-off kids were mixing the two, hence the 'Royal Borough' nickname for the combination.

'So, our little chum is at the cutting edge of juvenile stupidity, is he?' Slider said. 'How much did you find?'

'About fifty grams of charlie and twenty-five of K,' Hart said. 'Plus, like I said, the papers for making the wraps.'

'So we could make dealing stick all right?'

'Yes, guv, and there was something else,' McLaren added eagerly. 'In the bathroom there was a hairbrush on the shelf in front of the mirror, and there were some long blonde hairs in it, along with the black.'

'We brought 'em back in an evidence bag, guv, in case you want to do a DNA test,' Hart concluded. "O" course, he might have had some other blonde bird up there, but . . .'

'Quite,' said Slider. This was good. It gave him more to work with in putting pressure on Carmichael, and if enough pressure were exerted it would probably not be necessary to send the hair to be expensively analysed. 'All right, get it written up and the samples booked. I'm off to see a man about a drug.'

Michael Carmichael was looking both furious and sulky, which Slider thought a promising combination. Both states of mind were the enemy of rational thought, and without rational thought there could be no cunning.

'I'm not talking to you!' he shouted as soon as Slider came in.

Slider had brought Mackay with him, in case of trouble, and nodded to him to stand inconspicuously in the corner, while Detton, the duty constable, went to stand outside the door. He wanted the conversation, if it took place at all, to seem like a one-to-one.

It didn't start well. Carmichael fixed angry eyes on Slider and snarled, 'I'm not telling you anything. I want a lawyer.'

Slider looked fatherly concern. 'Oh, don't say that! I was hoping to have a friendly chat, just between the two of us.'

'I know my rights,' Carmichael said, and thumped the table to emphasise his determination. 'I'm not saying anything without a lawyer. You get me one, or that's it.'

'Well, I'm sure you do know your rights,' Slider said, 'but the thing is this: we've found a lot of drugs in your flat. If you insist on a lawyer, we'll have to charge you with dealing, and that means prison.'

'You planted 'em there. You'd never make it stick.'

'Yes, we would. Don't be silly.'

He knew it, too. He changed tack. 'It's just a bit for my own use. You don't go down for that. You'd have to let me go with a slap on the wrist.'

'Don't let's waste time. You know the quantities you had up there, far more than for your own use – plus the papers all ready for making the wraps. It's a clear charge of dealing, for which it's a couple of years inside.' He paused long enough to let it sink in. Carmichael's face was dark with anger and frustration, and for a moment he seemed to struggle for escape, moving his head this way and that, rocking the chair back on its hind legs and letting it drop with a crash. Finally he let loose with a flood of foul language, beating his fists on the table. Slider watched him unmoved until the storm abated, and then said, 'Calm down and listen. *Listen!*' Carmichael shut his mouth and looked at Slider, trembling slightly, nostrils flaring. 'As it happens,' Slider went on, 'I'm not minded to follow up the drugs thing – *if* you co-operate.'

'Co-operate?' Carmichael said at last, with deep suspicion. 'What are you talking about?'

'It's not the drugs I want to talk to you about, so if you calm down and talk to me sensibly without babbling about your rights and wanting a lawyer, I can forget we found anything in your flat.'

'What do you want to talk about?' he said, but Slider could see he knew the answer to that.

'Zellah Wilding.'

'Oh, shit. You're going to try to pin that on me now, are you? Just 'cos I come from Woodley South. Stick a label on someone and hang him. You fascist bastard! You and the Nazis would've got along great.'

'I'm not trying to pin anything on you. I'm trying to find out the truth. I want to hear your side of the story. But if you want to go the other way, I can charge you for dealing and pass you over to someone else to do the questioning.' Carmichael watched him with narrowed eyes. 'We've got plenty against you already,' Slider said. 'Maybe you've got a good explanation for everything. I'd like to hear. But if you don't want to tell me about it, we can just as easily assemble the evidence without your input.'

'Frame me, you mean. Fit me up.'

Slider enumerated on his fingers. 'We found Zellah's hair in your flat. You claimed you hadn't seen her in months but we've got eyewitnesses who saw you with her on the night she was murdered. And they saw you quarrelling with her.' He laid the hand on the table and shrugged, looking away indifferently. 'Your call, son. If you're innocent, talk to me, tell me what really happened. Otherwise let's book you and get it over with. But don't waste my time.'

There was a breathless pause – breathless for Slider, anyway – before Carmichael said sulkily, 'All right, I'll talk.'

'You'll waive seeing a lawyer at this time?'

'And the drugs thing goes away?'

'On that understanding.'

'All right.' He rocked his chair back on to its hind legs again, and stuffed his hands into his pockets – no easy feat, given their tightness. 'What do you want to know?'

'Tell me about meeting Zellah that night.'

'It was her idea,' he said. 'I'd forgotten about her. I hadn't seen her in months – that's the truth.'

'How many months? When did you last see her before that night?'

'It must've been . . . May, probably. It was, like, Easter when I took her home that time on my bike and her dad give me the bollocking. I'd have dropped her then – I mean, she was a nice enough bird, but who needs that kind of aggro? – but she was all over me. It was all *her*, you know,' he insisted in an aggrieved tone. 'She made the running. So we went out a few more weeks, and then she dropped me.'

'Dropped you how? Said she didn't want to see you any more?'

'No, she just didn't ring me. I never rang her, in case her dad was around. He wasn't above answering her phone if it rang when he was there, so she told me never to ring her. And when she stopped ringing me, I thought it was over. *I* didn't care,' he added, to make it clear. 'I had other fish to fry. I don't go short of birds, I promise you.'

'I'm sure you don't. So tell me about the date on Sunday.'

'Well, she rang me up out of the blue, Sunday morning, and said let's get together that night. I said I was busy. Well, I wasn't going to let her think I was at her beck and call. I said I could see her some other time, but she said that night or nothing, so in the end I thought, what the hell. I mean, she was a right little raver in bed, and I'd got nothing better to do. So I said OK. She said would I pick her up and we arranged a place.'

'The Black Lion in Chiswick,' Slider mentioned, just to keep the pressure on. Carmichael stared at him. 'They have a CCTV camera trained on the car park,' Slider assured him. 'We have the tape.'

Carmichael felt the need to express some feelings about the fascist state and Big Brother surveillance before he could go on. In the end, Slider prompted him. 'You picked her up, and took her back to your flat?'

'Yeah,' Carmichael agreed, though his mind was evidently still on his political grievances. 'Free country? Don't make me laugh.'

'To your flat,' Slider prompted. 'And did what?'

'Had a drink. Put some sounds on. Talked a bit. I had a smoke. She was sort of wandering about. Restless.'

'Nervous?'

He shrugged. 'I dunno. Maybe. She was in a funny mood all right. I thought she wanted to get it on – I mean, I thought that was why she phoned me in the first place. We had a bit of a cuddle, but when I started kissing her she pulled away. Then she said she wanted to go to the fair. I thought she was playing hard to get and we'd do it later, so I didn't care. Girls like to play games like that. But she was hot stuff in bed. You wouldn't think to look at her, but she was all over me when we went out together. Tore the clothes off me, practically.'

'Did she love you? Was she in love with you?'

The question seemed to surprise him, as if love didn't normally come into his calculations. 'She was mad for me,' he said at last doubtfully, making a distinction. 'Couldn't get enough.'

Slider left that line for the moment. 'How do you know Oliver Paulson?' he asked. Carmichael looked surprised and uneasy. 'Who?'

'Chloë's brother. You met Zellah through him. Chloë, Zellah and Sophy were at his flat one day and the five of you went out to lunch. Surely you can't have forgotten him?'

'Well, why shouldn't I know him?' Carmichael tried, unconvincingly.

'A bit out of your normal circle, isn't he? An ex-public-schoolboy City dealer with a million-pound flat in Notting Hill.'

'And I'm a kid from a sink estate, yeah, I get it,' he said bitterly.

'You've obviously bettered yourself,' Slider said. 'You've got a nice pad in Ladbroke Grove, an expensive Harley, nice clothes, posh friends. What's your secret?' Carmichael only glowered. 'I told you I wasn't interested in the drugs thing, so let's just get it out of the way, shall we? You knew Oliver Paulson because you were supplying him with drugs.'

A pause, and then, with a kind of sigh of release, Carmichael said, 'He contacted me through a bloke in a pub I know. I got him charlie, and then CK when they went over to that. A lot of 'em changed over because they said it interfered with work less, when they're doing it three–four times a week, like most of these City whizzes, instead of just weekends. I don't care,' he shrugged. 'I charge 'em the same for Calvin Klein, and it costs me less. They could get ket cheaper on the street, but they don't want to get their hands dirty, and they know they can trust me. So then Olly put me on to some other friends of his and I've made a good thing out of it. I do parties and everything. Some of 'em contact me before they even ring the caterers. It's meant I could give up the risky end of the business, and good riddance. I never liked hanging about on the Woodley South, standing on corners with all those scag dealers and crack heads, and the stupid bloody gangstas with their knives and attitude. I hate that bloody place!' he cried with sudden vehemence. 'I wouldn't ever go back there, ever, if it weren't for my mum.' He turned his gaze to Slider, and for a moment a younger Mike Carmichael looked out from his eyes, a scared and uncertain boy who had been left to fend for himself, in a fast-moving and dangerous world, by the inexplicable withdrawal of his mother. 'I've tried to get her out, but she won't leave. And I've tried to get her off the shit, but she won't even try. The only thing I can do for her is make sure she doesn't get in with any of the really dangerous dealers, or get hold of shit that's cut with something that'll kill her. That's why I get her the stuff – because she'd go somewhere else if I didn't, and end up dead, or worse. I give her money and try and make her eat and take care of herself. What else can I do? I mean, what am I supposed to do? You tell me!'

Slider resisted the call to sympathy and the urge to ask himself what he would have done in the same circumstances. His habit of empathizing was both one of the strengths of his character and one of its weaknesses, and he knew it. Instead he asked, 'Did Zellah take drugs?'

'No, she wasn't interested. She thought it was stupid to mess with your brain like that. Mind you, she *had* a brain, not like those friends of hers. I don't think they even knew how clever she was. She tried to hide it from them, but it came out all over the place – to me, at least. *I* noticed. She was, like, brilliant. She could have been a rocket scientist if she wanted. But she was one messed-up kid. Didn't know what she wanted. Except sex. She liked that.'

Slider thought of the drawings, of the bleak poem, of what Markov had said of her. 'Do you think she had doubts about her sexuality?' he asked.

'Doubts?' Carmichael stared. 'What are you talking about?'

'A lot of young people go through a phase of wondering about their . . . orientation.' He hated using the word, but he couldn't think how else to phrase it. 'Sometimes they try to hide it from themselves by going too far in the other direction.'

'You mean, did she pretend to like sex because she was secretly a lezzer?' he said brutally, and then laughed. 'No chance! That girl was a natural in bed. Who told you that crap?'

'I was just speculating aloud,' Slider said. 'Trying to understand her.' On an impulse, he said, 'Do you know Alex Markov?'

To his surprise, Carmichael said at once, 'Yeah, he's one of Oliver's mates. I met him at Olly's. I sell him stuff, too. They call him the Magic Marker, because he's an artist and he used to be into psychedelics, speed, mushrooms and that, when he was at college.' Slider smiled inwardly at this derivation of his sobriquet. Magic Markov indeed! 'Olly bought a painting off him once.'

'Have you been to his house?'

'No. I take him the gear at Olly's or we meet in a pub. He's married and I don't think his wife knows he does drugs. She's a top nurse on shifts, so they don't see much of each other. I don't think they're getting on, to tell you the truth. Olly says it's a good lesson in why you should never get married.' Carmichael seemed to be enjoying himself now, was becoming almost garrulous, as if he had forgotten why they were having this conversation. 'Why do you want to know about him?'

'No reason. Let's go back to Sunday. So you and Zellah went to the fair.'

The elation dropped away. He gave Slider a resentful look, like a person realizing he had been duped. '*I* didn't want to go. I mean, that's kids' stuff. But I thought if it put her in the mood . . .'

'You went on your bike?'

'Well, we weren't walking,' he said, as though that was out of the question, though it was not much more than a mile.

'You seemed to be having fun there, according to witnesses.'

He shrugged. 'Oh well – it was all right. I didn't mind it. And she was having a great time, screaming her head off on the rides and hanging on to me.'

'Did you notice a funny-looking little man watching you or following you?'

'I didn't notice anyone. I wasn't looking at anyone except Zellah,' he said. 'Why?'

'Skip it. Go on – you said she was having fun.'

'Yeah at first, but then she starts going quiet, and then, all of a sudden, out of the blue, she says I should go because she's meeting someone else. I say who and she says another man.'

'You must have been angry,' Slider suggested.

'You kidding me? I couldn't believe it. I tell her she can think again about bloody that, when I'd picked her up, and then paid for all those rides. I said if she was just using me for transport I'd snatch her bald-headed. I wasn't having her treating me like a chauffeur, the cow!'

'But it was a bit late for a second date, wasn't it? Everything would be closing round about then.'

'What are you talking about? It was only about ten o'clock. Most parties don't *start* until then. And all the pubs had extensions.'

Slider had to tread carefully. 'It was later than ten o'clock when you had your row with her. It was nearer midnight. The evening was over.'

'It wasn't midnight. I'm telling you. We'd only been at the fair an hour, an hour and a half maybe. It couldn't have been much after ten.'

'Then you had two rows. Made it up after the first, then got into it again.'

'There was no two rows. She walked off.'

Slider shook his head. 'You were seen. We have a witness saw you quarrelling with Zellah at about midnight.'

Carmichael set his jaw. 'Well, they're lying. Or you are. You're trying to fit me up.'

'I'm just trying to get to the truth,' Slider said. 'You quarrelled with Zellah, whenever it was—'

'It was about *ten*!' he shouted.

'All right. Just tell me what happened.'

'We got into it a bit. She said I'd only ever wanted her for sex, and I said what else did *she* want *me* for, and she was lucky to get me with a dad like hers. I said what did she call me up for that day, then, and she looks kind of mad and desperate and says she thought we could be friends. I say yeah, friends, and then you prance off with another bloke?' He paused. 'Anyway, we shout back and forth a bit and then she said she was sorry but that was how it was, and she walked off. I went the other way, because to tell you the truth I wanted to hit her, and I didn't think I'd better see the bitch again until I'd cooled off.'

'Very commendable. And where did you go?'

'I went to the pub.'

'The North Pole?'

'Nah, I don't drink there,' he said scornfully. 'I went up the Windsor Castle.'

'In Campden Hill Road?'

'Yeah. I go there sometimes. It's quieter.'

'You do business there?' It was in a better class of area, more like Oliver Paulson's Lansdowne Crescent. Carmichael shrugged. 'Did you see anyone you knew in there?'

'Nah. I bought a pint and took it outside. I didn't want to talk to anyone. I was in a temper. I'd had it with all this for one night.' He made the yacking sign with his hand.

'How long did you stay?'

'I dunno. An hour, hour and a half. I had a couple of pints, and then I'd cooled off a bit so I got a takeaway and went home.'

'You didn't speak to anyone in the pub?'

'I told you.'

'So no one can vouch for you? Would the barman remember you?'

His expression changed. 'Maybe. I dunno. I don't remember which one it was. It might have been a temporary. They get extra staff in on Bank Holidays, all the pubs.'

'Which takeaway did you go to?'

'I don't know. It was Chinese. One in Portobello Road. I don't remember.'

'I think you should try.'

'Why? What does it matter?' He sounded panicky now. 'I told you, Zellah left me to see another bloke. It's him you should be asking. I never saw her again, and that's the truth.'

'You were seen around the Old Oak Common area on your bike in the early hours of the morning,' Slider said, taking a chance. 'We've got an eyewitness who saw you.'

'They're lying. You're trying to fit me up. I never went down there.'

'Where did you go?'

'When?'

'After you bought the takeaway on Sunday night. When d'you think?' Slider said impatiently.

'Well, I was gonna go to bed, but I was still a bit wound up—'

'You said you'd cooled down.'

'A bit. I said I'd cooled down a bit. I didn't want to smack her any more, but I was still too angry to go to bed. Well, I was going down to Brighton the next day. There's a bikers' rally Bank Holiday Monday, and, well . . .' He hesitated a beat. 'All right, I do some business down there. They're good business, those rallies. So I decided to go straight away, instead of waiting for morning. I like driving in the night. The roads are clear and you can go faster. Nobody bothers you, and I'd had enough of being bothered.'

'I see. So what time did you arrive in Brighton?'

'I dunno exactly. About three, ha' past three maybe.'

'And where did you go?'

'I stayed at a mate's flat. I slept on his sofa.'

'You must have woken him up when you arrived.'

He looked away. 'I got a key. I let myself in.'

'So he couldn't vouch for what time you arrived?'

'I suppose not.'

'How unfortunate for you.' As a matter of fact, since Zellah was killed before two o'clock and Brighton was sixty or seventy miles away, he could have killed her and still have made it there by three thirty, especially as he said he was driving fast. But Slider didn't point that out. They had kept the time of death back from any statements: you never knew when it would come in useful. 'So,' he went on, 'you can't really give us any evidence of your whereabouts on Sunday night and Monday morning. Unless a barman remembers you, or a Chinese takeaway happens to recall your memorable order of one sweet and sour pork and a special fried rice.'

Carmichael looked sulky. 'I can't help it. That's what happened.'

'Maybe. So when did you come back from Brighton?' Slider asked next.

'Wednesday.'

'Why have you been avoiding your own place? And why did you run when you saw us?'

'*You* know. You found the gear. I thought you were after me for that. I've been staked out before by you cops. You never leave a bloke alone once you've got your claws into him. I spotted your lot a mile off – that big, stupid-looking plod. But he went off to have a slash or something, and I slipped in. I looked out the window this morning but I didn't spot the black girl, or I wouldn't have come out. I didn't know you weren't interested in the gear.' He looked at Slider in appeal. 'You *said* you weren't interested in it. You said you were forgetting it.'

'I'm not interested in it, except as part of a larger story. What I am interested in is the lies you're telling me, and why you're telling them.'

'I'm *not* lying!' he shouted.

'Well, of course you'd say that. But the fact remains that we know you were with Zellah at midnight, and you can't account for yourself for the rest of the night. You had a violent quarrel with her, and later that night she turns up dead. Now, don't you want to tell me a bit more about it? Because there may be mitigating circumstances – if it was a fit of temper, say, and she was winding you up. You may be able to get off with a lighter sentence if it was a sudden, uncontrollable impulse. But if you lie and try to cover it up, that will make it look like premeditated, and no one will be able to help you. Certainly not me. I won't even want to try, if you lie to me.'

'I'm not lying!' he shouted, his face ominously red. 'You bastard!' He flung himself out of the chair and lunged across the desk at Slider. Slider was ready and moved back out of reach, Mackay jumped forward, and Detton hurried in from the corridor. Carmichael raged and struggled for a while before he gave in to the two burly men who were both much bigger than him, but he still had the spirit to howl abuse at Slider as he passed.

After a bit, Mackay came back, straightening himself. 'Feisty little bugger, isn't he, guv?' he said mildly. 'But not much of an alibi. A pint, a takeaway and a midnight drive? I could've thought of something better than that with one hand tied behind my back. Get a mate to vouch for you, at least.'

'Maybe his mates wouldn't have wanted to cover for him when it was a matter of murder,' Slider said. 'Do you get the impression he's the sort to have loyal pals who love him for himself alone?'

'Point,' Mackay conceded. 'Blokes you sell ket and charlie to wouldn't be the most reliable.'

'We'll have to waste time checking out his alibi anyway, inadequate as it is.'

'Even with Oates in the can? You're not writing him off, then – Carmichael?'

'If he hadn't lied to me I might have,' Slider said. 'But he must have something to hide, if he wants to convince me he wasn't with Zellah after ten o'clock, when we know he was.'

'Yeah, and what's that bollocks about her having another date? I can't buy that. He's just trying to make us think there was someone else with her later – the "mysterious stranger" who offed her. That's feeble.'

'Yes,' Slider said, deep in thought. 'But at least he didn't hint who it might be. At least he didn't try to drop anyone else in it.'

'Only because he couldn't think of anyone,' Mackay said robustly.

FOURTEEN

Salmon Chanted Evening

Hart and McLaren went up to the canteen and came down with a couple of trays of teas and coffees and a selection of buns, and everyone piled in for a discussion. Missing were Hollis, still with Oates, and Atherton, who was on the computer in what he now fondly thought of as Emily's Room. When they had been investigating the murder of her father, they had set up a desk and computer for her in the photocopy room so that she could do research for the case, and it had proved so useful to have a quiet place for internet surfing they had made it permanent.

While the mugs were being distributed, Mackay recounted the interview with Carmichael.

'Nah, I don't buy it,' Hart said, slipping her delectable bottom on to the edge of her own desk. 'It's a load of carp.'

'Carp?' Slider wasn't sure he had heard correctly.

'A fishy story. Look, if she had a date with someone else, why did she need Biker Boy to pick her up?'

'Maybe the date didn't have a car,' said Fathom.

'She could have gone by bus or tube, or taxi even. What sort of girl gets an old boyfriend to pick her up just for that? "Sorry, love, I'm off with someone else, ta for the lift"? I don't think so. Especially when she knows he's got a temper. He's trying to cover for himself and making a pathetic job of it. The worst load of rubbish I've heard in a long time.'

'And going off to Brighton looks like running away,' Fathom said.

'If that's where he went,' Slider said. 'I shall have to use precious manpower checking his alibi – the friend in Brighton whose sofa he slept on; trying to find one Chinese takeaway in a road thick with them.'

'Yeah, funny he don't remember which one it was,' McLaren said cynically.

'*You'd* remember,' Hart said, but it wasn't approval.

'Still, it means we can keep him in while we do it,' Slider said. 'I wonder who *did* initiate the date. He says he never phoned Zellah because her father might pick up the phone, but he could be lying.'

Connolly started. 'Oh, Jaysus, I forgot – we got the dump from Zellah's mobile, sir. I meant to tell you. It just slipped my mind.'

'You're not allowed to forget anything in this job,' McLaren said indistinctly through a mouthful of bun. 'You have to train your memory if you want to stay. I did.'

'Go on, Maurice,' Hart urged. 'Recite "My one thousand most memorable curries". It's a classic.'

'Tell me about the mobile record,' Slider interrupted.

'Well, sir,' Connolly said, 'she didn't use it much. She wasn't one of these obsessive texters. And the calls were to the people you'd expect. The only one she made on the Sunday was to Mike Carmichael, which sort of confirms that she made the date with him at the last minute, like he said.'

'What, no long chat with her mate Sophy that she was going to visit?' Mackay said with ironic surprise.

'She could have rung *her* on the house phone,' Connolly pointed out.

'True,' said Hart. 'But I bet if she did it'd be a short one.'

'Who else did she ring?' Slider prompted.

'Well, in the days before it was only Sophy and Chloë, and going back further it was mostly them and another girl they mentioned, Frieda Mossman. Otherwise just a sprinkling of calls you might expect – the home number, the ballet school, the art-master Markov, Oliver Paulson's flat, Domino's Pizza, a What's On in London information line, the central library at Hammersmith, that sort of thing.'

'What about Carmichael?' Hart said.

'Before Sunday, the last previous call she made to him on her mobile was the beginning of June.'

'So that rather confirms what he said,' Slider mused. 'That they hadn't been seeing each other recently.'

'If she did make a date with another bloke,' Hart said, 'how did she do it? Not on her mobile. Not on her dad's phone for obvious reasons. So how?'

'Maybe Sophy or Chloë made it for her,' Connolly suggested.

'But they didn't know about it, or who it was,' Slider reminded her. 'I suppose she could have made the date face to face at some point.'

'Or it could be that Biker Boy's story is the load of Tottenham we know it to be,' Hart finished.

'Yeah, that gets my vote,' said McLaren.

'There's a lot about Carmichael that bothers me,' Slider said, 'but there's also a lot about him as a suspect that bothers me – mainly a motive.'

'Fit of temper,' Mackay said. 'Why not?'

'Because of the tights,' Slider answered. 'The tights make it premeditated, which requires a motive, and I can't see what motive he had – apart from annoyance over the second date, which we don't believe in anyway.'

'And we're forgetting Ronnie Oates,' McLaren said, just as Hollis appeared in the doorway. 'How's it goin', Col?'

'Got it all down,' Hollis said. 'He's signed it and now he's cheery and comfortable, tucked up for the night. They're getting him shepherd's pie and beans for his tea. You never saw such a happy felon. Good job he's got an unhappy solicitor to make up the balance.'

'Which one was it?' Mackay asked with professional interest.

'That Jane Dormer,' Hollis said. 'She was next on the list. Came in with a face like a boot, and it just got longer.'

'Didn't Atherton go out with her once?' McLaren said.

'More than once,' said Hart. 'I remember Swilley bollocking him about it. "You've got to stop doinking the enemy, Jim," she said.'

'The enemy? He doesn't go out with criminals, does he?' Connolly said, shocked.

'The legal profession,' Hart clarified.

Hollis went on. 'Anyway, La Dormer was not happy that we'd questioned Ronnie without her, and very suspicious about him waiving his right to her divine presence, but there was nothing she could do about it, because he repeated it all in front of her, and she could see he wasn't cowed and didn't have any bruises or missing teeth. Well, no more missing teeth than usual. He couldn't wait to do his confession all over again, with no prompting from me. Loving the whole thing. So she was stymied. All she could do was give me a lecture about oppressing minorities and trampling on civil liberties, etcetera, etcetera.'

'That's something, coming from her,' McLaren said. 'It was her got that Dave Gammel, the Pensioner Mugger, off on a technicality. Wasn't worried about the civil liberties of his victims, was she?'

'The main thing,' Slider recaptured the thread, 'is that he repeated his confession – is that right?'

Hollis nodded, but made a wry face. 'Trouble is, he wasn't very good on the details of the actual murder. Nice and circumstantial about going to the fair and watching her and following her at a distance across the Scrubs. Then it starts to fall apart. He seems to have lost sight of her for a bit. Says he watched a couple snogging by the changing rooms, but that doesn't seem to have been Zellah and her feller. Then he says Zellah was asleep when he first saw her.'

'Which is what he told you from the beginning,' Slider said uneasily.

'Yes, then he contradicts that and says she came on to him. And when he comes to the murder itself, he seems to be mixing it up with Wanda Lempowski. Says she asked for money and said he could do what he liked, so he started strangling her, but she started screaming so he pulled tighter to stop her, and the next thing she was dead. Said he didn't mean to. Begged us not to tell his mum.'

'It couldn't have been like that,' Slider said. 'Zellah wasn't a prostitute.'

'Unless,' Connolly said, 'she was just doing it to sort of get back at her dad. Not the strangling, obviously, but having sex for money. You know, "You don't trust me so I'll give you something not to trust", sort of thing. Not knowing what Ronnie liked to do.'

'Cutting off her nose to spite her face, you mean?' Slider said.

Hart said thoughtfully, 'Yeah. If she'd had a rotten evening and was looking forward to a row with her dad, she might just decide to throw everything over and be as bad as she could for the hell of it. Might as well be hung for a sheep as a lamb, sort o' style.'

Slider said, 'Ye–es. It's a theory. There's just one tiny snag with it.'

'Ronnie,' said Hollis. 'Even to get back at her old man, would she really come on to Ronnie Oates?'

'Exactly.'

'So what d'you think is going on, then, sir?' Connolly asked.

'Ronnie's attention-seeking,' Slider said. 'He doesn't grasp the significance of what he's doing; he's just enjoying being a big man and having everyone listen to him.'

'Not to mention whatever he wants to eat, plus waiter service,' Hollis added. 'The trouble is—'

'It still could have been him,' Slider concluded. 'The fact that this present account doesn't add up doesn't mean there isn't another one somewhere that does, that he's not remembering. We have to get more confirmation, someone who saw something. Connolly, you were on that. Anything?'

'Not yet, sir. I'm still trying to find out who the snogging couple were. They seem to have been around a lot of the time. And the blue or black car parked under the bridge comes up a bit, but no one remembers the number.'

'Keep working on it,' Slider said. 'Something will come up. Meanwhile—'

'Meanwhile,' Atherton interrupted, walking in at that moment, 'Wilding has flitted again.'

'Wojjer mean, again?' Hart said. 'How can you flit from a flit?'

'I found the wife's sister,' Atherton said, perching on a desk and looking round. 'No tea for me?'

'We didn't know you were coming,' Hart said. 'Have a bun and get on with it.'

He took the last remaining Bath bun and began picking the currants out with his long, precise fingers, like a doctor removing buckshot from a bottom. 'I traced Mrs Wilding's sister, and rang up to see if they had gone there, which they had. The sister – a Mrs Peachey – sounded nervous and twitchy, so I asked to speak to Mr Wilding, and the next thing, Mrs Wilding came on, distraught. It seems they'd had a huge row about Zellah. Our Pam, having the usual unregulated emotions of the cerebrally challenged, apparently expressed her grief over the loss of her daughter by attacking her husband for having been too strict with the girl all her life. The logic of her position escaping the fond father, he attacked her right back for having persuaded him to let Zellah go to Sophy's for a sleepover against his better judgement. He said it was her fault Zellah was dead. She responded that, *au contraire*, if he'd let her have a normal life she'd have known how to take care of herself. Little Pam screamed that he had killed his precious as surely as if he had strangled her himself, upon which he bellowed loud enough to shake the chandeliers, belted her round the side of the head, and rushed from the house shouting that he was going to kill himself. She yelled he should get on with it and do everyone a favour. However, when he didn't return, she cooled off and started to wonder whether he really meant it, and now she's in a state of complete meltdown. End of Act Two, audience goes wild, curtain, lights up and ice cream all round.'

'Them as says it, never does it,' Hollis suggested.

'Unless, of course, they are already racked with guilt because they actually *did* strangle the precious,' Atherton said. 'It's looking better, isn't it? He was out all night and didn't tell us; he knew what time the murder happened without our telling him; he had her phone at home – what girl ever goes out without her mobile? – and he did a runner. Now he's done a runner from a runner.'

'She didn't use the mobile after that morning,' Slider said. 'We got the records. She phoned Carmichael from it that morning, and that was the last call made. So it's quite possible she did just leave it behind by mistake.'

Atherton looked pleased. 'That's even better. She left it behind. Daddy, creeping about her bedroom trying to catch her out – because I'd bet anything he did snoop around when she wasn't there – finds it, does last number recall and discovers she's rung the boyfriend from the sink estate when he's forbidden her to. He blows a fuse and decides she has to go. Actually,' he concluded, 'it's *better* if she really did leave the mobile behind.'

Slider couldn't deny that. Deceit was something that really could enrage a controller like Wilding. He thought of the sketch book, not quite properly concealed under the mattress. Had Wilding found that as well? Had he realized that all the rules he could make wouldn't stop his little girl from slipping away from him eventually? Had he seen in these successful deceits the inevitable end of the game, where she grew up and left home and he never saw her again? In his passion, rage and grief did he perhaps decide that the only solution was that she must never grow up?

'We'll have to find him, that's certain,' Slider said. 'For his own safety if nothing else.'

'Sceptic!' Atherton snorted. He discovered he was hungry, having missed lunch, and demolished the denuded bun in three chomps.

'Did Mrs Wilding have any idea where he might have gone?'

'She could only think he must have gone home, but she's been ringing there without getting an answer.'

'Any other relatives he might have gone to?'

'I asked that. Wilding was an only child. Mrs W only has the one sister. Parents all dead. A couple of cousins they aren't close to. And they've never really had any friends. Why am I not surprised? Besides, she's convinced he's gone to "do something stupid" as she so elegantly puts it, which I gather is either kill himself or someone else.'

'Who else could he kill?' Connolly asked. 'If he's blaming his wife and she's blaming him?'

'Sophy, for leading Zellah astray,' Atherton suggested. 'Sophy's parents for not bringing her up right. Carmichael for trying to corrupt the perfect lily.'

'We've got Carmichael here,' Mackay pointed out.

'I don't suppose Wilding knows that,' Atherton said. 'And if my idea about last number recall is right, he might have gone off to slaughter the Goth before doing himself in.'

'All right,' Slider said. 'We'll ask Basingstoke police to look out for him. Alert Reading police in case he goes to Woodley South estate. We'll have to have someone watch the house in Violet Street in case he goes home. And we'll put out a Met-wide alert for him. We've got the make and reg number of his car?' Atherton nodded. 'All right, get those and a description of him out to every borough.'

'Wanted for murder?' McLaren asked eagerly.

'For questioning.' Slider still felt a father's tenderness about suspecting him, however bad things looked. 'And to stop him committing suicide—'

'Which would bugger up the investigation,' Hart concluded.

'Where do Londoners go to kill themselves?' Slider asked.

'The river,' said Connolly.

'Or the railway,' Mackay added.

'There's plenty of railway right next to the murder site,' McLaren pointed out.

'And a dog returns to his vomit,' Atherton said.

'Must you?' Hart complained, still bun in hand.

'That's a good point,' Slider intervened. 'If he doesn't go home, he might go back to the scene of the crime, whether he did it or not. It was the last place she was alive.'

'We've still got it taped off,' Atherton pointed out.

'Better alert the uniforms there to keep an eye out for him,' Slider said. 'Connolly, run down and do that, will you? Impress on them the importance of nabbing him if sighted. Is that everything covered? Can anyone think of anything else?' No answer. 'Right, then, let's get organized. And meanwhile,' he added with a sigh, 'I'd better go and see Mr Porson about the extra expense.'

'Not our fault, guv,' Hart said smartly. 'It was that organ, Organ, for letting him go. What a dipstick!'

'Organ Organ?' said McLaren eagerly. 'That's as bad as Michael Carmichael.'

Hart gave him her most exasperated huff. 'You're so slow, you should have your own time zone.'

Atherton appeared at the door to Slider's office where he was toiling over the essential paperwork. 'I was thinking it was time to go home.'

'Hmm?' Slider looked up vaguely. 'So, go.'

'But you've got my woman. I can't have her back until you go home and release her.'

'Point,' said Slider.

'I thought that if we went together, I could pick her up and drive her home. She was going to get a taxi, but . . .'

'Oh. Right.'

'And then I thought, how about picking up some fish and chips on the way? I'm certainly starving and you must be too.'

'Fish and chips,' Slider said. He imagined the smell – the crisp batter, the fragrant chips, the delicate hint of vinegar – and his stomach groaned audibly. 'What a good idea.'

'It was one of mine,' Atherton said modestly. 'Of course it's good.'

Slider stretched crackingly. 'I can do the rest of this tomorrow.' He put his pen down, stood up, reached for his jacket, and the phone rang.

'Leave it,' Atherton urged. 'You're not here. If you'd been fifteen seconds nimbler on your feet you'd have been halfway down the corridor by now.'

'It might be important,' Slider said.

'A ringing phone is like an unopened letter,' Atherton said. 'Leave it long enough and it doesn't need answering.'

But Slider had already picked it up.

'Bill! How's life?' It was Freddie.

'You should ask someone who has one.'

'I didn't think you'd still be there.'

'Then why did you *phone* me?'

'Don't be so literal. I've done your post.'

'Oh,' said Slider, and sat down. 'It's Freddie Cameron. He's done the post,' he said to Atherton.

'Can't it wait?' Atherton complained from the depth of his day-long hunger.

'Who's that, Atherton?' Freddie heard him. 'I'd have thought he'd be down at the gym or something by now.'

'Why the gym?'

'Exercise. Healthy mind in a healthy body. I assume he'd pick the one he has a chance at.'

'Listen, insult him on your own time. I want to go home,' Slider said. 'Any surprises in the post?'

'Not insofar as the murder's concerned,' Freddie said. 'The cause of death was the strangulation all right, as I said at the time.'

'I knew you'd be right. I have complete faith in you.'

Cameron expanded on the warm zephyr of regard. 'Raised venous pressure, if you want a precise cause of death. Most lay people think the cause of death in strangulation is hypoxia, but in fact in a case like this—'

'Freddie, it's me.'

'Oh, sorry. My long way round of telling you considerable force was used. The hyoid and cricoid were both fractured. Obstruction of the carotid arteries was severe enough to cause cerebral ischaemia, and there was bleeding into the neck muscles.'

'And the ligature was, in fact, the ligature?' Slider asked.

'Yes, no doubt about that. It woz the tights wot done it. And there are no signs of any other injury, or of poisons, drugs or excess alcohol. You're looking for a strangler all right.' It was important to say this, because there had been a case not so long ago where the strangling had been faked to conceal a death by poison.

'Right,' said Slider. 'Well, thank you. It's as well to have that cleared up. You sent the tights off for testing?'

'Yes, of course, and all her clothing, but don't get your hopes up.'

'My hopes don't know which way up is. Any defensive injuries?'

'I'm afraid not, and nothing under the fingernails. I think she must have grabbed at the ligature instead of trying to fight him off. Big mistake, of course,' he added sadly. 'I imagine the attacker was so much bigger and stronger than her that she was overwhelmed very quickly, and had little chance to resist.'

That rather ruled out Carmichael, then, Slider thought. He was neither tall nor heavy. Though he did have strong biker's hands. Ronnie Oates was not tall or muscular, either, though he might have the proverbial strength of the madman. But Wilding was a big man in every dimension. Damn. He really didn't want it to be Wilding. 'Anything else?'

'Just one thing – the reason I thought I ought to ring you tonight rather than waiting until tomorrow, in case the consideration changed anything.'

'I *was* wondering.'

'She was pregnant.'

'Come again?'

'You heard me.'

Slider stared at nothing. Oh, this was a whole new can of worms, kettle of fish, any receptacle you liked of any multiple zoological specimens you cared to name. 'How long?' he asked at last.

'About eight weeks,' Cameron said. 'I'm sorry, Bill.' He knew his friend would mind. It always made things worse when the victim was pregnant – two lives taken at one blow.

'It's all right,' Slider said automatically. 'Thanks for letting me know.'

'I sent a sample of foetal tissue off right away to the DNA lab for typing. Of course, it's up to you whether you want to pay for the express service. I just sent it with the standard forms. I don't know what stage your investigation is at . . .'

'More suspects than you can shake a stick at,' Slider said rather absently.

'That bad, eh? But this might filter them out somewhat, perhaps?' Slider didn't answer, and he went on, 'Well, I'll love you and leave you. I'm off home to the memsahib. We ought to get together some time, you know. Have dinner, or what-not. When the rush is over.'

Slider pulled himself together. 'If we wait that long we'll both be dead. Let's make it sooner rather than later.'

'Right-o. Be in touch.'

And he was gone. Slider replaced the receiver and looked up at Atherton, who was straining at the leash with curiosity.

'She was pregnant. Eight weeks pregnant.'

Atherton sighed with what appeared to be immense satisfaction. Strange how his reactions were so different, Slider thought; but then he had never had any children – or not that he knew about, as he always said when asked.

'*Now* we've got a game,' Atherton said. 'That's a whole new tin of sardines. DNA will out. You always said the problem with Carmichael was the lack of a motive. Now you've got one, hot and strong.'

'But she's only two months pregnant, and he hadn't seen her for three months.'

'That's only what *he* says. What better reason could he have for lying about it? This is just what we needed – the grit in the oyster, round which the theory forms.'

Slider looked unhappy. 'My life is all grit. I should like to have a bit of oyster round it. It occurs to me that this feeds in to your alternative theory just as well – that Wilding did it. If he knew about it.'

'Suits me,' said Atherton cheerfully. 'Either one.'

'Except, would he really kill his own grandchild, if he knew about it?'

'Then perhaps he *didn't* know. Look, enough thinking for now. I'm hungry. You're hungry. The brain needs feeding. Out there somewhere there's a piece of rock salmon with your name on it, and the gnomes down at the chip face are this moment hewing out potato delicacies and hand-carving them to your exacting requirements.'

Slider stood up again with a tired smile. 'Enough. I get the picture. No more thought.'

Atherton handed him his jacket. 'Keep that promise, and there's a pickled egg in it for you.' They walked out into the corridor. 'Reminds me of the old saying,' he went on. 'You know the one: give a man a fish, and he'll eat for a day. *Teach* a man to fish, and he'll sit in a boat and drink beer all day.'

'You are certifiably nuts,' Slider said, but he laughed, which was what Atherton had been aiming for.

FIFTEEN

Whores de Combat

The fish and chips definitely came under the category of Things That Sounded Like A Good Idea At The Time. The Chizzick Chippy – as they had taken to spelling themselves lately for inscrutable Lebanese reasons – did a rock and chips to die for, and during the short hours of the night Slider thought he was going to.

As Atherton had bought Emily a poke of chips to keep them company, it was natural for Slider to offer a drink to go with, and he happened to have some bottles of Marston's Pedigree in the kitchen cupboard. By the time Joanna got back they had settled in for conversation. She wasn't sleepy yet and wanted a beer too, and chip envy drove her to propose making herself a toasted cheese sandwich. Naturally Atherton, who cooked even better than he made love (according to his CV) jumped up chivalrously and offered to do the making. Pretty soon it was toasted cheese all round, which on top of the fish and chips was like signing a pact never to sleep again this side of the Apocalypse (which took place later in Slider's large intestine).

They talked about the case of course, and the sad and interesting news that Zellah had been pregnant.

'Maybe that's why she suddenly wanted to see this Carmichael bloke,' Emily said. 'To persuade him to help her. Pay for an abortion, if nothing else.' She looked round at them. 'She must have been terrified, poor thing. Think of having to face a father like that, or having him find out! And from what you've said she wouldn't have any money, or access to any. I don't know whether she knew Carmichael was a drug dealer—'

'I don't know either,' Slider said. 'But it would have been apparent that he had a reasonable amount of money, anyway. His own flat, a very expensive motorbike . . .'

'And she must have thought at least that he was cool and streetwise, the sort of person who would know how to arrange it.'

'That's a very good point,' Joanna said. 'Who else could she turn to?'

'But she hadn't rung Carmichael on her mobile since the beginning of June, and assuming for the moment that means she wasn't seeing him, why would she think he'd believe it was his baby?' Slider said. 'And if it wasn't, why would he help her?'

'Well,' said Joanna, 'as to point one, how would she know how far along she was if she hadn't seen a doctor? OK, she must have missed periods to suspect she was pregnant, and maybe she bought one of those kits at a chemist and tested herself, but she might not have been savvy enough to work it back to an exact date. She might have thought it *was* him, or at least thought it was possible. As to point two . . . I've forgotten what point two was.'

'Why would he help her?' Atherton supplied.

'Oh. Well, as I said before, who else *could* she ask? If you're desperate, you don't worry too much about motivation. You just yell "help!"'

'Carmichael's the one I'd go to,' Emily said. 'In her situation,' she added, intercepting Atherton's look. 'What did he say about it?'

'Carmichael? About the pregnancy? We haven't spoken to him about it yet,' Slider said. '*He* didn't mention it to *us*, which is odd, because it would make a much better reason for them to have had a big row, especially as he's claiming he hadn't been out with her since May, which would mean it wasn't his.'

'Maybe he chose May as the cut-off point for that very reason,' Joanna said.

'Maybe,' Slider agreed. 'But as a story it still makes more sense than this stuff about her meeting someone else, making a second date after the one with him.'

'That,' Joanna said, finishing the last crusty corner of her sandwich with obvious relish, 'is so lame it might just be true.'

'Anyway,' Atherton said, 'once we've got the DNA typed we can prove it was his baby, and then we've got him.'

'Have you?' Emily said.

They exchanged a long look; the sort that passes between people who have talked together so much they know each other's thought processes.

'I take your point,' Atherton said. 'We don't all kill our firstborn. Even if it was Carmichael's baby, it doesn't mean Wilding didn't find out and decide in a Biblical rage that Zellah had to die.'

'Poor old Bible,' Emily said. 'It does get a bad press. Did she keep a diary?'

'Not that we've found,' Slider said. 'But I suppose her father might have destroyed it.'

'It's just that it's usual to mark in your diary when your period's due . . .'

'Don't add more complications, please.'

'I'm sorry to have to say it,' Joanna said, 'but in a small house like that, he may have been aware anyway that she hadn't had a period for a couple of months. A period's not an easy thing to keep secret when you share a bathroom.'

'Yucky, but true,' Atherton consented. 'Well, we've got to find him first. And then of course there's still Ronnie Oates, the Acton Strangler.'

'I thought you'd ruled him out,' Emily said.

'Not at all. You can never be sure that someone irrational didn't do something irrational, especially when his account of what he *was* doing is irrational,' Atherton said. 'And when you know he was on the spot. And has a predilection for seeing ladies wearing their tights round their necks. But then, who doesn't? On which note,' he stood up, 'I think I'd better take you home.'

'You give me so much confidence in my personal safety,' Emily assured him.

'Sometimes I'm ashamed to be a man,' he said. 'But if I switched now, I'd have to buy a whole new wardrobe.'

There was nothing like standing in for a major acid manufacturing plant to make you feel glad about being woken up early by a crying baby. He could have kissed little George – in fact he did, and whisked him away to change his nappy and make his breakfast. While he was busy, he heard Joanna go to the bathroom, and a few moments later she came into the kitchen, looking a little bleary, but ready to do her duty.

'I'll take over, if you like.'

'I didn't want you to wake up. I tried not to disturb you,' Slider said.

'Are you kidding me? It was like sleeping with a harpooned octopus in its dying throes. What was it? Indijaggers?'

'Fish and chips, Marstons and toasted cheese.'

'Sounds elegant to me.'

'Not at that time of night.'

'You always told me you could eat nails.'

'That was then. This is now. I hate to mention it, but I'm not twenty-two any more.'

She slipped her body against his. 'Now he tells me.' They kissed. 'Give me that spoon,' she said when they untangled themselves. 'You're doing it all wrong. The food goes in through the mouth, not the nostrils.'

'Now she tells me.'

'Go and have your shower. I'll make you breakfast with my other hand, show you how we women multi-task.'

He groaned. 'Not breakfast. Please, never mention food to me again.'

'Don't be daft. I'll make you some nice plain porridge, and you'll feel better for it.'

She was right, of course. She always was. The porridge soaked up the molten asphalt in his stomach, and allowed him to take a couple of aspirin to clear his head; after which, though it was still early, he was ready to go in to the office and tackle the rest of the paperwork while it was still quiet, and before it drove him to despair.

'I get to feel more and more like a faithless bureaucrat,' he said, kissing her goodbye.

'You know who's a really sinister character that you haven't investigated yet?' Joanna said, following him to the door. 'This rich banker type, Oliver what's-his-face.'

'Oliver Paulson.'

'If you say so. From what you've told me, he seems to have known all the protagonists, but you've never asked him a single question.'

'Only because we haven't got round to it. He works in the City so he'd have to be an evening interview.'

'If he was a suspect you'd go right to his office and winkle him out.'

'But why should he be a suspect?'

'He's a mega-rich banker,' she said in a logic-for-the-simple tone. 'Everyone hates *those*. Like estate agents in the old days. Maybe it was *his* baby.'

He patted her shoulder. 'You just keep thinking, Butch. That's what you're good at.'

'I could think you under the table any day.'

In the quiet of his office without the phone ringing, he got through the leftover paperwork in record time, and felt chipper enough to go down and see Carmichael, to see if he could catch him off balance.

Carmichael was not happy. 'You can't keep me here,' he fumed. 'You've got nothing on me. You got to let me go. I know my rights.'

'There's the little matter of the drugs we found in your place,' Slider reminded him.

His face fell like a lift in a disaster movie. 'You said you were forgetting them.'

'I may still do. If you co-operate fully.'

'I co-operated! You bastard!' He let loose with a mouthful.

'Hey! Enough of that,' Slider said. 'Watch your lip. My people have to check your alibi, such as it is, which all takes time.'

'What d'y mean, "such as it is"? I've told you—'

'Yes, you've told me, but you haven't given me anything concrete to cover the hours during which Zellah was killed. And you didn't tell me,' he added sternly, 'that she was pregnant.'

Carmichael's face was a picture. His mouth opened, but nothing came out. Messages worked across his eyes, trying to connect up with something in his brain. At last he managed, 'But she . . . Pregnant? She never . . . It's nothing to do with me!'

'Come on,' Slider said encouragingly. 'You can't tell me she didn't tell you that. Isn't that the whole reason she suddenly wanted to see you?'

'No!' he said strenuously. 'She never said a word! I swear! Anyway . . .' More mental conflict. 'She couldn't have been. Not by me.'

'Don't make me give you the talk your father should have had with you. The one where a girl and a boy do certain things together in the privacy of his flat.'

'But I mean . . . why wouldn't she tell me, if she thought it was mine? Anyway, I hadn't seen her for months. How far on was she?'

'Look, son,' Slider said, avoiding that one, 'a simple DNA test is going to establish that it was your child. Now, if you really didn't know she was pregnant, I can see it's going to be pretty upsetting to think you killed the baby along with her—'

'*I didn't kill her!* Why won't you believe me? And if it *was* mine . . .' Something occurred to him. His eyes widened. 'I bet that's who she was going to see afterwards – some other bloke she'd been banging. Going the rounds to see who she could palm the kid off on.'

'Is that what the row was about?' Slider asked smoothly. 'She told you she was pregnant and you told her she was on her own? No use coming to you? You wouldn't even pay for an abortion?'

He shook his head, suddenly thoughtful. 'She would never have done that,' he said. 'She was, like, very religious. She'd never have had an abortion.'

'What, even though she was terrified of her father? If it was a choice between telling him, and getting rid of it . . .'

'No. You didn't know her. She would never have done that,' he said, quiet now. 'And she didn't tell me. I swear. If she had, I would have . . . I'd have helped her. I'd . . . I'd like a kid. I mean, I wouldn't have wanted one right now, for choice, but if that's how it had to be . . . I'd have helped. If it was mine. I'd have looked after her.'

'You have a softer side to you, I see,' Slider said, poking him for the reaction.

His face grew bitter. 'Yeah, that's a big laugh to you lot, isn't it? Comes from the Woodley South, so he's no good. Mother's a smack-head prostitute, no dad, brought up on the street. It's a big laugh someone like me would want a clean life and a family. Split your sides, why don't you?'

'Don't come all pious with me, son. Clean life? You sell drugs,' Slider reminded him.

'To rich kids, who are going to buy them anyway. If they didn't get 'em from me, they'd get 'em from someone else. At least I don't rob 'em, or cut the charlie with something worse. Anyway, it's not like they're street junkies robbing old ladies for a fix. It's just what they do to relax in the evenings after work, instead of having a drink. What's the difference from that and selling booze in a pub?'

'Selling alcohol isn't illegal.'

'And that's your answer, is it?' he said bitterly.

Actually, it was, but it didn't help his present campaign, so he sidestepped the argument. Instead he said, 'It makes much more sense that she told you she was pregnant, you had a row about it, she walked off, and later you met up again, had another row, and in the heat of the moment you strangled her. Come on, isn't that really what happened? I know you've got a temper. She went on and on and on about it, just wouldn't stop yacking, and then she started crying – they always turn on the waterworks to get their own way, don't they? You suspected anyway she was trying to shove the kid off on you when she'd been seeing someone else, and when she started to get hysterical and make a scene – well, anyone would snap. Isn't that what happened? Come on, you can tell me. Get it off your chest.'

No line had ever so singularly *not* worked. Carmichael looked at him, utterly unmoved, still thinking things out. Then he said quietly, 'I bet you it was her dad. If he found out – well, he'd kill her. Literally.'

Slider sighed. 'And after that he'd kill you. It's lucky for you that you're in here where it's safe.'

Carmichael turned his face away, stony with something that Slider was horribly afraid was sorrow of some kind. He *really* didn't want to like Carmichael, even the slightest bit. On the other hand, he found himself fairly convinced that he *hadn't* known Zellah was pregnant, though quite where that got him he wasn't sure.

As he was passing through behind the shop on his way back upstairs, Nicholls popped his head out and said, 'Oh, Bill, there you are. There's a guy wants to see you about the Wilding case.'

'Did he ask for me by name?'

'Officer in charge. But I think he's pukka. Looks like a cit.'

Slider sighed. 'All right. Shove him in . . . what's empty?'

'This time o' day? All of them. Have number two – no one's thrown up in that since the weekend.'

'Always grateful,' Slider said.

He was not sure, when he first caught sight of the man, that Nicholls' description was accurate. He looked more like a nutcase than a cit, though Slider had to confess that that was mostly because the man was wearing shorts, and he had a pathological suspicion of grown men who wore shorts in urban areas. He was tallish, scrawny, in his forties, with scanty hair and, as if to compensate, a large beard, above which an all-weather tan matched the brown of the sinewy legs exposed between shorts and sandals.

'The name's Eden,' he said briskly, extending his hand towards Slider.

Slider never liked touching members of the public if he could help it, and used his own hand to gesture the man to a seat, avoiding the contact.

'Detective Inspector Slider. What can I do for you, Mr Eden?'

'They tell me you're the person in charge of the case – the murder – that poor girl on Old Oak Common? I thought it was my duty to come forward, though I don't know whether my information will be of any help or not.'

'You have information about Zellah Wilding?'

'Yes, if that's her name. At least, I suppose it was her I saw. On Sunday night.'

'Why didn't you come forward before now?' Slider asked sternly.

The man bridled. 'I've been away for a few days. I went away early on Monday and I've only just got back.'

'How come you didn't hear about it? Don't you watch television or read the newspapers?'

'As a matter of fact,' he said, sounding annoyed, 'I've been walking in the Lake District, camping out, and no, I don't read the papers when I'm away. I like to commune with nature and get away from civilization. And I must say I don't like your attitude. It's only when I saw the police tape round the area and my neighbour told me what had happened that I heard about it, and I thought perhaps my information might be useful to you. But I can go away right now if you're going to talk to me like that.'

'Please tell me what you know, Mr Eden. Whether you think it's important or not. You say you saw Zellah Wilding on Sunday?'

'I tell you, I don't know if it was her,' he said, unmollified. 'I was coming home late on Sunday night. I'd been to see a friend for supper, and we'd sat talking longer than I realized, and I only just got the last train. I walked home from East Acton Station – I live in Braybrook Street, on the corner of Wulfstan Street?'

'Yes, I know.'

'Well, I wasn't really noticing anyone consciously, you understand, because I was thinking about my holiday, and thinking I'd better pack before I went to bed as I had to get up so early, and how I ought to set both alarm clocks, because I'm a sound sleeper, and I wasn't going to get much sleep as it was because I was so late.'

'Yes, I understand. Go on. What did you see?'

'Well, when I turned into Braybrook Street there was a young girl sitting on the grass on the other side of the road, putting her shoes on. A girl in a very short skirt and one of those tops that leaves the middle bare.'

'Did she have a pendant round her neck?'

He considered. 'Yes, I think so. Some kind of ornament, some dangly thing. Anyway, she put her shoes on, then stood up, and just stood there, as if she was waiting for someone. She looked across at me as I came along, and I looked away – avoiding her eyes, you see, so I didn't get a really good look at her. I took her for a prostitute, if you must know,' he added, blushing again, 'and I wanted to make sure she didn't come over and bother me. Because they can be very nasty, especially if they're drunk. Foul mouthed, you know. I don't like bad language.'

'Did she look drunk?'

'I can't really say. I didn't stare at her. She looked the sort that might be drunk. Blonde hair, and those very high heels, and the skimpy clothes, like I said. Anyway, just then a car went past me, and she looked at it and started walking after it. It slowed down, and stopped under the railway bridge, and she went up to it.'

'Did she run?'

'No, just walked quite quickly, tottering on those heels, you know. When she reached it the door opened and she got in.'

'Did you see who was in the car?'

'Well, no. I wasn't really looking, you see. I got the impression it was a man.' He screwed up his face as if that would help memory. 'In my mind it's just a shape inside the car, but a bigger shape than if it was a woman. A tall man, probably. That's all I can say.'

'All right. So she got in the car, and it drove off?'

'No,' he said, sounding annoyed. 'I didn't say that. It didn't drive off. She got in, and it just stayed there, under the bridge. It's dark there, because there's no street light nearby, so I thought it was another of those kerb crawlers. We had trouble that way a while back, people picking up prostitutes and doing it in their cars under the bridge. Disgusting! And leaving their condoms lying around afterwards for anyone to see! I complained to the police, if you want to know, and we had a patrol car come round at night for a couple of weeks and eventually they moved on, the girls did. That was back in the spring. It's been all right since then. So I thought, hello, it's starting up again. Which was why, when I went upstairs to my bedroom, I looked out of the window to see if the car was still there.'

'And was it?'

'Yes, it was. I was quite upset about it, I can tell you, thinking we were going to have all that trouble again, those foul-mouthed girls shouting things at you as you went past, making fun of you, throwing those things in the garden. One of them put one through my letter-box once, because I'd told her to clear off. Made me feel quite sick, having to deal with it. And once you've got them hanging around, the drug dealers come next, and your life isn't worth living. So that's why I was looking out from behind the curtain, with the light off, so they wouldn't be able to see me. The car was still there, and as I watched, the door opened on the passenger side again and she got out – the same girl.'

He looked at Slider for encouragement.

'Yes?'

'And she sort of stumbled away from the car – trying to hurry, you know, over the grass, but in those heels – and she put her hands to her face, as if she was crying. Or she might just have been rubbing her eyes, of course, but given what happened later, maybe she was crying.'

'What did happen later?' Slider asked.

He stared. 'Well, she was murdered, wasn't she?'

'You saw that?'

'No!' He was indignant. '*You* said she was murdered, not me.'

'Please, just tell me what you saw,' Slider said patiently.

'Well, that's all,' Eden said reluctantly. 'I stopped watching then. I mean, I wasn't that interested. I didn't know she was going to be murdered, did I? It wasn't my fault.'

'Of course not,' Slider said soothingly. 'Nobody said it was. You saw her get out of the car and run away—'

'She didn't run, really. Just sort of – hurried, but clumsily. Those heels . . .'

'Quite. And did you see the man get out and follow her?'

'No. I told you, I stopped watching. I'd only looked out to see if the car was still there, and she happened to get out at that moment. I didn't want to see any more. I pulled the curtains and went to bed. In the morning the car was gone, of course, and I didn't see her. I understand she – her body – was hidden in the bushes. But I left very early, and of course I turned the other way out of the house, towards the station, so I wouldn't have been looking in that direction anyway.'

'Can you tell me anything about the car? Make, colour, registration number?'

He looked regretful. 'I'm not very good on cars. I don't have one myself – never taken the test, as a matter of fact. I prefer walking, and trains for long distances. Much more rational mode of transport. The car is the curse of modern society in my opinion. All I can tell you is that it was medium sized – not a Mini, for instance, and not one of those Chelsea Tractors, either. Just an ordinary car – a saloon, do you call them? It was dark blue, I think. I didn't notice the number plate, I'm afraid.'

'Well, thank you,' Slider said, with an inward sigh. 'That does help. Can you give me an estimate of the time this happened?'

'Well, as I said, I got the last train to East Acton, which got in just before one o'clock. You could look it up if you wanted to be absolutely accurate. It's only a few minutes to walk home from there. Then when I got in, I pottered around a bit, got some things together, laid the table for my breakfast, so it might have been a quarter past or twenty past one when I went upstairs. Maybe half past one. I don't think it could have been later than that.'

'Right,' said Slider. Given that they knew she had died before two o'clock, the moment when she stumbled from the car was probably the beginning of the last scene, and unfortunately the audience had drawn the curtain on it. 'Did you see anyone else about on your walk home?'

'Only the other people who got off the tube with me. I think there were three or four – half a dozen, perhaps – but they scattered outside the station. No one else came in my direction. Oh, there was a couple standing by the council sports changing rooms – you know that concrete block on the edge of the common?'

'Yes, I know. A couple?'

'Well, a youth and a girl. Kissing, and – you know, fondling each other.'

'Could you describe them?'

'Certainly not,' he said. 'I most *definitely* didn't look in their direction. I just caught sight of them out of the corner of my eye. Once when I accidentally looked at a couple doing that, the boy came over and was *very* rude and aggressive, asking who I was staring at and threatening to "punch my lights out". And I hadn't even been looking at them, just glanced in their direction and away again. As if I *would* look! There's nothing to interest me in human beings acting like dogs on heat, I can assure you! There's all too much of it around. So I made very sure *not* to look at them.'

'Were they still there when you looked out of your bedroom window?'

'I don't know. I couldn't have seen them from my window because they were at the other end, on the side away from the road. I could only see them coming from that end. There always seems to be *someone* doing that sort of thing around the changing rooms,' he added with a burst of annoyance. 'Why they have to go there I can't think. And if it's not couples it's groups of youths in those hooded tops, smoking and drinking lager and making a noise. I feel quite threatened sometimes, and it must be worse for my neighbours, some of whom are quite elderly. But the police don't seem to want to do anything about it.' He had red spots of indignation on his cheeks now. 'Well, perhaps now there's been a murder they'll take our complaints more seriously. There was a time when, if you rang the police, they came round. Not any more.'

Much as Slider sympathized with people like him whose lives were made hideous by gatherings of youths, he didn't want to get into that. He had one last question to ask.

'So apart from the young couple kissing, did you see anyone else hanging around? A funny-looking little man perhaps?' He described Oates.

'No, no one else. Just the couple by the sheds, and the girl further along putting her shoes on.'

'And I suppose you don't know who the young couple are?'

'Well, I'd have said so if I did,' he said, with indignation again. He seemed to have an inexhaustible supply of it. 'I have the feeling I've seen them around locally, but I couldn't say more than that. As I said, I try not to look at people on the streets late at night. It doesn't pay. But they likely would be local, wouldn't they, at that time of night and on foot?'

'Very likely. Oh, you weren't passed by a motorbike, I suppose? Or did you hear one going round the streets nearby?'

'No, not that I noticed. But there's so much traffic all the time, I might not necessarily hear it if there was one. It's a sound you learn to shut out. That's one of the reasons I have to get away from time to time, to the wilderness, just me and nature in all its primitive glory. With my little tent and my backpack, I can go where I please, and get right away from so-called civilization. It restores me. I don't think I could cope otherwise.'

Which was all well and good, Slider thought afterwards as he went away, for those not actually fighting in the front line. But at least now he had a more solid time; and he knew that the car under the railway bridge was involved. Which looked rather like eliminating both Carmichael and Ronnie Oates.

And that left Wilding, damn it.

SIXTEEN

Post Hoc Ergo Propter Hoc

'Well, that's always the problem, isn't it?' Atherton said. 'When the delicate mayfly of theory meets the speeding windscreen of evidence . . .'

'You needn't sound so pleased about it,' said Slider.

'I know you have a father's sensibilities. But although I would never dream of saying "I told you so"—'

'Try it, and you'll be walking funny for the rest of the day.'

'—I *did* always favour Wilding for suspect,' Atherton concluded. 'And there's no difficulty about him. Motive – tick. Opportunity – tick. Means – a car and a pair of tights – tick. Alibi – big cross. And he lied to us.'

'Motive depends on his knowing about Zellah's external activities. And on disapproving of them being enough of a reason to kill your beloved only child,' said Slider. 'And if you say the words "religious nut" one more time you're going home with a note.'

'I wouldn't dream of it,' Atherton said with large sincerity. 'His religion is neither here nor there. His possessiveness and control-freakery are quite sufficient. Are you going to let Carmichael and Ronnie go?'

'Not quite yet,' Slider said. 'If I let Ronnie out before naming another suspect the press will be all over him and wild stories will proliferate like triffids. And with Carmichael, I still want confirmation of his alibi. If we accept that the man in the car was the murderer, Ronnie's ruled out because he can't drive. But Carmichael could have borrowed a car.'

'Or stolen one.'

'Uncharitable. Anyway, I still have to make a decision about the drugs charge. I know I promised him I'd forget it, but there is the public good to consider.'

191

'Not to mention your career if it ever got out,' Atherton added. 'A caution at least might be indicated.'

'Meanwhile, we put everyone we can spare on looking for Wilding.'

'We might get more response if we put out a public appeal.'

'I thought of that. But I don't want to spook him into killing himself before we've had a chance to talk to him.'

'How cold you are,' Atherton said with mock admiration. 'The inference being that you don't mind him killing himself afterwards.'

'What else is there left for him?' Slider said starkly.

Connolly was still plodding round the Old Oak Common area, re-interviewing those people covered in the original canvass, and knocking on new doors in case there were others like Mr Eden who had not yet come forward. In particular she was looking for what the others were shorthanding as the Snogging Couple, who – thanks to Eden – they now knew had been on the scene as late as one o'clock, and possibly later. They might have seen . . . well, anything!

And given the excitement in the area over the publicity it was receiving, and the usual burning desire of people to be famous, it was odd they *hadn't* come forward. Of course, the other burning motivation the police came across was 'not wanting to get involved', but in Connolly's experience it was usually older people who went with that, while the younger ones went with seeing their names in the newspapers or, grail of grails, their faces on the telly.

She had gone as far as Wells House Road, not because anyone living there could have seen anything from their windows, being on the far side of the railway bridge and tucked away down a side turning, but because they might have been going home late that night. Having drawn a blank, she stepped out on to Old Oak Common Lane again and stood for a moment, wondering what to do next. Opposite her were the sidings and sheds of the railway depot, sandwiched between the high-speed line from Paddington and the Grand Union Canal, and it occurred to her that there could hardly have been a place more fertile of suicide opportunities. It was a bleak kind of place, and the houses along here were grim, sooty and run down. There was something about the hinterland of railways that always gave her the creeps, and she decided on the spur of that moment not to pursue her enquiries any further afield but to get back to the comparative comfort of the ex-council houses near the common.

There were, in fact, two railway bridges over Old Oak Common Lane: one for the local line and one for the main line. Connolly had just stepped into the shade of the first bridge when she noticed a man standing under the second one.

He had his back to her, standing under the shadow of the bridge, but at the further side, nearest to the common. He seemed to be staring at the place where Zellah had died, which was still taped off and had two peelers on duty, guarding the forensic tent and the patch of earth and bushes it covered. She had spoken to them earlier, on one of her passes down Braybrook Street, so she knew they were PCs Gostyn and D'Arblay. Gostyn was fairly new to the station, but D'Arblay had known this ground for years, and she had worked with him often, and liked him. In fact, it was he who had encouraged her to apply for a try-out in DI Slider's firm. He admired Slider and said he was a very fair boss, and a brilliant detective. These considerations rushed through her mind, because the man under the bridge, cut out for her against the bright sunshine beyond, but probably hidden in shadow to the PCs, was Wilding.

She was sure it was. She had been to his house and had a good look at him when Atherton interviewed him; she knew his height and shape, the big shoulders, the large head with the thick bushy hair, the corner of his glasses just visible because of the angle of his head. She couldn't see his face, but she was sure it was him. He was wearing grey trousers and a dark-red checked short-sleeved shirt that could have been brother to the dark-blue one she had seen him in before. He was just standing there, unnaturally still, not fidgeting or shifting his weight, and his hands hung loosely at the end of his arms in a way that, to her, suggested despair. A normal man stuffed his hands in his pockets, or clasped them, fiddled with a button or scratched his ear, but in the time she watched him he didn't move them at all. It was the pose, the immobility, of a man who had given up.

Obviously she must approach him, but what if he ran, or resisted? He was considerably taller and stronger than her and she'd have a job restraining him. She stepped back carefully around the edge of the railway arch, where she could conceal herself but still keep an eye on her quarry, and radioed in.

Nicholls was still the relief sergeant, and she asked to speak to him personally. He was quick on the uptake when she explained the situation to him.

'I want to try going up to him quietly, Skip, and see if he'll come with me, which he might just do. He looks totally banjoed. But if he runs, I'll need help catching him. He's a lot bigger than me. Could you radio D'Arblay and warn him? But tell him *not to look.*'

'Aye, I'm with you. You don't want them staring at him and spooking him. I'll tell him to warn Gostyn. But d'you think Wilding's likely to be violent? I don't want you taking any chances.'

'I don't think he'll hurt me, Skip. He's not that kind of desperate. But he may run, and if we have to bring him down he'll struggle.'

'OK, lassie,' Nicholls said. 'I'll get straight on to them. Let me know how it comes out.'

Cautiously, Connolly moved forward again under the bridge to a position where she could see the two PCs. They were just standing there in the sun, not talking. She saw D'Arblay bend his head and put his hand up to the radio switch, but she couldn't hear anything from this distance. She willed him not to look across at Wilding and, bless him, he didn't. With a wonderfully casual movement he stretched his arms and then took a couple of steps, as though needing to ease his muscles, turning his back on the railway bridge and blocking Gostyn for a moment as he spoke to him. Connolly saw D'Arblay grip Gostyn's arm, and could imagine the low, urgent command, 'Don't look over there, whatever you do.' She moved forward quietly, on the further side of the road from Wilding because she didn't want to creep up on him and startle him. He saw the movement and turned his head towards her at the same instant that Gostyn, unable to control his impulse, looked directly across at Wilding.

There was a breathless moment of tension as Connolly's system flooded with adrenalin and her nerves and muscles prepared to leap into action. She felt the hair lift on her scalp in animal reaction. It was Wilding all right, now she could see his face. He was unshaven, his hair was unkempt, and he had bags under his eyes you could have travelled to Australia with, but mostly it was the expression of his face that made her shiver. He looked like a man who had looked down into Hell.

'Mr Wilding,' she said, trying for a normal rather than a humouring-lunatics tone. 'You remember me? I'm PC Connolly. I came to your house on Tuesday. I've been hoping we could have another word with you.'

He shook his head slowly, though it seemed rather in bewilderment than as a negative. She stepped closer. He looked at her dully, as if not understanding what she had said, and not caring much to try.

'Would you come with me? Just for a chat?' she said. Another step, and she was able to lay her hand on his arm. She didn't want to touch his bare skin – she was afraid that would be too intimate a contact – so she laid it against his upper arm, just below his shoulder. She felt him trembling, a faint, fast vibration. Exhaustion, she wouldn't wonder. Still he looked at her. His lips were dry. 'How about a cup of tea?' she said. 'I bet you could do with one.'

The word 'tea' made him try to lick his lips, and his tongue was so dry it stuck to them. He closed his eyes a moment and lowered his head with a sigh. Then he opened them, and looked at her with resignation. He was too tired, she thought, to care any more what he did.

'Come on,' she said kindly. 'My car's just down here.' And with only a little urging, she got him to start walking. Out of the corner of her eyes, she saw D'Arblay speaking into his radio again, presumably reporting her success. Gostyn, the big goon, was staring as if his career depended on it, and she was afraid any moment he'd come running at them and Wilding would take off. She didn't feel safe until she had let him into her car and closed the door on him. When she got in at her side, the smell of his sweat was filling the hot interior, intensifying her sense of him and his distress. It was like shutting herself into a confined space with a dangerously wounded animal – a bear, perhaps, or a lion – which might turn in its pain and kill her. The journey back to the station seemed horribly long, and she had never been more aware of the fragility of the female human frame.

Slider had tea and sandwiches sent in to Wilding, and despatched one of his uniforms, armed with Wilding's car keys, to fetch in his car, which he said was in Wulfstan Street. Not that it would be any help to the investigation, for even if they found traces of Zellah in it, why wouldn't they? But you never knew.

Wilding drank two cups of tea, but didn't touch the sandwiches. When Slider went in with Atherton to question him, he saw this, and asked if Wilding would like something different to eat.

'I want nothing,' he said stonily. 'My life is over. I have no wish to preserve it.'

'I understand,' Slider began.

'Spare me your empty pieties. You don't understand.'

It was a little flash of spirit, and Slider was glad of it. There was still something there to work with, a spark that cared a tiny bit about *something*, whatever it was.

'What were you doing at Old Oak Common?' he asked.

'Why should I tell you?'

'Is there some reason I shouldn't know?' Slider countered conversationally.

Wilding stared heavily at nothing. 'I wanted to see . . . the place where she died. I couldn't get close to it. I was waiting for those men to go away.'

'They'll be there for some time yet,' Slider told him.

'I can wait,' Wilding said with massive indifference.

'There's nothing to see there. Why do you want to?' No answer. 'If you had come to me, I could probably have arranged for you to go in.'

'With you there, and the constables, and all the paraphernalia of your futile investigation? No, thank you. I will wait until you have gone away and left it as it was before, when she was alive. I want to stand there, where she was.'

'And what then?'

'I will kill myself.'

No, Slider thought; despite those words he was not quite at the last gate. He still wanted to 'tell' – that human urge that was of such value to policemen like him. But to tell what?

'Why do you call the investigation futile?' he asked. 'Do you think we won't find out who did it? We always do.'

'I don't care if you do. What difference does it make? It won't bring her back.' Tears began to seep out of his eyes, and he pulled out a handkerchief and pressed it against them. 'Don't imagine that it's anything you can say that makes me weep. I can't stop, that's all. It's a nervous reaction.'

The handkerchief was filthy, and Slider pushed a box of tissues across to him. He ignored it. 'What do you want from me?' he asked after a moment, when the tears seem to be stopped. 'What do you want?'

'I want to know the truth,' Slider said.

Wilding looked at him bitterly. 'Oh yes, you have the luxury of intellectual curiosity. And the vanity. You haven't lost everything that gave meaning to your life. What does the truth matter to me? I don't care about it. My daughter is dead.'

'Then why did you tell lies and sign your name to them? Your daughter was dead then. It seems you cared then about concealing the truth.'

A consciousness stirred in his eyes. 'What are you talking about?'

'In your statement about your whereabouts that evening, you said you were at home the whole time. But you weren't. You went out in your car shortly after Zellah left. You followed her, didn't you?'

The tears began to leak again. He pressed them back, Canute-like, with the filthy handkerchief.

'You knew where she was going,' Slider tried. 'Why follow her? Or did you, perhaps, think that she *wasn't* going to Sophy's house? Did you think there was some deception going on?' Wilding still didn't answer, but now he reached for a tissue and blew his nose, and then took another to blot at his eyes. He had done it in what seemed an automatic gesture, but Slider saw it as a sign of lowered resistance, and pressed a little more. 'I'm surprised you should suspect your lovely daughter of hiding something from you. Or did you have some reason to think her friends were conspiring to do her harm?'

That provoked him. 'Zellah would never have done anything like that if it hadn't been for those others corrupting her,' he cried in a little flash of defensive spirit.

'Done anything like what?' Slider asked.

Wilding didn't answer that, but he talked. 'I tried to keep her safe. I tried to keep her away from bad influences. That was all I ever wanted, to keep her as she was – so beautiful, so perfect. Was that wrong?' He laid his big, hard hands on the table in a gesture of finality. Even after only three days away from his bench, the little nicks and scratches were healing, the recent scars fading. Life could be very cruel, in its thoughtless regeneration. 'But everything was against me. The whole of modern society is a disease. What can one man do against it?'

'Her friends, Sophy and Chloë . . .' Slider began.

The fire lit in him. 'Those girls! *She* wanted them as Zellah's friends – my wife. Her own *mother* was complicit in corrupting her. *Friends*? What kind of mother would want her child to mix with creatures like that? Trollops with empty minds. Hussies with no interest in *anything*, beyond sex and celebrities and clothes.' He rocked back and forth in an anguish of mourning. 'But that's what her mother wanted. She wanted my daughter, with all her wonderful intelligence and talent, to be . . . a *model*.'

His tone of disgust and outrage and grief said this was the worst fate a girl could encounter. Worse than death? Well, perhaps. Perhaps.

'And what did you want for her?' Slider asked quietly, hoping to slip his questions in isotonically so Wilding would hardly notice.

'To be something that mattered. To be herself. To use all her abilities, not just her looks. Not to waste herself. But all the time I was fighting against the world. The foul, trivial, dirty, corrupting world.' Slider felt Atherton's ears prick, though he was not looking at him. 'It was the world that took my Zellah from me,' Wilding cried. 'I tried to save her, but in the end . . .'

He didn't finish the sentence, which was a pity, because the conclusion of it might have been 'the only way I could save her was to kill her' or words to that effect. The tears were seeping out again and Wilding took another tissue. Atherton stirred just very slightly, so that Slider knew he thought Wilding was hiding in there and ought to be winkled out. But Slider didn't think so. There was a momentum now. He just had to keep it going.

'What made you decide that particular day that something was going to happen?' he asked, without emphasis. 'Was it the fact that she was staying over?'

'I was always against that,' Wilding answered without pause. 'I could understand Zellah wanting to – the other girls often did it, and she was too innocent to see the danger they represented. But her mother wanted it, too. There's no excuse for *her*. Good God, she *prides* herself on being worldly!' he said bitterly. 'They both asked, over and over. Zellah sounded so wistful. Pam – well, I knew she wouldn't let up. In the end . . . But I shouldn't have given in. I shall always blame myself for that.'

'What were you afraid was going to happen?'

'I had no specific apprehension. I just knew it would not be good for her to spend time unsupervised with those creatures. But then...' He paused so long that Slider was on the brink of prompting him when he went on, very low, his head bent, so it was hard even in the silent room to hear him.

'It was the deceit that was so hard to bear. I was used to it from Pam. I expected it from her. But not Zellah. Not... my little girl.'

Slider took a chance. 'You found her mobile phone,' he suggested.

'Almost as soon as she'd left the house,' he said. 'I went up to her room. It was lying on her bed. I was worried about her being out without it. I thought I could catch her up in the car and give it to her.'

Slider shook his head. 'That wasn't the way it was,' he said, gently but firmly. 'If that was your intention, you would have gone openly and told your wife about it. But you left secretly without her knowing. You decided to follow Zellah and see what she was up to. Why was that? What aroused your suspicion?'

It was a rule they were taught early on in the CID, never to ask a question you don't already know the answer to. Sometimes you couldn't help it, but in the present case it was a useful tool. Wilding didn't answer, and Slider was able to say, 'You used the last-number recall to see who she'd been speaking to, and found she had called the young man you had forbidden her to see.'

Wilding raised his head and his voice was anguished, a cry of pain. 'She deceived me! She must have been deceiving me for months with that – that piece of trash! I had to know! You must see that! I had to know how far things had gone, how far he had corrupted her! You must see I had to!'

'I do see,' Slider said. 'If she felt she had to hide it from you, you were afraid it might be very bad.'

'She was so innocent, she wouldn't know – she wouldn't see it coming. I didn't want her to be shocked. I wanted to step in before that happened, before he exposed her to things she wouldn't understand. So I drove to the Cooper-Hutchinsons' house and waited there until she arrived. I saw her go in. For a moment I was relieved. And then I thought, what if that was a ruse? What if they were conniving at her ruin? So I waited. And sure enough, she came out again, alone. Dressed like . . . dressed like . . .' Tears flowed so freely Slider wondered where all the moisture could be coming from, in a man who had been dehydrated. 'They weren't her clothes. Those girls – her *friends* – had dressed her like a *prostitute*.'

Slider took a bunch of tissues from the box and pushed them into his hands, but he couldn't afford to let the momentum drop. 'Why didn't you stop her then?' he asked, though he knew it would hurt. But hurt, in this case, might be a useful weapon.

'I had to *know*!' he cried out in pain. 'I had to know the worst. If I'd stopped her then, she might have lied to me. I couldn't bear my child to lie to my face. If it was bad, I had to know so I could face her with it.'

Interesting, Slider thought – the same rule of interrogation he had just been thinking about. Know the answer before you ask the question.

'So you followed her to the pub.'

Wilding didn't seem to wonder how Slider knew. He said, 'I thought she was meeting him inside. I was going to go in and confront her, but there wasn't a parking space, and I was afraid if I drove off to find one, she might come out and I'd miss her. And while I was still debating what to do, she *did* come out. She was obviously waiting for someone. And in a moment he drove up on his motorbike. Before I could get out and stop her, she got on and drove off with him. I followed, but he could weave in and out of the traffic. I couldn't catch him up, and I lost him at the lights.' He blew his nose again. The tears had stopped, perhaps from exhaustion of the reservoir.

'What did you do?'

'I drove about looking for them. It was hopeless.'

'Why didn't you go to his flat?'

'I had no idea where he lived. I thought he lived with his mother in Reading, but I didn't know the address. I didn't think he would be taking her there. I thought, in fact, he was taking her to the Carnival. She wanted to go, but I'd forbidden it. It was too dangerous for a young girl. But it was the sort of thing I assumed *he'd* like.'

'So did you go there?'

'I tried to. But of course you can't get near it in a car. It's all cordoned off. I looked for a parking space and the nearest I could get was in Barlby Road. I parked there and tried walking down Ladbroke Grove, but the streets were packed. So many people – all that noise – it was bedlam. How could I find her in that crowd? It was hopeless. I was jostled and deafened – I thought I was going to be robbed – but I kept going. I was sure she was there somewhere, and I had to find her – save her . . .' He stopped, staring dully at his hands.

'Was it just by chance that you found them again?' Slider asked after a moment.

'What?' Wilding said. He raised his head at the question. Was that wariness?

'You were parked in Barlby Road. Your way home was back down North Pole Road. Opposite the end of North Pole Road was the fair. You thought they might have gone there – something Zellah would like, but that wouldn't be so dangerous. She'd accepted your edict that she mustn't go to the Carnival, but the fair was safe enough, and nearly as much fun. Did you spot them going in, or did you go in and find them inside?'

'I didn't see her,' he said. He looked bewildered. 'I didn't think about the fair. After being jostled in the crowds for a while I couldn't stand it any more and I went back to my car. But I couldn't go home without her. I just drove about the streets. It was stupid – pointless. I suppose in the back of my mind I hoped I might just spot her by chance. I didn't know what else to do. I knew she was in danger, but I couldn't get to her.' His hands clenched. 'Do you know what that's like? To be so helpless . . . If I could have found them, I'd have saved her.'

'But by the time you did find her, it was too late to save her,' Slider said. 'So there was only one thing left to do.'

'I tell you, I never found her,' he said. 'In the end I went home without her. I'll never forgive myself. Not to be there when she needed me . . .'

'What made you look around Old Oak Common? You were driving around the streets. Was it just chance you saw her there?'

'I never thought to go there. Why should I?'

'You saw her standing by the side of the road. You stopped the car. She ran and jumped in. Then you asked her what she'd been up to. There was a terrible row. Believe me, I understand. It's the worst thing for a father to go through, the realization that he hasn't been able to keep his daughter safe. She defied you and jumped out of the car. In anguish, you followed. You were too late to save her body, but you could still save her soul.'

'What are you saying?' Wilding's eyes were wide, his face a gape of horror.

Slider hardened his voice. 'But you'd known all along it was going to come to that, hadn't you? From the moment you knew she was deceiving you to see that man. You knew it was too late. Which was why you'd gone prepared. You knew what you would have to do, and when the moment came—'

'You're saying . . .' Wilding's voice was hoarse. 'You mean . . . you think *I killed her*?' He started to rise from his seat, and it was horribly primordial, like a rock being forced up by tectonic pressures. '*No!* You can't say that! You can't say that! My Zellah! My own precious love! Take it back! You *take it back*!'

He lunged across the table, reaching for Slider's throat – an interesting reaction, Slider thought, even as his adrenalin was taking charge, bypassing his brain and saving his bacon. Throttling was evidently Wilding's preferred option for choking off unpleasant speeches and the unpleasant thoughts behind them. So what had Zellah said in the car that had finally convinced her father there was no other option? Because mad as he must have been at the beginning of the trail – and he would have had to be furious to the point of madness to take the tights with him – there had obviously been time between that and the final act for other feelings and thoughts to assert themselves. The sight of Zellah, still dressed like a prostitute, and standing beside the road like one, could have been enough to restore the default fury, but he didn't kill her right there and then, in the car. There had been speech, and Zellah had got out, apparently weeping. Slider had a fair idea what the speech must have been about – the thing that must have been on Zellah's mind all that last day, and for who knew how many days before.

It was a few minutes before order was restored, and Wilding was seated again, trembling visibly, staring at nothing again, but this time in what looked more like shock than despair. Shock at having been found out? Or was he one of those murderers who managed to distance themselves from their crime, so that it was a shock suddenly to be made to register it again?

'Mr Wilding, let's have it over with,' Slider resumed, quite kindly. 'You strangled Zellah with a pair of tights you'd brought from home for the purpose. You did it for the best possible motives – to save her from what you saw as a life of degradation, sin and vice, which would have endangered her immortal soul.'

'You don't believe that? You don't really believe that?' Wilding said, screwing up his face in what looked like pain. 'That I would kill what I loved the most?'

'To *save* what you loved most. The world was taking her away from you, corrupting her, ruining her. This way, you could keep her for ever, as she was – yours, and yours alone.' Wilding only shook his head, slowly back and forth in a goaded manner, as if trying to avoid blows coming at him in slow motion. 'Perhaps you didn't really think in the end you could do it. But she told you something, as you sat in the car. She told you something that made it clear you were at the last resort.'

'She told me something.' Was it a question, or was he just repeating the words? Slider couldn't tell.

'She told you about the baby.' He watched closely for reaction. 'She told you she was pregnant.'

It came – the reaction – after a measurable pause; and the flesh of the big, exhausted face cringed as from a blow. He stared, and then he screwed up his eyes, and put his fists to his cheeks, and his lower lip dropped and trembled. 'No,' he said, as one pleading with a torturer. 'No. Please, no. You're making it up. She wasn't. *Please!*'

'Zellah was two months pregnant,' Slider said.

After a long moment, the next words – with steel under them – were, 'Who did it? Who did that to her? Was it that Carmichael boy? I will kill him! I swear I will kill him!'

And with sadness, Slider decided that he hadn't known about the pregnancy, and he was rather sorry to have been the one to let that particular cat out of the bag.

'Nevertheless,' Atherton said as they went back upstairs, 'he's still the best suspect. He didn't have to know she was pregnant for the rest to work.' He counted the points off. 'He admits he knew she'd been seeing Carmichael. He admits suspecting her of being on the slippery slope to damnation. He admits he followed her. He lied to us about it and can't give any good reason why.'

'He was ashamed. Following Zellah was not open, honest behaviour: it was a lapse from his own standards. And he'd done it behind his wife's back.'

'*Exactly*,' Atherton said, as though that were a triumph. 'And he still hasn't told his wife. Why? Because she'd suspect what we suspect – that it was him what done her in.'

'Would she?' Slider objected mildly.

'Wouldn't she?' Atherton countered. 'Plus, he was out all night, he can't account for his whereabouts at any point, and he admits he was looking for Zellah. Then he does a runner. And where do we finally find him? Hanging around the scene of his crime – as murderers are commonly known not to be able to resist doing – and talking about suicide. Guilty men in his position usually want to kill themselves afterwards, because they can't live with the knowledge of what they've done.'

'I know,' Slider said.

Atherton looked at him sidelong. 'I can't tell whether you really think he didn't do it, or you're just playing devil's advocate as usual.'

'I don't know.'

'Don't know which?'

'Both.' Slider paused at the top of the stairs and sighed. 'If he did it, he may well have hidden the knowledge from himself, and we may never get it out.'

'We can enjoy trying.'

'Enjoy?'

'He called her his own precious love. That's creepy.'

Slider sighed again, thinking of Kate. He might not have used those words out loud, but there were times when he had felt like that about her. Atherton, who had no daughter, didn't understand. It wasn't a sexual thing or even a possessive thing: it was that a father had a particular vulnerability where his daughter was concerned, a love that sometimes made him go weak at the knees. And a particular set of worries about her, which, for obvious reasons, you didn't have about a son.

'We need more evidence,' he said briskly. 'We've nothing concrete to link him to the scene of the crime. We need a witness who can identify him, or remembers the reg number of his car. Or a scrap of DNA from the tights.'

'We've got his car,' Atherton said, 'and a good reason now to go over it. If we could find a bit of soil on the floor that matches the murder scene—'

'And if it isn't the same as the soil in his garden or elsewhere in East Acton,' Slider said. 'And if we can be sure he didn't walk on the grass that day when Connolly found him there.'

'Always with the negativity!' Atherton sighed, growing more buoyant as he always did with resistance. 'Kindly don't take the bloom off the peach.'

'That's what you call a peach?' Slider said derisively, and peeled off from him as they hit the corridor. 'I have to go and see Mr Porson.'

SEVENTEEN

You Can't Tell a Buck by its Clover

Porson was encouraging. 'Rhodes wasn't built in a day,' he said. 'Give yourself time. Keep on at him and he'll crack eventually. They always do. In his position he *wants* to talk, you have to remember that. Meanwhile, find that evidence. Confession is one thing, but you can't make huts without straw.'

Straw huts? Slider thought. Or straw hats? Or was the old man thinking in a subliminal way of the three little pigs, one of whom built his house of straw instead of bricks? Boy, you wouldn't want to get lost in Porson's mind without a miner's lamp and a ball of string!

'So what have you got to go on?' Porson asked in conclusion.

Slider pulled himself together. 'We've brought his car in. It's a Ford Focus – dark blue, so that's all right – and we're going to look for soil or grass from the murder site. There's an outside chance we might get something from the tights or the necklace chain. And we're looking for more witnesses. If we can find someone who saw his car's reg number at or near Old Oak Common . . .'

'Hmm,' said Porson, evidently unimpressed. 'Better get that confession. What about the other two? Can't keep cluttering up the cells with old suspects. I take it you've gone right off them?'

'I think we can rule out Oates, sir. He can't drive and he has no access to a car. And his confession seems to be more to do with Wanda Lempowski than Zellah Wilding. The problem with him is his confession. If we let him go now he's going to repeat it to the press *ad nauseam*—'

'—and stir up a hermit's nest, yes. Well, no need to show everyone our hand. You can hold him for another twelve hours, for his own good, but after that we'll have to have a clear-out. What about Carmichael?'

'I'm still not a hundred per cent happy about him. Haven't managed to confirm his alibi so far, and it's still possible he borrowed a car and that it was him at the Common with Zellah.'

Porson scowled. 'I can't keep giving bed and breakfast to everyone in West London. D'you think he'll skip if you let him out?'

'If he's guilty, yes. I think he'd disappear and take a lot of finding. He's streetwise and his business is highly mobile.'

'And Wilding?'

'If he's guilty he'll kill himself. And if he's innocent he'll kill Carmichael.'

Porson walked a few tempestuous steps up and down behind his desk. 'Well, what *do* you want? Three suspects is two too many.'

'Just a little more time, sir,' Slider said, unhappily aware that this was not all he wanted. 'I think it would help if we could establish who the father of the baby was. It would certainly give us more of an edge with Carmichael.'

Porson nodded, seeing the point. 'All right. Fast-track the DNA test. I'll authorise the expense. We'll have to cut back somewhere, though. Can I send some of the uniform back?'

'Yes, sir. I can manage with my own people.'

'All right, get on with it, then. Time and tide gathers no moss.'

Slider trudged away.

On his way back to his office, Joanna's words came back to him – that Oliver Paulson was the one character he hadn't interviewed who knew everybody. Not that there was any reason to suspect Paulson had anything to do with it, but it was possible he might have some knowledge that would give Slider a fresh angle, or a new insight. He was desperate for either. Time was passing, and the old adage that you solved a murder in the first forty-eight hours, while less true than it used to be, still hung around in the back of a copper's mind. And he felt no nearer to understanding Zellah. *Someone* must have known her. He didn't suppose it was Oliver Paulson, but he might know someone who had.

A couple of telephone calls brought him a bit of luck. Paulson had been working from home that day (Slider had forgotten it was Friday); furthermore, he was actually *there*, not using the home-working day to get a start on a long weekend. Slider put a few things in train, and then took himself over to Lansdowne Crescent.

The semicircular street, together with its opposite half, Stanley Crescent, marked the position of the old horse-racing track, famous in the eighteenth century. The circular green which had been the centre of the racecourse had once been bisected by a lane which was hardly more than a dirt track. Now the dirt track had grown up to be Ladbroke Grove, a serious, tarmacked thoroughfare, and all that was left of the green was two little half moons of garden surrounded by -railings, one for each of the crescents.

But these railinged gardens were a feature of nineteenth-century London which was highly prized in the twentieth, and added a significant number of thousands to the value of a property. Lansdowne Crescent was an 1850s terrace of typical Kensington houses in white stucco, with steps up to a pillared portico over a semi-basement. The Golden Rectangle architecture and big sash windows provided the grand and harmonious proportions that gave north-west London so much of its handsomeness, while inside the rooms were lofty, airy and ample.

The flat Oliver Paulson shared occupied the top three floors of the five-storey building, the ground floor and basement being a separate flat. Paulson and his friends therefore had the original drawing-room floor for their living rooms, and the original bedroom floors above, plus the servants' rooms under the roof.

Most of the parking spaces were occupied, but Slider managed to find an empty Residents Only spot a few doors down, slipped in between a silver Mazda and a black Focus, and slapped his POLICE ON CALL notice on the dashboard in case of passing wardens. He found Paulson alone – the other flatmates still being at work. He was taking full advantage of the home-working day: he had evidently not shaved that morning, and was slobbing out in grey tracksuit bottoms with what looked like a coffee-stain on one knee, bare feet and an elderly T-shirt with the Hard Rock Café motif on the back.

He seemed a well-toned young man, arguing frequent trips to the gym, and his face and arms were expensively tanned. The family likeness to his sister was immediately obvious: he had the same undistinguished, slightly pudgy features, and a similar open-eyed, guileless look which hardly went with the traditional idea of a Master of the Universe, for all the evidence of high life around him.

But with friendly frankness, he immediately disabused Slider of the notion that he was one of those. 'Oh, no, I'm just a back-room boy. A grubber. Analysis and research. I don't do the risky, nuts-on-the-block stuff – though I do share in the bonuses, thank God!' he added with a happy laugh. 'Otherwise, how could I afford a place like this?' He looked round at the wide, high-ceilinged, glamorous room as if he could hardly believe he was really here. 'My dad thinks I'm such a fool, I must have got in by mistake. He keeps telling me to put away every penny I can, because they're going to cotton on sooner or later that they hired the wrong bloke, and chuck me out!'

'And do you?' Slider asked, smiling. You could no more dislike this boy than slap a baby. He had to remind himself that in taking drugs, Paulson was a casual lawbreaker and therefore on the wrong side of the them-and-us divide.

'What, save? Me? Are you kidding? Easy come, easy go, that's me. I know it can't last for ever. All the more reason to enjoy it while I can. Can I get you something? Coffee? Herbal tea?'

'Nothing, thank you. I just wanted to talk to you about Zellah Wilding.'

The cheery face fell. 'God, yes, that poor kid! What a rotten thing to happen. Do you know who did it yet?'

'We're working on that,' Slider said. 'Can we sit down?'

'Of course. Sorry. Will over here do?'

There were two modern armchairs framing a low table in front of the French windows, beyond which was a narrow balcony with a wrought-iron railing, looking on to the crescent and its garden. They sat facing each other, sideways-on to the view. Paulson sat on the edge of the seat, leaning forward slightly, resting his forearms on his thighs, knees out, his hands dangling into the space between. They fidgeted with each other and with anything else that came into their orbit. This unrest, together with the pinkness of his eyes and the fact that he sniffed constantly, and frequently pulled out a handkerchief to wipe his nose, told Slider he had celebrated the night before, anticipating the fact that he didn't have to go to the office today.

'So what did you want to know?' he asked, jiggling his knees.

'It's very hard to get an idea of what Zellah was really like. I thought you might give me your impression of her.'

'I don't do impressions,' he said, giggling. 'Though I've done a bit of amateur dramatics in the past.'

It was a good joke, but Slider did not want to encourage this state of mind. He made his face stern and said, 'She *is* dead, sir.'

It was probably the 'sir' that dampened him as much as anything. 'I'm sorry. I'm a bit nervous. Police, murder, that sort of thing. Poor old Zellah. She didn't deserve that. I really did feel awful when I heard.'

'She came here quite often, I believe?'

'Oh, yes. Well, she was mates with my sister, Chloë, and her mate, Sophy?' He looked at Slider to see if he knew, and Slider nodded. 'The three of them used to come here a lot. Mostly on Saturday mornings. I didn't mind. I'm fond of old Chlo. We've always got on. She was my favourite sister at home. And Soph – well, that girl's a nutter. But she's a laugh. Well, she and Zellah did ballet class together on Saturday mornings, and they used to come here afterwards to meet up with Chlo. Sometimes they'd go off together and do stuff, sometimes they'd hang around here, or I'd take them out to lunch if I wasn't doing anything. It was a laugh. There were four of them at one time – this girl Frieda Mossman was one of the gang, but they dropped her for some reason. Some girly fight or other. I didn't ask. After that, the three of them were even tighter. Sometimes they'd call round after school, as well. I wasn't usually here, but Chlo had a key and let them in. She and Soph could have seen each other at home, but Zellah couldn't have people back to her house, so it was somewhere for them to hang.'

Slider noticed that Zellah wasn't 'Zell'. 'How did Zellah fit in with the other two? Was it an equal, three-way relationship?' he asked.

'Oh, Soph was the ringleader. She's the noisy one. She's a laugh, that girl! Zellah was the quiet one.' He frowned in thought. 'It was hard to make her out, really. She never seemed to say much. You couldn't tell what she was thinking. Sort of . . . closed up, if you know what I mean. But you couldn't push her around. I mean, Sophy's the sort to walk all over you if you let her. Old Chloë was pretty much putty in her hands, but I've heard Zellah put her foot down. Just quietly, you know – no fuss – but that was it. If she said she didn't want to do something, Soph couldn't make her. And vice versa.'

'Vice versa?'

'If she wanted to do something, they couldn't talk her out of it.'

'Have you an instance in mind when they tried to talk her out of something?'

He looked uneasy, jiggling his knees faster, rubbing his nose, scratching his head. 'Well, not really. Nothing in particular. Just . . . general observation.'

Slider tried a slightly different question. 'What did she want to do that the others disapproved of?'

'Oh, it wasn't Chlo, it was Sophy. She didn't like . . .' He cast Slider an anxious look as he clammed up.

Slider took a punt. 'She didn't like Mike Carmichael?'

'Oh, you know about him?' It was only partly relief. The jiggling went on as he patently tried to work out how much Slider knew about Carmichael and his usefulness to society.

Slider sighed. 'Mr Paulson, we have to have a frank conversation. I am involved in a murder investigation, and I can't have it clogged up with lesser considerations. So let me just tell you that I know Carmichael was supplying you and your friends with drugs for your personal recreational use, and that I'm not concerned with that.'

'You mean you're not going to . . .? I mean, even if I *were*, you know – not that I'm saying I *was* – but you wouldn't, you know, take it any further?'

'Just answer my questions without holding anything back. If you are completely honest with me there will be no consequences for you or your friends over anything Carmichael has supplied you with in the past. Does that satisfy you?'

'I suppose so,' he said, though with a hint of puzzlement, as if he were trying to analyse the actual words of the treaty, in case they could be made to mean something different. Slider could see why Paulson's father was surprised by his good job and large income. 'So, what were you asking?' Paulson continued at last. 'I've forgotten where we were.'

'Sophy objected to Mike Carmichael.'

'She didn't like him,' Paulson said plainly. 'She thought he was a drone. I'm afraid our Soph is a bit of a snob, and once she knew he came from a housing estate, that was him. So when Zellah was obviously smitten with him, Soph went at her like fury. Harsh words were said. Well, poor old Zellah's background is a bit on the gnarly side, you know? Sophy was well out of order, some of the things she said. But they made up, the way girls do. And the upshot was that Zellah was going out with Mike and there was nothing anyone could do about it.'

'Zellah met Carmichael here, I understand?'

'Oh, you know that? Well, yes. They called round one Saturday, the girls, when Mike was here. They all liked him right away – even Soph, until she found out he was from the Woodley South – but you could see Zellah was struck all of a heap. Well, he's a good-looking guy, and a smooth operator, and I don't think Zellah had much experience with boys. One smile from him and that kid was toast.'

'Didn't that worry you?'

He looked puzzled, then it cleared. 'What, you mean because Mike's a . . . because of the . . .? No, Mike's a stand-up guy. I like him. He's a decent bloke. He wouldn't give drugs to a kid like her. And you could see he liked her.'

'Did any of the girls take drugs?'

'No!' he said, seeming shocked at the question. 'I'm certain Chlo doesn't, and I'm pretty sure Zellah wouldn't – she was very strait-laced about some things. Sophy – well, she's a savvy kid, and she doesn't care what she does. But I reckon that's more talk than action. They never took drugs here. And I don't keep anything in the house, so they couldn't have found anything by accident, I promise you that.'

'You say Zellah was strait-laced about some things. What *wasn't* she strait-laced about?'

'Well . . .' He looked uncomfortable. 'She and Mike – I mean, she's just a kid, but they weren't just friends, if you know what I mean.'

'You mean they were having sex,' Slider said calmly. Odd that *he* was so embarrassed about it. Grown-up-ness seemed to exist in discrete patches in his generation.

'Mike talked about it a bit,' he said awkwardly. 'I mean, not *details*, obviously, but he said she was really uninhibited. Wild in bed. He seemed a bit uneasy about it sometimes. I mean, he was obviously into her, but I think he thought she was a bit *too* into him, if you know what I mean. I mean, she was very young. It must have been a bit of a responsibility.'

'Were Sophy and Chloë having sexual relationships as well?'

'I doubt it. Chloë's as innocent as the day is long. They talked about it a lot – honestly, sometimes they could make *me* blush, the way they talked about sex and boys and so on. But I think that was all bluff. Sophy wanted to sound like a hard case, and Chlo would do whatever Soph did. I'd bet they never went further than snogging. But then little Zellah, who wouldn't say boo to a goose, steps right in and does the deed. No fuss, no muss. All the way. It'd make you laugh.' But he didn't laugh. He was thoughtful now. 'I think maybe that's partly why Soph was so mad about her and Mike – not just that Mike was lower class, but that Zellah had done what she didn't dare to do.'

'Do you think she disapproved?'

'What, of the whole sex thing? Yeah, maybe she did. But she'd run her mouth so often about doing it and not caring that she couldn't go back on it now.' He looked at Slider propitiatingly. 'You know what girls are like. Worse than boys for boasting and talking dirty. They egg each other on. It'd make a cat blush, sometimes, the things they say.'

'Do you think Zellah was in love with Mike?'

He thought about it. 'I think she was – at first, anyway. She was mad about him, and it wasn't just sex. It must have been a lonely life for her, the way things were at home. But it was always hard to tell with Zellah what she really thought about anything. And of course she did dump him in the end.'

'Ending it was her idea, was it?'

'Well, according to Mike she just stopped phoning him. He couldn't understand it.'

'She didn't give a reason?'

'Mike never said. I think he was a bit miffed, so he didn't like talking about it.'

'Do you remember when that was – when they stopped seeing each other?'

He shook his head slowly. 'I can't say exactly. A couple of months ago, anyway. It's not like I wrote it down in my diary, you know?'

'Try to think. It may be important.'

He screwed up his face. 'I can't remember,' he said at last. 'Some time after Easter. They were still together in the Easter holidays, I remember that, because of all the planning that went on, for them to be able to see each other. So it was after that. Beginning, middle of May, maybe.'

'But of course they may still have been seeing each other secretly,' Slider threw in casually.

'I don't think so,' Paulson said at once. 'She was seeing someone else.'

'Are you sure about that?'

'Oh, yes,' he said. 'But I don't know who,' he added, anticipating the question. 'She was very secretive about it.'

'She didn't ever meet him at your house?'

'No. I don't know where they met. He must have had his own place. You see, when she was going out with Mike, I didn't see her here so much, because she was meeting him at his flat. And when she broke off with him, she came here a bit more often, but not as much as before Mike. So I reckon she was seeing the new bloke at his place.'

Slider pondered this. 'What did Chloë and Sophy think about the new boyfriend?'

'I don't think they knew about him. I think she was keeping him a secret from them. I never heard her talk about him.'

'Then how do you know there *was* anybody?' Slider said, frustrated.

He found this question difficult to answer. 'I just *know* there was someone. She was in love. You could see it – that look they have, sort of dreamy and always thinking about something else. She was like that about Mike at first, but she wasn't secretive about him – not with us, anyway. No, I'm certain there *was* someone. But it was a big secret.'

'Why did it have to be a secret?' Slider asked. He felt a sense of doom creeping up on him. Not a whole new person to investigate, not at this stage!

'I don't know. Maybe it was someone she thought Sophy would disapprove of. Maybe she just didn't want to go through all that again.' He stretched. 'Anything else? 'Cause I've got a bit of work I ought to finish up, and I'm going out tonight.'

'Just a couple more questions,' Slider said. Because of the way he was sitting he had been staring, over Paulson's shoulder, at an enormous painting on the wall over the fireplace, and it reminded him of something Carmichael had said. 'I understand you know Alex Markov?'

'Yeah, I've met him at parties and things. We're not close mates or anything, but I know him.'

'He's another customer of Mike Carmichael's, I understand.'

He looked cautious. 'Well, I don't know about that.'

'Oh, come on, if you've met him at parties you must know he likes the same jollies as you. Anyway, Mike told me so.'

'Well, why are you asking me, then?' he said sulkily. 'Yeah, he does a line or two. So what? Everyone does.'

'More than a line or two?'

'I'm not his keeper. But I've seen him get monged occasionally. Well, more than occasionally. What of it?'

'Has he been here to your flat?'

'Yeah, once or twice,' he said reluctantly. Evidently Markov was not someone he wanted to have associated with his name – at least, not in front of a police officer. Slider found that interesting. He had been enthusiastic about Carmichael, who on the face of it was a far more dangerous acquaintance to admit.

'Has he met the girls here?' he asked.

'I don't think so. But they know him anyway – he's a teacher at their school. He's not like an ordinary teacher, though,' he added quickly, in case Slider thought him uncool to hang with a member of the NUT. 'He teaches art, and he's an artist himself. The teaching's just to pay the rent, you know. The painting's his real career. He's good. I bought one of his things once – that's it, over there. Cool, isn't it?'

The massive canvas, about six feet by four, was painted with two oblongs of different shades of red, which overlapped near the middle making a third shade. It dominated that end of the room, but cool was the last thing Slider would have said about all that redness.

'I don't know anything about modern art,' he excused himself.

'Well, I don't either,' Paulson confessed endearingly, 'but I liked the colour, and the poor bloke was short of a bob or two and I'd just had a bonus, so I thought it couldn't hurt. An original Markov – maybe it'll be worth a fortune one day. Who knows?'

'Why was he short of money?'

'I don't know,' Paulson said with easy indifference. 'Expensive lifestyle, I suppose.' Slider thought of the flat, the skiing holidays, and above all the drug habit. 'I don't think the teaching pays much – it's not full-time.'

'There's his painting,' Slider suggested.

'When he sells one. I don't suppose it's that often. Anyway, he told me once it was his wife who had to take out the mortgage in her name, because he didn't have enough equity in his salary to cover the loan.'

'Have you met her?'

'No, they don't really go around together. She's a high-up nurse and she works shifts. To tell you the truth, I think they're having problems. But I don't really know. You'd have to ask him about that. All I can say is, I've never seen them out together. Why do you want to know about Alex, anyway?'

'No particular reason. He was just mentioned in passing in a conversation. One last thing. Can you tell me what you were doing on Sunday night?'

He entirely failed to be alarmed by the question. He laughed. 'When did you last see your father, eh? Well, let me see. I got home Sunday morning from a party about four-ish, went to bed, got up about midday, went down the pub with the others and met some friends. One of them's married with a family and everything, and he invited us back to his place in Holland Park for Sunday lunch. Stayed there for the rest of the day. Then about nine we went on to a party in Clapham, at a friend of Jeremy's. He's my flatmate, Jeremy? Jeremy, Jamie, Ben and me share this flat.'

'You didn't come back here to change or anything?'

'No, you want to keep away from the area when the Carnival's on,' he said. 'That's why we were glad to go to Gary and Stella's for Sunday lunch. So then the four of us went on to this party in Clapham and stayed there all night. We came back Monday morning about ten-ish, got cleaned up, and then Ben and Jamie went to see their parents, and Jeremy and I went out to see a friend who lives in Hampstead.'

'Did you drive there?'

'Tube. I don't have a car. I don't think it's worth it in London. The parking's horrendous.'

This chimed with something in Slider's memory and he stared at the big, red painting for a moment until it clicked. Alex Markov had said almost the same thing. 'How did you get that painting home on the tube?' he asked. 'It must have been awkward.'

Paulson turned round and looked at it. 'Oh, I didn't. Alex delivered it.'

'Still must have been awkward on the tube.'

Paulson looked puzzled. 'He brought it in his car.'

'I thought he didn't have one.'

'*I* don't know,' Paulson said with a broad shrug. 'He *came* in a car, that's all I know. Maybe he borrowed one.'

'Maybe that was it,' Slider said. He stood up to take his leave. The alibi, given freely and unhesitatingly, as from the depths of a clear conscience, was eminently checkable, so Slider wasn't going to check it. He hadn't suspected Paulson of anything anyway. He had only hoped he might have been around to see something. But that was out.

At the door, Oliver Paulson became serious again, remembering what it was all about. 'I can't believe poor little Zellah got murdered,' he said. 'Why would anyone do that? I read in the paper you'd arrested a serial killer for it, but if it was a serial killer, why would you come round here asking me about Mike? You don't think he had anything to do with it?'

'Don't you think he's capable of it?' Slider countered.

'Well, he's got a bit of a temper on him. I suppose he's had to fight his way out a few times, coming from the Woodley South. But

I always thought he was a decent bloke underneath. I mean, I wouldn't have introduced him to my sister otherwise.'

Ah, that was it, Slider thought. He was feeling guilty for having brought Mike and Zellah together in the first place. Or maybe there had been things said at home, by the parents.

'When it comes to unregulated passions, anyone can be capable of anything,' Slider said neutrally.

'I suppose so,' Paulson said, still troubled. 'But I wouldn't have thought Mike would do something like that. *Was* that why you were asking about him?'

He evidently meant to have an answer. Slider said, 'I'm asking about everyone in Zellah's life. Trying to find out what she was really like.'

'Good luck with that,' Paulson said shortly. 'She was a hard one to know, that one. An enigma.'

A riddle wrapped in a mystery inside an enigma, Slider thought, going back to his car. Perhaps, as with Russia, the key lay in self-interest. He just had to find what, in Zellah's case, that had been.

EIGHTEEN
How Do I Love Thee?
Let Me Ring You Back

Slider idled back to the station, through the home-going traffic, allowing his thoughts to disconnect in the hope that a lot of small things that were bothering him would join forces and present him with a petition.

O'Flaherty was the duty sergeant. 'Ah, Billy, me boy, dere y'are!' he said largely. His 'Simple Man o' the Bogs' act, begun years before as a defence mechanism, had become a mere mannerism now. 'Someone waiting to see you.'

'That's what they'll put on my tombstone,' Slider said.

'Well, now,' Fergus said, leaning on the door frame as one settling in for a bunny, 'in a very real an' metaphysical sense that'd be true.'

'This is not the moment to convert me to Catholicism. Can we have the unreal and non-metaphysical news first?'

'Ye're a disappointment to me, darlin',' Fergus said with a fat sigh. 'I could ha' given it to Atherton, but I thought y'd be grateful, and y'd see me right for it. I only need another five conversions now to get me sainthood.'

'I'll convert later,' Slider said, 'though why you should care whether I'm analogue or digital . . . Who's waiting for me?'

O'Flaherty gestured into the shop, and Slider peered round the door, to see a brace of teenagers sitting on the bench, looking resigned.

'I think it could be your Snogging Couple,' Fergus said. 'Now isn't that worth something?'

Slider patted his pockets. 'I'd give you a Hail Mary but I've left my wallet upstairs.'

'I can make change for a Paternoster,' Fergus said hopefully. 'Ah, you CID types are all tight. Short arms and long pockets. Where d'yiz want Janet and John?'

'Stick them in an interview room.' Slider sighed. 'I wish you *had* given them to Atherton. I've got a lot to think about.'

'He's out. Ah, go on, take 'em! Me instinct tells me they've somethin' to say. And they did come in of their own free will.'

'If it's the Snogging Couple, they should have come in days ago,' Slider grumbled. 'Oh well, I'd better talk to them, I suppose. They won't have anything to tell me, of course. Just want to be noticed.'

'Don't we all?' Fergus said.

'I thought as a Catholic you were always being noticed.'

'Glad to see y' haven't lost y' sense a humour, darlin',' Fergus said, and went off to fetch the witnesses.

The Snogging Couple – for so it turned out to be – were Chantelle Watts and Tyler Burton. She was a meaty, pallid girl with straight fair hair, spots on her chin, an outsize bust and a stud in her eyebrow. He was slim, remarkably unpierced in any dimension, and had the thick black hair and tan skin that suggested Italian heritage. He looked a lot younger than her, though that may have been the effect of his slightness against her bulk, and the world-weary air that she felt suitable to the present situation.

'My mum said we oughta come in,' Chantelle said, when the introductions and social niceties had been got over. 'She said there might be a reward.'

'I'm afraid that's not likely to happen,' Slider said. 'But you are doing the right thing in coming forward. That should be reward enough, to know you are helping.'

This idea wandered about the ether looking for a home, but evidently found Chantelle's environment inhospitable. After an extensive gape she said, 'What, you mean there's no money in it?'

'No one has offered a reward for information – yet. But I tell you what, I'll make a note of your names and everything you tell me, and if there's a reward offered later, you'll be in line for it.'

Tyler, who seemed to be marginally the sharper tack of the two, jumped in while she was still construing this, and said, 'I don't want me name in the papers. Me dad'd kill me if he knew I was round 'ere. He don't like us talking to the fuzz.'

'Why don't you just tell me what you know,' Slider said patiently, cursing Atherton's absence, Fergus's instincts, and the lack of tea in his bloodstream, 'and we'll see how it goes. You saw something on Sunday night, did you?'

It took a degree of coaxing and carefully designed questions to extract the story, though after the first few sentences they were not unwilling to talk. Being noticed by a policeman was better than not being noticed by anyone, which was their usual fate. It was just that they had no idea how to string two sentences together – indeed, stringing words together was almost beyond them. Their real linguistic skill lay at the phoneme level. Chantelle could have snorted and grunted for Britain.

The story, as Slider painstakingly reconstructed it, was that they had been 'messing around' together most of Sunday, having met at Chantelle's house in the afternoon, watched a film on telly, eaten some frozen pizza (though not, Slider was relieved to hear, until after it had been microwaved by Chantelle's mum) and then, when the film was over, had become bored enough to heave themselves out of the sofa and go out in search of some mates.

That, he managed to work out, was about six o'clock. They had gone to a friend's house, hung about there for a bit, then they and the friend had 'gone down The Fairway', where there was a patch of open green in front of the houses where they and their peers generally 'hung about'. They had loitered around there for some time, 'having a laugh', which meant, as Slider knew, gossiping, teasing and insulting each other, texting and phoning other friends on their mobiles, and playing electronic games on the same. There were about ten of them, ranging in age from Tyler, who was just fifteen, through Chantelle who was sixteen, to a youth called Dean Scraggs who was eighteen but 'a bit daft', and therefore not welcome with any of the older gangs.

Finally some householders had objected to the noise and had come out to tell them to clear off, and having become bored with the scene, they obliged. They had wandered down to East Acton Lane, shedding a couple of bodies on the way, and fetched up at the Goldsmith's Arms, where they had hung about outside while Dean Scraggs went in and bought two pints of lager. He brought them out and they shared them between them, standing on the pavement, where a number of other clients were enjoying the warm evening.

Eventually they had got noisy and drawn attention to themselves, and the publican, worried for his licence, came out and told them to clear off. There was another patch of green at the junction of East Acton Lane and Friar's Place Lane, and they had hung about there for a bit, then wandered back the way they had come, losing more of the group. At the off-licence on Western Parade they had had a whip round and accumulated enough for Dean to go in and buy a bottle of cider. The remaining six of them had gone up to Old Oak Common and sat on the grass and drunk the cider and 'had a laugh' until it and the cigarettes had run out, at which point the other four had departed.

The recitation of this emptiness would have depressed Slider if he hadn't heard it so many times before, and if it hadn't seemed to be leading to something he needed to know.

'What time do you think that was?' he asked. 'When the others left?'

Chantelle shrugged, but Tyler said, 'It musta bin about eleven, summing like that. Cos when I texted Bazza it said eleven-fifteen on the phone, and that was after.'

This generation, Slider reflected, told the time more often by their mobiles than by watches. 'Go on,' he said. 'What happened next?'

Alone together, the couple had chatted a bit and texted some friends, and then had grown amorous. They had started 'snogging', but after a bit they got annoyed because there were so many people coming past, and some of them tutted, and some of them stared, and Chantelle 'lost it' and mouthed off at them. Tyler didn't want to get in a fight because he was more interested in Chantelle's jugs and the prospect of investigating her knickers, so he proposed that they move round behind the council changing-room block. In its shadow, and concealed from the road, they would have a bit of privacy. And there they stayed, preoccupied with each other, until the girl had come along.

Chantelle, who had had her back to the wall, had seen her first across Tyler's shoulder, coming across the Scrubs from the direction of the fair. She was carrying her shoes, and looked 'pissed off'.

'Was she crying?' Slider asked.

'Nah. But she might've been crying before.' An effort of thought dredged up a detail. 'She 'ad, like, mascara under here.' She pointed under her eyes. 'Like it'd run.'

'What did she do next?'

The girl had passed by, and at this point Tyler had first seen her, going past the building and down towards the edge of the common, where it joined the pavement and the road. He described her as blonde, about his age, wearing a mauve top and a black skirt, and agreed she was carrying her shoes. She had stood around a bit, and then come back towards them.

'She'd def'nitely bin crying,' Tyler said. 'You could see she was upset.'

'I was gonna give 'er a mouf-ful,' Chantelle admitted. 'I mean, can't a person get no privacy? But Tyler's a softy.'

'So she comes up and says she's sorry for disturbing us,' Tyler took up the story. 'She had, like, this posh voice.'

'Snobby cow,' Chantelle said with automatic viciousness.

'But it was manners, Chant, to say sorry an' that,' Tyler urged. Chantelle sniffed and rolled her eyes, unwilling to be convinced. 'Anyway, she says – this girl says – she's left her mobile at home, and can she use mine to make a call.'

'I says no. Bloody cheek! Who'd she think she was?' Chantelle interrupted.

'But she said she'd pay for the call,' said Tyler. 'She says she needs to call someone to pick her up.'

'She said that?' Slider's ears pricked with interest. 'Did she say who? Her dad, maybe?' But she was so close to home she could have walked it easily. Yet where else could she be taken at that time of night? Perhaps she wanted to speak to him out of earshot of her mother. Of course, she didn't know Wilding had been out all evening – although he might have gone home by then: his timings under interview had been very vague.

'No, she never said,' Tyler answered. 'I said go on then, and give her my phone, and she made a call.'

'Did you hear anything of what she said? Anything at all?'

'Nah, she took it and walked off a bit, and turned her back.'

'I said to 'im you wanter watch she don't nick it,' Chantelle contributed.

'She never wanted to nick it, Chant. She just wanted to call somebody. Anyway, she brings the phone back and says thank you, all posh, and offers me money. A two-quid piece it was. I said forget it.'

'I told you he was a softy. I'd've took it.'

'Well, she was upset,' Tyler excused himself. 'She weren't on long.'

'I'd've still took it. Snobby cow.'

There was a pause. 'So what happened next?' Slider asked.

Tyler and Chantelle had gone back to their kissing. Glancing that way from time to time, Tyler had seen the girl sit on the grass and put her shoes on. Then she stood by the side of the road as if she was waiting for someone. After a bit, a car came past, and Tyler had seen her perk up, as if she recognised it. It had gone past and stopped under the bridge, and she had hurried down to it, and got in.

'What sort of car was it?' Slider asked, mental fingers crossed.

'It was a Ford Focus,' Chantelle said. 'I know, because my dad's got one.'

'What colour?'

'I dunno. Black I think. I never see it proper till it was under the bridge, an' it's dark under there.'

'Could it have been dark blue?' Slider asked.

'Coulda bin,' Chantelle said after thought. 'A right dark blue, though.'

'Did you see the registration number?'

She was scornful. 'What am I, a kid? Car numbers? I 'ad better fings to fink about.'

Slider turned to Tyler, and tried to give him a man-to-man, women-don't-understand-these-things look. 'You didn't happen to notice the registration number, did you?'

'Well,' Tyler said, with deep reluctance to rupture the bond. 'No. I never. I didn't know it was important.'

'Of course not,' Slider said comfortingly. 'But even if you remember part of it, it would help. A couple of letters?'

'No,' he said. 'I never looked at it. But it weren't a Focus, it was a Toyota Corolla.'

'Shut up! It was a Focus,' Chantelle said hotly. 'D'you fink I don't know me own dad's car?'

'Honest, Chant, it was a Corolla. They look the same from the back,' he added placatingly. He looked at Slider. 'Honest.'

'What colour?' Slider asked, his mind on tiptoe.

'It was black, but that new black that's, like, a bit blue. Sapphire Black they call it, but it looks blue sometimes, if you catch it that way. I see it as it come past, under the lights. But it *was* dark under the bridge.' He glanced at his mate, obviously afraid of a handbagging for contradiction. Chantelle looked as though she could pack a punch. Her chubby fists were connected to meaty arms, and decorated with enough cheap rings to constitute a knuckle duster.

'Did you see who was in the car as it went past?' Slider asked next.

'Nah, but I see him later when he got out,' Tyler said.

'Yeah,' Chantelle took over, sensing the glory bit was coming, the bit that might earn the reward. 'Tyler says she's got out the car again, this girl, so I looks over there, and she's like, running across the grass, or, like, half-running, cause her heels were, like, sticking in.'

'Was she crying?'

'Yeah, she might've been.'

'I see her put her hands up to her face,' Tyler said. 'Like this.' He mimed wiping his eyes. 'And then I see this man get out the car and go after her.'

Slider breathed a breath of pure happiness. 'So you got a look at him? Can you describe him to me?'

'Well,' Tyler said, exchanging a glance with his beloved which broke Slider's heart. 'See, the thing is, when I see him get out, I says to Chantelle, "That bloke's getting out the car," and she says, "Bloody 'ell, it's like Piccadilly Bleeding Circus, let's go 'ome".'

'I was fed up of being stared at, and all these people around,' she defended herself. 'If him and this girl was going to 'ave a row, I'd 'ad enough. I says to Tyler, "Let's go".'

'She, like, pulls me arm, so I turned the other way, and we went,' Tyler said unhappily, realizing he had blown his chance of fame. 'So I never really got a look at him. He was tall, though,' he added eagerly, offering a crumb.

'Anything else?' Slider asked. 'How old?'

They both shook their heads. Tyler said, 'Not young. I mean, he was a grown-up. I dunno how old.'

'Like me? Older? Younger?'

'I dunno,' Tyler said, and Chantelle shook her head again. Evidently the relative age of grown-ups was an esoteric business to them.

'Was he dark-haired? Or fair?' Slider persisted.

'I dunno,' Tyler said sadly. 'I never got a real look at him. I just see him get out the car and then I turns to Chantelle and the next thing we went.'

There seemed nothing more to say. After a moment, Slider said, 'I'll need you to write down what you've told me and sign it. I'll have someone come and help you with that. But tell me, why didn't you come in sooner? Didn't you read about the murder, or see it on the telly?'

They looked at each other. 'I never fought about it,' Chantelle said.

Tyler said, 'This lady come round this morning and spoke to Chantelle's mum, asking if she'd seen anyfing, an' that, and her mum told Chantelle when she come in, and Chantelle told her mum about this girl and the bloke in the car, and her mum said we should come in. So Chantelle rung me up, and we come.' He looked at Slider helplessly. Evidently doing your civic duty simply didn't come into their thought processes. Police investigations and murders happened in another world, far removed from the one they inhabited. It was like the world of the telly, which was both real and unreal, pertinent and unimportant, in varying degrees and baffling combination. Most of all, Slider supposed, it was the world of the grown-ups, which was not only nothing to do with them, but never would be. Their self-absorption was developed to an evolution-ary degree, like a giraffe's neck or a narwhal's tusk, the one immediately noticeable thing about them. *Oh, brave new world*, he thought, *that hath such people in it.*

Up in his office, Slider wrote on a piece of paper the reg number he had automatically noted from the car parked in front of Markov's building, and called Connolly in.

'Good work on finding the Snogging Couple,' he said.

'I didn't think I had, sir,' she said, puzzled.

'The mother of half of it received a visit this morning from "a lady" asking for information about the murder. I assume that was you. She mentioned it to her daughter, the daughter admitted she had been there, and the mother propelled her and the boy in our direction.'

'Oh, that's good.' She looked pleased. 'And did they see anything?'

'They did indeed. So well done. Your diligence paid off.' He smiled at her. 'Don't let anyone tell you this job requires brilliance. Just dogged determination and the ability to ask the same question a thousand times and still listen to the answer.'

'You make it sound so glamorous, sir,' she said, greatly daring.

'Changing your mind about joining us?' he said.

'No, sir. Is there a chance?'

'A very good one,' Slider said. 'Meanwhile, I've got a job for you. A bit of research, and I need it asap.' He gave her the slip of paper. 'Find out who owns that car, the keeper's address, how it's insured, whether there's any finance on it, involvement in accidents, outstanding tickets – everything you can.'

'Is that the car under the bridge?' she asked.

'I don't know. That's what I hope to find out.'

'It's like a French farce,' Atherton said, when he came back from interviewing Mrs Wilding again, and Slider told him what the Snogging Couple had said. 'You say they saw the murderer but didn't see Ronnie Oates or Eden; Eden didn't see them but saw the murderer; Oates didn't see anyone but the victim. And presumably the murderer didn't see anyone at all, or he wouldn't have done it there and then. All of them popping in and out of doors on one small road within one small window of time, and just missing each other.'

'Such is life,' Slider said.

'And death. So where are we now?'

'I don't think it was Wilding.'

'Oh, don't say that! I've invested so much in him. His wife now hates him so much for what happened she's willing to swear he did it. And he's softening up nicely in the pokey. Another couple of interviews and he'll sing like a lark. Chantelle said it was a blue Focus. What more do you want?'

'Tyler says it wasn't, and I'd trust him about cars more than I'd trust her,' Slider said.

'He had his tongue down her throat at the time and his mind on lower things,' Atherton said. 'He was terminally confused. And I really, *really* don't like Wilding.'

'Never mind,' Slider consoled him. 'We've got a terrific new lead. As soon as we get Tyler's mobile phone record back, we'll know who Zellah phoned. And therefore, who came to meet her at the common.'

Atherton frowned. 'But who would she call to fetch her apart from her father?'

'I didn't say "fetch", I said "meet".'

'Classic misdirection,' Atherton said, surveying his boss's face. 'You're up to something. What do you know?'

'Only what you know. I'm just putting it together differently.'

'Aren't you going to tell me?'

'I've just got one more visit to pay.'

'I'll come with you.'

'I won't be long. You can go home. We can't do anything until we get the various bits of information in – phone records and DNA results.'

Atherton pretended a sulk. 'I'll work it out for myself, you see if I don't.'

'I wish you would,' Slider said. 'It would give me a bit of confirmation that I'm not completely out to lunch.'

'Hand me my dressing-gown, violin and the customary ounce of shag,' Atherton said, 'and I will bend my mighty brain to it.'

On his way down to his car, Slider had a thought, and diverted his steps to the lock-ups, signed himself in and had Mike Carmichael brought to him. He looked tired and much more frightened, the attitude, sulks and anger all dissolved. He had had plenty of time to think, and realized now, perhaps, how bad things looked.

'Sit down,' Slider said. 'I just want to ask you something.'

'When are you going to let me go?' Carmichael demanded, but with more of a plea and less assurance behind it. 'You can't keep me here like this.'

'Don't let's get into that again. What's the matter? You've only been here a day and a bit. Aren't they treating you well?'

'I don't wanna *be* here,' Carmichael said, balling his fists with frustration; but it looked more as though he might burst into tears than lash out at Slider. 'I've not *done* anything. I didn't kill Zellah! I was . . . I was *fond* of her. She was all right, for a kid. And I hadn't seen her for months, anyway. Why would I want to kill her?'

'Take it easy, son,' Slider said. 'It won't be much longer.'

'What do you want to ask me? I've told you everything I know. I didn't kill her.'

'Was Zellah in love with you?' Slider asked, abruptly, in the hope of surprising an answer out of him.

His eyebrows went up, but he thought about it. 'I dunno. I guess – maybe. When we were going out, she was mad for me. It was a bit scary. But I liked her. She was so clever, and funny in a way, and good fun, but . . .' He paused, thinking it out.

'Vulnerable?' Slider tried after a bit.

He looked up. 'Yeah, I suppose. It was like – I dunno – like nobody had ever touched her before, or taken any notice of her.'

'As if no one had ever loved her?'

He looked cautious at the use of the word. 'Yeah, maybe. Sort of. But we never talked about love, you know. I never promised her anything.'

'I didn't suppose you had,' said Slider.

He seemed to take that as a criticism. 'She was just a kid! I was fond of her, but that was it. What do you want from me?'

'Did she ever tell you she loved you?'

'Yeah, but that was just talk. Anyway,' he went on defensively, '*she* broke up with *me*. I didn't dump her.'

'But you would have.'

'I don't know. Probably, in the end. I mean, it wasn't a lifetime commitment. It wasn't like we were going to get married or anything.'

'What did you think when she broke up with you? That she'd met someone else?'

'That's what Olly said. But I didn't see her after that, not until that Sunday, so I didn't know.'

'We've got the records from her mobile phone, and she rang you up at the beginning of June – one phone call, after quite a gap. What was that about?'

He looked surprised and then puzzled, and then his brow cleared. 'Oh yeah. I remember. She just rang me out of the blue. That was weird. I'd not seen her for a couple of weeks, then suddenly she rings and she's, like, just sort of chatting. And I said d'you want to meet up, and she says no, that's all over. She says she can't see me any more. Well, I thought it was a bit cool, but I didn't care, really. You know, I'd sort of moved on. So I said, whatever you like, babe. And then she says, "I'm happy now. I just wanted to be sure you were."'

'Those were her words?'

'Fact,' he said. '"I'm happy, I just wanted to be sure you were."'

'What did you think she meant?'

'*I* don't know. I tell you, she was one messed-up kid.' He looked thoughtful. 'I'd forgotten about that until you mentioned it.'

'Did she *sound* happy?'

'Yeah, now I think about it, she did.' He frowned. 'But that Sunday, she was different. I couldn't make out what was going on with her, but I tell you one thing: she wasn't happy. You know, I was angry yesterday that she got me into this. But now I just feel sorry for her. Poor little cow.'

Slider felt again that unwanted sympathy. Carmichael wasn't the unmitigated villain he ought to have been in the circumstances.

'There's one other thing I wanted to ask you. While Zellah was at your flat, did she make a phone call?'

He thought for a moment and then said, 'Yeah, she did.'

'When, exactly?'

He frowned with effort. 'We'd been talking. Then we cuddled a bit. Then when I tried to kiss her she pulled away. Then she went to the bathroom, and when she come out she said she had to phone someone. I said she knew where the phone was, and she went.'

'Did you hear any of the conversation?'

'No. The phone's in the kitchen.'

'You didn't ask her anything about it?'

'No. She used to have to check in with her dad now and then. I assumed that was what she was doing.'

'So you don't actually know it was her father she phoned?'

'Why? Does it matter?'

'Was it before or after the phone call that she said she wanted to go to the fair?'

He stared. 'After. It was after. You mean . . .?' He was thinking hard. 'She phoned him – the other bloke – and that was when she made the date with him?'

'I don't know,' Slider said. 'It's possible. When I get your phone records, we'll see what number she dialled.'

His anger was returning, darkening his face. 'She did that? Rang him up from my flat, while she was with me? The sly little bitch! She really played me for a fool!'

'Oh,' said Slider sadly, 'I don't think that's what she was doing.'

NINETEEN

100-What Brain

The Mossmans lived in Doyle Gardens, between Harlesden and Kensal Rise, areas which were in any case so close together it was impossible to say where one began and the other ended. It was a large semi-detached house in what had once been quite a posh street, but was now creeping arthritically downhill; but the house had a large garden which backed on to the sports ground, which perhaps accounted for the family's staying put. There was an elderly but well-kept Mercedes saloon on the hardstanding, and a space where the ghostly outline on the paving said another car was customarily parked. Slider, detective faculties working at full tilt, deduced that Mrs Mossman was home but Mr Mossman was still at his place of business.

So it proved. She was a comfortable rather than glamorous woman, upholstered of figure and sensibly dressed, and the house smelled of soup and furniture polish. The motherly and wifely arts were evidently her forte. A dog came bouncing to meet Slider – mongrel, but with a large injection of black lab – and halfway down the passage a cat appeared and wound sinuously round his legs before galloping for the kitchen.

It was to the kitchen that Mrs Mossman led him, excusing herself that she was in the middle of something.

'That's all right,' Slider said. 'I like kitchens.'

This one looked over the garden, was not newly refurbished, and was full of the clutter of living. On the stove, stock bubbled in a pot. Pastry was lying out on a marble slab waiting to be rolled, and there were cubes of meat and onion seething gently in a frying pan.

'Steak and kidney pie?' he suggested.

She gave him a small, brief smile. 'Steak and onion pie. Cyril doesn't care for kidneys. I suppose it's Frieda you want to speak to? It *is* about this awful business, isn't it – poor Zellah Wilding?'

'Yes, I'm afraid so.'

'It's so terrible.' Behind her glasses, her brown eyes were large and moist, as if ready to overflow. 'I keep thinking how it could have been Frieda – not that we'd have let her roam about the Scrubs alone like that. I can't think what the Wildings were up to. They were always so strict with Zellah. I don't understand how they suddenly let her go wandering about in the middle of the night in a place like that. But then you can be killed right outside your own front door these days, in broad daylight, can't you? Oh, it's a terrible world! But I try not to frighten Frieda too much. Cyril and I want her to be strong and independent. It's such a problem, balancing that against keeping her safe. I hate even letting her go to school on her own, but you have to untie the apron strings, don't you? I don't want her to be one of those girls who can't do anything for herself, or find her way anywhere. There are plenty of those at school, I can tell you – get driven to school in the morning and collected at night, and taken everywhere in a car. Their parents are nothing but unpaid chauffeurs, and it's not *good* for the girls to be so dependent. When we were seventeen we went everywhere on our own. But then something like this happens, and it makes you pause. You just don't know what to think, what to do for the best.'

Slider said, 'I know exactly what you mean. I have a daughter myself.' He was surprised at himself for offering the fact, but he felt her dilemma acutely. 'If it helps, I don't think it was a random killing.'

'Oh?' She was surprised, and didn't know quite how to take it. 'I thought I read that you'd arrested some awful serial killer.'

'We have to follow lines of enquiry as they arise. They don't all lead to the right conclusion. In fact, I believe now that the killer knew Zellah.'

'They do say,' she said introspectively, 'that it's more often someone the victim knows.'

'That's true,' Slider said.

'I don't know that it makes me feel any safer,' she concluded.

'I sometimes wonder,' Slider said, 'whether feeling safe isn't a modern luxury we've got used to comparatively recently. Historically, life was always dangerous and uncertain.'

'I suppose you're right,' she said with the brief, tight smile again. 'But the fact is we *have* got used to it. Well, I mustn't keep you. You'll want to talk to Frieda. She's upstairs studying. I'll just turn the gas down and go and fetch her. You can talk to her in the lounge – I expect you'd sooner be alone with her?'

Slider was impressed by her understanding and generosity. 'If you don't mind.'

'No, I know there are things girls won't say in front of their parents. You'll try not to frighten her, though, won't you? No gory details or anything?'

'Of course not; nothing like that. I shan't mention the murder itself. I only want to talk to her about what Zellah was like.'

She nodded, but with a penetrating look that both sought reassurance and threatened reprisal if he got it wrong. She led him through into the lounge, an expensively, rather heavily furnished room, well-kept and comfortable but not the least fashionable. There were framed photographs on every surface; an upright piano against one wall, open and with music on the stand as if it were regularly used; bright dahlias put, rather than arranged, in a vase on the windowsill. A gas coal-effect fire occupied the grate under the 1930s mantelpiece, and the dog, who followed them in, lay down on the rug in front of it as though it were his habitual spot. The cat pranced in too, sprang up on to the back of an armchair and arched its back, inviting caress. Everything here spoke of a family home, of belonging and care and custom, of a little interknit tribe pursuing its innocent routines. It was so different from the Wildings' jarring, comfortless mismatch. Here was a small haven of a world, built inside the larger chaos of a great metropolis and the twenty-first century. He hoped desperately that nothing bad would ever come to blast it open.

In a little while Mrs Mossman appeared at the door and ushered in a small, plumpish girl with frizzy hair and glasses, wearing blue cotton Capri pants and a plain white T-shirt. She looked at Slider uncertainly, her bare toes curling for comfort into the carpet pile.

'This is Frieda,' Mrs Mossman said. 'Frieda, this is Detective Inspector Slider. He wants to talk to you about Zellah. You must talk to him absolutely honestly, darling. I shall be in the kitchen if you want me.' She looked at Slider. 'Do you mind dogs? Shall I take him away?'

'I like dogs,' Slider said. He thought its presence would be comforting to the girl. 'He's fine. What's his name?'

'Barney.' The dog looked up and beat his tail at the sound of his name. 'I'll leave you to it, then,' Mrs Mossman said, and departed.

Frieda remained at the door, watching Slider alertly, like an animal poised for flight. She seemed pale, and looked as though she had been crying a lot recently. She appeared younger than seventeen, and there was little under her T-shirt to disturb the shape of it. Her plump face was still a child's, her whole posture unaware of the power of the female body. He looked with sympathy at the impossible hair and the strong glasses. He imagined Sophy's cruel remarks and the hurt they had caused: behind the lenses, the eyes, intensely dark as coffee beans, were intelligent. There was nothing wrong with her features: she had good skin, and one day she would switch to contacts, subdue her hair and be as attractive as the next girl, but there was no use in saying that to a teenage girl. His own daughter thought she had a big nose, and when she looked in the mirror that was all she saw. We all have to pin our disappointments on something.

'Come and sit down,' he said. He sat himself in one of the armchairs. It was the one the cat was decorating, and it jumped down at once on to his lap and started kneading bread. The sound of its purr filled the room like the sound of a trapped bumble bee.

'He likes you,' Frieda said. Her voice was light and small, as though she was trying not to make an impression on the world.

'I like cats, too,' he said.

'People are mostly cat people or dog people,' she said. 'It's quite rare to be both.' She drifted across the room and perched on the edge of the chair opposite, but only, said her demeanour, so that she could stroke Barney. Barney at once flopped on to his side and presented his belly – the gesture of a nice dog who knew his place in the hierarchy.

'I like all animals,' Slider said. 'My father was a farmer.' Two revelations in five minutes – what was wrong with him? He was too comfortable here. It was dangerous.

'I'd have liked to be a farmer,' Frieda said. 'But there's no money in it, and it's terribly hard work. A lot of the girls want to be vets, but they're just sentimental about animals. They don't understand what it really means.'

'What do you want to do, now you're not going to be a farmer?'

She looked at him carefully, to see if he was teasing her, and then said, 'I'm going to be a doctor.' She said it with unemphatic firmness, as though there were no doubt about it, so no need to be dogmatic.

'Good for you,' he said.

'Why "good for me"?' Her voice was light and sharp. She didn't want to be patronized.

'The country needs doctors,' he said. 'Is your father one?'

'No, Daddy's in the wine trade. He used to deal futures on Liv-ex, but now he's a buyer for a big wholesaler. It's more fun because he gets to go on trips all the time.' She sat up, abandoning the dog's belly, and said, 'But you didn't come here to talk about careers. You don't need to put me at ease with small talk, you know. I'm perfectly all right.'

'I can see that,' Slider said. Her light, clipped voice said she was at ease, but her eyes said differently.

'You want to talk to me about Zellah.'

'Of course. I want to know what she was like.'

'In what way?' It was a wary question.

'I believe she was very bright,' Slider said, for somewhere to start. 'Intelligent?'

'Yes, she was. She and I did classes together. We were both doing science A levels. That's not popular, you know. The popular girls do arts, and non-subjects like media and fashion.' She mentioned them witheringly. 'Nowadays it's more important to be pretty and fashionable than clever. Even those that have a brain try to hide it. It's so stupid.'

'Even Zellah? Did she try to hide it?'

'Not at first,' Frieda said. 'Frankly, she was even more intelligent than me. She was brilliant. And not just at academic subjects. She could draw, too, and she did music, and ballet.' She saw Slider's glance towards the piano and said, 'Yes, I can play. I've taken piano since I was six. But I'll never be any good at it. A lot of music is mathematics, and I can do that side of it all right, but I don't have the artistic talent. I can't put the feeling into it.'

'And Zellah could?'

'Yes. She was artistic *and* academic. It's very rare.'

'Like being both a cat person and a dog person.'

She looked at him with something like scorn, as if he just didn't get it. 'She was a polymath,' she said sternly.

'So what changed?' he asked.

Her mouth turned down. '*Boys*,' she said witheringly. 'She started to get silly about boys. That's all they think about, the popular girls – people like Chloë Paulson and Sophy Cooper-Hutchinson. Always preening themselves and wearing make-up and hanging around waiting for the St Martin's boys to come out. It's so *stupid*.' She looked at him sharply as if he had said something. 'Oh, I know what you're thinking – that it's just sour grapes? It's not. I *know* what I look like. And I know I'm never going to look any different. But it's *not* that. I don't care, you see. I've got a brain, and that's worth any amount of good looks. Good looks go off, you know, but your brain lasts your whole life. I mean to *do* something with mine. And before you ask, no, I'm not worried about getting married. I don't care about it. Not now. I've got too much else to think about. Anyway, I expect in the end I'll marry one of my cousins – I've got hundreds, and they all seem to marry each other. But not until I've excelled in my field.'

'Have you chosen your field yet?' he asked, hoping to get back in her good books with an intelligent question.

'Genetics,' she said with the same light sureness. 'There's the potential to cure every known disease, condition and syndrome through genetic manipulation. The possibilities are literally endless. All the great medical discoveries of this century are going to be in genetics.'

'I see you set yourself high standards,' Slider said. 'And I can understand how you felt Zellah had let herself down.'

'She *did*,' Frieda said hotly. 'She had everything – brains, talent. She was even *beautiful*. I mean, she really was – ten times more beautiful than those other girls, if that *means* anything, which it doesn't. But she never seemed to know how lucky she was. Suddenly she wanted to be popular, and hang around with the *in* girls, no matter how vapid they were.'

'You didn't understand it,' Slider suggested.

'Not from her. I mean, when we were younger, we all used to hang out together, and it didn't matter. Sophy and Chloë and Zellah and me, and another couple of girls, Matilda and Polly, but they've left now. And then it all changed.'

'When did it change?'

'About eighteen months, two years ago. It used to be that ballet and ponies were the thing, and then suddenly it was nothing but boys. I stopped really liking Sophy and Chloë, but I thought Zellah was different. But she seemed to want to be in with them, so I stayed with her too, for a while. But it all got too silly.'

'In what way?'

'Sophy and Chloë were obsessed with sex,' Frieda said scornfully. She clasped her hands between her knees, her toes pointing away from each other. A child's unselfconscious pose. 'It was all they talked about. It was like a competition between them over who could be most outrageous, have the most boyfriends, be the first to go all the way. It was just pathetic.'

'Do you think they did go all the way?'

'It doesn't matter,' she said shortly. 'The thing was, Zellah went along with it, competed with them, boasted even worse than them. I'm sure they were convinced *she* had. They thought she was terrific for it. For being the first. How could anyone be so shallow? I couldn't understand why Zellah did it.'

'Maybe she just wanted to be liked.'

'For that? Why?' She seemed angry about it.

'Did she have a lot of other friends?'

'Not really. I was her best friend, up till then. She wasn't allowed to have girls home, or to go out much after school, so it made it difficult for her. She was always a bit of a loner.'

'Well, doesn't that explain why she might want to try to fit in with girls like Sophy and Chloë?' Slider said.

He was also thinking *puberty*, but the onset of that was not something he could or would discuss with Frieda, who didn't look as if she was much bothered with it yet.

'But she had *me*,' Frieda said. 'Or she did until she took up with that awful Mike.'

'Was he awful?'

'*She* didn't think so. She was mad for him. Sophy hated him. After that they didn't hang around together so much. Oh, but then she remembered she *did* have another friend,' she added with a hint of bitterness. 'When it was convenient to her.'

'You?'

'I covered for her. When she wanted to see Mike, I let her pretend she was visiting me. It was one of the few things her father let her do. She'd say she was coming to see me after ballet on Saturday, or after school, but really she was seeing Mike.'

'Do you think she was in love with him?' Slider asked, stroking the cat. It had settled, couching on his lap, eyes closed with bliss.

She considered carefully. 'I think she was *infatuated*,' she said decidedly. It was almost comical, the contrast between the adult vocabulary, and the little-girl form before him. 'She thought she was in love, but when the real thing came along, she realized it was different from what she felt for Mike.' She looked at him sternly, determined to keep him straight. 'She didn't *say* all this to me, you understand. It's what I *deduced*. She never spoke much about her feelings. She was a very *private* person, really. But she was mad about Mike, but when she met the new man, she dropped Mike like a hot potato. I almost felt sorry for him – not that I think he was the type to care. But she really, really loved the new man. It was different. I could see it was different.'

Slider was almost holding his breath. 'And who was the new man?'

'I don't know,' Frieda said.

Well, what had he hoped for? It was never that easy.

'All I know,' she went on, 'is that he lived not far from here, because she spoke once about walking from here to his house. And he was a lot older than her. She said something about it being nice to be with a real grown-up and not just a boy like Mike. She went all dreamy-eyed when she mentioned him. But if ever I asked who he was, or anything about him, she clammed up. I got the *impression*,' she said in her careful way, 'that there was something wrong.' She stared down at the dog for a moment, who wagged hopefully back, but her mind was elsewhere. 'I know it's a terrible thing to say,' she said at last, looking up at him, 'but I've wondered if . . . well, if he was *married*.'

'What makes you think that?'

'Oh, I don't know. But if he wasn't, why did it all have to be such a secret?'

'Because her parents wouldn't have liked her to have a boyfriend?'

'Oh, I don't mean secret from them. *Obviously* it had to be a secret from them,' she said, shaking her head at his stupidity. 'But why keep it a secret from me? She didn't keep Mike a secret from me. Or from Sophy and Chloë. But I don't think they even knew she *had* a new boyfriend.'

'I don't think they did either,' Slider said encouragingly. 'I think you knew Zellah much better than they did.'

'I was her only real friend,' she said bleakly, 'but still she didn't trust me enough to tell me about him. I wish I knew why. Nothing's ever so bad if you can *understand*.'

'Can you think of anything, anything at all, that she told you about the new boyfriend? Anything that might help us find him.'

Now her gaze sharpened behind the glasses. 'Why do you want to find him? Do you think he was the one that . . . that killed her?'

'I don't know,' Slider said, glad to be able to fall back on that. 'But obviously we want to talk to anyone who knew her well, particularly in the last two or three months.'

'Well, I can't think of anything she said, apart from what I've told you. Mostly she just said how wonderful he was. And how he understood her. She said that *a lot.*' She nodded at Slider emphatically. 'She really thought he was her soulmate. She didn't like her parents much. They were always fighting over her. I've seen them with her, at parents' day, and it was true. Everyone says how proud they were of her, but I don't think they actually really *saw* her, as a person. They just wanted to own her. For reflected glory. You know,' she added seriously, 'I don't think it could have been the new man that killed her. I mean, she loved him. And I suppose he must have loved her. So why would he?'

For all her intellectual maturity, she was still untried where emotions were concerned. She couldn't conceive why love might lead to death.

Atherton was still there when Slider got back to the station, sitting on his windowsill.

'I thought I told you to go home.'

'With my boss going solo, risking his all out in the wilderness? No way,' said Atherton. 'You might have needed rescuing, and who else was going to go out with the barrel of brandy round his neck? Besides, you'll want to hear this. Connolly?'

Connolly came in from the CID room with a piece of paper in her hand. 'I got the gen on the car, sir,' she said. 'Two-year-old Toyota Corolla, colour sapphire black.' She looked up from the paper. 'That's—'

'I know what that is, thank you, Constable,' he said. 'I had a lecture earlier today from a career TDA artist.'

'Registered keeper is a Miss Stephanie Barstowe, address 6 Shirland House, Bravington Road, Kensal Town. Bought new on finance from Kensal Motors, Harrow Road – payments all up to date so far. You asked about tickets – there's half a dozen outstanding, all around London. No other violations. Insurance is with Liverpool Victoria, fully comp, fifty-pound windscreen excess, self and named driver covered. And,' she looked up here, with an expression of triumph, 'the named driver is Alexander Markov of the same address.'

Slider sat down behind his desk. 'Go on.'

'I got talking to another nurse in the same unit, and they *are* married, but she uses her maiden name. I suppose that's because of her career – she's manager of the intensive-care unit, so she's a bit of a player. Also, I asked did Stephanie drive the car to work. Apparently she drives in when the weather's bad, otherwise she cycles.'

'The weather was fine on Sunday,' Atherton said.

'And I did a bit of checking with the management about her shifts. The parking tickets are all at times Stephanie was working. So someone else was driving the car at those times.'

'You said the car under the railway bridge was a Toyota Corolla,' Atherton said to Slider. 'But I'm not sure where you're going with this, or what made you connect the two. There must be hundreds of Corollas in the area.'

'Just as there are Focuses,' Slider replied, 'but you were happy for it to be Wilding's.'

'Well, obviously, because it belongs to someone connected with the victim,' he said, and stopped abruptly.

'Sir,' Connolly said, frowning as she tried to catch up, 'I thought Markov said Zellah was a lezzer. It said in your notes—'

'Classic misdirection,' Slider said.

'Hey, I said that,' Atherton protested.

'About a completely different subject. Markov threw out the suggestion about Zellah in the hope that I wouldn't make a connection between him, Zellah and sex. He didn't say she *was* a lesbian. He said he *wondered* if she had doubts about her sexuality, as many young girls do. He also told me that he *didn't own a car.* And then he said it was hardly worth it in London. And he said his wife cycled to work. Every one of those statements is true. But he didn't say he never *drove* a car, though that was the impression he hoped to leave.'

'Misdirection,' Connolly said. 'I see. So you think . . .?'

Slider turned to Atherton. 'Emily said Carmichael's account of the last meeting with Zellah was so dumb it could almost be true.'

'The thing about having two dates?' he remembered.

'It was school holidays. She couldn't use the after-school activity excuse. The sleepover with Sophy and Chloë was her one chance to get in touch with the father of the baby,' Slider went on. 'She must have been desperate and terrified by then. Imagine if you were her, having to tell *that* father you were pregnant.'

'Yes,' Atherton said. 'That would frighten a triple DSO.'

'She couldn't ring Markov from home. I don't know if she tried to ring him from Sophy's house. Maybe she did, and he wasn't in, or his wife answered. I suspect she felt she had to see him face to face to tell him – it's not something you can do over the phone.'

'So where did Carmichael come into it?' Atherton asked. 'Was she really just using him for transport?'

'I think she thought of him as a friend – someone she could talk to. She must have felt lonely, isolated with her problem.'

'You got that right,' Connolly said. 'Couldn't talk to her parents. And nobody would confide something like that to Sophy Cooper-Hutchinson.'

'And I've learned enough about Frieda Mossman today to know she wouldn't have confided in her, either,' Slider said. 'Not about that. At least Mike wouldn't be shocked or dis-approving. Probably she hoped to be able to talk to him. But he quickly showed he was just interested in sex,' he said sadly. 'So all that was left was to get in touch with Markov. Now, the scenario I'm working on is that she phoned Markov from Mike's flat – he says she made a phone call. She told him she must see him. They agreed a time and a place – the fairground, ten o'clock. She had time to kill, so she got Mike to take her to the fair, and tried to have a good time.'

'The condemned man eating a hearty meal?' Atherton said.

'Something like that.' He thought of her going on the rides and screaming, hugging Mike's arm to her, being a normal girlfriend for the last time in her life. He couldn't blame her for using Carmichael. Hadn't he used her? 'But then she told Mike she was meeting someone else, and naturally enough he didn't like that and they quarrelled.'

'But,' said Atherton, 'the fat lady said the quarrel was later, near midnight.'

'I've looked at the write-ups. She said there was *a* quarrel. The rifle-range man's description matches Carmichael all right, but the fat lady said a tall man – Carmichael is not notably tall – older than Zellah – Carmichael doesn't look particularly older than her – and she said he had brown hair, where Carmichael is notably dark. When Emily said that thing about the dumb excuse being true, I started to wonder if Zellah didn't meet two men after all, and have two quarrels: one at ten, and a second, serious one at twelve.'

'Yes,' said Atherton, staring at nothing, 'it works. She fights with Markov. She runs off across the Scrubs weeping, thinking her world is at an end. But after a while and some walking, she wonders if there isn't still hope. She sees the Snogging Couple and asks to use their phone, rings Markov again, he comes to meet her.'

'Meet, you see, not fetch,' said Slider.

'They have another row, she jumps out of the car, he chases her and kills her.'

They were silent.

'But, sir,' said Connolly, 'if she told him she was up the pole the first time they met, why would he come to see her a second time? Why did they quarrel again? And why did that quarrel lead him to kill her?'

'And why,' Atherton said, 'did he take a pair of tights with him when he went to meet her the second time?'

'That,' said Slider, 'is something I think we'll have to ask him.'

'But first we need the phone records,' Atherton said. 'If it wasn't Markov she phoned, the whole theory is a crock.'

'We can't expect to get them tonight. I think we should all go home and get a good night's sleep.'

Atherton cocked his head. 'Dollars to doughnuts *you* won't sleep tonight.'

'That's entirely my problem,' Slider said with dignity.

Joanna, holding Slider in bed, could feel both his weariness and his tension. The intense sympathy he always felt with a murder victim, even when it was a low-life scumbag, was partly what made him a good detective, but it also wore him out. He would find it hard to get to sleep tonight. He was keeping quite still, so as not to disturb her, but it was not a restful stillness. She sought for something to take his mind off the case.

'Your father rang again this evening,' she said, quietly, so as not to wake the baby.

'Hmm?'

'He sounded wistful.'

Slider sighed. 'I'll ring him tomorrow. I'll *make* time. I've got him on my conscience.'

'You haven't got room on your conscience for anything else. I looked at more flats today.'

'Oh?'

'Nothing we could afford. You wouldn't believe what a broom-cupboard costs these days. The only thing in our range was a lock-up garage. But it had no plumbing.'

'What about . . .?'

'I looked at rentals, too,' she anticipated. 'The rents are as much as a mortgage would be. The only reason I can afford this place is that I've been here so long the rent's protected.'

'I've let you down.'

'Don't start that. I'm not your dependant. But I just can't think of a way out. We can't increase our incomes, and we've nothing to sell. Unless . . .'

'Unless what?'

'Well, I did think perhaps we could sell George and lease him back. You get a big tax advantage with lease-back.'

'I'm glad you've still got your sensa yuma,' he said. 'You'll need it, living with me. We can't even get a council flat, since I was foolish enough to marry you. They only give them to unmarried mothers.'

'I was just wondering about your dad, though. If he's selling his place, perhaps we could pool our resources and live together.'

'You wouldn't mind?' Slider was amazed and touched.

'I love your dad.'

'But it's different having him to live with us.'

'Well, it'd be the other way round, really, since the money would be his.'

He kissed her brow tenderly. 'Thank you for the thought. I'm glad you like the old man that much. But you don't know that he'd want to live with us.'

'I think he would. He was hinting that he'd like to move closer to us.'

'Closer and with aren't the same thing. But anyway, that cottage can't be worth much – not enough to buy somewhere in London, let alone something big enough for the four of us.'

'Oh well,' she said comfortably, 'we'll just have to stay put. At least we've got a roof over our heads. People in past times lived in small spaces and shared rooms.'

'People in past times had surgery without anaesthetic.'

'Not the same thing. I think we've just got too nice. We're all going to have to trim our nails if the recession gets bad.'

'Hmm.'

She could feel he had relaxed, and the 'hmm' was much more contented than the first one. They were silent a moment, and then she thought of something that infallibly relaxed him and put him to sleep afterwards. She laid her lips against his ear, and whispered, 'How would you feel about a close encounter of the marital kind?'

'Hmm,' he murmured into her neck. And one second later she felt the infinitesimal thud as he fell off the cliff of consciousness and into the void of sleep. It was that quick when you were as tired as he was. Smiling in the darkness, she held him until he was deep enough under for her to release herself without waking him, then turned over into her own sleep position.

TWENTY

You Must Remember This;
A Kiss is Still a Coordinated
Interpersonal Labial Spasm

Tufnell 'Tufty' Arceneaux, who described himself as 'The Bodily Fluids Man' with more than a coincidental accuracy, rang Slider as soon as he was at his desk in the morning. 'Bill, old chum!' he roared (everything about Tufty was larger than life). 'How's the world treating you? How's the wife? How's the nipper?'

'He's great fun,' Slider said. 'He's just started crawling.'

'That'll be useful training for later life! Especially if he wants to get on in the police force.'

'We're not allowed to call it that. It's the police service now.'

'Makes you sound like a lot of bloody tennis players.'

'How's Diana? Is she enjoying the job?' Tufty's wife had recently gone back to work in an advertising agency.

'Loves it. A prank a minute. They've just taken on a new product, Galaxy-type chocolate bar called Destiny. She put up a whole folder, artwork and everything, with the slogan "It's the Destiny that shapes our ends". Did it with a straight face,' he concluded admiringly.

'They'll sack her if she's not careful.'

'Oh, no, they love her. All the others are under twenty-five. She's the only one who can spell. Anyway, I've pulled every digit out of every orifice, done the impossible, and got all your analyses done.'

'All of them? That's amazing,' Slider said. 'I thought I'd have to wait until Monday at least.'

'What are you talking about? I've had them since Tuesday.'

'I know you had the first ones on Tuesday, but Freddie only sent the foetal tissue on Thursday.'

'I can do it in thirty-six hours when I have to. Come to think of it, I've done it *for* thirty-six hours when I've had to, but that's another story.'

'Well, I'm very grateful.'

'Special service for my old and bestest chum. Fact is, when the foetal tissue came in, I thought there's no point in the one lot without t'other, so I got on with it without waiting for you to fast-track. Now, if that doesn't warrant an invite to dinner with you and your charming mate, I don't know what does.'

'Absolutely as soon as I've got this case sorted out, we'll do it,' Slider said, thinking doubtfully of how easy it would be to fit Tufty's large frame and its even more enormous appetite into Joanna's small sitting room, where the only table was.

'Excellent, old chum-bum. Nosh-date, potential, duly noted in the almanac. Now, regarding your samples – the foetal tissue does *not* match the profile you gave me from the records – Michael Carmichael? God, what a name!'

'Carmichael is not the father?'

'Not in those trousers. Have you got anyone else you want me to check it against?'

'Not yet, but I hope to very soon.'

'Ah, a hot suspect in the offing, eh?'

'What about DNA from the tights and the chain?'

'Couldn't get anything from the tights, just a few of the victim's own skin cells. But there was a trace of blood and a few cells on the chain. I managed to work it up, and we have a match between that and the foetal DNA. Whoever cut his hand on the chain was also the baby's progenitor. I'd say father but it doesn't seem a very fatherly act to kill the mother, now does it?'

'Not when I was a boy scout. Thanks, Tufty. That's a great help.'

'Let me know when you've got something to match it against, and I'll put it through on the express till. Five items or less. You've got room in your basket. Well, back to the grindstone. Dyb dyb, old horse.'

'Dob dob,' Slider responded absently, his mind already on the next thing.

Porson was late in, having gone to Hammersmith first, straight from home, and he was still inhaling his first mug of coffee when Slider arrived at his door.

'Good news, sir,' he said.

'I'm up for that,' Porson said.

Slider told him about the DNA typing, and went on, 'And we've just had the phone records back, for Carmichael's home phone and Tyler Burton's mobile. The number Zellah called from each was the same. It was Alex Markov's.'

Porson put down his mug so sharply a slurp of coffee sprang over the rim. 'Bloody hell, that's a relief,' he said, giving himself away completely.

'That's how I felt, sir,' Slider admitted. A theory's all very well, but one is as good as another until you get something solid to back it up. 'And we've got a good possibility the car under the bridge was his. Same make and colour, anyway, though it's a pity we haven't got a reg number.'

'Plus he lied to you about not having a car,' Porson added, dragging a handkerchief from his pocket and mopping the spilled coffee with it. His wife was dead and he did his own laundry now, Slider reflected. 'Right, how do you want to proceed?'

'I need to get a DNA sample from him so I can check it against the foetus and the sample from the chain,' he said.

'You could arrest him,' Porson said, stuffing the handkerchief back into his pocket. 'You've got enough to be going on with.'

'I've been thinking about it, sir,' Slider said, 'and I'd like to get him to come in voluntarily, get him relaxed and then catch him unawares. I think with the right handling we could get a confession out of him, and that would make things much easier.'

Porson nodded. 'I'm all for that. But how are you going to get him to come in?'

'I think I know how,' Slider said.

'Well, go to it, laddie, and best of luck. It'd be good to get this cleared up today. Mr Wetherspoon was asking me -questions this morning. He's got a new protégé he'd like to parachute into a front-line unit for experience. If it comes our way I want to refuse, but I need a bit of leverage to fight it off, and a quick result in the hand is worth a nod to a blind horse.'

'Absolutely, sir,' said Slider. 'I'll do my best.'

'I know, laddie. You always do,' said Porson.

'How are you going to get him in?' Atherton asked.

'Stop breathing down my neck. I have a plan.'

'A man with a plan: Panama.'

'Right. And if it doesn't work, I'll eat my hat.'

'It was a *canal*!'

'Stop burbling, it's ringing. Hello? Mr Markov? It's Detective Inspector Slider here. Shepherd's Bush police station. You remember I called on you – yes, that's right. Oh, coming along slowly. These things take time. Mr Markov, there are just a couple more questions I'd like to ask you. It's just a small thing, but it's as well to get these things cleared up. Well, I wondered if you could pop into the station here this morning? If you wouldn't mind. Yes, I could come out to you, but,' he lowered his voice, 'I assume your wife is there, and I would hate to disturb her. There are some aspects of the case I'm sure you'd prefer not to expose her to. Quite. There's no need for her to be involved in any unpleasantness. Everything said here will be confidential. Indeed. Yes. Thank you so much. I'll expect you shortly, then.'

He put down the phone and smiled like a cat. 'He thinks I've cottoned on that he and Zellah were making the beast with two backs. He'll come in to explain it away somehow.'

'Devious and unscrupulous,' Atherton said. 'I like it!'

Markov looked as though he hadn't slept much for days. He had shaved for the occasion and put on clean clothes, but his skin was slack with too much alcohol, and there were bags under his eyes. The eyes themselves were bloodshot, and his nose was red around the nostrils and kept running. 'I think I'm getting a cold,' he said, to excuse the constant need to sniff and wipe. 'These summer colds are the devil – worse than the winter sort, I always think.'

'Yes, very nasty,' Slider said in a friendly way. 'And so unfair, somehow. One feels far more put upon.' He gestured Markov into a seat in the interview room, and went round to the other side of the table. 'Can I offer you tea, or coffee?'

'No, thank you. I wouldn't mind some water, though.'

Slider had him brought a small bottle of mineral water and a plastic cup, and sat with hands relaxed on the table in front of him while Markov unscrewed the cap, poured some water and drank it. The action and Slider's demeanour were working on him. The wariness with which he had entered had evaporated. He obviously thought that he was going to be able to talk his way out of whatever was coming.

'Well, now,' Slider said, with a comfortable smile, 'I expect you're wondering what all this is about. It's quite a small thing, but I do need to have it cleared up. It's about your wife's car.'

'Oh yes?' Markov said. He frowned, as if he were trying to remember what, if anything, he had ever said about the car.

'You did say that she cycled to work?'

'That's right.'

'Then I wonder why you didn't report it missing on Sunday night.'

'Missing?'

'If you knew she hadn't taken it, it must have been stolen, mustn't it?'

'It wasn't stolen,' he said, looking puzzled. 'It was there this morning.' A blush spread through his waxy face as he remembered he had previously repudiated all knowledge of a car. 'Oh! I mean – when I said before . . . it was . . . I didn't . . .'

'You said you didn't own a car. Quite.'

'It was the truth,' he protested.

'Yes, I know – your wife owns it. What I want to know is, what was it doing under the railway bridge at Old Oak Common on Sunday night?' Markov looked absolutely stumped, his face rigid, his eyes stationary. 'We know your wife was at work on Sunday night. You can't work in an intensive-care unit without having plenty of witnesses to the fact. You, on the other hand, were at home, with no one to vouch for you.'

'I was at home all evening,' he blurted. 'I was working on a painting. I can't help it if there was no one else there.' He thought so hard you could hear the creak. 'Maybe a joyrider took it, and then brought it back.'

'Did you drive here today?' Slider asked. Markov's eyes flitted about, looking for escape. 'We know that you are insured to drive it. Did you drive it here today? Is it downstairs?'

'Well . . . yes,' Markov admitted, like someone swallowing a too-large lump of steak.

'Then we'd like to have a look at it, if you don't mind. Do some tests.'

'What sort of tests?' he asked faintly.

'Forensic tests. Whoever took the car will have left traces of themselves – hair, skin cells, sweat and sebaceous oil on the steering wheel and so on. You can't get into a car without leaving DNA behind. Everyone who was ever in it will be there.'

'You'll find my DNA in there,' Markov said in a dry voice. 'And Steph's.'

'Of course we'll have to eliminate those. We could start with yours – if you'd be so kind as to let us take a buccal swab.' He brought out the kit. Markov was sweating now, but he still couldn't see where this was going. 'You'd have no objection to that, would you?'

'Well, I—'

'Thank you. This won't take a moment.' It was done in seconds. 'Thank you,' Slider said. 'And if we could have the car keys . . .?'

Markov handed them over. Atherton handed them and the swab to the constable outside the door and returned to his seat. Markov's eyes flitted between them anxiously.

'Of course,' Slider said amiably, 'the other traces we'll find in the car will be Zellah's, but we already have her DNA typed, so we'll recognise those.'

'Zellah? She . . .' He stopped.

'You won't try to pretend she was never in your car, I hope,' Slider said lightly. 'You *were* having an affair with her.' Markov only stared, helpless as a rabbit before headlights. 'Quite clever to try to make me think she was a lesbian,' he went on conversationally. 'Throw me off the scent. Unfortunately, there was too much evidence the other way. Including the sad fact that she was pregnant.'

Markov went so white Slider thought for an electric moment that he might throw up. 'You said – my wife – you implied she needn't know. That's why I came here. You won't tell her?'

'I won't tell her you were having an affair,' Slider said, 'but I think she's going to find out anyway. Your DNA will match the baby's, and when that's added to all the other evidence we have against you, we will be charging you with Zellah's murder. I think your wife is bound to hear about that sooner or later, don't you?'

Markov's mouth opened and shut a few times, but he didn't seem to be able to get any words out. At last he said, 'I didn't. I didn't. I didn't. You've got it wrong. It wasn't me.'

'Let me see your hands,' Slider said.

Markov's hands were on the table, balled into fists. He looked at them as if he didn't know what they were, and lay them flat, palm down. Slider reached across the table, took hold of a forefinger of each, and turned them over, palm up. Across the palm of the right hand was a thin, faint red mark, the healing scar of a long but minor cut. 'How did you do that?' he asked.

'I – I cut myself by accident. With a palette knife. Grabbed the wrong end. I'd had a glass of wine or two,' he added with an attempt at a light laugh.

Inventive, Slider thought. Even at this stage. He shook his head and said, 'You cut it on the chain around Zellah's neck. We have a DNA sample from that, too, and it will match yours, just as the foetal tissue will. I think, Mr Markov, the time has come for you to tell me everything. We know you killed her, you see. We have all the evidence we need to charge you. There is just this one window of opportunity for you to tell your side of the story, mention any mitigating circumstances we might not know about. Now's the time to talk. Otherwise, it's premeditated murder of the worst kind, and nothing will save you from the full penalty of the law.'

To his surprise, Markov began to weep. 'I didn't mean to! It was a mistake! An accident! I never meant to hurt her! You don't understand. It wasn't my fault.'

They were tears, Slider decided, of self-pity. Understandable, but not very noble. He thought of Zellah, and wished her nemesis had been a bit more of a man, even though that would have made his job harder.

'I never meant things to get out of hand,' Markov said, his hands folded round a mug of tea as if it were a cold day. He was shaking a little. 'I mean, I teach pubescent girls all the time, and they all fall in love with me. Well, most of them. It's the whole art-master thing. I could have had dozens of them if I was that way inclined. But I'm no Humbert. But Zellah . . . Zellah was different. She was . . .' He paused a long time, thinking, and then drew out his handkerchief and wiped his nose. It was still leaking, though whether from the recent tears or last night's snow, Slider couldn't tell.

'She had a talent,' he resumed at last. 'It wasn't just in drawing. She was brilliant academically, and she had a real feeling for music, painting, dance – everything. There was something about that girl – an artistic spirit. And she was beautiful. I don't mean just physically. She was remote, shut away, like a frozen princess on an ice mountain, waiting for the prince who could ride his horse to the top and rescue her.' He wiped his nose again, and then looked sharply at Slider, coming down to earth with a bump. 'I don't mean I ever intended to *do* anything about it. I'm an artist. I can look without touching. It all came from her side. She *threw* herself at me.'

'And you and your wife weren't getting on.'

'We haven't been for a long time,' he said with a sigh. 'We should never have married. Steph and I – well, we're not right for each other. She's too practical; I'm too romantic. And – well, there are money troubles. The mortgage is hefty, and I'm maxed out on my credit cards. I've got an overdraft, too. Painting in oils is expensive. Steph refuses to understand that. Of course, when I sell something, I pay the loans off.'

'So, like many a man whose wife doesn't understand him, you started an affair,' Slider said.

Markov looked sulky. 'I told you, that was her idea. She was crazy about me. I could take it or leave it.'

'But you took it,' Slider said. 'Your wife working shifts made it easy for you to fit it in.' Markov wanted to protest, but Slider waved that line away. 'What happened on Sunday?'

'I hadn't seen her for a while. It wasn't so easy for her to get away in school holidays. It must have been over a week – two weeks, probably. I was hoping, actually, that she was cooling off. You see, much as I liked her, I was afraid of Steph finding out. She owns the flat, you see. She could make it very awkward for me. If there was a divorce, I'd lose everything. I wouldn't even have a roof over my head. OK, I've got the teaching job, but it's part-time, and it doesn't pay much, and if I took a full-time job I wouldn't have time to paint.'

'And you have an expensive drugs habit, and your wife's income helps pay for that,' Atherton said neutrally.

Markov looked at him resentfully. 'It's all right for you to sit in judgement over me. You don't know what an artist suffers. The pressures,' he put his hands to his head, 'are unbearable sometimes. I *need* cocaine to be able to relax—'

'Let's get back to Sunday,' Slider interrupted. He didn't want to go off on the drugs line again. 'You hadn't seen Zellah for a while, and then suddenly she telephoned you. Oh yes,' he added, 'we know about that. Telephone calls are all logged, you know.'

'Oh,' he said blankly. 'Well, yes, she phoned me and said she wanted to see me. Could she come over, she asked. Steph had gone to work, fortunately. But I was doing a bit of painting and I didn't want to break off. I said I was busy. She said it was really important and she must see me. So I said OK, I'd meet her later. We agreed ten o'clock, in the fairground opposite the North Pole.' He moved restlessly. 'I was thinking this might be a good opportunity to break up with her, and it would be easier in a crowded place like that, where she couldn't make a fuss.'

'Good thought,' said Slider drily.

'But when I met her, she started talking about us, and our relationship and all that sort of thing, and how much she loved me, and next thing she was asking me when I was going to leave my wife for her.'

'Amazing.'

'I'd never said anything to her about that! Never so much as mentioned marriage! Well, I didn't want a scene, so I tried to put her off gently, but she wouldn't change the subject. Went on and on about it. Eventually I got fed up and, well, lost my temper a bit, and we ended up shouting at each other. And then she tells me she's having a baby.'

'How did you react to that?'

'I was dumbfounded. I mean, we'd always used a condom. I said I didn't see how she could possibly hold me responsible for her condition. I said she must have been seeing someone else. She started crying. She said she loved me, and that there wasn't anyone but me. She said condoms weren't always reliable. She begged me to leave my wife and marry her. She said her father would kill her otherwise. I said I was sorry for her but there was no question of it. It went on like that for a bit. We'd walked right to the back of the fair by that time, where the caravans and lorries are. Finally she rushes off in tears, runs away across the Scrubs.'

'Why didn't you follow her?'

'I didn't want to get into it all over again. I thought she'd calm down and just go home in the end. She was heading in the right direction. I didn't want any more trouble.' He seemed to see something in Slider's face and went on, self-exculpatory. 'I was angry, if you want to know. I knew if I went after her there'd be an even worse row. I thought it best to go home. I'd . . . I'd had a few drinks during the evening.'

'Drinks?' Slider queried.

Markov looked at him, and then shrugged. 'I suppose it doesn't matter now. You know about it anyway. All right, I was a bit wired. I'd had a couple of lines. I generally do a bit when I'm working. It helps clear my mind, gives me an edge.'

'I see. And what happened then?'

'Well, I was still angry when I got home. And worried. I paced about a bit. I had a couple of stiff drinks, to bring me down. And then she phoned again. She said she was at Old Oak Common, and she couldn't go home because she was supposed to be staying over with friends that night. She said if she went home at this time of night when she wasn't expected, it would all come out, and her father would kill her and then come after me. She wanted me to pick her up and drive her to her friend's house. I didn't see any way out of it, so I went.'

'She was waiting by the side of the road when you went past,' Slider said. 'You drove on under the bridge and stopped, and she came and got in.'

Markov blinked. 'How do you know?

'There were witnesses.'

'I didn't see anyone.'

'Never mind, they were there. Go on.'

'Well, she got in, and I asked where did she want to go. She started crying again, and said she only wanted to be with me, begged me to marry her. I said I wasn't going to listen to all that again. I said I wasn't going to marry her, and she'd better get used to the idea. I told her she should have an abortion. I even offered to help her pay for it. She stopped crying, as if it was turned off with a tap. She looked at me.' He paused, and shivered unconsciously. 'I've never seen such a look on anyone's face. I wish I could have painted it. She said she'd never have an abortion. And then she said, in this horrible, hard voice, that I'd have to marry her because she was going to tell my wife.'

'Ah,' said Slider. That was the last section of the jigsaw. He had wondered what it was that had triggered the final rage.

'The blackmailing little trollop!' Markov said, angered all over again at the memory. 'She was going to ruin everything! And when I'd just offered to help her! She jumped out of the car and ran across the grass. I went after her. I shouted at her to stop, but she didn't. I caught up with her and grabbed for her, but I only got the chain of that thing round her neck. It broke – cut my hand – but it jerked her off balance. I think the heel of her shoe broke. Anyway, she stumbled and I caught her arm. She turned round to face me. We were right on the embankment by then. She said nothing I could say would change her mind. Either I could tell my wife or she would, but one way or the other I was going to marry her. And so . . .' He stopped. He didn't seem to want to go on. He looked at Slider almost in appeal.

'And so you killed her,' Slider said unemotionally.

'I didn't mean to!' he cried. 'I was just so mad at her! I didn't know what I was doing. I thought of the trouble she was going to cause me, how she was going to ruin my whole life. And Steph, too, she didn't deserve that. She was blackmailing me! All that talk about love was rubbish! All she wanted was marriage, and she didn't care who she destroyed to get it. I was so mad, I just . . . I just . . . well, before I knew what was happening she was dead. I didn't mean to, I swear it. I didn't mean to hurt her. Something came over me. If I could take it back, I would. I never meant to hurt her.'

The appeal was blatant now, and tears started to leak from his eyes again.

Slider looked at him without pity. 'If you didn't mean to hurt her, why did you take a pair of tights with you?'

'What?' He looked dumbfounded.

'You strangled Zellah with a pair of tights. They weren't hers, and I doubt you drive around with a pair of women's tights in your pocket. So you must have taken them with you for the purpose of killing her. Which means it was premeditated murder.'

He stared, whitening. 'No,' he said in a whisper of a voice. He must have read his fate in Slider's face, because he began crying in earnest now. 'I'm sorry!' he gasped through the tears. 'I'm sorry.'

'I'm sure you are,' Slider said. *Sorry for yourself*, he added inside his head.

They got enough of everything done by the end of the day to go for a celebratory drink in the British Queen. Emily joined them, and Joanna came, bringing the baby, so they sat out in the garden. It was a warm evening, the threatening storm having passed over without breaking. The landlord brought out a platter of sandwiches, pork pies and scotch eggs, the low sun flickered through the trees, there was a blackbird singing nearby. It was all very pleasant. George got passed around from hand to hand and had the time of his life. Everyone wanted to pet him, and he held court like a confirmed *bon viveur*, half a ham sandwich in one hand and somebody's biro in the other, munching and conducting by turns.

Slider leaned tiredly against Joanna on the only bench with a back, and let the others talk. Atherton and Hart led the way in telling the story to her and Emily, though Atherton generously called on Connolly to add a sentence or two.

She had the last word of the story. 'The tights were his wife's, of course. She kept a spare pair in the car because she laddered so many at work. When Zellah jumped out to do a legger, she must've hit the storage bin yoke with her knee – it fell open and the tights fell out. He was so mad at her by then he picked them up and – well, enda story. We found the wrapper from the tights under the driver's seat. Shoved it there when he got out the car, and didn't shift it afterwards, the eejit. Don't know if he was too stupid, too upset – or maybe just a stone mentaller who thought he could get away with anything.'

Hart blew crumbs, waving her sandwich urgently. 'That third thing.'

'I think he was in such a blind panic he was on automatic,' Hollis said. 'Otherwise he'd have taken the tights away with him, or tried to hide the body. He just killed her and ran away.'

'And put the whole thing out of his mind,' Connolly finished, 'and hoped it'd go away.'

Atherton said. 'He'd just offered to pay for Zellah to have an abortion, but his only money was his wife's. A prince among men.'

Slider reached for his pint. It was time for the toasts. 'To all of us,' he proposed. 'Good work, everybody. We did it!'

Atherton proposed the next one. 'To the criminal – without whom police work would be merely theory.'

Then Connolly said, 'To the boss – sir – Mr Slider.'

'The guv!' the others roared, and drank with gusto.

'Oh shucks,' Slider said.

'They love you, you fool,' Joanna said.

'Shups,' said George, who had arrived back with him at that moment, passed over from Hart.

'He's a bit damp,' Hart explained, half apologetically.

'Like the guv's eyes,' said Joanna, laughing. 'Let's have another round. I'm up.' And to the polite protests, 'It must be my turn by now.'

Connolly turned to Hart when she'd gone. 'D'y'know what I'm going to tellya? That one,' she jerked her head in Joanna's direction, 'is one smart ban.'

In bed that night, Joanna said, 'You've hardly spoken about her. Is she bothering you so much?'

'Who?'

'Don't be a mug. Zellah, of course.'

'Yes, she bothers me. I keep thinking about her, so lonely, her parents fighting over her like two dogs over a juicy bone. She was desperate for love, trying to fit in with the other girls, trying to be what Mike Carmichael wanted, then finding what she thought was her soul mate in Alex Markov. She told Frieda he really understood her.'

'Poor kid.'

'Yes, she was just a kid, in spite of everything. And then that last day, pregnant, alone, desperately afraid, not knowing what to do or who to turn to. I can't help thinking she knew all along Markov was going to let her down. She couldn't have known he was going to kill her, though.'

'Do you think she really loved Markov?'

'Of course it was a fantasy. But yes, she loved him. That was what it was all about.' He thought of that poem. The thrush, sobbing in darkness. How lonely, how utterly alone she had felt herself. She had thought Markov was her sunlit freedom. Poor little sap. 'She gave him what he wanted – sex – in exchange for what she wanted – warmth. Just to be touched, held. Not to be alone.'

'Well, she wouldn't be the first woman to do that. In fact, I'd think it's probably how most relationships go. Sex in exchange for a cuddle.'

'That's a comforting thought.'

'Strange how she repeated her mother's past. Fell for a married man and got pregnant. Subconscious copying, I suppose. But what a hellish life she must have had, with a father like that.'

'He did his best for her, according to his own lights. It's all anyone can do.'

'What will happen now?' she asked after a moment. 'Will Markov go down?'

'Yes, the tights will do for him as surely as they did for Zellah. If only he'd used his hands, he might have claimed it was a momentary lapse. But the tights made it premeditated; malice aforethought. His fell purpose.'

'He'll get life?'

'Which means twenty years. Out in fourteen. Still young enough for a new life. Even to start a family. It's the Wildings who get the real life sentence.'

'What will Mr Wilding do now, I wonder?'

'I don't know. We've taken the possibility of revenge away from him. I've managed to convince him it wasn't Carmichael. And he can't get at Markov, because we've got him banged up. All he had left to keep him going was the determination to kill the person responsible.'

'Then I suppose he'll kill himself,' Joanna said.

'That's not my problem,' Slider said after a moment.

'Then stop sounding as if it is. You won, you fool. What do you think that drink at the pub was all about?'

'You can't ever win in a situation like this,' he said. 'That poor child. She was just a little girl.'

Joanna folded him close to her. She knew he was close to crying. 'You avenge them, the wronged dead. They're lucky, the ones who have you. Don't you know that? They can lie quiet. You've done what she needed. She won't walk tonight.'

After a bit he sighed, and she felt him relax. Time to come back to earth. 'You forgot to phone your father again,' she said.

'Oh hell,' he muttered. 'Remind me to phone him tomorrow, without fail.'

'I understand congratulations are in order?' Mr Slider said.

'How did you know that?' Slider said, sitting out in Joanna's pocket handkerchief of a garden with his Sunday morning coffee, while George sat on the grass nearby, considering what to eat – grass, stick, stone, worm? It was all so tempting . . .

'Joanna told me yesterday. She rang to say you'd broken the case and probably wouldn't have a chance to ring me.'

'I'm sorry. You know how much there is to do.'

'I know. It didn't matter, anyway, son. I've gone ahead and done it.'

'Done what?'

'Sold the cottage. Well, you said you didn't mind.'

'It was your decision,' Slider said, but he feared that his father, old and commercially innocent, might have been rooked. He wished he had waited until Slider could help him. 'I hope you got a decent price for it,' he said anxiously.

'Don't worry. Your old dad's not so green as he's grass-looking. Listen, Bill, there's something I want to ask you. But I want you to promise to say no if you feel that way. There'll be no hard feelings. You just be honest with me.'

'Dad—'

'No, let me say my piece. I bin practising,' he said with a smile in his voice. 'I know you and Joanna are looking to move, and I was wondering whether we couldn't throw in together, and get a place a bit bigger, with room for me. A granny-flat or whatever they call it. I don't need much – just a bed-sitting room with a gas ring, and a bathroom.'

'Oh, Dad, it would be lovely, but—'

'I wouldn't be underfoot, don't you think that. You wouldn't even see me unless you asked to. But I'd like to be closer, now I'm getting on a bit. And, see, I could stop in for the gas man, that sort of thing. And I could babysit for you any time, if you wanted to go out. I'd be on hand, like. And what I thought was, if I give you the money right off, I only got to live another seven years, and you wouldn't be hit with those old death-duties when I do pop off.'

'Dad, it would be wonderful,' Slider said, desperate to stop him, 'but we could never afford a place big enough. We can't find anything we can afford even for us.'

'I'd be putting in my money, you know.'

'I know, but what you could get for the cottage just wouldn't be enough in London.'

Mr Slider chuckled. 'Oh, I got a fair bit for it. A tidy bit. I sold it to a developer, you see.'

'A developer?'

'That's right, son. It seems the government's told the County Council they've got to build six thousand more houses in Essex, and the only way they can do that is on greenfield sites. Well, my bit of land's handy to the main road, and there's the lane all the way up to the cottage, with the sewage and water and electric already laid on. And it's not conservation land or prime farmland. So it's ideal.'

Slider felt breathless. 'You seem to know a lot about it,' he managed to say.

'I told you, I'm not so green as you think. Once they approached me and made an offer, I said I'd think about it, and I went and did a bit of homework. Talked to the planning officer at the council, had a look at some other plans, spoke to a solicitor. The developers offered me two hundred and fifty thousand for the cottage.'

'Two hundred and fifty?' Slider was pleasantly surprised. It was a lot for that little place, and it was all clear profit – no mortgage to pay off. Despite himself, his brain went instantly into calculation mode. A quarter of a million was far too little for anywhere round here, of course, but it was a handsome deposit in anyone's language, and say he and Jo could get a hefty mortgage, and they looked further out – a *lot* further out . . .

Mr Slider said, chuckling again, 'Ah, but that's just for the cottage. Near on four acres I got there. They could put sixteen executive homes on that, or twenty-four luxury dwellings. I took advice and asked 'em for one and a quarter million, and we settled in the end on one-point-oh-five. What that oh-five was about, don't ask me! But it makes one-point-three altogether. That'll be enough to get somewhere with a little annexe for me, won't it? If you want me, that is.'

Slider found his voice at last. 'For the chance of a live-in babysitter? Are you kidding?'

'And don't forget house-sitting,' Mr Slider said calmly. 'I read an article about it in the paper. If you have someone living in your house when you go on holiday, you can get a reduction on your insurance. Now that's *most* important, son.'

Helplessly, and perhaps even with a touch of hysteria, Slider began to laugh.